Joseph Waddell Clokey

David's Harp in Song and Story

Joseph Waddell Clokey

David's Harp in Song and Story

ISBN/EAN: 9783337181840

Printed in Europe, USA, Canada, Australia, Japan

Cover: Foto ©Andreas Hilbeck / pixelio.de

More available books at **www.hansebooks.com**

DAVID'S HARP

IN

SONG AND STORY,

BY

JOSEPH WADDELL CLOKEY. D. D.

WITH AN INTRODUCTION BY

W. J. ROBINSON, D. D.

"The Harp the Hebrew minstrel swept,
　　The King of Men, the loved of Heaven,
Which Music hallow'd while she wept
　　O'er tones her heart of hearts had given,
　　Redoubled be her tears, its chords are riven!
It soften'd men of iron mold,
　　It gave them virtues not their own;
No ear so dull, no soul so cold,
　　That felt not, fired not to the tone,
　　Till David's lyre grew mightier than his throne."
　　　　　　　　　　　　　　　—*Byron.*

PITTSBURGH:
UNITED PRESBYTERIAN BOARD OF PUBLICATION,
53 AND 55 NINTH STREET,
1896

DEDICATION.

To the memory of my Sainted Parents is dedicated this History of the Bible Psalms, which supplied for their lifetime the sole material of their praise, both in their church and home. If they are now, in the other life, in conscious touch with us in this, it will be a pleasant thought to them to know that they have children in earth who will never cease to be grateful to them that they led their feet in childlife by the green pastures and still waters of a Holy Bible and a Holy Psalmody.

New Albany, Ind.

CONTENTS.

PAGE.

Introduction by Dr. Robinson...................... 6

Chapter I.   The Psalms........................ 11

     II.   The Psalms in the Jewish Church........ 18

    III.   "   "   "   Primitive Church..... 46

    IV.   "   "   "   Dark Ages.......... 64

     V.   "   "   "   Reformation.......... 90

    VI.   "   "   "   Swiss and French Ref-
                               ormation.........107

   VII.   "   "   "   Netherlands.........134

  VIII.   "   "   "   English Reformation..149

    IX.   "   "   "   Scotch Reformation...177

     X.   "   "   "   American Colonies....207

    XI.   "   "   "   American Presbyterian
                                 Churches.........225

   XII.   Psalm Singing Among the Early New
             England Puritans.................249

PREFACE.

At one of the last sessions of the Presbyterian General Assembly held in Pittsburg in the month of May, the following communication was read by the stated clerk:

"To the General Assembly of the Presbyterian Church, now in session in Pittsburg:

"Dear Fathers and Brethren—The undersigned beg leave to state that they are chairmen of committees appointed by the General Assembly of the United Presbyterian church now in this city and by the synod of the Reformed Presbyterian church, respectively, for the purpose of securing a metrical version of the Book of Psalms which will be correct and elegant and conform to the present canons of literary taste in the English tongue. The object proposed is not to commit any body of Christians to the use of such book in whole or in part when completed, but to secure, if possible, a metrical translation of the Psalter of such excellence as will commend it to the taste and judgment of all who may desire to use the Psalms in praise, and as will secure it a place in the hymnody of all the churches.

"It is believed that the material for such a version is already in hand and is to be found in the many versions and the many manuals of the churches, as also in many separate individual renderings. Thus, while new renderings would not be excluded from consideration, the proposed work would be chiefly that of collation, selection and compilation of metrical translations now in existence.

"We are instructed by the bodies which we represent to solicit the co-operation in this revision of other bodies of Christians which have authorized in their standards the use of the Psalms in praise.

"We therefore request this General Assembly, representing the largest and most influential of the Presbyterian bodies, to consider this proposal favorably and to appoint a committee to co-operate in this work, being assured that your example in so doing would be readily followed by all the Reformed churches.

"W. J. ROBINSON,
"Chair. Com. United Presbyterians.
"W. J. COLEMAN,
"Chair. Com. Reformed Presbyterians."

May 27, 1895.

The members of the Assembly at the time, perhaps, looked on a favorable response to this communication more in the light of a courtesy than anything else, and so appointed a corresponding committee. The question of her Psalmody had not been one of the agitated topics of the church, and few, if any, of the delegates felt that here was a proposition of serious import. The falling of the communication among such a body intensely stirred by questions connected with seminary control, was like the dropping of a leaf in a tempest, yet, it was a leaf borne by a dove to the ark that told of the subsidence of the flood, and the reappearing of the forests and the soil that had been for months covered from sight. So may not this communication from two bodies of Presbyterians to a third, by a prophetic leaf, omening such a settling down of denominational agitations as will bring to the surface, as never before, the Psalms of the Bible, which have been so often obscured amid the contentions over other important affairs. To this united committee from these three leading bodies of Christians this little work goes with its silent plea. It is sent to you that the Psalms may tell their own story. They come in no spirit of dispute ; they do not propose to take issue with you on any of the questions of your Psalmody over which you conscientiously differ. At present they only plead for greater prominence in the praises of Zion. We are part of God's Inspired Word, they say to you, sent down from Heaven through the movings of the Holy Spirit that we may be sung in the praises of God's people. For more than twenty-five centuries we have been in the worship of the church, and what we have done in all these long ages, in comforting and inspiring the people of God, we are still capable of doing for the ages to come. Are you, and are your difficulties and dangers, and experiences, so different from your fathers who loved us, that you can afford to consign us to an obscure corner in your Books of Song ! We claim a high place in your material of praise. Read our story and consider our plea.

5

INTRODUCTION.

The Book of Psalms is a unique portion of the Inspired volume. While it is vitally, as well as structurally, a part of the sacred Book, breathing the same spirit, and throbbing with the pulsations of the same divine life which animates the whole, yet in its structure, matter, style and tone, it differs from all the other books of the Bible. As another has well said, "It is not the history of God's people, or of God's ways with them, nor is it the inculcation of positive doctrines or duties, nor the formal prophetic announcement of coming events. These are in the Psalms, it is true, but only in a subordinate way. History, prophecy, providence, doctrine and law are all here, but these form nothing more than the frame around which the Spirit of God has built the praise, prayer and adoration of the Lord's people." Dr. Addison Alexander, in his learned exegetical Commentary on the Psalms, points out the following distinctive characteristics of the book: "These hundred and fifty independent pieces, different as they are, have this in common, that they are all poetical, not merely imaginative and expressive of feeling, but stamped externally with that peculiar character of parallelism which distinguishes the higher style of Hebrew composition from ordinary prose. A still more marked resemblance is that they are all not only poetical, but lyrical, i. e., songs, poems intended to be sung, and with musical accompaniment. Thirdly, they are all religious lyrics, even those which seem at first sight the most secular in theme and spirit, but which are all found on inquiry to be strongly expressive of religious feeling. In the fourth place, they are all ecclesiastical lyrics, Psalms or Hymns, intended to be permanently used in public worship, not excepting those which bear the clearest impress of original connection with the social, domestic or personal relations and experiences of the writers." Like every other portion of the Sacred Volume, the Book of Psalms is the Word of God, the expression of the Divine mind toward sinful men, "The revelation of the will of God for human salvation," and is profitable for doctrine, for reproof, for correction, for instruction in righteousness." But unlike every other portion of the Volume, in its structure, matter, style and form, it seems to be specially adapted to the use of formal praise and worship. It is a book complete in itself. It depends for its interpretation, and for its highest uses, upon every other part of the Word, yet it stands out with a recognized prominence that distinguishes it as "the Divinest of these Divine Words." In its themes

6

it compasses the whole range of revealed truth. It opens the door into the very inner sanctuary of the Divine mind. It lays bare the secrets of the human heart. It sweeps every chord in the entire gamut of human feeling, and attunes its voice to all the varying moods, and changing experiences, which make up the spiritual life of the child of God on earth. "There," says Luther, "you look right down into the heart of saints, and behold all manner of joys and joyous hearts toward God and his love springing lustily into life! Again, you look into the heart of saints as into death and hell! How gloomy and dark their mournful visions of God." What notes of joy, outbursts of gladness and songs of praise echo and re-echo through this wonderful book! And yet how much of the song is modulated to the expression of grief and sorrow. "The Book is a 'Psalm of Life'", and it sings in both the major and minor keys, because human life has both joys and sorrows. What a mirror it is of the human heart burdened with sin, redeemed by grace, struggling against ten thousand enemies within and without, helpless in itself, laying hold upon the divine strength, in the depths to-day, and crying out in fear and anguish on the Rock to-morrow, and shouting the songs of deliverance, now wailing the cry of utter despair, and anon rising exultant on the wings of hope, "faint, yet pursuing!" It is no wonder that the true child of God finds the Book of Psalms the very manual of his spiritual life. Though written ages before the fuller revelation of the Gospel had been given, this Book is irradiated with the brightest beams of Gospel light. It was rich and full as the honey-comb to the Old Testament saint, but it has a richer fulness and a sweeter taste to him who has entered most largely into "the fulness of the blessing of the Gospel of Christ." Spurgeon writes in the Preface to the last volume of "The Treasury of David," as the testimony of his experience in the study of the Book, "The Book of Psalms instructs us in the use of wings as well as words; it sets us both mounting and singing. Often have I ceased my commenting upon the text, that I might rise with the Psalm, and gaze upon the visions of God." And what multitudes of the best and holiest of the followers of Jesus have found in this Book, the songs which have made melody "in the house of their pilgrimage!" Well may the celebrated Tholuck say, "Songs, which like the Psalms have stood the test of three thousand years, contain a germ for eternity." And yet another distinction belongs to this Book. These songs, so rich, full and complete in all the material for the worship of God, so adapted in their clear and graphic expression of all the emotions and experiences of true piety, to the purposes of worship, so adequate to all the uses of worship, are declared by their very style and structure to have been designed by their Author, for the service of worship. This is the conclusion to which all scholarly study of the Book invariably leads. Few, if any, competent Expositors have failed to express this conviction. The great and prominent purpose of the Book of Psalms, as indicated by its matter, style and structure, was to furnish the Church with an inspired Psalter for her service of praise on earth. Has the Church accepted and acted upon this divine intent in giving the Book? Has she made use of it as the manual of her formal Praise in the worship of her God? A glance at the Church to-day suggests a negative answer to the question. With the exception of a few of the smaller branches, the great Church of Jesus Christ has found other, and in her judgment, better and more appropriate material for rendering the high praises of God in her public worship than is furnished by the inspired Psalter. The genius of un-inspired men has created a hymnody for praise and worship, drawn from the inspired Word, and from the store-house of human experience, which has been accepted by the Church, as better fitted to express the reverent adoration, praise and homage due from the creature to the great Creator, than the inspired Psalms and Hymns of the Sacred Scrip-tures. And hence, the voice of inspired Psalm is seldom heard in the public worship of the modern Church. Has it always been thus? Has this divinely-given Book of Praises never approved itself to the mind and heart of the Church? Or is its exclusion from the service of praise a modern innovation? These are inquiries which cannot but be of great interest to every lover of the inspired Word. It is believed that these inquiries find a very satisfactory answer in the pages of this Work. The Author has undertaken to show, by a careful study of the history of the Church, what is the estimate which the Church in all past ages has placed upon the inspired Psalter, and what is the place she has given it in her service of worship. Well fitted for the necessary study and re-search, by his taste, his scholarly attainments, his mental acumen, dis-cipline and equipment, and his access to the Authorities, Dr. Clokey has traced the history of the Psalter from its first appearance in the Hebrew Church, down through all the Christian ages to the present time. And by an accumulation of undisputed testimonies, he has shown that this incomparable Book of Praises has not only furnished the material for the Church's praise through all the ages past, but has also been her sup-port in the times of her severest trials, her "Battle Cry" in her great conflicts with the powers of darkness, and the inspiration to her glorious "Works of faith, and labors of love." He has disclosed the fact that these inspired Psalms have played an important part in the great "Revivals" and Reformation movements, which have so often awakened the slumbering Church, and lifted her up to a higher plane of life. He has also made prominent the fact that these Psalms have been a great conserving power in the Church, standing as a bulwark of defense to the truth against the assaults of error. And thus we believe that this

8

volume is not only a timely and valuable contribution to the religious literature of the day, but also a full vindication of the claims of the inspired Psalter to be the divinely-appointed and all-sufficient Hymnody of the Church on earth, and a mighty plea for its restoration to its rightful place in the modern Church. The work is commended to the Christian public, with the full assurance that a careful perusal of its contents will awaken a new interest in this most precious portion of the Word of God, and with the hope that it will give a mighty impulse to the movement which has already begun, to unite the whole Church of Jesus Christ in the use of God's own Songs, in the service of his praise and worship.

W. J. ROBINSON.

ALLEGHENY, PA., Feb., 1896.

CHAPTER I.

THE PSALMS.

A French infidel has called the Psalms "the poetry of religious souls." This compliment is full of meaning and reveals more than usual acquaintance with the history and character of the Psalms. Were his "Life of Jesus" as faithful a portrayal of truth, the world would acknowledge itself under an eternal debt of gratitude to him. The poetic merits of these Bible lyrics have never been disputed. They have been extolled by literature's most eminent critics. The very greatest of our poets frankly confess their indebtedness to them for that which gives life to their numbers—poetic inspiration. The Psalms possess no instance of the extravagance of an excited fancy; yet have they the sublimity of the most exalted genius. They never descend to triteness nor vulgarity; yet are they grand in their simplicity. They are nature's own poetry. Like the swelling of the sea or the murmur of the brook; like the rushing of the storm or the silent falling of the sunshine, they move, not as if controlled and impelled by some force from without, but as by the impulse of a principle and under the guidance of a law. They are a true representative of the poetry of that age when the imagination and the heart were not constrained by a narrow poetic creed, but roamed in freedom and yielded only to nature's inspirings. The soul, in all the variety of its experience; in the enthusiasm of its joy or the depression of its grief; in the buoyancy of its hopes, the agitation of its fears, the harassing of its doubts, can find no freer, fuller utterance than in the Psalms of Holy Writ.

The Psalms exhibit that without which no poem can be

a portraiture of true human experience—piety. It is because of their eminently religious character, that they have
formed the staple of the sacred songs of the Church for
three thousand years.

The "new creature" in Christ being the same in all
ages, the harp of Judah has never ceased to awaken sympathy
in the hearts of God's people. Truly remarkable is the
endurance of the Psalms ; their changes from age to age,
from race to race, from clime to clime, have left no evidences
of decay. For centuries they served in the temple ; for
centuries they have mingled in the devotions of the New
Economy, yet are they as new and vigorous as when first
they sprung from the souls of their inspired authors. Well
has Tholuck said, "Songs, which, like the Psalms, have
stood the test of three thousand years, contain a germ for
eternity." The universal appreciation of the Psalms has been
no less remarkable. Like a sparkling spring they have
welcomed and refreshed every soul that has sought their
cooling waters. We do not wonder that genius has been
attracted to their beauty. They bear the impress of a divine
origin, and must possess depths of excellence that will, to
human intellects, ever reveal new truths or known truth
in new attractions. These Psalms comforted Chrysostom,
Athanasius, Savonarola—great minds of earlier years—in
their retreat from persecution. Polycarp, Columba, Hilde-
brand, Bernard, Francis of Assisi, Columbus, Huss, Edward
VI., Ximenes, Xavier, Melancthon, and Jewell, varying in
their creeds and characters, yet, in common, great in birth
or intellect, all breathed their last utterances in words from
the Psalms. Sentiments from his Psalter were the last
words that fell upon the ear of Charles V., the imperial foe
to the Reformation. Locke, in his last days, bade a friend

read the Psalms aloud, and it was while in wrapt attention to them that the stroke of death fell upon him. So dear to Wallace, in his wanderings, was his psalm book that when brought to the place of execution, he had it hung before him, and his eyes remained fixed upon it as the consolation of his dying hours. Henry V., of England, at his death-bed had the penitential Psalms read to him. When the priest came to the words of the Fifty-first Psalm, "Build thou the walls of Jerusalem," the warlike genius of the dying King was aroused, and he exclaimed : "Ah, had God suffered me to live out my days and bring this French war to a close, I am the man who would have conquered the Holy Land." The great Addison found the Twenty-third Psalm, throughout his life, the best expression of his devotion. "I have lost a world of time," said the learned Salmasius on his death-bed ; "If I had one year more, I would spend it in reading the Psalms of David and Paul's Epistles."

Humbolt was an especial admirer of the One hundred and fourth Psalm. He called it a picture of the entire cosmos, and adds, "We are astonished to see within the compass of a poem of such small dimensions, the universe, the heavens, and the earth drawn with a few grand strokes." The unhappy Darnley was soothed in the toils of his enemies by the Fifty-fifth Psalm.

Burleigh selected the Psalms—over the rest of the Bible—as his especial delight. Luther called them his "Little Bible," and made them the framework of his devotions, and the substance of his war cries. "This sweet-smelling bundle of Psalms," said Dickson, of Scotland.

But the burden of the history of these sacred songs comes from the homes of the lowly and obscure. Where the names of Homer, Dante, Byron, Shelley, Milton are never heard, the Psalms are sung, read, committed to memory, repeated, as though the exclusive boon of earth's unknown. From how many lips, now closed in death, have gone up the sweet music of Judea's hallowed songs! From how many cots of disease; from how many deserts and rocks, and caves, and forests; from how many crosses and guillotines have echoed back to ancient Jerusalem the vibrations of David's Psaltery! The history of the Psalms as they nourished and comforted the captives in Babylon, the hunted worshipers under the cruelty of Roman Emperors, the Waldenses, in their mountain retreats, the Huguenots, in their desert worship or in banishment, and the Covenanters among the rugged resorts of the Highlands—in all they have done for unnumbered hearts and homes, can never be written.

Whence this agreement in love and admiration for the book of Psalms? Doubtless in the fact that they are the poems of the heart. However men may differ in their habits of thought, their tastes, education, position and origin, the workings of the human heart are everywhere the same. A tear is a tear, whether it fall upon the cheek of the galley slave or of a King or a poet; so with joy, grief, love, fear, doubt, distress; external distinctions do not run into the bosoms of men. In the heart is the unity of the human race. The Psalms are the pure offspring of emotion; go forth saturated with the feeling of natures deeply stirred by the experiences of the inner life, and so are profoundly human. Men everywhere and in all times and positions love them, because every one sees in them the exact and full mirroring of his own soul. Nor can they ever be despised or even find a successful rival till the race ceases to be what it is, and its living myriads rise to sing heaven's new Psalms, or sink to the wailings of despair.

The selection of a few of the many eloquent encomiums upon the Psalms may claim a place here as a part of their history and literature :

"So far from questioning the poetry of the Psalms of David, there existed no productions which could be conceived more *poetical, harmonious* and *heart-stirring* and mostly more *ecstatic* than just the Psalms."—Henry Stephanus.

"The use of the Psalms became the blessing of humanity, not only on account of their *contents,* but also on account of the *form.* Just as no lyric poet among the Greeks and the Romans furnished such a mass of doctrine, consolation and instruction, so there is hardly anywhere to be found so rich a variety of tone in every species of song as here. *For two thousand years have the Psalms frequently and differently been translated and imitated, and still there are many new formations of their much-embracing and rich manner possible. They are flowers which change their appearance in every time and in every soil—but always bloom in the beauty of youth.* Just because the Psalter contains the simplest lyrical expressions of the most diversified feelings—it is *the hymn-book* for all times."—Herder.

"David yields me every day the most delightful hour. There is nothing Greek, nothing Roman, nothing in the West, nor in the land towards midnight to equal David, when the God of Israel chose to praise him higher than the gods of the nations. The utterance of his mind sinks deep into my heart, and *never in my life, never have I thus seen God.*"—John Mueller.

"One word from the Psalms was a sunbeam to me ; like a lark, I settled on the pinions of that eagle ; carried by her, I scaled the rock, and beheld from that eminence the world, with *its* cares and *mine,* stretched out beneath me ; I acquired to think, infer, mourn, pray, wait, hope and speak in the spirit of David : 'I thank thee, O Lord, that thou hast humbled me.' * * * * 'Next to the writings of the New Testament, these are to me my dearest and most precious book—the golden mirror, the cyclopædia of the most blessed and fruitful knowledge and experience of my life ; to thoroughly understand them will be the occupation of eternity, and our second life will form their commentary."—John Jacob Moser.

" The Book of Psalms is a vase of perfume broken on the steps of the temple and shedding abroad its odors to the heart of all humanity. The little Shepherd has become the master of the sacred choir of the universe. A chord of his harp is to be found in all choirs, resounding forever in unison with the echoes of Horeb and Engedi. David is the psalmist of eternity. What power hath poetry when inspired by the Almighty God!''—Lamartine.

"These works (the Psalms, allegories of Solomon, and prophecies of Isaiah) are set forth with a splendor and a sublimity which, considered merely as poetry, excite our wonder and disdain all comparison with any other composition ; they form a fountain of fiery and God-like inspiration of which the greatest modern poets have never been weary of drinking, which has suggested to them their noblest images and animated them for their most magnificent flights.''—Schlegel.

"It is in the main owing to the religious and devotional qualities of the Hebrew poetry that the Book of Psalms still, after the lapse of so many centuries, and the rise and fall of so many modes of thought and forms of social life, holds an empire over the hearts of men far wider and deeper and more influential than what any other influence has possessed, save only that which is and will ever be exercised by David's greater Son.''—Kitto.

"The Psalms thus applied have advantages that no fresh compositions, however finely executed, can possibly have. Since, besides their incomparable fineness to express our sentiments, they are, at the same time, memorials of and appeals to former mercies and deliverances ; they are acknowledgments of prophecies accomplished ; they point out the connection between the old and new dispensations, whereby teaching us to admire and adore the wisdom of God displayed in both and furnishing while we read or sing them, an inexhaustible variety of the noblest matter that can engage the contemplations of men.''—Horne.

"Those holy songs are nothing else than the expressions and breathings of devout and holy affections : such as an humble and fervent love to God, admiration of His glorious perfections and wonderful works, earnest desires, thirstings and pantings of soul after Him. And these expressions of holy affection of which the Psalms of David are everywhere full, are the more to our present purpose, because those Psalms are not only the expression of the religion of so eminent a Saint, but were also by the direction of the Holy Spirit penned for the use of the Church, not only in that age but in after ages.''—Jonathan Edwards.

"The soul of the reformer has vibrated under them (the Psalms) to its depths ; and the lone hand of Luther holding his banner before the eyes of Europe, has trembled less that it was stretched out to the time of David's heroic Psalms. On them the freed spirit of the Martyr has soared away. And have not destruction and death heard their fame, when on the brown heaths of Scotland, the stern lay was lifted, by the persecuted, like a new drawn sword and waved flashing before the eyes of the foemen—

'In Judah's land God is well known,
His name's in Israel great,' etc.

"Wild, holy, tameless strains ; how have ye run down through ages, in which large poems, systems and religions have perished, firing the souls of poets, kissing the lips of children, smoothing the pillows of the dying, stirring the warrior to heroic rage, perfuming the chambers of solitary Saints and clasping into one the hearts and voices of thousands of assembled worshipers ; tinging many a literature and finding a room in many a land, and still ye are as fresh and young and powerful as ever ; yea, perhaps preparing for even mightier triumphs than when first chanted ! Britain, Germany, America, now sing you, but you must yet awaken the dumb millions of China and Japan."—Gilfillan.

"We need not dwell on this universality as found in the Psalms of David. Devout feeling, and the most learned critical research, alike concur in the thought, that the key to their best interpretation is found in that view which regards them as the divine songs of all truly religious souls, the standing temple service of all ages, so adapted to the expression of temporal and spiritual sorrows, temporal and spiritual joys, temporal and spiritual salvation, that each may be regarded as the primary or secondary significance, according to the state of soul in which the incipient reads or chants the wondrously adapted words. There is nowhere in the physical world any such evidence of adaptedness or design as this. The historical world certainly furnishes nothing like it. Let it be called accommodation, if any prefer the word ; we could not thus accommodate one of the lyric hymns of Greece, or a song of the Rig Veda."—Tayler Lewis.

CHAPTER II.

THE PSALMS IN THE JEWISH CHURCH.

Some of the old Jewish writers, proud of the antiquity of their Psalms, have taken pains to prove to us that Abraham, Melchisedec, and even Adam, are to be classed among the sacred Psalmists. But more modern critics are content with claiming the church's first great Lawgiver as her first great inspired Poet. To Moses, in the present collection of the Psalms, is given but one—the Ninetieth. When that was composed, where, on what occasion, no one has told us. Its title is its sole history—"A Prayer of Moses." That its strains came from a soul when in sorrow and oppressed by the consciousness of some present or foreknown calamity, our own experience tells us, as we pass over the sentiments of that Psalm. Let the reader place himself by the Red Sea, with the hosts of Egypt struggling hopelessly before him; let him visit the camp of Sennacherib, with its countless dead covering the sods of the valley; or let him listen to the wailings at the final fall of Jerusalem, her streets in blood from a million of her slain; let him view these scenes as one personally interested in the dead, and how fully will his religious feelings find expression in the pathos of these sad words:

"3. Thou turnest man to destruction; and sayest, Return, ye children of men.

"4. For a thousand years in thy sight are but as yesterday when it is past, and as a watch in the night.

"5. Thou carriest them away as with a flood; they are as a sleep; in the morning they are like grass which groweth up.

"6. In the morning it flourisheth, and groweth up; in the evening it is cut down, and withereth.

"7. For we are consumed by thine anger, and by thy wrath are we troubled."

How much of this world's history has the "Prayer of Moses" seen? More than five hundred years passed away with it, before Homer penned his immortal Iliad ; or before David played his harp in the royal chamber of Saul. Was the Ninetieth Psalm sung in the Wilderness pilgrimage? Did its strains help express the joy at the crossing of the Jordan, or at the falling of Jericho's walls? Perhaps the young minstrel prophets that met Saul were chanting to the music of their instruments, "Lord, thou hast been our dwelling place."

Wonderful song! Since its inditing, Greece has begun and ended its career of martial and literary splendor ; Romulus built a city that grew, mastered the world ; that fell, and is now only remembered as the great Rome—all since Moses sang. Fifteen hundred years of the past, and eighteen hundred of the present dispensation have gone by— thirty-three centuries, yet the "Prayer of Moses" survives. Worn in the bearing upward of countless prayers, in the soothings of countless troubled and penitent souls, it has lost none of its simple, sublime beauty ; but now awaits the bidding of new-born souls, as fresh as in its Wilderness days.

Leaving Moses, one cannot pass over the centuries that intervene in the authorship of the Psalter without lamenting the loss of the many inspired songs that comforted and cheered the Israelites in the days of their pilgrimage and during the rule of the judges. Did God provide inspired men to indite new songs from period to period? It is not passing the bounds of probability to suppose that Israel was frequently supplied with Psalms by the prophets to be sung in connection with any that may have descended to them from the days of Moses and Job. But God has for some wise purpose shut out of the Psalter all but one of the ante-Davidic Psalms.

The next Psalmist we meet with comes upon a throne, and so surrounds his sacred poetry with the dignity of royal authorship.   While the first King of Israel was enjoying the undisputed authority of his reign, a shepherd lad was feeding his father's sheep on the plains about the ancient city of Bethlehem.   He possessed no external distinction, save that which was in common with his race—he was a Jew.   His father was from one of the most noted lines of Jewish ancestry, but spent his days, like his brethren, in the peaceable pursuits of a shepherd's life; and young David was passing quietly into the same calling, unambitious and unsuspecting of a bright destiny.   The choice of the grave old prophet was his first intimation of greatness.   The glory of a successful combat against the giant champion of the Philistines, and the songs of Israel's daughters over his triumphs were further premonitions that his valor was not always to be exercised against the foes of his father's flocks, but had been consecrated by an overruling power to the exploits of a soldier and a king.

Religious in spirit, beautiful in person, heroic in danger, a poet, a musician, David grew in favor with God and men. His royal preferment, coming not from inheritance nor civil suffrage, but from heaven, an unseen hand safely guided his footsteps up from the humble home at Bethlehem, through the praises of his fellow-countrymen, to a long and successful sway over a proud and powerful race.

But the world thinks least of David, the King; most of David, the sweet Psalmist of Israel.   The sovereignty of his sceptre extended over one people and in one generation. When in the tomb of the kings, his authority reclined with him; for the mere name of royalty, however green-preserved in memory, can win no victories. As a poet prince, David rules as he never ruled before; though dead, the music of his voice still successfully summons obeying nations, and though none now bow at his throne, millions list and are moved at the touching of his Psaltery.

David was called as a Psalmist as well as a King. His education referred to his songs as well as to his commands. Continually under the influence of the Spirit, led by Him in every pathway of life, and through every form of experience, David's Psalms are a miracle in their vast depth of feeling and in their comprehension of every shade of life between deep sorrow and exultant joy. "His harp was full-stringed, and every angel of joy and sorrow swept over the cords as he passed. For the hearts of one hundred men strove and struggled together in the narrow continent of his single heart; and will the scornful men have no sympathy for one so conditioned, but scorn him, because he ruled not with constant quietness the unruly hosts of divers natures which dwelt within his single soul? With the defense of his backslidings, which he had more keenly scrutinized, more clearly discerned against, and more bitterly lamented than any of his censors, we do not charge ourselves, because they were in a manner necessary, that he might be the full-orbed man that needed to utter every form of Spiritual feeling."

"The Lord did not intend that his Church should be without a rule for uttering its grief; and to bring such a rule and institute into being He raised up his servant David as he had formerly raised up Moses to give to the Church an institute of law, and to that end he led him the round of all human conditions, that he might catch the Spirit proper to everyone and utter it according to truth. He allowed him not to curtail his being by treading the round of one function, but every variety of function. He cultivated his whole being, and filled his soul with wisdom and feeling. He found him objects for every affection, that the affection might not slumber and die. He brought him up in the sheep pastures, that the ground-work of his character might be laid among the simple and univeral forms of feeling. He took him to the camp and made him a conqueror that he might be filled with nobleness of soul and ideas of glory. He placed him in the palace that he might be filled with ideas of majesty and sovereign might. He carried him to the Wilderness and placed him in solitudes that his soul might dwell alone in the sublime conceptions of God and his mighty works. And he kept him there for long years with only one step between him and death that he might be well schooled to trust and depend upon the Providence of God."— Irving's Introduction to the Psalms.

Much difference of opinion prevails as to the number of the canonical Psalms of which David was the author. From the general appellation, David's Psalms, as commonly applied to the Psalter, the impression of the masses is that David composed all of the one hundred and fifty. With this impression corresponds the opinion of some of the old Greek and Latin fathers. Some eminent archæologists credit to him only seventy-three, and others even less than this, while some of the Jewish writers regard David as only the compiler of the Psalms. But by the best authorities David is regarded as the author of at least seventy Psalms.

By consulting the titles of the Psalms in our English Bibles we find that seventy-three are assigned to David. This classification of King James' version agrees with the Hebrew. In the Latin Vulgate only seventy Psalms are attributed to the Hebrew Psalmist. As some of the Psalms bear no names of authors, and as there is no possible way of ascertaining their authorship, it is possible that some or all these came from the pen of David. Of two things only are we certain, that David composed more of the Psalms than any other poet, and that he did not compose all of them.

Following the titles of the English and Hebrew Psalters, the Psalmist immediately succeeding David is Solomon, to whom are attributed the Seventy-second and One hundred and twenty-seventh Psalms. It is doubtful, however, whether either of these Psalms was composed by Solomon. While most of the versions ascribe the Seventy-second to him, the Syriac ascribes it to David, which seems very probable since the conclusion reads, "The prayers of David the son of Jesse are ended."

The title of the One hundred and twenty-seventh Psalm in the Syriac reads, "A Psalm of David concerning Solomon; and that it was spoken also concerning Haggai and Zechariah, who forwarded the building of the temple." In the Septuagint, Æthiopic, Arabic and Anglo-Saxon, the title is simply "A Psalm of Degrees." The Psalm bears internal evidence of having been written at the time of the building of one of the temples, but which one is not known. It is not probable that the Psalms can claim Solomon, the gifted king and poet, among their authors, unless for some of those inserted without titles.

Twelve Psalms bear the name of Asaph. The first Asaph of whom we have any knowledge, was a celebrated musician in the days of David, and the son of Berachiah of the tribe of Levi. He was one of three chief leaders in the choir, first of the tabernacle, and afterwards of the temple. He was a prophet as well as a poet and musician, and in the days of Hezekiah is placed alongside of David in the estimation of the Jews—"moreover, Hezekiah the king, and the princes commanded the Levites to sing praise unto the Lord, with the words of David and of Asaph the seer."

It has been supposed by some that Asaph was only a composer of the music to which the Psalms bearing his name were sung. This may be; it is plain that the full twelve Psalms were not written by the Asaph of David's time, as some of them bear marked evidence of having been composed over the downfall of Jerusalem at the time of the captivity in Babylon. The apparent discrepancy between the title and the occasion of the writing of these Babylonish Psalms is no doubt explained by the supposition that some other Asaph, who was among the captives, was their author. That there was an Asaph among the returned captives, we learn from Nehemiah 2:8. This Asaph, in the land of the captivity, was held in esteem, as he had been appointed keeper of the king's forest, and held communications with Artaxerxes.

In the Psalter, Heman and Ethan have each one Psalm. These two were both Levites, Ezrahites, and leaders in the choir in the days of David and Solomon. They were men so distinguished for wisdom that they were among the specified few who in 1 Kings 4 : 31, are said to have excelled. Ethan is sometimes called Jeduthan.

There have been those who have referred the Eighty-eighth and Eighty-ninth Psalms to the Heman and Ethan mentioned in 1 Chron. 2:6, as the grandsons of Judah by his daughter-in-law Tamar. If this conjecture were correct, these Psalms are the oldest specimens of poetry extant, as these two persons lived nearly two hundred years before Moses.

In the Arabic the Eighty-ninth Psalm is credited to Nathan, the Israelite.

Korah was confederate with Dathan, Abiram, and two hundred and fifty of the principal Levites in their rebellion against the authority of Moses and Aaron, and with them was swallowed up in the cleaving of the earth. As all the children of Korah did not perish with him, it is thought by Professor Stuart that the "sons of Korah," to whom are attributed ten Psalms, were his descendants. In the days of David, the Korahites "were over the work of the service, keepers of the gates of the tabernacle; and their fathers, being over the host of the Lord, were keepers of the entry."

The Korahites were also singers in the temple in the days of Jehoshaphat. The authors of the ten Psalms may have been some of these who served in the tabernacle or sang in the temple.

Many of the Psalms composed during, or after the captivity, are variously ascribed to Haggai, Ezra, Zechariah and Nehemiah; but the name of neither of these persons appears in the titles of what are regarded the captivity Psalms.

There are not wanting learned men who bring some of the Psalms down to the age of the Maccabees. Certain Jewish authorities include in this period all of the Hallelujah Psalms. By Rudinger, the First, Forty-fourth, Forty-sixth, Forty-ninth and One hundred and eighth; by Herman Von Hardt, the One hundred and nineteenth ; by Venema, the Eighty-fifth, Ninety-third and One hundred and eighth; and by others, in addition to these, the Sixtieth, Seventy-fourth, Seventy-ninth, Eightieth, Eighty-third, are considered Maccabæan. Hitzig represented few Psalms as belonging to any earlier date: according to his hypothesis Psalms First, Second, Forty-fourth, Sixtieth and the last three books, including all from the Seventy-third to the One hundred and fiftieth Psalm, were of Maccabæan origin. He is followed in his opinion by Lengerke and Justus Olshausen.

Westcott, late Fellow of Trinity College, Cambridge, thus sums up the objections to a Maccabæan authorship in the Psalter: "But if it be admitted that the Psalms in question are of a later date than the captivity, it by no means follows that they are Maccabæan. On the contrary, they do not contain the slightest trace of those internal divisions of the people which were the marked features of the Maccabæan struggle. The dangers then were as much from within as without; and party jealousies brought the divine cause to the greatest peril. It is incredible that a series of Maccabæan

Psalms should contain no allusion to a system of enforced idolatry, or to a temporizing priesthood, or to a faithless multitude. And while the obscurity that hangs over the history of the Persian supremacy from the time of Nehemiah to the invasion of Alexander, makes it impossible to fix with any precision a date to which the Psalms can be referred, the one glimpse which is given of the state of Jerusalem in the interval, is such as to show that they may well have found some sufficient occasion in the wars and disorders which attended the decline of the Persian power.''

It may be stated in addition to this that the closing of the Old Testament canon in the fourth century before Christ, and the translation of the Septuagint, containing the entire Psalter, in the third century before the Christian era, contradict the supposition of any Psalms having been composed as late as the time of the Maccabees.

The question of the authorship of the Psalms, though perplexing, does not affect the integrity, inspiration and sublimity of the Psalms themselves. The one hundred and fifty are in the canon of the sacred Scriptures, and ''whether David or any other prophet was employed as the instrument of communicating to the Church such and such a particular Psalm, is a question which, if it cannot always be satisfactorily answered, need not disquiet our minds. When we discern in an epistle the well-known hand of a friend, we are not solicitous about the pen with which it was written.''

At this point may be introduced an inquiry of no little importance : What was the design of the Almighty in directing the gradual collection of the Psalms and the final fixing of them in the canon of his inspired Word? As each of the other books of the Bible is only a selection, and has for some wise purpose been compiled from much more that might have been included, we must conclude that there was some special design also in choosing out of the Jewish Psalmody of more than one thousand years, the one hundred and fifty Psalms, and setting them as a part of a complete Bible. What this design was, does not appear from any express declaration in the Scriptures. The individual and general titles of the Psalms throw no light on the subject, for they either make no reference to it, or are of an origin that cannot be regarded as authoritative. Nowhere in the Old Testament does God inform us why he had the one hundred and fifty Psalms collected, and placed where they are. The supposition that he was governed by a desire simply to provide a Liturgical Psalm-book for the temple worship does not harmonize with the delay of a complete collection until within five hundred years of the final overthrow of the temple service, nor with the fact of a limited selection from the many inspired songs sung from time to time by the Jewish people.

By consulting the New Testament, we conclude that the primary design of the present selection from all the songs of the Hebrews was, that these specially foreshadowed the coming of Christ. That the Psalms are prophetic of Christ no good commentator pretends to deny. That Psalms prophetic should be gathered because of their prophecies, seems just as probable as that the writings of Isaiah and Jeremiah should be collected and made canonical for theirs.

Bishop Horsley, in his preface to the book of Psalms, remarks: "It is true that many of the Psalms are commemorative of the miraculous interpositions of God in behalf of his chosen people; for, indeed, the history of the Jews is a fundamental part of revealed religion. Many were probably composed upon the occasion of remarkable passages in David's life, his dangers, his afflictions, his deliverances. But of those which relate to the public history of the natural Israel, there are few in which the fortunes of the mystical

Israel, the Christian Church, are not adumbrated; and of those which allude to the life of David, there are none in which the Son of David is not the principal and immediate subject. David's complaints against his enemies are Messiah's complaints, first of the unbelieving Jews, then of the heathen persecutors and of the apostate faction in the latter ages. David's afflictions are the Messiah's sufferings; David's penitential supplications are the supplications of the Messiah in agony; David's songs of triumph and thanksgiving are Messiah's songs of triumph and thanksgiving for his victory over sin and death and hell. In a word, there is not a page of this book of Psalms in which the pious reader will not find his Saviour, if he reads with a view of finding him.''

That the Psalms which David himself wrote, were prophetic, David himself states : '' David the son of Jesse said, and the man who was raised up on high, the anointed of the God of Jacob, and the sweet Psalmist of Israel said, The Spirit of Jehovah speaks by me, and his word was on my tongue.''

In the New Testament the principal use made of the Psalter is of it as a collection of prophecies. The Second, Eighth, Sixteenth, Eighteenth, Nineteenth, Twenty-second, Fortieth, Forty-first, Forty-fourth, Forty-fifth, Sixty-eighth, Sixty-ninth, Seventy-third, Ninety-first, Ninety-fifth, One hundred and tenth, One hundred and seventeenth, One hundred and eighteenth and One hundred and thirty-second are expressly quoted from as containing prophecies of Christ in his life, death and exaltation. Christ himself referred to the Psalms as prophecies. After his resurrection he appeared to his disciples and in the course of his conversation with them said, ''These are the words which I spake unto you while I was yet with you, that all things must be fulfilled which were written in the law of Moses, and in the prophets, *and in the Psalms concerning me.*''

That the prophecies concerning the Messiah should be composed in the form of Psalms or songs, and be sung in the stated services of the Jewish Church, does not seem strange. There is nothing in the material of a prophecy that need render it unfit for psalmody; and there is a peculiar beauty and appropriateness in making the Psalms of a great people reflect the glories of an approaching Saviour.

It seems probable that in early days the terms to designate prophecies and psalms were synonymous. The students whom Saul met after leaving Samuel, are called "prophets," and they are said to have been prophesying "with a psaltery, and a tabret, and a pipe, and a harp;" by which we understand that they were psalming their prophecies.

In 1 Chron. 25:2, Jeduthan is represented as one who "*prophesied with a harp*, to give thanks and to praise the Lord." "Moreover, David and the captains of the host separated to the service of the sons of Asaph, and of Heman, and of Jeduthan, who should *prophesy* with harps, with psalteries, and with cymbals."

That God also designed the Psalter as a book of praise for his Church has been a commonly-received opinion, both in the earlier and later days of the New Testament Church. Without such a design could not be well explained the adaptability of the Psalms for psalmody, their use by Christ and his disciples, and their influence in the sacred music of God's people in every age. At whatever time the general title of the book was given, the Psalter was regarded as a book for praise, for the "Schillim" of the Hebrews, and the "Psalmor" and "Psalterion" of the Septuagint Greek, were given to designate the Psalms as material to be sung in divine worship, rather than as a collection of prophecies, or of divine precepts.

Although the New Testament Scriptures make but little

mention of the matter of sacred melodies, yet, in what they
do say, the Psalms of David are clearly recognized as commended as proper songs for the edifying and comforting of
God's people.   As in Eph. 5 : 19 : "Speaking to yourselves in Psalms and hymns and spiritual songs, singing and
making melody in your hearts " ; and in Col. 3 : 16 : " Let
the word of God dwell in you richly in all wisdom ; teaching and admonishing one another in Psalms and hymns and
spiritual songs, singing with grace in your hearts unto the
Lord " ; and in James 5 : 13 : " Is any merry?   Let him
sing Psalms."

Over the character of Hebrew poetry hangs a cloud
whose gloom eminent critics for centuries have vexed themselves to remove.   That the Psalms, the Book of Job and
other parts of the Scriptures are sublimely poetic, all fully
agree.   That poetry, of whether sacred or secular, should
assume a measure and find its utterance in numbers, all fully
accord as an essential in its composition.   What was the
measure ?   Was there any form of metre ?   These are the
mysterious problems which the learned have labored to solve.

The rules regulating the composition of Hebrew poetry
have been lost, and to restore them at this date is as difficult
as to transfer ourselves back to the times and into the circumstances when the poems of the Bible were recorded, and
created anew the numbers of their inditing.   There was a
period when there were no *rules* for the poet; all that he
had, in common with the poets of his own times, and of all
times, was the genius and inspiration that give birth to
poetic sentiment.   Having no mould for his utterance, the
poet must create one for himself.   The poems of Homer
and of the Bible were probably the first of their kind, composed at a time when the measures, like the poet himself,
were born.   Poetic genius, when creating, is no more likely

to create the same measures in the utterances of two individuals, or in two localities, or in two eras, than it is to create sameness of sentiment. Originality must be peculiar to every composer in the first days of poesy. For this reason, Homer might write in Greece, and Solomon at the same time in Jerusalem, and no known rules guide them, and so their poetry would differ as widely in the numbers as in the sentiment. For the same reason the numbers of modern tunes and those of the tunes of the Hebrew poets would bear no resemblance to one another. To trace the measures of the Psalms in the Iliad or Odyssey, or to seek their discovery in the rules of modern poetry and rhetoric, assumes the poets to have had common rules, and to have written according to them. Had the Psalms themselves been totally lost, how foolish to attempt to resurrect their sentiments by taking the Iliad or Paradise Lost as a starting point! To restore lost sentiment is to create it; to restore lost measures is to create them.

It is highly probable that many of the later Psalms were composed upon some model; but this model was in earlier Psalms, or earlier poems, the rules of whose composing are lost, so that these possess the same difficulty as though written when rules were unknown.

That there should be some resemblance between the utterance of the Psalms and the works of Homer, Hesiod or Pindar is natural. All poems, however widely they may differ in their origin, or their eras, possess resemblances. Resemblances in poetry are inborn; hence in any age, or any land, we can, as by instinct, detect a poem, though totally ignorant of its general construction.

But resemblances do not argue even the *existence* of rules.

The Psalms, like the Iliad, were written too soon for rhyme. Rhyme was neither born nor created, nor discov-

ered ; it was invented. It is mechanical, and must be
classed with the locomotive and the reaper, and not with the
offspring of poetic inspiration. He who invented *rhyme*
invented manacles for the hands that should freely guide the
pen. Still a history of the Psalms would not be complete
without certain spectral theories concerning the style of their
poetry. These, if they will throw no light into dark places,
will be useful in summing up the estimation in which the
Psalms have been held, and the relative degree of attention
and investigation they have attracted.

Some of the early writers speak with as much confidence
upon the measures of the Psalms as though the Hebrew
system of poetic numbers was fully known in their times.
Josephus affirms that the Songs of Moses, the Ninetieth
Psalm among them, were composed in the Greek heroic
verse, and that David composed odes and hymns in pentameters and trimeters—verses of five and three feet. Origin
and Eusebius followed his opinion. Eusebius states that
the One hundred and nineteenth Psalm was composed in
heroic verse of sixteen syllables. Julian, in reply to
Eusebius, undertakes to prove that the Hebrews had no
culture, and that their poetry, like the poetry of all un-
civilized nations, was rude. Jerome fancied he could trace
in the Psalms the iambic, alcaic and saphic verses of Horace,
Pindar, Alcaceus and Sappho. Gregory, of Nyssa, denies
the existence of classic metres in the Psalms. Augustine
favored the view that they were in metre, and Scaliger responds to him by saying that the poetic books of the Bible
were mostly composed in prose, only animated by a poetic
spirit, the Song of Moses, the Proverbs and Job being the
only exceptions. Gerhard Vossius argued for a rhythm, but
no metre, while Gomarus, in the seventeenth century, contended for both rhythm and meters. Marcus Meibomius,

toward the close of the same century, professed to have discovered the lost system of Hebrew metres, and proposed
to restore the whole Scriptures to their original state, provided six thousand men would contribute each £5 sterling for
a copy of his book.   Failing in his scheme, he published some
specimens of restored poems.   The whole book of Psalms,
according to his view, was written in distichs, and were intended to be sung by two choirs.

Sir W. Jones attempted to apply the Arabic meters to
the Psalms, but succeeded in establishing no system.   M.
de Lacy, the French Orientalist, Herder and other eminent
German writers believed that the Psalms had no proper
meter, consisting of cadences and measured syllables, but
"simply of periods artificially constructed and balanced,
resembling a well-trellessed garland or a row of pearls arranged in just proportions."   Dr. Kitto thought the ancient
Hebrews had too much simple majesty and too much gravity
for the jingling play of rhyme.   "Rhyme is indeed entirely
foreign to the genius of the ancient Hebrew poetry ; and
although a rhyme may here and there be met with, it may
safely be presumed to be the result of accident rather than
design, or any part of poetical contrivance.   It is of more
consequence to notice this, because later Hebrew poetry has
both rhythm and metre."

Says Bishop Horsley :—" The Psalms are all poems of a lyric kind—
that is, adapted to music, but with great variety in the style of the composition.   Some are simply odes—some are of the kind called eliagic,
which are pathetic compositions upon mournful subjects ; some are
ethic, delivering grave maxims of life or the precepts of religion, in
solemn, but for the most part, simple strains ; some are enigmatic, delivering the doctrines of religion in enigmas contributed to strike the
imagination forcibly, and yet easy to be understood.   In all these the
author delivers the whole matter in his own person.   But a very great,
I believe the far greater, part are a sort of dramatic ode, consisting of
dialogues between persons sustaining certain characters.   In these dia-

logue Psalms, the persons are frequently the Psalmist himself, or the
chorus of Priests and Levites, or the leader of the Levitical Band, opening the ode with a proem, declarative of the subject, and very often
closing the whole with a solemn admonition drawn from what the other
persons say; the other persons are Jehovah, sometimes as one, sometimes as another, of the three persons; Christ, in his incarnate state,
sometimes before, sometimes after his resurrection; the human soul of
Christ as distinguished from the divine essence. Christ, in his incarnate
state, is personified sometimes as a priest, sometimes as a king, and
sometimes as a conquerer."

A novelty in the Psalms in the Hebrew, which is not
seen in our English Bible, is in the acrostic or alphabetical
Psalms. These are considered by Bishop Lowth as one of
the leading features in the effusions of Hebrew music. In
these Psalms, the number, order of the lines, or system of
lines and periods are regulated by the number and order of
the twenty-two letters of the Hebrew alphabet; each letter
beginning a line or stanza. It is supposed that poems among
the Hebrews were written in this method to aid the memory
in committing and retaining them. It bears something of
the same relation to poetry as does the rhyme of later times,
and no doubt answered much the same purpose.

The only evidence of the feature of Hebrew poetry that
presents itself in the English Bible, is in the One hundred
and nineteenth Psalm, where the English spelling and naming
of the Hebrew characters occur at regular intervals through
the Psalm, and which serve no other end than to mystify the
mass of readers, and probably to divide the Psalm into portions of convenient length to be sung.

Of the multitude of versifyers of the Psalms only two
have attempted to transfer into English metre the acros-
ticisms of the alphabetical Psalms. These are Montagu and
Burges.

The following specimen from Montagu, will give the
reader some idea of the Hebrew acrostics:

PSALM 100.

All ye lands now come in throng,
Be ye joyful in the Lord:
Come before him with a song,
Do him homage in accord.
Earth ! all nations ! Him adore,
Fear and serve him evermore.
God provides for all our needs;
He 'twas made us ; his we are ;
In his pastures, Jah us feeds,
Keeps us with a Shepherd's care,
Laud to him raise every voice;
Mirthful in the Lord rejoice.
Now him in his temple sue,
Offer up your thanks and praise !
Pay him your oblation due,
Quicken ye, your voices raise,
Raising high, his praises frame;
Singing, bless his holy name.
Truth and mercy are the Lord's
Unto everlastingness.
Vast his works are, wise his words,
Xcellent. Him all confess,
Yield him homage and adore;
Zealous serve him evermore.

Concerning the use of the Psalms in the early Jewish
Church, we know little more than that they were sung.
Whether they were sung in family worship, or sung by the
common people, we can only conjecture, as the specialties of
the home devotions of Israel are not given to us either in the
Old Testament or at the hand of any uninspired chronicler.

Of the Psalm-singing in the Tabernacle and Temple and
on great festive occasions there are few items recorded, and
those few refer mostly to the manner of the Jewish Psalmody
rather than to the matter of it. Judging from what we
know, and from the structure of the several Psalms, there is
warrant for saying that the Psalms we now have in the
Psalter are given us, not simply as the offspring of inspiration,
but of great and special occasions for which they were com-

posed. Could we have a full history of the inditing of each Psalm, these records would no doubt give us an insight into the great occasions and remarkable vicissitudes of the Hebrew nations.

May not our Psalter be composed only of the *gems* of the Hebrew Psalm-books, thrown up into view and use by the extraordinary experiences of a thousand years?

Whilst reliable records give us little insight into the distribution of the Psalms in the services of the Jewish Church, tradition comes to our assistance. In the work of Lightfoot on the Temple Service, in Brown's Jewish Antiquities and other similar works are given what are reputed to be the customs of the Jews at or about the time of Christ. The Hebrew worship was liturgical, and the Book of Order contained certain Psalms arranged as stated songs for certain occasions, just as we now see in the liturgies of the Greek, Roman and English churches.

In connection with the morning service of the Temple, a stated Psalm was sung for each day of the week. On the first day :

Psalm 24 was sung, because, as the gamara states, it celebrates the creating of the world by the Lord upon the first day of the week. "The earth is the Lord's and the fullness thereof : the world and all that dwell therein," etc.

Psalm 48 was sung on the second day of the week, because the Lord on this day divided the waters and reigned over them.

Psalm 82 was sung, because on this day the earth appeared, on which were judges and judging, and by his wisdom he established the world.

Psalm 94 was sung on the fourth day, because God on it made the sun and moon and stars, and will be avenged on them that worship them.

Psalm 81 was sung on the fifth day, because of the variety of creatures made on that day to praise God's name.

Psalm 93 was sung on the sixth day, because the Lord finished his work by making man, who can give glory to the Creator.

Psalm 92 was sung on the seventh day. It is entitled a Psalm for the Sabbath.

No mention is made by tradition of what Psalms were sung during each day and at evening service. According to some authorities, Psalms 9, 104, 118 were set apart for Sabbath Psalmody. These Psalms, when sung, were divided into three parts, with pauses between the parts, where the priests could blow their ordinary blasts, and the people worship. Thus, in the Twenty-fourth Psalm, the whole band probably sang verses first and second : "The earth is the Lord's and the fullness thereof : the world and they that dwell therein," etc. Here, in the pause, the trumpets sounded, and the people worshipped. The second division begins with one-half the choir asking in the third verse : "Who shall ascend into the hill of the Lord?" etc., and the other half answers in verses 4, 5, 6, "He that hath clean hands and a pure heart," etc. Here the whole band sound "Selah," and the second pause begins. The third division begins with one-half of the band singing : "Lift up your heads, O ye gates, and be ye lifted up, ye everlasting doors, and the King of glory shall come in." The other half responds : "Who is this King of glory?" The first again answers : "The Lord strong and mighty, the Lord mighty in battle," etc. The second half again asks in the tenth verse : "Who is this King of glory?" The first half again reply : "The Lord of hosts, he is the King of glory" : when the whole band ends the Psalm by sounding "Selah."

The singing of the Psalms was not confined to the regular services of the Temple.

Dr. Loroth supposes that the Hundred and thirty-fourth Psalm was sung by the two divisions of those who watched the Temple by night, and sung with such intervals as to indicate the hours of the night. Tholuck thus translates and divides this Psalm :

A SONG FROM THE HIGHER CHOIR.

THE COMING TEMPLE GUARD.

1. Behold, bless ye the Lord,
   All ye the servants of the Lord,
   Which by night stand in the house of the Lord.

2. Lift up your hands to the sanctuary,
   And bless the Lord.

THE RETIRING TEMPLE GUARD.

3. The Lord that made heaven and earth,
   Bless thee out of Zion.

Some Psalms were no doubt considered as especially appropriate for occasions of war, and were sung in march or at the attack. In the days of the Maccabees the Psalms were sung in the procession of the people, who bore branches and the boughs of firs and palms in their hands in token of triumph. The young warriors under Judas Maccabees sung them at the siege of Gazara ; and Judas himself "sung Psalms with a loud voice," as he and his company charged against the soldiers of Gorgias, the Governor of Idumea. From 2 Chron., 20: 21, we learn that as early as the days of Jehoshaphat, the Psalms were sung in battle. Jehoshaphat, when he had gone forth against Moab and Ammon, appointed singers unto the Lord, who should praise the beauty of holiness, as they went out before the army, and to say, " Praise the Lord ; for His mercy endureth forever." It was while this martial choir was singing the One hundred and thirty-sixth Psalm that the Lord sent ambushments against the enemy and they were smitten.'' After the victory, the whole army, with Jehoshaphat in the front, marched in a triumphal procession to the house of the Lord, singing to the music of their harps and psalteries.

Psalm-singing was a prominent feature in the worship of the great Jehovah festivals. The first great festive occasion was the Passover, fixed for the appearance of the new moon in the Jewish first month, or our month of March.

In the original institution of the Passover, each family was to have a lamb for sacrifice. But in the time of our Saviour this rule was so modified as to allow a lamb for a group, or society of not less than ten. These groups were called in Hebrew Hebure, and were generally made up four days before the day of the Passover. It was while these companies were offering their lambs in the court of the priest, about the middle of the afternoon, that the Levites sang the Egyptian Hallel, comprising Psalms One hundred and thirteenth, One hundred and fourteenth, One hundred and fifteenth, One hundred and sixteenth, One hundred and seventeenth, One hundred and eighteenth. The companies entered the court in three divisions, hence the Hallel was begun three times, and almost finished a third time when the last company completed its offering. The Egyptian Hallel was so called from its being a Hallelujah in remembrance of the deliverance from Egypt. Sometimes it was called the Lesser Hallel to distinguish it from the greater Hallel sung at a later period on passover occasions.

On the evening of the 14th of the month, or, according to Jewish reckoning, on the beginning of the 15th day, the several companies gathered around their tables to eat the paschal lambs. During the continuance of the meal the Jews were to drink four cups of mingled wine and water. Between the drinking of the first and second cup, there was to be, among other things, an explanation of the passover by the presiding officers. This was generally done by taking the Hallel Psalms and commenting on a part of them. The fourth cup of wine was called the Hallel cup because the President finished with it his reading of the Hallel Psalms, begun over the second cup. It is supposed that the cup Christ blessed and gave to his disciples was the third of the evening, and that it was the concluding part of the Hallel Psalms that he and his disciples sang before retiring to the Mount of Olives.

After the fourth, or Hallel cup, the usual custom on these festive occasions was to close the ceremonies for the evening. But there was a tradition that a fifth cup might be taken by such as felt so disposed, provided they would repeat the great Hallel over it. There is a division of opinion as to what constituted the Great Hallel. Rabbi Judah says it was Psalm One hundred and thirty-six ; Rabbi Johanan, that it was from One hundred and twenty to One hundred and thirty-seventh Psalm ; Rabbi Ahabar Jacob, that it was from Psalm One hundred and thirty-fifth, fourth verse, to Psalm One hundred and thirty-seventh.

In the treatise, Erachin, to the above Psalms, the One hundred and fifth is added as part of the great Hallel. The second of the three great Jewish festivals was the feast of Pentecost—sometimes called the feast of Weeks, sometimes the feast of Harvest, sometimes the day of the first fruits. The time of the observance was on the fiftieth day after the first day of unleavened bread, or sometimes in the month of May. Brown, in his Antiquities of the Jews, thus describes the gathering of the Jews on this occasion, and their singing the One hundred and twenty-second Psalm. They tell us that all the males

within the limits of the several districts throughout the
land, having met at the principal cities in these districts,
with a view of going up to Jerusalem to the feast of Pentecost, lodged in the streets during the night, for fear of pol-
lution ; and, as the air was mild, they could do it without
injury to their health ; that on the morning of the following
day, the President of each company called them betimes,
" Arise, and let us go up to Zion, to the Lord, thy God ; "
that they set out on their journey, preceded by a bullock,
intended for the sacrifice, whose horns were gilded (like that
afterward vowed by Diomed to Pallers, and of Nestor to
Minerva) ; and whose head was decorated with a garland of
olive branches ; and that a person playing on a pipe went
also before them, to cheer them on their journey, whilst
bursts of religious fervor were frequently heard by the
people, exclaiming as in Psalm One hundred and twenty-two,
" I was glad when they said unto me, let us go up to the house
of the Lord." Delightful, indeed, must the sight have been
to observe the companies coming from the different districts
of the land to Jerusalem, as to a common center, to worship
God. We are informed, that to avoid fatigue, they traveled
only two parts of the day, and that when they came near the
city they sent a messenger to announce their approach ; on
which, some of the chiefs of the priesthood went out to
meet them. Their entry into the city was exceedingly
picturesque. Each carried his basket of wheat, grapes, figs,
apricots, olives or dates. The baskets of the rich were of
gold or silver, and those of the poor were of wicker work,
fancifully ornamented with flowers. As they entered the
city they joyfully exclaimed, ' Our feet shall stand within
thy gates, O Jerusalem ; ' and all the artificers in their
shops rose as they passed and bade them welcome. Indeed
the whole of Psalm One hundred and twenty-two receives

an additional beauty if we consider it as expressive of what would naturally happen on this occasion.

"Let us suppose the several tribes to be near the walls of the city and preparing to enter it, headed by the several chiefs of the priesthood: what was more natural for them to say in holy exultation, as in verses 1, 2, 'I was glad when they said unto me, Let us go up into the house of the Lord. Our feet shall stand within thy gates, O Jerusalem.' Having entered the city and seen the private and public buildings, which to many of them would be new and wonderful, they would naturally exclaim, as in verses 3, 4, 5, 'Jerusalem is builded as a city that is compact together, whither the tribes go up, the tribes of the Lord unto the testimony of Israel, to give thanks unto the name of the Lord; for there are set thrones of judgment, the thrones of the house of David.' The very welcome that was given to them as they passed, by the artificers and other inhabitants, from the doors of their shops, and the tops of their houses, seemed to be contained in verse 6, 'Pray for the peace of Jerusalem.' To which the tribes would naturally reply, 'They shall prosper that love thee. Peace be within thy walls, and prosperity within thy palaces. For my brethren and companions' sakes, I will now say, Peace be within thee. Because of the house of the Lord our God, I will seek thy good.' Thus did they proceed with the sound of music to the mountain on which the temple stood ; at the foot of which every individual, of whatever rank, took his basket on his shoulder and repeated as he ascended, the whole of the One hundred and fiftieth Psalm, probably in a kind of musical cadence, to make the procession more solemn and impressive. When come into the court of the priests, the band of the temple sang the Thirtieth Psalm, and the president of the company, with his basket on his shoulder, in the name of the

rest, repeated the words which God had enjoined on the occasion, as we have already transcribed them from Deut. 26:
3-10, 'I profess this day,' etc.; a priest in the meantime
putting his hand under the president's basket and waving it
before the Lord."

During the days of the Feast of Pentecost, the Psalms
were frequently sung, but what Psalms we are not informed
till the eighth and last day of the festivities. The Psalms
sung on this day were the Egyptian Hallel, already mentioned, in the celebration of the Passover.

The third of the three principal Jewish festivals was the
Feast of Tabernacles, which came in the latter part of the
month of Tizri, or September. In the original appointment
on the occasion of this feast, the people were required to
dwell in booths; but in the time of Christ the Pharisees so
explained the commandments as to establish the custom of
bearing branches in the hands rather than dwelling in booths.
Accordingly the first thing the Jews did when the feast began, was to supply themselves with branches of the palm
and myrtle, and then to resort to a place called *Mutsa*, a
short distance below Jerusalem, and on the banks of the Kid-
ron, for willow branches. Each person procured two willow
branches; one to place on the altar, and the other to be bound
by means of a golden, or silver cord, or by a twig, with the
branches of palm and myrtle. This last was called the *luleb*,
which was to be carried during the whole of the first day of
the feast.

During the days of the feast, the ordinary Psalms for
the week were dispensed with and the Egyptian Hallel sung:
" that being renewed daily," as the Jerusalem Targum expresses it, "because their lulebs were renewed daily." During the performing of the psalmody by the band the crowds
were accustomed to express the ardor of their feelings by
outward tokens. When the beginning of the 118th Psalm
was sung, "O give thanks unto the Lord," they shook the
branches they held in their hands. The same thing was
done when the 25th verse was repeated ; and at the concluding verse, the whole multitude joined in shaking their lulebs
"on the right hand and on the left, upwards and downwards."

During the sacrifices of the first day of the Feast of Tabernacles, the Levitical band sang the 105th Psalm. After the completion of the sacrifices, and before the Jews left the mountain of the Lord's house, they went in procession round the altar, setting each one his branch against it, and repeating Psalm 118:25, "Save now, I beseech thee, O Lord; O Lord, I beseech thee, send now prosperity." As they passed through the gates of the court of Israel they solemnly pronounced this benediction, "Beauty be to thee, O altar;" "beauty be to thee, O altar." Among the Jews of some countries at the present day this custom still prevails, the people walking around the desk in the middle of the synagogue, singing Psalm 118:25.

At the Feast of Tabernacles the people did not leave the temple at the end of the evening sacrifice, as was their custom on other festive days. They remained at night and engaged in the rejoicing for the pouring out of the water, as it was called. "Their manner of observing it was as follows: They all met in the court of the women; the women above in the balconies which surrounded three sides of the court, and the men below on the ground. The court was lighted by four golden lamps, one on each side, which were raised to a great height, and kept burning, by four young men of the priesthood, who ascended them by a ladder, poured into each of them one hundred and twenty logs of oil, and supplied them with wicks that had formerly been prepared from the old coats and girdles of the priests." Prominent in the exercises of this evening was the music. The pipe of the temple was played, and on the steps leading from the court of the women to the gate of Nicanor, sat the Levites with their instruments, those belonging to the vocal department singing, as stated by some authorities, the fifteen Psalms of Degrees, from Psalm 120th to Psalm 134th, while the members of the Sanhedrin, the rulers of the synagogues and the doctors and the eminent in rank and piety amused themselves and the audience by dancing to the sacred music, and promenading with torches in their hands.

On the morning of the second day of the Feast of Tabernacles, instead of the regular Psalm of the morning, the Hallel was again sung. During the offering of the special sacrifices of this day, the Twenty-ninth Psalm was sung, and at the close of the ceremonies the Jews passed round the altar, singing Psalm One hundred and eighteenth, twenty-fifth verse. The Hallel was sung again on the third day, and the special Psalm sung was the Fiftieth, from the eighteenth verse to the close. The exercises of the fourth day were similar to those preceding, only the Ninety-fourth Psalm was sung from the sixteenth verse to the end; on the fifth day, during the special offering, the Ninety-fourth Psalm was sung from the eighth verse to the end. On the sixth day, the Eighty-first Psalm was sung from verse sixth to the end; on the seventh day, the Eighty-second Psalm, from verse fifth to the end, was sung. On this day the modern Jews lay aside their myrtle and palm branches, and take only the willow, while they make seven revolutions round the desk of the synagogue, singing the Twenty-ninth Psalm. The Psalm of the eighth day of the feast is not mentioned in the authorities relied on.

At the Feast of Trumpets, appointed for the first day of the moon of the month Tizri, the Levites sang Psalm Eighty-first; if, however, "the first day of the year fell upon the fifth day of the week, on which day this Psalm was appointed always to be sung during the offering of the morning sacrifice, they then sang it twice over, viz., once at the daily sacrifice and once at the additional sacrifice, beginning one of the times at the sixth verse, but whether the first or last time is not said. And if the new year fell upon the Sabbath the Psalms for the first day of the year were sung, and took the place of the Psalms which in that section were said to be appointed for the Sabbath."

The foregoing account, while it does not contain the full story of the Psalm-singing of the Jews, will suffice to show the high estimation in which the Psalms were held and the manner in which they were woven into the whole warp and woof of the devotions of God's ancient people.

CHAPTER III.

The Psalms in the Primitive Church.

Two of our prominent historians seem to have discovered no traces of the universal use of the Psalms before the fourth century. Says Spanheim : "Besides hymns and songs, and private Psalms, of which there was a great number in their solemn assemblies, the Psalm-book of David was brought into the Western Church in this age" (the fourth century). Mosheim, basing his opinion on the testimony of Cyril, of Jerusalem ; of the Apostolical Constitutions, and of Beansobre, states that the "Psalms of David were now (fourth century) sung as part of divine service." How far Mosheim's opinion is rendered plausible by the statements of Cyril and Beansobre, the author cannot say, for the writings of these persons could not be consulted ; but the Apostolical Constitutions make no mention of the Psalms except in connection with the singing and reading of them in the regular worship of the Church, thus giving no more ground for the inference that this is the first use made of them, than is given by the English Liturgy, or Scotch Liturgy for the conclusion that the Psalms were not sung in Great Britain till after the Reformation.

Were there no direct testimony as to Psalm-singing in the earliest days of the New Testament worship, there is circumstantial evidence strong enough to justify the conclusion that it was universal.

The founders and first converts of the primitive Church were Jews, the habits, convictions, and tastes of whom would, in every absence of divine institution and direction, give to the new system of worship a shape corresponding to that of the old. We need no more confirmation of this conjecture than a knowledge of human nature, a principle of which is to reproduce in new places, and under new systems, old and long-cherished customs, except where necessity or new convictions would call for a change. So powerfully

(46)

does this principle operate, that often antique ways and manners are preserved in spite of the claims of duty, necessity, and reason for reform, thus occasioning the de-nunciation of bigotry.

The whole Jewish people at the coming of Christ were Psalm-singers. They were early brought into contact with the temple services, where the music of the Levites would, more than anything else, make a pleasing impression upon their youthful hearts. Their fondness for the temple and the temple exercises would naturally include the Psalter. After the Babylonish captivity, there is a probability that the Psalms became, as they were not fully before, the common property of the people, and the families. The Levites still held their place and observed the sacred rites of their office and the people attended their services, but the worship of the Church was not so fully as before performed by representation. The people began to meet in synagogues by themselves and for themselves, and their Psalmody was diffused among the homes of the nation. At the beginning of the Christian Dispensation, we may suppose that wherever there was a religious family there the Psalms were sung and taught. These home customs would tend to deepen the love of the Jews for their Psalms. In middle life and old age they would be invested with tender recollections and pleasing memories of early years and of home. Christ himself was a Jew, of strictly Jewish training, and grew up familiar with, and fondly attached to, the Book of Psalms. Paul's attachment to Judaism in all of its features is well seen in his early persecutions. With all of the Apostles of the primitive Church, there were habits and preferences such as would insure the transfer of the Jewish songs into the new worship.

In addition to the reference of early impressions and early recollections, the Psalter had a history that would beget for it strong attachment in the Jewish mind. The biography of their Psalmists is a gallery of the nation's most honored characters. The tabernacle days are represented by but one song, but that one is sufficient to hallow the whole Psalter with the memory of Moses. David is the first of their greatest kings and warriors, and to this day he is honored as the nation's sweetest bard. Here are the Psalms of their warrior kings; Psalms from the days of Hezekiah, and Josiah; and from the poets of the returning captives. These are the Psalms the fathers have sung for centuries ; they have comforted them in trouble, soothed them in captivity, nerved them for battle, gladdened them in their triumphs and pilgrimages. The Psalter is identified with the whole history of the race from the escape out of Egypt to that out of Babylon, and is a mirroring of its successes and misfortunes. What a precious relic of the past ! What a sweet souvenir of departed greatness—these old lyrics ! Every Jew would be highly susceptible to the influence of such reflections, and would grow proud of his Psalter as of his home and his race. Conversion to the faith of Jesus, as the Messiah, would not change his preferences for the songs of his people, unless plain precept would identify them with the things that were to pass away. Rather would his faith deepen his fondness for them, as in the Saviour it would perceive the substance of their foreshadowings.

Why, the converted Hebrew might ask, may I not sing the Psalms of the fathers in my own worship? Christ has nowhere forbidden it. His apostles have not forbidden it.

These Psalms were no part of the ceremonial law, and so need not necessarily pass away with the bullock and the blood of the altar. The tone of them is against Jewish ritualism, and is eminently in harmony with the spirituality of the new Faith. Instead of a bleeding lamb, their offering is a bleeding heart; a broken spirit instead of a mangled sacrifice. What an emphasis are they upon the fundamental Gospel idea, "Not by the flesh of bulls and goats, but by the precious blood of Jesus Christ."

It would be unnatural to suppose an entire and abrupt cessation in the singing of the Psalms at the change of dispensation.

The positive testimony to the use of the Psalms in the primitive Church is by no means full, but there remains sufficient to place the question beyond a doubt. In Ephesians 5:19; Colossians 3:16, and James 5:13, the use of the term "Psalms" or Psalmoi, as it is in the Greek, certainly refers to the Psalms, and intimates that they were sung at Colosse and Ephesus, and among "the twelve tribes" which were "scattered abroad." Christ and the writers of the New Testament frequently quote from the Psalter, and call it the "Psalms," and that, no doubt, from the title given them in the Septuagint translated many years before their day. The expression in 1 Cor. 14: 15, "I will sing with the spirit, and I will sing with the understanding," reads in the original, "I will psalm with the spirit and I will psalm with the understanding," and seems to be a clear indication that the Psalms were sung at Corinth. The occasions on which the Psalms were sung in the early primitive Church and the manner of singing them are enveloped in darkness.

That the "Hymn" sung by Christ and his disciples at the institution of the Lord's Supper was the usual Psalm of the old Passover, as prescribed by the Jewish liturgy, there can be scarcely a doubt. Says Albert Barnes, "The One hundred and thirteenth and One hundred and fourteenth Psalms were sung during the observance of the Passover, and the One hundred and fifteenth, One hundred and sixteenth, One hundred and seventeenth, and One hundred and eighteenth Psalms at the close. There can be no doubt that our Saviour and the apostles also used the same Psalms in their observance of the Passover." With this view agrees Dr. Lange in his "Life of Christ. "The celebration was now concluded by singing at its close the usual Song of Praise (Psalms One hundred and fifteenth to One hundred and eighteenth inclusive)." At the time of Christ, the Greek words "Psalms" and "Hymns" were both applied to the Psalms of the Bible. In the Septuagint "Hymns" is employed in the titles of some of the Psalms, as in Psalms Six, Fifty-four, Fifty-five.

In the "Antiquity of the Jews," published about the year 93 A. D., Josephus speaks of the Psalms as hymns: "And now David, being freed from wars and dangers, and enjoying for the future a profound peace, composed songs and *hymns* to God of several sorts of metre; some of those which he made were trimeters, and some were pentameters; He also made instruments of music, and taught the Levites to sing *hymns* to God." In the apostolical constitutions, a liturgy belonging to the fourth century, "the Psalms are called hymns." "Let another sing the *hymns* of David and let the people repeat the concluding line."

During the latter part of the first century and early part of the second, concerning which profane history says but little, we may suppose that the Psalms still held the principal place in the Psalmody of the Christians. Still hallowed by the same memories as when first sung by the primitive converts from Judaism, and sanctified by the practice of Jesus and his disciples, they would commend themselves to that age almost immediately connected with the days of the founding of the Church. The custom from the latter part of the second to the fifth century shows that from a very early date the Psalms were in prominent use at communion, on the Sabbath, during the extraordinary gatherings of the people preparatory to the sacred festivals, and in the private worship of home. As Christianity spread itself over the world the Psalms went with it, until by the fourth century, they were sung on the banks of the Rhine and the Danube, amid the mountains of Persia, in the deserts of Arabia, in Egypt and Abyssinia, along the north coast of Africa, and in the British Isles, as well as in the crowded congregations of Palestine, Asia Minor, Greece and Rome. They became everywhere identified with the New Testament Church, as with the Church before the days of Christ; and their varied use now forms a prominent and interesting feature of ecclesiastical history. During the persecutions of the first centuries, begun by Nero, and carried on by his successors, the singing of Psalms was one of the most prominent and most frequent exercises of the persecuted as they gathered in the Roman Catacombs, in the caves, and wilderness places, or in the deserts and cemeteries.

Tertulian, who was a presbyter at Carthage about the close of the second century, informs us that the Psalms took their place in his day in the regular worship of the African Church, and that the singing of them usually followed the reading of the Scriptures. "The Scriptures are read and Psalms sung." The same custom existed still in the fourth century, as

Jerome testifies.   In speaking of the assemblies of Christians in his time, he says the services began with the reading of Scripture and the singing of Psalms.   "When they are assembled together, Psalms are sung and Scriptures read; then prayers being read, they all sit down and the father begins a discourse to them."

Eusebius, a Bishop of Cæsarea, in the fourth century, tells us the Psalms were sung in his day and his country, in all the assemblies of the Christians.   St. Basil, of the same century and belonging to the same country as Eusebius, says that the Christians in their assemblies offered their confessions on their knees, and then rose and sang Psalms to God. John Chrysostom, born at Antioch, about the year 354, and made Bishop of Constantinople in 398, testifies to the use of the Psalms in his bishopric.   In a sermon at Constantinople he remarks to his audience, "All of us, young and old, rich and poor, bond and free, men and women, what have we now enjoyed in our united Psalm !   With one voice, and, as it were with one heart, we have sung the prayer.   As the hand of the harper unites all the strings to one song, so the Psalm brought together our hearts into one prayer.   And the royal poet who wrote ages agone by, has been present with us to-day by his Psalm and has joined in our worship." The singing of Psalms was in great repute in Alexandria during the fourth century, and especially while Athanasius resided there as the Bishop of that church, as is stated by Augustine, a writer of the fifth century.   It was equally popular in the church at Milan, while St. Ambrose was its Bishop.

Psalm-singing was not confined to the assemblies of the Christians, but became a popular pastime, and a part of social and family festivities and devotions.   Jerome says : "You could not go into the fields but you might hear the plowman at his hallelujahs and the vine dresser chanting the Psalms of David."   In the "Apostolical Constitutions," which may be taken as a fair representation of the customs of Psalmody during the fourth century, it is stated, "the women, the children, and humblest mechanic, could repeat all the Psalms of David ; they chanted them at home and abroad ;

they made them the exercises of their piety and the refreshments of their minds. They thus had answers ready to oppose temptation, and were always prepared to pray to God, and to praise him in any circumstance in a form of their own inditing."

The same custom prevailed among the Christians at Constantinople. Says Chrysostom, in his Homily on Penitence: "All Christians employ themselves in David's Psalms more frequently than in any other part of the Old or New Testament. The grace of the Holy Ghost hath so ordered it, that they should be recited and sang every night and day. In the Church's vigils, the first, the midst, the last are David's Psalms. In the morning David's Psalms are sought for; and David is the first, the midst and the last. At funeral solemnities, the first, the midst and the last is David. Many who know not a letter can say David's Psalms by heart. In all the private houses, where the virgins spin—in the monasteries—in the deserts, where men converse with God, the first, the midst and the last is David. In the night, when men are asleep, he wakes them up to sing; and collecting the servants of God into angelic troops, turns earth into heaven, and of men makes angels, chanting David's Psalms."

The popularity of Psalm-singing among the people as early as the second century may be seen in the act of Bardesanes in conforming the number of his private Psalms to the one hundred and fifty Psalms of the Psalter, so that his sentiments might more easily gain access to the people and be adopted by them.

Although, it has been surmised, by writers favorable to that view, that during the third century, the compositions of uninspired men were to some extent sung by Christians, yet any attempt to set aside the Psalms and to substitute in their place any other songs was firmly withstood. An instance of this occurs in the case of Paul, of Samosata, after the middle of the third century. Paul was Bishop of Antioch at the time he began to promulgate his Socinian heresy. Two councils were convened concerning him, at the second of which, about 269, A. D., he was deposed from his office, excluded from the privileges of the Church, and an epistle was written and dispersed through the Roman world explaining the errors of Paul, and the decision of the council. The following extract is taken from Milner's translation of that epistle as it is recorded by the historian, Eusebius : " Vain, and fond of secular dignity, he preferred the name of Judge to that of Bishop ; he erected for himself a tribunal and lofty throne, after the manner of civil magistrates, and not like a disciple of Christ. He was accustomed to walk through the streets with a numerous guard, in great state, receiving letters and dictating answers ; insomuch that great scandal has accrued to the faith through his pride and haughtiness. In Church assemblies he used theatrical artifices, to amaze, surprise and procure applause from weak people, such as striking his thigh with his hand, and stamping with his feet. Then, if there were any who did not applaud him, nor shake their handkerchiefs, nor make loud acclamations, as is usual in the theater, nor leap up and down as his partisans do, but behaved with decent and reverent attentions as becomes the house of God, he reproved and even reviled such persons. He openly inveighed against the deceased expositors of the Scripture in the most impudent and scornful terms, and magnified himself exactly in the manner of sophists and impostors. *He suppressed the Psalms made in honor of Jesus Christ, and called them modern compositions; and he directed others to be sung in the Church in his own commendation;* which very much shocked his hearers ; he also encouraged similar practices, as far as it was in his power, among the neighboring Bishops."

From this epistle it will appear that a part of the charge against Paul was that he interfered with the Psalm-singing, long in practice at Antioch, and instituted songs in his own honor, an encroachment that a council composed of seventy Bishops decided as contrary to the custom of the Church and the spirit of Christianity. This case of Paul, however, has been a matter of controversy. It is claimed by many that the Psalms displaced by Paul were the hymns of the earlier days composed in honor of Christ as divine, and that he is the first who introduced and defended the exclusive use

of the Psalms of the Bible.   The testimony on which such an
opinion is based is that of Neander in his Ecclesiastical
History.   He states the case of Paul thus : "The Church
hymns, which had been in use since the second century, he
banished as an innovation,   *   *   *   on the principle that
only passages out of the Holy Scripture ought to be sung ;
and thus he probably suffered nothing but the Psalms to be
used."

It is difficult to determine how historians become so
widely different in their views, when having access to the
same records.   It is equally difficult to conjecture how Paul
could expect any aid in his errors from the exclusive use of
the Psalms, since they have always been regarded as prophetic of a divine Saviour, and are so quoted in the New
Testament.

It was no uncommon circumstance for the Christians to
be condemned by heretics for their Psalm-singing. Augustine
says of one Hilary, that he "took every opportunity of
loading with malicious censure the customs—that hymns
from the Book of Psalms should be sung at the altar."
Such was the conduct of this person that Augustine, at the
request of his brethren, replied to his reproaches.   The
same author says of the Donatists that they reproached the
Orthodox "because they sang with sobriety the divine songs
of the prophets, while they (the Donatists) inflamed their
minds with the poetic effusions of human genius."

Concerning the distribution of the Psalms in the public
services, whether a liturgical method of stated Psalms for
stated occasions prevailed to any great extent, as among the
Jews, is not known.   It appears that certain Psalms were
popular on special occasions before the fifth century, but it
is not probable any rule on the subject was generally followed.   In the second century, Tertullian says that the
One hundred and thirty-third Psalm was generally sung on
communion occasions, and he complains of those who use it
only on that occasion.   In the third century it was customary
in the Africk churches to sing the Thirty-third Psalm at communion: "I will bless the Lord at all times ; his praise shall
be continually in my mouth," etc.—corresponding to the

Thirty-fourth of the English Psalter. This Psalm is also recommended by the author of the Apostolical Constitutions, and was used at the Lord's Supper by Jerome. In Jerome's day, the Forty-fifth was a communion Psalm : "My heart is inditing a good matter," &c. In the Africk churches about the same time the One hundred and thirty-third was sung. Of this Psalm, St. Augustin says it was so noted and well known that they who knew nothing of the Psalter could repeat it from hearing it so frequently sung at the altar.

In the Liturgy of St. James the Thirty-fourth Psalm is appointed for communion seasons, chiefly because of the words in the eighth verse, " O taste and see that the Lord is good; blessed is the man that trusteth in him." St. Mark's Liturgy appoints Psalm Forty-second, " As a hart panteth after the water-brooks, so panteth my soul after thee, O God," &c. According to Cotelerius, in some of the ancient rituals, at the end of Gregory's Sacramentarium, the One hundred and thirty-ninth Psalm is recommended, " O Lord, thou has searched me and known me," &c. St. Chrysostom says the One hundred and forty-fifth Psalm was, in his day, sung at communion, chiefly because of the words, "The eyes of all wait upon thee, and thou givest them their meat in due season."

In a Liturgy attributed to St. Chrysostom the One hundred and thirteenth and Thirty-fourth Psalms are appointed to be sung.

The Liturgy of St. James recommended the singing of the Fifty-seventh Psalm after the communion, " Be merciful unto me, O God," &c.; also the Seventy-first, because of verse eighth, "Let my mouth be filled with thy praise, and with thy honor all the day." In some of the churches it was customary to sing Psalms while the communicants were partaking of the supper, as well as before and after it, but what Psalms, or whether any particular ones, were selected, is not stated. It was also customary in some places for the minister to lecture through the Psalms regularly, in which case the precentor was required to give out the Psalms in their order for the people to sing. This method was followed by Augustine, for he speaks of the Sixty-fifth as being sung in this way.

Psalm-singing was a part of the exercises connected with the burial of the dead. At first there do not seem to have been any set Psalms for such occasions ; but after liturgies had come into use the Psalms for funerals, as well as the prayers and chapters from the Scriptures, were appointed and regularly sung. This custom came into the New Testament church from the Jews, among whom it was customary to follow the dead to their graves singing and playing upon instruments of music.

An incident related by Gibbon in his History of the Decline and Fall of the Roman Empire will illustrate the use of Psalmody at funerals, and give some idea of the enthusiasm with which the Psalms were sung in the time of Julian, the apostate. Julian, who, until his manhood, was trained in the doctrines of Christianity, became one of the last defenders of ancient paganism. He restored the worship of the sun, filled his gardens with the statues and altars of the gods, rebuilt the temples and sacred places that Christianity had been instrumental in destroying, and spent the greater part of his revenue in refitting the groves once dedicated to some heathen deity, bringing birds from distant countries to bleed on the altars, and procuring oxen, a whole hecatomb of which he would sometimes sacrifice at a single offering, all for the purpose of resurrecting the magnificent pageantry of heroic and mythological ages.

Julian, in his zeal for his new faith, tried a weapon often tried after his day by the church he then sought to destroy—persecution. Such was his fervor that blood did not satisfy; but even the dead bodies of the Christians that for a century had been in their graves must be removed from the sacred places and buried elsewhere. The demonstration of the Christians connected with the removal of the body of one of their early bishops, and its reburial at Antioch, is graphically described by Gibbon in his seventy-third chapter. After the body of Babyeas, bishop of Antioch, had rested near a century in its grave it was reburied in the Grove of Daphne and a magnificent temple erected over his remains. By the order of Julian this temple was demolished and the remains of the bishop removed to their former resting place within the walls of Antioch. "The scene of infection was purified according to the forms of ancient rituals; the bodies were decently removed, and the ministers of the church were permitted to convey the remains of St. Babylas to their former habitation within the walls of Antioch. The modest behavior which might have assuaged the jealousy of a hostile government was neglected on this occasion by the zeal of the Christians. The lofty car that transported the relics of Babylas was followed and accompanied and received by an innumerable multitude, *who chanted, with thundering acclamations, the Psalms of David, the most expressive of their contempt for idols and idolaters.* The return of the saint was a triumph; and the triumph was an insult to the religion of the Emperor, who exerted his pride to dissemble his resentment. During the night which terminated this indiscreet procession the temple of Daphne was in flames; the statue of Apollo was consumed, and the walls of the edifice were left a naked and awful monument of ruin." The Psalm chanted on this occasion was the Ninety-seventh, chosen particularly for the sentiment, "Confounded be all they that serve graven images, that boast themselves of idols." The ringleader in the movement of the Christians was Theodorus, a pious young man. Julian, enraged, commanded him to be seized and put to the torture. But though tormented by the pains of the rack for a whole day, Theodorus continued cheerful and persevered in singing "Confounded be all they that serve graven images," &c.

In Antioch lived, during these excitements, a Christian lady named Publia. It was her custom when Julian would pass by her window to sing from the One hundred and fifteenth Psalm, "Their idols are silver and gold, the work of men's hands," &c. When commanded on one occasion to be silent, she responded to the command by singing from Psalm Sixty-eighth, "Let God arise, let his enemies be scattered," &c. For her Psalm-singing Julian commanded her to be brought before him, where she was beaten till she was covered with blood. She bore her suffering patiently,

and, on her release, returned to her home to continue singing with her companions.

An interesting feature in the history of the Psalms during the fourth century, and while Julian was still in power,
is the use made of them by the Christians for comfort and
encouragement under the Arian persecution.   It was no uncommon thing for the Christians to be surrounded in their
churches by Arian soldiers, and besieged while at their devotions.   Under such circumstances the bishop, or presbyter,
would order his precentor to give out some Psalm, which he
and the people would sing.   Sometimes whole nights and
days were spent in Psalm-singing, and not unfrequently the
besiegers were baffled by the valor and Psalmody of the
besieged.

An instance of this occurred in the church at Alexandria, under the rule of the celebrated Athanasius, often known
as the Father of Orthodoxy.   The duke of Egypt, with five
thousand soldiers, suddenly invested the church of St. The-
onas, where Athanasius and part of his clergy and people
were performing their midnight devotions.   While the soldiers were breaking open the sacred edifice, "the archbishop,
seated on his throne, expected, with calm and intrepid dignity, the approach of death; while the public devotion was
interrupted by shouts of rage and cries of terror, he animated his trembling congregation to express their religious
confidence by chanting one of the Psalms of David which
celebrates the triumph of the God of Israel over the haughty
and imperious tyrant of Egypt."   The Psalm sung was the
One hundred and thirty-sixth, which was performed by the
deacon singing:

O give thanks unto the Lord; for he is good:
And the people responding—

For his mercy endureth forever.

As the Psalm concluded the soldiers rushed into the building, but Athanasius, through the importunities of the clergy
and monks, made his escape and spent six years in impene-
trable obscurity among the lonely monasteries by the Nile.

In Syria, among other depredations, the Arians perverted the Doxology, "Glory be to the Father, the Son and

the Holy Ghost," which contained a recognition of the Trinity of the Godhead, and made it read, "Glory be to the Father, *by* the Son and the Holy Ghost." Leontius, the Arian Bishop of Antioch, adopted this Unitarian doxology, when Flavian and Diodorus, two pastors, and both earnest supporters of the orthodox faith, withdrew from his communion, and assembled their followers at the monuments of the martyrs, where, dividing them into two parts, they taught them to sing alternately the Psalms of the Bible and the orthodox doxology, Glory be to the Father, and the Son, and the Holy Ghost. According to Theodoret, Flavian and Diodorus and their adherents, wandered for days and nights in the palm groves of Syria, and the desert, now reclining under the open sky, again resting near the foot of some mountain, having nothing to console them but the Psalms, which, however, they sang everywhere. "At length they led the flock beside the banks of a neighboring stream; they did not, like the captives of Babylon, hang their harps on the willows, for they sang praises to their Creator in every part of his kingdom." The zeal of these Trinitarians was so great that swarms of monks were attracted to their meetings and took part in their Psalmody. Leontius, the Bishop of Antioch, was in danger of losing his whole congregation, and was compelled to recall the two protesting pastors and introduce the orthodox doxology. Milner states that Flavian was the first to use the present doxology, as sung in our evangelical churches, and that he was induced to introduce it as an offset to the Arian doxology established first in his day.

To the fourth century has been referred a relic brought by Dr. Hogg from Egypt, in 1843. It is a portion of the book of Psalms, written on papyrus, and is thus described: "Among the various objects of antiquity which were purchased from the Arabs at Thebes were two papyri, the one Coptic, the other Greek; both in the form of books. The subject of the Coptic papyrus, now in the hands of Sir William Gill, at Naples, has not yet been ascertained, but since my return to England, the Greek papyrus has been discovered to contain a portion of the Psalms. The leaves are of about ten inches in length, by seven in width, and are arranged and have been sewed together like a book. They are formed of strips of the papyrus plant crossing each other at right angles. The writing, continued on both sides, is perfectly legible, the letters partaking both of the uncial and cursive forms, sometimes standing quite apart, unconnected by cursive strokes, with accents occasionally but not regularly inserted. The beginning of the manuscript is imperfect, and it concludes with the second verse of the Thirty-fourth Psalm. The text, as far as it has been collated, has been found to be a good one, and to possess some interesting variations not found in other ancient versions. These papyri were both discovered among the rubbish of an ancient convent at Thebes, remarkable as still presenting some fragments of an inscription purporting to be a pastoral letter from Athanasius, patriarch of Alexandria, who died A. D. 371, which has been conjectured to be the age of the manuscript." This was no doubt the form of the Psalm books used by the monks in their devotions in that early day, and as used in the church in Alexandria while Athanasius was Bishop.

The Book of Psalms was highly esteemed by the early Christian fathers, not simply because they afforded excellent material for public and private psalmody, but because of the influence the reading, singing and studying of them had in forming character and promoting virtue. Most of the early authors prepared commentaries on the Psalms, in which their sentiments may be seen.

Says St. Basil, of the fourth century, "What is it, I pray, which you cannot find in the Psalms? Do not they teach you the most honorable fortitude, the most exact justice, a grave temperance, a discerning prudence, a right manner of repentance, the rules of patience, and every good thing that can be mentioned?"

St. Ambrose was a great admirer of what he called "The sweet book of Psalms." The One hundred and nineteenth was especially a favorite with him.

Augustine, after he had heard the Psalms sung in the church at Milan, wrote, "I read with pleasure the Psalms of David—the hymns and songs of thy church moved my soul intensely; thy truth was distilled by them into my heart; the flame of piety was kindled, and my tears flowed for joy." From the tenth book of his Confessions we learn that the "hymns and songs" sung at the church at Milan were the Psalms of the Bible. In his last sickness this distinguished divine exhibited his attachment to the Psalms by having those called the Penitential Psalms inscribed upon the wall of his bed chamber in a position and in such sized characters that he could easily read them. He usually read them with eyes filled with tears. Bingham, in his Antiquities, states the same thing as having been commanded by St. Austine while he lay sick.

Jerome was the author of "Commentaries on the Psalms;" and he was so much of an admirer of them that he was accustomed to recommend the reading, singing and committing of them to his pupils. He directed Rusticus "to learn the Psalms by heart, and to repeat them in turn as in the monks' assemblies," saying that he himself had learned them by heart when he was young, and sang them every day when old. His advice to the Lady Paula, with reference to the training of her daughter, was, "Let her never hear bad words, but as soon as she can speak let her learn some parts of the Psalms." He relates of Marcella, Paula, Blesilla and Eustochinno that they could recite with ease the Psalter in the Hebrew, Greek and Latin tongues.

The Psalms are still read and sung in those churches of the present day that have descended from the primitive Asiatic, African and European congregations. While we lament their degeneracy in the faith and piety of early days, and that they are now regarded, alongside of Mohamedanism and Budhism, as missionary ground, yet their present practices and attachments with reference to the Psalms and remnants of other portions of the Scriptures, are a pleasing episode in a history otherwise so full of superstition and folly.

Among the Nestorians, the nearest orthodoxy of all the relics of primitive churches, the Psalms are sung exclusively in worship. The whole book of Psalms, or portions of it, may be still found among the native Abyssinians, Copts, Armenians, and all the Eastern churches. The following extracts are from a letter written years ago to the author by Rev. John Crawford, a missionary of the United Presbyterian Church in Damascus, Syria : "The Psalms of David are, I believe, used more or less in all the Eastern churches. These churches are not all represented in Damascus, or in Syria, although the most of them are. There are, for example, no Nestorians in Syria, and no Copts in this part of it, and I cannot therefore speak positively in regard to them; but I presume that, in respect to the matter under consideration, there is little difference between them and the other churches. In the Greek, the Armenian, the Syrian and the Maronite churches the Psalms are much used in their different services. The Liturgy of the Greek church, which I have before me in Arabic, contains a large number of Psalms. Some of these are merely read, or used as prayers; others are sung. In the Greek church here in Syria they are sung sometimes in Arabic, sometimes in modern Greek, although few of the people understand Greek. In the Syrian and Maronite churches they are sung in Syriac only, a language which few of the worshipers now understand. In the Armenian church, the Armenian language, which is the language of the people, is, I think, used alone.

"In all the schools in these churches the children are taught to read the Psalms. No other portion of the Scriptures is used, and the book of Psalms is almost the only reading book, so that the children become very familiar with the Psalms and can repeat many of them from memory.

"So far as I am informed, none of the churches have metrical versions of the Psalms, but all use the prose version. They are, of course, chanted, although, I should say, their mode of chanting differs a good deal from the mode of chanting in the West. I have not, however, sufficient knowledge of music to describe the difference."

It is an interesting fact, amid the many changes that have passed over the spirit of the Oriental churches, during a period of more than two thousand years, that the music of Judah's Psalmists in no instance has lost its exercise or its power. In the Revolution of Christ and his Apostles that overturned a system having its existence from the days of Moses, the Psalms received a lustre they never possessed before, and so continued the songs of Zion.

In the decay of primitive Christianity, they preserved a place and an influence, when for the most part superstition and formalism covered and concealed all else. Whatever efforts have been made, to further change the features of eastern religion, it has been Psalm-singers converting Psalm-singers to Psalm-singing. Judaism, in its efforts to reclaim the fair country of Palestine to the faith and the forms of the kings and the prophets, still sings the Psalms of David. Catholicism sent over her missionaries to persuade the Greeks, Syrians, Egyptians, Abyssinians, to pay respect to the Holy See, but she sent the Psalter as the music of her schools. From the evangelical churches of Great Britain and the United States have been sent missionaries to bring back the descendants of the primitive worshipers to the purity and simplicity of the truth as it is in Christ, but in their Sabbath Schools and congregations in Asia Minor, Palestine, along the Nile, the Copts, Armenians, Maronites, are taught to sing the same Psalms that they and their fathers before them had sung in their native worship.

CHAPTER IV.

The Psalms in the Dark Ages.

The term Dark Ages has been applied in its widest sense to that period of intellectual depression in the history of Europe, from the establishment of the barbarian supremacy in the fifth century to the revival of learning, about the beginning of the fifteenth century. During these thousand years the pall of ignorance, superstition and crime rested upon the Church, as well as the state, and her forms of worship, like her priests and people, became greatly corrupted. The Scriptures gradually passed out of the hands of the people, so that Luther could consult a Bible only as he found it in a dead language, and chained in a monastery. It is an exceedingly interesting fact, that in this period of darkness the Psalms of David were almost the only portion of the Sacred Volume that continued its influence upon the minds of men. Though the practice of Psalmody was greatly corrupted, the chain in the story of the Hebrew Psalter remains an unbroken one.

This is the era of the reign of the monastic system, which, in the fourth century, swept with the rapidity of a contagion from the highlands of Upper Egypt, through Palestine and Syria and Italy, into Gaul and Great Britain. What was at first a vast confusion, gradually became reduced to a rigid system of religious forms and services under the influence of such monks as St. Anthony and Pachomius.

Of the devotions of the monasteries it may be said that David's Psalms were "the first, the middle and the last." It was a part of the exercise of each day to learn a portion of the Psalms by heart. Outside of the cloister exercises the monks sang Psalms at their labors, in their recreations, in their wanderings. Friends were received into the dwellings of the monks by Psalm-singing in imitation of Christ's entrance into Jerusalem. They sang them at their meals, in their social gatherings, and at all hours during the night and day. This they did without books, having committed to memory the Psalms according to the rules of their orders. Psalm-singing was so universal among the monks that an ancient author says of those in Palestine, "At Bethlehem there was nothing to be heard but Psalms; one could not go into the fields but he would hear the mower solacing himself with hymns, and the vinedresser tuning David's Psalms."

As may be supposed, in an age of extravagance, and among fanatics, Psalm-singing among these ascetics was carried to excess. A single instance will exhibit this. Socrates in his Ecclesiastical History, when speaking of the monks of Egypt, mentions one Pambos, an illiterate man who spent nineteen years in singing one verse of a Psalm: he "went to some one for the purpose of being taught a Psalm; and having heard the first verse of the Thirty-eighth, 'I said, I will take heed to my ways that I offend not with my tongue,' he departed without staying to hear the second verse, saying, this one would suffice if he could practically acquire it. And when the person who had given him the verse, reproved him because he had not seen him for the space of six months, he answered that he had not yet learned to practice the verse of the Psalm. After a considerable lapse of time, being asked by one of his friends whether he had made himself master of the verse, he answered, 'I have scarcely succeeded in accomplishing it during nineteen years.'"

In the monasteries Psalms were sung at all the canonical hours. In Egypt, according to St. Jerome, the monks met at 9 o'clock, when Psalms were sung, Scriptures read, prayer offered and remarks made. The author of the Constitutions prescribes for the devotions, the reading of the Old Testament, then the singing of Psalms; to the Bishops he gives direction: "When you teach the people, O Bishop, command them to come to church morning and evening, every day— do you assemble yourselves together every day, morning and evening, singing Psalms, and praying in the Lord's house. But especially on the Sabbath day, do you meet together more diligently." In many cases the superintendence of these Bishops extended to the monasteries.

St. Basil, in speaking of the nocturnal worship of the monks, mentions their confessing on their knees, and their rising to sing Psalms.

In connection with certain hours, certain Psalms were chosen and sung regularly because of some supposed fitness for those hours.

The Psalm that was sung statedly in the morning service was the Sixty-third, being selected because of the words, "Early will I seek thee." The monkish fathers highly prized this Psalm "as a spiritual song and medicine to blot out our sins, to kindle in us a desire of God; to raise our souls and inflame them with a mighty fire of devotion." It was known as the Morning Psalm. The stated Psalm for the evening service was that numbered One hundred and fortieth in the Latin Psalter, but in the English One hundred and forty-first. It was selected for the words, "Let my prayer be set forth before thee as incense, and the lifting up of my hands as the evening sacrifice," and was called the Evening Psalm. In some monasteries stated Psalms were selected for the hours between the morning and evening services, and in others not, such being sung as the leader or abbot might choose. According to St. Basil, in some places the Ninety-first Psalm was sung regularly at the sixth hour or noon-day. It was used to guard against the incursions of noon-day devils, and was selected chiefly because of the words in verses fourth, fifth and sixth:

"4. He shall cover thee with his feathers, and under his wings shalt thou trust ; his truth shalt be thy shield and buckler.

"5. Thou shalt not be afraid of the terror by night, nor for the arrow that flieth by day ;

"6. Nor for the pestilence that walketh in darkness; nor for the destruction that wasteth at noonday."

The stated Psalm was not the only one sung at the hour for which it was appointed. Other Psalms were usually selected at the option of whoever conducted the worship.

Cassian tells us that in Italy the Fifty-first and Nine-tieth Psalms were sung in addition to the Sixty-third, the regular morning Psalm, the Ninetieth being thought appropriate because of the words :

"5. Thou carriest them away as with a flood; they are as a sleep; in the morning they are like grass which groweth up.

"6. In the morning it flourisheth and groweth up; in the evening is cut down and withereth."

Frequently the Psalms were selected with reference to their appropriateness to those hours at which occurred the condemnation, crucifixion, burial and resurrection of Jesus Christ; thus the Twenty-second Psalm, "My God, my God, why hast thou forsaken me," etc., was a crucifixion Psalm.

In all of the nocturnal services, or the vigils, Psalms were sung, but seldom were any fixed for stated singing. When the Matutina or new morning services were begun in Bethlehem, and were fixed at 6 o'clock, the Fifty-first Psalm was appointed to be sung as a Psalm of confession:

"Have mercy upon me, O God, according to thy loving kindness; according unto the multitude of thy tender mercies blot out my transgressions," etc.

In other places, however, this Psalm was sung at the close of the nocturnal devotions or at the break of day.

In Egypt, the vigils were concluded with the One hundred and forty-eighth, One hundred and forty-ninth, and One hundred and fiftieth Psalms. St. Basil, speaking of these vigils, says that "the people rise while it is yet night, and come to the place of prayer, and there, with much labor and affliction and contrition and tears, make confession of their sins to God."

"When this is done, they rise from prayer, and dispose themselves to Psalmody; sometimes dividing themselves into two parts, they answer one another in singing, or sing alternately; after this again, they permit one alone to begin the Psalm, and the rest join in the close of every verse. And thus, with this variety of Psalmody, they carry on the night, praying betwixt whiles, or intermingling prayers, with their Psalms. At last, when the day begins to dawn, they all in common, as with one mouth and one heart, offer up to God the Psalm of confession (Fifty-first), every one making the words of their Psalm to be the expression of his own repentance."

The number of Psalms sung at the canonical hours,

has differed in different localities and ages. At first there was no uniform rule on this point, each monastery having been left to its own choice.

Cassian tells us that in Egypt, at the beginning of the Monastic life, the monks, in some places, sang ten Psalms in immediate succession; in other places eighteen were sung; in others twenty; in some as high as fifty were sung without intermission. At last, by common consent, the number for the morning and evening was reduced to twelve Psalms. After the full complement of canonical hours was introduced, many monasteries regulated the number of the Psalms by the number of the hour—three Psalms at the third hour, six at the sixth, nine at the ninth. Finally, the custom was established of singing only three Psalms at all the diurnal hours, the singing of the twelve being reserved for the regular morning and evening service.

The Psalms in the vigils of the night usually numbered more than during the day, in some monasteries as high as sixty being sung.

In the Gallican church, at the time of the second council of Tours, an order prevailed differing from that of the eastern countries. In one of the canons of this council, which met about the year 567 A. D., it was ordered that the new morning service, beginning at 6 o'clock, should be performed with six antiphonies and two Psalms, in the height of summer; in September there were to be seven antiphonies and two Psalms; in October, eight antiphonies and three Psalms; in November, nine antiphonies and three Psalms; in January and February until Easter, ten antiphonies and three Psalms. At the sixth hour, there were to be six Psalms and the Allelujah, and at the twelfth hour, twelve Psalms and the Allelujah. In the month of August, there were to be manications—early matins, or morning service, without Psalms, because it was the harvest time, and men were in haste to go to their labors.

This nocturnal Psalm-singing was increased to almost perpetual Psalmody in the vigils preceding the days appointed for great festive occasions. These special days grew in number, till there was an average of two for each week.

The Psalmody in the monasteries was usually performed in a standing posture, and after the manner of the church itself. In Egyptian monasteries, only the leader sang, and he "with a plain, even voice." In some cases more than one person was appointed to conduct the singing, in which case one person would follow another; if there were four persons, each would chant three of the twelve Psalms; if three, each would chant four; if two, each would chant six Psalms. Never more than four persons were appointed at one time.

Beside the regular monasteries, there were other communities of ascetics, which practiced what they called perpetual Psalmody. This custom was begun by the Watchers, founded in Constantinople during the fifth century, by Alexander, a monk. They divided themselves into three classes, which succeeded each other at stated hours, so that the exercises of prayer and praise never ceased. This they carried on, day and night, to guard against the incursions of midday and midnight devils. Besides these, were the Graziers, who lived after the manner of flocks and herds, and who performed their Psalm-singing in the fields and mountains as their cloisters. It was contrary to their custom to dwell in a house, to eat bread or flesh and to drink wine. They would usually sing and pray till meal-time and then take their knives and cut grass for their food. In the nunneries, the customs of the Psalmody as performed in the monasteries were followed. St. Jerome speaks of virgins singing Psalms at the canonical hours and in the night vigils, and says they were obliged to learn portions of the Psalter every day.

After the revolution produced by the Northern hordes, though the monastic institutions underwent some changes, yet the canonical hours, and the Psalms for those hours were retained. Cassian, writing about the fifth century, says, in a vindication of the Egyptian monks, what may be said of those in the West: "Our elders have not changed the ancient customs of singing, but the devotions are performed in the same manner as formerly in the meetings by night. The hymns, which it had been the custom to sing at the end of the night vigils, were the same hymns they sing at this day, namely, the Fifty-first, Sixty-third, Ninetieth and One hundred and forty-ninth." The changes of St. Benedict referred to agriculture, the distribution of monastic duties, the conduct of the monks in sleeping, eating, &c.

Not only was the ancient Psalm-singing continued by Benedict, but there was in his order something of the early enthusiasm of Psalmody. The Benedictines were "advised to separate the soul from the body by divine contemplations and for that purpose to emaciate and enervate the body by watching and singing of Psalms." Benedict desired to divide the day equally between agricultural pursuits and religious exercises ; but many of his disciples forgot the rules of their leader and spent their days in singing and prayer. The fanaticism among such became so great, as we are informed by Fosbrook, that the "best man was looked on as a barrel organ set to Psalm tunes ; and this was carried to such excess in some places that they established the Laus Perennis or Perpetual Psalmody—an infinite series of psalmody continued by relays of monks day and night forever without coming to an end. Not to wonder, when Psalm-singing was in high repute, that the monks should soon get up some marvelous tales about St. Benedict, the founder of their order ; it was asserted that he sang Psalms in his mother's womb ; and, at his birth, came singing into the world."

About the middle of the sixth century Columba, an Irishman, founded many churches and monasteries among the Irish and Scots. He was of royal blood, and was born, 521, in Gastan, County of Tyrconnel, Ireland. In 563 or 565, "he set out in a wicker boat, covered with hides, accompanied by twelve of his friends and followers, and landed in the isle of Hi, or Iona, near the confines of the Scottish and Pictish territories," being resolved to become the Apostle of the Highlands.

"By the preaching and virtues of Columba, many of the northern Picts were led to embrace Christianity, who gave him the small island on which he first landed. Here he built his monastery, which became the chief seminary of learning of that time, perhaps in Europe, and the nursery from which not only the monasteries of his own island, and above three hundred churches, which he himself had established, but also many of those in neighboring nations, were supplied with learned divines and able pastors. In this seminary, which might justly be called a missionary college, the students spent much of their time in reading, and in transcribing the Scriptures and sacred hymns, which Columba was at pains should be done with the greatest care and accuracy, in which he was surprisingly successful.''

Columba, like Basil, Athanasius and Benedict, was a monk and a Psalm-singer, and taught the singing of the Psalms in his monastery. A part of each day's duties for his pupils was the copying of the Psalter. On one occasion Baithen, a disciple of Columba, requested that a Psalter which he had copied should be examined by one of his brethren, but Columba replied that it had already been examined, and that there was but *one* error in it, which was the absence of the letter *i* from a word.

It is not until the time of Benedict and Columba that we find the Psalms a part of the disciplinary inflictions of the monasteries. It was a custom, in the old English monasteries, to fine the monks who were rich according to their wealth, but to impose a penalty of singing fifty Psalms on those unable to pay a fine in money.

In the rules of Columba it was ordained, ''A year's penance for him who loses a consecrated wafer; six months for him who lets it turn red; forty days for him who contemptuously flings it into the water; twenty days for him who brings it up through weakness of stomach. He who neglects his Amen to the Benedicite, who speaks when eating, who forgets to make the sign of the cross on his spoon, or on a lantern lighted by a younger brother, is to receive six or twelve stripes as the case may deserve, and repeat *twelve Psalms* . . . Fifty stripes for him who does not kneel at prayer, who has sung badly or has coughed while chanting the Psalms.''

In the flogging of the monks, a valuation of so many Psalms was placed alongside of so many lashes, and when the valuation superceded what was demanded by individuals for penance or penalty, the superabundant value of stripes went into a common fund for the benefit of those who could not pay what they owed.

"The monks of Fonte Avellana determined that thirty Psalms sung with an accompaniment of one hundred lashes to each Psalm, making three thousand lashes, should be set off for one year of purgatory. By a fantastic species of arithmetic three thousand lashes were valued at £4. The whole Psalter, with fifteen thousand lashes, was set off for five years; and twenty Psalters with thirty thousand lashes entered into the book of the Recording Angel as receipt in full for one hundred years of purgatory. This scale seems to have been sanctioned by the Pope."

None was more ambitious, if we may believe a legend, to lay up this kind of spiritual and heavenly treasure than St. Dominic, the Cuirassier—so called from wearing an iron cuirass next his skin. He taxed himself ordinarily at ten Psalters and thirty thousand lashes for each day: at which rate, three thousand six hundred and fifty years of purgatory could be redeemed in a single year. During Lent, the ordinary task was not sufficient for this benevolent monk. His superiors were petitioned to supplement till his daily task was two and a half Psalters and thirty-four thousand five hundred stripes for each day, the valuation of one hundred years of purgatory. But even this did not satisfy him. During Lent again, he petitioned for the privilege of redeeming one thousand years of purgatory. During the forty days of Lent, says Damian, he sang two hundred Psalters and inflicted sixty millions of stripes! Well might Yepes say of this saint, "I neither know how his head should be capable of repeating so many Psalms, nor how his arms should have strength to give him so many blows, nor how his flesh should be able to endure so inhuman a battery." But as the legend runs, St. Dominic gained flesh under his castigations. His appetite grew by what it fed on until, in jockey phrase, he flogged himself against time. He commenced one evening singing and flogging and in twenty-four hours went twelve times through the Psalter and had begun the thirteenth and gone to beati quorum in the Thirty-second Psalm, taking one hundred and eighty-one thousand one hundred lashes, equal to sixty-one years, twelve days and thirty-three minutes of purgatory!! Now as old St. Dominic only sinned once, in accepting the present of a furred robe, he stood creditor to an immense amount on the angel's books; but as no good works are lost, all went to the great sinking fund of the Holy Catholic Church." Pietro Damiano, a cardinal and saint, related these events as occurring to his own personal knowledge. His relation of them is in a letter written to Pope Alexander II. "A Protestant might have asked how Dominic counted the stripes while singing the Psalms, and also what *became of the cuirass all the time,* for it has been well said, if he kept it on, he might have laid on as lustily as Sancho on the trees, and still have kept a whole skin."

In the Brotherhood of the Eleven Thousand Virgins, founded by Elector Frederick the Wise, the community had accumulated vast fortunes in spiritual treasures, which was to be set at the disposal of its members to help them on the road to salvation. They were entitled to draw on a fund of no less than six thousand, four hundred and fifty-five masses; three thousand, five hundred and fifty entire Psalters; two hundred thousand rosaries, besides eleven thousand prayers of the Patroness of St. Ursula, and "six hundred and thirty-eleven thousand Paternosters and Ave Marias."

It was partly because many of the monks had come behind in their yearly penance of Psalters and stripes—some of them to the extent of three hundred years in purgatory, and nine hundred thousand lashes, valued at £1,200—that the Crusades took so largely from these monastic orders. The Pope proclaimed pardon and exemption to all who would go in the Crusades.

An interesting feature of the history of the Psalms as they are connected with the monasteries, is in the art of illuminating and illustrating manuscripts, as it was carried on extensively by the monks in their cells. The copying of the Scriptures in letters of gold was called chrysographia, or gold writing. It is evidently very ancient in its origin, having existed among the Arabs, and probably among the Jews, long before the Christian era. The copy of the sacred book sent to Ptolemy by the high priest Eleazar, and presented to him by the seventy-two interpreters, was written upon the finest vellum in letters of gold.

A number of Psalters are preserved embellished richly with gold letters and pictures.

Among the legacies of Count Everard we find bequeathed to his son Beringarius, a Psalter written in letters of gold. Of the few books belonging to the first church erected at Canterbury, England, was "a Psalter ornamented with a miniature painting of Samuel, the Priest, and adorned on the outside with the image of Christ and the four evangelists on a plate of silver." A Latin Psalter, ornamented with most beautiful miniatures and richly illuminated for Richard II. when but a youth, is preserved in the Cottonian Library. It contains a calendar and various tables, besides hymns and the Athanasian Creed. The King is represented in different places on his knees before the Virgin Mary, who has the infant Jesus in her arms.

Charlemagne, while King of the Franks, had a Psalter executed in letters of gold to present to Pope Hadrian II., as the dedicatory verses, written by himself, state. The Psalter is written on vellum and is a large octavo volume.

Scaliger tells us "his grandmother had a Psalter, the cover of which was two inches thick, in the inside of which was a kind of cupboard wherein was a silver crucifix, and behind it the name of Berenica Codrona, de la Scala."

A Latin Psalter, with an interlinear Saxon version, of the ninth century, is decorated on the exterior of the oaken boards with which it is bound, with a large brass crucifix, about seven or eight inches in height, formerly, perhaps, covered or washed with silver.

Ervene, one of the teachers of Wolstan, and Bishop of Worcester, to encourage his pupils to learn to read, had a Psalter and Sacramentary prepared whose capital letters were written in gold.

In the Cotton Library is a Psalter said to have been

used by Athelstan, in Saxon letters, written in 703. Every Psalm is begun with gilt capitals, with a title preceding it in red letters. It has several ornamental paintings.

Longfellow, in his History of Poetry, gives an idea of an ancient glee-man from an illuminated manuscript of the Psalms. The picture is "a frontispiece to the Psalms of David. The great Psalmist sits upon his throne with a harp in his hand and his masters of sacred song about him. Below stands the glee-man throwing three balls and three knives alternately into the air and catching them as they fall, like a modern juggler."

In the Egerton Collection is a Psalter, the corners of of whose binding are carved ivory. To protect the fragile binding it is encased in a portable glass box. The one side presents six incidents in the life of King David; the other, six works of mercy. A small shield with the text is placed between the figures in each. The figures are flat in execution, but the interlacing bands, strongly resembling the Saxon style of ornament, the graceful, though nondescript, animals that fill up the interstices, the borders, beautiful exceedingly, that surround each side, are exquisite in execution and taste. The middle of each foliaged scroll is finished with a turquoise, the centre ornaments have rubies, and scarcely could Queen Victoria receive a more royal gift-book than this remain of an age termed dark and barbarous. The Psalter belonged to one of the queens of Jerusalem about the twelfth century.

In 1299 Godfrey, abbot of Peterborough, presented to an Italian cardinal "a Psalter written in letters of azure and gold and wonderfully illuminated." In the Arundel collection is a Prayer-book containing a Psalter and antiphonal, the gift-book of Robert de Lyle to his daughter Audfrey. "The chief fault of the specimen is its profusion of gold. Nearly all the pictures are on a burnished gold ground; and so thick has the sizing been laid on, that in some instances the figures seem sunk within it. With the initial letters, raised gold forms the letter and the most graceful foliage enriches it, and sweeps downward almost to the foot of the page. Lighter foliage, vine or ivy leaves, some green, some bright gold, waves around the heavier portions and the masses

of shade and color are further carried off by most delicate
flourishes, with the finest pen. The music of the Psalter is
on four red lines. A border encircles some of the pages, finished off with fine pen flourishes, and sometimes with a small
vignette. These consist of birds and beasts. Figures of
the prophets and saints in oral meditation, on a ground of
bright pierced gold, and delicate armorial bearings, also meet
us. The initial letter of the Eighty-first Psalm encloses
King David, not playing on a harp, but striking a row of
silver bells, like a true Saxon, with hammers. Two figures,
one playing the violin, and the other the bagpipe, support
him; two graceful figures with a harp and a small organ,
occupy the lower corner of the page, and above two angels
are blowing burnished trumpets. The initial letter of the
Ninety-third Psalm gives us a group of choristers singing
from a long roll of music; the One hundred and tenth Psalm
(Dixit Dominus) has a representation of the Trinity finely
drawn, and the whole page is gorgeously ornamented."

There is a story told of the Cathack, a beautiful manuscript copy of the Psalms, said to have been written by St.
Columba. To exhibit veneration for the memory of this
great saint, this Psalter was enshrined in a magnificent case,
was carried as a sacred standard before the army in battle
and was so highly venerated from age to age, that it came
to be employed as a solemn sanction in the taking of oaths.
But the opening of this mysterious Psalter was forbidden
forever under the pain of some awful calamity.

In the monasteries of the present day, which may be
found in almost every country under the sun, the ancient
rules of Psalmody are to a great extent followed. The
Psalms are distributed throughout their liturgies for regular
reading and singing.

In the East, along the banks of the Nile, in Palestine,
Mesopotamia, Syria, where the ascetic system took its rise,
may be seen, everywhere, monastic buildings, some of which
are very ancient, and all of which are still occupied by a few
miserable and idle male and female monks. The libraries of
these monasteries are mostly composed of well-thumbed liturgies, in which the Psalms always hold a prominent place.

Lazy pilgrims may be met with who will perform upon one another the rite of baptism in the Jordan, or Red Sea, singing, as they baptize, the Psalms with a loud and boisterous noise.

But the history of the Psalms in the middle ages is not confined to the monasteries or to the churches whose ritual corresponded closely to that used by the monks. Their story is part of the every-day life of the era, and is always identified with the devoutness of such zealous Christians as survived the general decay.

The great Gregory, who was raised to the papal chair in 590, exhibited much attachment to the sacred Scriptures, which he knew by heart, and so loved the Psalms that he obliged his attendants to sing them with him when on his deathbed.

Charlemagne, the renowned warrior of France, whose name is associated with the military achievements of the close of the eighth and beginning of the ninth century, manifested great fondness for Psalm-singing. In his youth he had committed the Psalms to memory, and afterward sang them to the day of his death. A frequent charge of his to the priests was that they should gain proper views of the Scriptures and commit the Psalms to memory. He also recommended that when the Bishops and Abbots would have the poor with them at their meals, they should associate psalmody with their feasting. From his memorizing the Psalms, Alcuin, the historian of Charlemagne, has called him David.

A Latin Psalter, owned by Hildegard, wife of Charlemagne, and used by her during her lifetime, was, after her death, presented by the Emperor to the Cathedral of Bremen, where it was kept for several centuries, and annually exhibited to wondering and admiring multitudes.

During the Middle Ages there was a custom, largely observed in Roman Catholic countries, of perambulating, with great pomp and ceremony, the boundaries of the parish. This was done on what were called Gauge days—the Monday, Tuesday and Wednesday before Holy Thursday or Ascension Day. In the procession were borne banners, bells and lights, while occasionally the people engaged in singing Psalms and listened to the haranguing of some monk or priest, having the One hundred and fourth Psalm as his theme. The Psalms sung were thanksgiving psalms, such as exhibited best the festivities and hilarities of the occasion.

This custom of religious processions originated at a very early day, and was observed especially at funerals and marriages. Afterward it was adopted by the Arians, who awakened enthusiasm by their torchlight processions at night and their vociferous singing of Arian hymns. After the fourth or fifth century processions were frequent in connection with the installation of bishops, the consecration of relics, at feasts of thanksgiving, and often on occasions of danger or calamity. "Through the influence of Mamertus, Bishop of Vienna, 450 A. D., and Gregory the Great, processions became a regular ceremony which recurred at stated times, when the Gospels, costly crucifixes and banners, torches and burning candals, relics, pictures of the Virgin and of saints, were carried about, and Psalms or hymns sung. The religious services on these occasions were called Litanies. They consisted of prayers, and of the invocation of saints and angels, to which the people made response, 'Ora pro nobis!'"

Sometimes, during the Middle Ages, we meet with the Psalms in the novel customs of divination. This is at times called bibliomancy, at other, sortes sacrae, or sacred lots, and consisted in a sudden dipping into the Bible, or a sudden entrance into a religious assembly and a noting of the passage first striking the eye or the ear. This practice was a relic of heathenism, pagans at a very early day observing it with the poems of Homer and Virgil. Though it was repeatedly prohibited by successive councils in the fifth, sixth, seventh and eighth centuries, yet it prevailed extensively in the Roman Catholic Church. Prominent in these divinations were the Psalms, which became the oracle to which many resorted for intimations of the future.

When Clovis, the King of the Franks, was about to go to war with the Goths of Spain, he asked of heaven that he might have some revelation of the success of his project.

As he entered the Church of St. Martin, whither he had gone for the divine intimation, the choir was singing those words in the Eighteenth Psalm, "Thou hast given me the necks of mine enemies, that I might destroy them that hate me. They cried but there was none to save them, even unto the Lord, but he answered them not." This satisfied the superstitious monarch, and he went from the church convinced that heaven had decreed victory for him. Bibliomancy was resorted to frequently in appointing bishops, in which case, after a fast of three days, the Psalms, the Epistles of St. Paul and the Gospels were placed on one side of the altar, and on the other side small billets having on them the names of the candidates for the office. On one of these occasions when St. Agnan was chosen, it was done by St. Euvert calling a child and requiring it to act in the Sacred Lots. The child took up a billet that had the name of St. Agnan written on it. That the multitude might be satisfied that the call was of God, Euvert took the Psalter and opened suddenly where it said: "Blessed is the man whom thou choosest and causest to approach unto thee, that he may dwell in thy courts." Opening in the Epistle of St. Paul he found; "Other foundation can no man lay, than that is laid, which is Jesus Christ." In the Gospels he found: "Upon this rock will I build my church, and the gates of hell shall not prevail against it." These testimonies were satisfactory, and St. Agnan was proclaimed bishop.

This custom was continued in the cathedrals at Boulogne, Ypres, and at St. Omer till a period as late as 1744, the practice at Boulogne differing from that of earlier times in that the Psalms only were used in the divination.

The Psalms were sung in the canonization of the saints. From ten to twenty years after the death of some illustrious servant of the Church, canonization began by the proper authorities pitching a tent over the grave of the dead. Around the tent stood the great body of the attendants, whose office it was to chant the Psalms, while the Superior, accompanied by the more aged of the brotherhood, entered the tent, opened the grave, and prepared the bones, by washing and carefully wrapping them in linen or silk, for their deposition in the mortuary chest.

Psalm-singing accompanied unction at sick-beds. It was customary to perform unction on the eyelids, ears, lips, nostrils, neck, shoulders, breast, hands, feet and the principal parts affected by pain, a Psalm being chanted after each unction. If the sick died, the priests walked in front of the bier to the church and thence to the cemetery, chanting Psalms.

In the dedication of churches during the Middle Ages, Psalm-singing was a prominent feature of the ceremonies. The night preceding the solemn occasion was spent in watching and prayer. In the morning, the prelates, dressed in their pontifical robes, repaired to the porch of the church. Here the principal consecrator struck the door thrice with his crozier, saying, "Lift up your gates, O ye princes : and be ye lifted up, O eternal gates, and the King of glory shall come in." At the third stroke the door was opened. As the procession entered the church, the choir sang the Twenty-fourth Psalm, and the bishop exclaimed, "Peace to this house and all who dwell in it; peace to those who enter it ! Peace to those who go out." Proceeding to the foot of the altar, the consecrators lay prostrate till the litany was sung ; after which one of the bishops wrote two Roman alphabets on the floor in the form of a cross, and sprinkled the altar, walls and pavements with holy water. A prayer being chanted, the altars consecrated and mass said, the ceremonies ended with a banquet in the Episcopal palace.

In the devotions for the dead, the order consisted in frequent repetition of the Lord's Prayer, which was commonly called a belt of Pater-nosters; in the chanting of a number of Psalms, and in the people prostrating themselves upon their knees and intoning the anthem, "O Lord, according to thy great mercy give rest to his soul, and in consideration of thy infinite goodness grant that he may enjoy eternal light in company of the saints."

In the consecration of cemeteries, among other ceremonies, the bishop, followed by the clergy, walked around the limits intended for the burial of the dead, chanting the

Miserere—Fifty-first Psalm—and reading five prayers, one at each of the four corners and one in the middle of the ground. Absolution was one of the favorite practices of the Roman clergy, the ceremonies of which were attended with great pomp. Ash-Wednesday was the time appointed for this event. In the morning of this day, those who wished the imposition of penance, on account of some sin against the Moral Law, or some insult to religion, repaired publicly to the porch of the church, barefoot and clothed in robes of mourning. At the proper time the bishop led them into the church, and, himself, lay prostrate before the altar, while the choir chanted Psalms Thirty-seven, Fifty, Fifty-one and Fifty-three. After the offering of a prayer, the imposition of hands and the clothing of the head in sackcloth and ashes, the penitents, after the example of God's casting out Adam, were thrust from the church, and required, before their absolution would take effect, to perform the penitential services imposed upon them.

Psalm-singing mingled to some extent in the enthusiasm of the Crusades, which began in the eleventh century and continued to the middle of the thirteenth. This was not engaged in by the people, but by the priests and monks who performed the offices of the Church during the pilgrimages. It has been stated that the Crusades originated in a misinterpretation of a passage in the Psalms. The seventh verse of Psalm One hundred and thirty-second, which is properly rendered in the English version, "We will worship at his footstool," was translated in the Vulgate, "Let us adore the Lord in the spot where his feet were placed." Some of the most eminent fathers of the Church, such as Jerome and Eusebius, considered this as a prophecy and a command requiring the faithful to visit the Holy City and its surrounding sacred spots for the purpose of worshiping God where Christ himself had engaged in his devotions. Whether or not this verse gave rise to the Crusades, certain it is that it was the text of many a flaming discourse by bishops, priests and monks in their efforts to begin and carry on the holy wars against the infidels of the Holy Land.

Among the wonderful tales of the Crusade era is one

concerning the miraculous "Psalm-book of Quindreda," the sister of St. Kenelmus.   On the eve of the festival of St. Kenelmus, at Winchelcumbe, a crowd of women came from all the neighboring places to be present at the festivities given by the monks.   During the progress of the events connected with the occasion, one of the monks became guilty of an outrage in the corridors of the cloister.   On the next day he carried the Psalter of Quindreda in the procession; but when he wished to put it down, the book adhered to his hands.   He then remembered his sin of the preceding night, confessed, offered penance, and, by the assistance of the prayers of the brethren, succeeded in "breaking the chains the Divinity had imposed on him!"

This wonderful Psalter was the means of detecting guilt in Quindreda herself.   When the body of Kenelmus, her brother, was being carried to the grave, the people cried out, " He is a martyr."   Quindreda being suspected of committing the murder, she attempted a defense by saying, " It is as true that he has been assassinated as it is true that my eyes, drawn from my hand, are fastened on this Psalter." Scarcely had she uttered the words till both eyes fell from their sockets upon the book, leaving the stain of blood upon the leaves.   Such are some of the legends related by Baldwin, Archbishop of Canterbury, in a journal written in Wales.

It seems that this Psalter accompanied the crusaders in their marches and operated great prodigies by the way.

It is an item of no little interest that after the soldiers of the first Crusade scaled the walls of Jerusalem, July 15th, 1099, they marched by the light of burning buildings, and with feet treading in blood, to the church of the Resurrection, repeating Psalms.

The subject of the various versions of the Psalms meets us frequently during the progress of the Middle Ages.   The Hebrew was the original language of the Psalter.   There is no evidence of its having been rendered in any other dialect until about two hundred years before Christ.   This was the language of the Tabernacle, the Temple, a language that is now a dead tongue, except to some of the Jewish descendants, who have preserved a knowledge of it, by its use in the religious services of the synagogues.

The dialect in which Christ and his disciples employed the Psalms was the Greek, in what is commonly known as the Septuagint. At what time the Psalms, with the other inspired books, passed into the native dialects of the early Christian communities, is not known.

In the West the Scriptures were at first familiar only to those who could read the Greek, or who had learned them from those who had carried them there. But translations soon appeared. From Augustine we learn that the Latin Church very early possessed a number of versions in the native dialect of Italy. That translation which obtained the widest circulation passed under the name of Vetus Itala, or Ancient Italian. It was a translation from the Septuagint, and not from the Hebrew, there being few in the Western Church that were at that time acquainted with the native language of the Jews. It is supposed to have been prepared in the early part of the second century, as it is mentioned by Tertullian before the close of that century.

It was from this old Italic that the Psalms were sung by the western Christians for nearly three hundred years. But before the middle of the fourth century the Italic version of the Scriptures became extremely faulty, owing to errors in the copying of it from time to time. These errors gave opportunity to the enemies of the Church, especially to the Jews, to cavil concerning the doctrines and fidelity of the Christians. To remedy the evils and silence the objections of enemies, Jerome, under the patronage of Pope Damasus, undertook first a revision of the old version, and afterwards an entirely new one. The corrected edition appeared A. D. 390 or 391. The Psalms, which are all that remain of this edition, were called the Roman Psalter, because it began the soonest, and lasted the longest in the Roman offices. Its use began in the churches of Gaul almost as soon as at Rome, and prevailed there until, in the sixth century, Gregory of Tours, introduced that known as the Gallican Psalter.

The Gallican Psalter was also prepared by Jerome. It

was made from Origen's corrected edition of the Greek version, but, where the Greek was supposed faulty, the rendering was taken directly from the Hebrew; this Psalter was completed in 389 and was first used in Gaul, hence called Gallican.   From Gaul it passed into the worship of the English churches, and into those of Germany and Spain.   But in Rome, Jerome's first corrected edition continued in use, though the popes connived at its introduction in the western churches, even in those of some parts of Italy.   This version was publicly authorized by the Council of Trent and was soon afterwards introduced into the Church at Rome itself.   It is this ancient Psalter, corrected somewhat by Coverdale and others, that is still continued in the English Liturgy as the *reading Psalms*, and in the offices of the Catholic Church.

Augustine at first violently opposed the use of the Gallican Psalms, but afterwards became so highly pleased with them that he selected passages from them and embodied them in his Speculum, or Mirror, a work which contained choice selections from the Scriptures, and which he designed for those who were too poor to purchase the whole of the sacred Word, or too busily employed to read it all.

So highly pleased with this translation was Lucinius Boeticus, a Spaniard, and a warm friend to the Scriptures, that in 394 he sent six short-hand copyists from Spain to Palestine, where Jerome was when he prepared it, to take copies of it and of the other works of Jerome.

Jerome prepared also a Psalter directly from the Hebrew, which has been called the Hebraic-Latin Psalter. This was completed in 391, but though much admired, was never introduced into the offices of the Church.

During the Middle Ages many translations of the Psalms were made into the dialects of those nations among whom the Catholic Church sent her missionaries.   In many cases the Psalms were published in a volume by themselves, owing to their being essential to the performances of the Liturgy. Sometimes versions were translated by individuals on their own responsibility.   This was especially the case toward the close of the Middle Ages, when the Papal Church prohibited the use of the Scriptures to the people in their own dialects.

In the Ninth Century appeared a metrical version of the Psalms in the German, by Otfrid. Otfrid was a German by birth, and a monk of the Order of St. Benedict. He was at first a hearer, then a disciple of the celebrated Abbot of Fulda, Rabanus Maurus. Trithemus says of Otfrid: "He was profoundly versed in the knowledge of the Scriptures, and extensively acquainted with literature in general: a philosopher, a rhetorician, and a famous poet; eloquent in speech and excellent in disposition. His prose and poetical works were numerous, and have transmitted his name with honor to posterity. After the example of Charlemagne, he attempted to reduce the barbarous language of the ancient Germans to grammatical rule, and partially succeeded." A manuscript copy of his metrical Psalms is preserved in the Imperial Library at Vienna.

In the same century the Roman Liturgy with the Roman Psalter was translated into the Slavonic by Cyril and Methodius, brothers, and natives of Thessalonica, and both missionating monks. The letter of Pope John VIII, to these monks, approving of their works, will show that the Catholic Church had not yet, 880 A. D., shut out the Scriptures from the native languages. He says: "We approve of the Slavonic letters invented by the philosopher Constantine; and we order that the praises of Christ may be published in that language. It is not contrary to the faith to employ it in the prayers of the Church, and in reading the Holy Scriptures. He who made the three principal languages, Latin, Greek and Hebrew, made the rest also for his own glory. Nevertheless to show the more respect to the Gospel, let it first be read in the Latin, and then in the Slavonican for the sake of the people who understand not Latin."

In the latter part of the Tenth Century, Notker, surnamed Labeo, translated the Psalter into the Teutonic or Old German. He undertook the translation of the Psalms that the monks, under his care, who could not understand the Latin, might understand what they sang.

Schilter, who published a corrected edition of this Psalter, gives the title of it in Latin,—"*Notkeri Tertii Tabeonis Psalterium: e Latino in Theotiscam Veterem Linguam versum, et Paraphrasi illustratum. E Manuscripto codice pervetusto Du de la Lonbere, Primus eruit, et describi, dum viveret, curavit. Tum interpretatione et notis ornavit Io. Schilterus. Ulmae, 1726.*

A copy of this Psalter was written for the use of the Empress Cunegundis, wife of Henry II, A. D. 1004, by the younger Ekkerard, a monk of Mentz.

The following will give an idea of this translation:

PSALM I.

1. Der man ist salig, der in dero argon rat ne gegieng,
   Noh an dero sundigon unege ne stuont;
   Noh an demo suhstnole ne saz.
2. Nube ner ist salig, tes unillo an gotes eo ist, une der
   dara ana denchet tag unde naht.

In the Library of Trinity College, Cambridge, are two translations of the Psalms, one into the Norman-French, and the other a Polyglot, belonging to the Eleventh Century. The Polyglot contains the three most celebrated versions of the Latin Psalms, the Gallican, Roman and Hebraic, with a preface, prayer and commentary subjoined to each Psalm. With the Gallican version is a gloss or brief commentary; with the Roman is an interlineary Normano-Saxon version; and with the Hebraic, the Norman-French version. The whole is written on vellum, and is a beautiful specimen of an illuminated manuscript.

In the year 1229, met the Council of Toulouse, made infamous in history by its prohibiting the translation of the Scriptures into the languages of the people. The celebrated Canon is in the following terms: "We also forbid the laity to possess any of the Old or New Testaments, except perhaps, some one out of devotion wishes to have the Psalter or Breviary for the divine offices, or the Hours of the Blessed Virgin. But we strictly forbid them having any of these books translated into the vulgar tongue."

But this Canon had little influence, for from the

Thirteenth to the Sixteenth Century, individual enterprise supplied the Psalms and all the other sacred books in many of the vulgar tongues of the times.

In the Fifteenth Century printing was invented, and so the world was destined no longer to look for its copies of the Word of God to the pens and parchments of the lazy monks.

The first book issued from type and the first printed book that bears the names of the printers, and the place and date of its publication, was a Latin Psalter, commonly known as the Mentz Psalter. The most perfect copy of it has been preserved in the library at Vienna. It was discovered near Inspruck, in the Castle of Ambras, in 1665, among a mass of MSS. and printed books collected by Francis Sigismund. "The book is printed in folio, on vellum, and of such extreme rarity, that not more than six or seven copies are known to be in existence, all of which, however, differ from each other in some respect or other. The Psalter occupies one hundred and thirty-five leaves, and the *recto* the one hundred and thirty-sixth; the remaining forty-one leaves are appropriated to the litany, prayers, responses, vigils, &c. The Psalms are executed in larger characters than the hymns; the capital letters are cut on wood, with a degree of delicacy and boldness which is truly surprising; the largest of them, the initial letters of the Psalms, which are black, red and blue, must have passed three times through the press."

This Psalter bears date of August 14, 1457. A second edition of it was executed in 1459, and contains, with it, the first printed text of the Athanasian Creed. It is supposed that the St. Alban and Benedictine monks were at the expense of issuing both of these editions. Before the close of the century more than thirty editions of the Latin Psalter were issued from the press of Faust and Schoeffer.

Since the Fifteenth Century, and especially since the Reformation, Psalters, either by themselves or bound up with the New Testament, have passed into almost every language upon the face of the globe, and are now read or sung by earth's millions.

But one more edition of the Psalter will be noticed in

this connection : it is the celebrated Polyglots of Justinian, or Giustiniani.   Concerning the rise of Polyglots, a learned writer in his " Succinct Account of Polyglot Bibles," remarks : "The taste that prevailed early in the Sixteenth Century for the cultivation of literature was partly the cause of, and partly owing to the publication of the sacred writings in different languages. Certain men, in whom were providentially meeted a taste for sound learning, together with ecclesiastical influence, and secular opulence, determined to publish, first, *parts*, and then the *whole* of the sacred writings, in such languages as were esteemed the learned languages of the universe.   These were principally Latin, Greek, Hebrew, Arabic, Chaldee and Syriac ; others of less importance were added to them.   Such publications attract- ed general attention, and became greatly studied.   Hence the taste, not only for sacred literature, but universal science, became widely diffused ; and the different nations of Europe seemed to vie with each other in the publication of those works which have since obtained the denomination of Polyglotts, that is, ' Books in many languages.' "

The Polyglott Psalter of Justinian, Bishop of Nebio, in the Island of Corsica, was the first of these great publica- tions.   Its title is, "Psalterium, Hebraicum, Græcum, Ara- bicum, et Chaldeum, cum tribus Latinis Interpretationibus at Glossis."   It was printed at Geneva, 1516, by Peter Paul Porrus, and is in folio.   The preface to the Psalter is ad- dressed by the author to Pope Leo X.   The work is divided into eight columns, the first containing the Hebrew, the second, Justinian's Latin translation, rendered word for word from the Hebrew ; the third, the Latin Vulgate ; the fourth, the Greek; the fifth, the Arabic; the sixth, the Chal- dee paraphrase in Hebrew characters ; the seventh, Justin- ian's Latin translation of the Chaldee paraphrase; the eighth, Latin Scholia, or notes.

The Arabic in this Psalter was the first ever printed, and the Psalter itself the first part of the Bible that ever ap- peared in so many languages.

Justinian's motive in preparing this work was to secure some means whereby he might assist his indigent relatives.

But in this he was grievously disappointed, as we learn from his own statement: "I had always imagined that my work would be largely sought after, and that the wealthy prelates and princes would have afforded me every assistance necessary for printing the rest of the Bible in such a diversity of languages. But I was mistaken; every one applauded the work, but suffered it to rest and sleep; for scarcely was a fourth part sold of the two thousand copies which I had printed, exclusive of fifty more copies printed upon vellum, which I had presented to all the kings of the world, whether Christian or pagan."

In the Scholia or comments on Psalm 19:4: "Their words are gone to the end of the world," Justinian has given, "by way of commentary, a curious sketch of the life of Columbus, and an account of his discovery of America, with a very singular description of the inhabitants, particularly of the female native Americans; and in which he affirms that Columbus often boasted himself to be the person appointed by God to fulfill this prophetic exclamation of David." But the account of Columbus, by Justinian, seems to have displeased the family of that great navigator, for in the life of Columbus, written by his son (See Churchill's Coll. of Voyages, &c., Vol. II, Page 560), he is accused of falsehood and contradiction; and it is even added, "that considering the many mistakes and falsehoods found in his Psalter and History, the Senate of Genoa has laid a penalty upon any person who shall read or keep it, and has caused it to be carefully sought out in all places it has been sent to, that it may by public decree be destroyed, and utterly extinguished."

CHAPTER V.

THE PSALMS IN THE REFORMATION.

The Reformation of the fifteenth and sixteenth centuries partook of the nature both of a reaction and a revival. For centuries the intelligence and piety of the Church had been lying in a relapse; ignorance, formality and idolatry had succeeded to primitive light and zeal, saints and relics had usurped the honors of the Messiah; traditions and visions had been valued above Revelation, and society was again growing grey in its sins. But, as has been often remarked, there is a point in the retrogression of human affairs beyond which the race does not seem to pass. Before ignorance entirely reaches the brutal, and the heart's passions grow thoroughly fiendish, the divine within us, as if impelled by the sudden consciousness of its terrible decline, wheels upon its course, and mounts rapidly in a reform. The historian need not pause to determine the philosophy of such a phenomenon. Whether attributable to a certain elasticity of the native intellect, to the immediate interposition of a higher Power, or to both, the fact remains, and history appears to us little else than a record of the successive ebbings and flowings of faith and intelligence. By the twelfth century Western Europe had touched the lowest mark of immorality and wretchedness, when began another of the seeming periodic returns. This reaction against superstition, priestcraft, idolatry, ignorance and corruption in a thousand forms, culminated in what is commonly termed the Reformation; and introduced an era surpassed in importance only by the coming of Christ himself. With the reactions began a revival of primitive piety; the Bible issued from the cloister, and the shackles of an unknown tongue to exert a new power in the dialects of the people; faith gained upon superstition; and the doctrines of pure and undefiled religion upon the legends of a barbarous age; Christ rose to the zenith of esteem; men sought again the truth from the lips of his faithful servants,

90

and the world once more beheld the fervor and heard the devotions of a great regeneration.

Few events have ever given to the world such a variety of blessings as the Reformation. So universal was the change it produced, that we seem to be ushered into the presence of a newer and higher economy. The human mind regained its independence, and with it followed naturally freedom of speech and of the press.

Conscience regained its lost rights, and men learned that they could worship God as their own convictions impelled them.

Education resumed her influence among the masses, bearing to the humblest the ability to read and study the divine records.

Civil liberty began to dawn, and at this remote day we have republican institutions, the fruits of the great reform.

Among all the secondary features of the Reformation none appear with greater interest than the revival of sacred Psalmody. During the Dark Ages, the human voice was not silent in the matter of song, but its tones were bent from the high and ennobling exercise of singing the Redeemer's praise, and of giving utterance to the workings of pious hearts, and became merely a medium for exhibiting the corruptions of depraved inner life, or for magnifying the names and attributes of Antichrist. The Reformation purified the Psalmody of Zion; the book of Sacred Songs was expurgated, those in the praise of the Virgin and the saints being cast out.

The Sacred Songs of the Reformation appeared in the native tongues of the people, instead of a language dead, and so its sentiments unknown. Psalms and Hymns rolled over Germany, rising from the lips of her thousands, in words and in a rythm with which all were familiar. Passing from the native land of Luther, these sacred songs retained their inspiration and truth, but dropped their dress and reappeared in the dialects of the Russian, the Pole, the Swiss, the Italian, the Spaniard, the Portuguese, the French, the Netherlander, the Norwegian, the English, the Scotch, the Irish, thus presenting to the world a Babel of tongues, but to God a unity of sentiment and praise.

In the reaction the *masses* regained their rights to sing praise to their God. The Psalmody of the Dark Ages was representative, a select and trained choir appearing for the people. By an enactment the congregation sat silent. In the revival the Church heard the voices of all her sons and daughters praising her Lord as in primitive days.

Many of those agencies that prepared the way for a return to pure and evangelical faith and worship contributed also to the influence and universality of sacred Psalmody.

The invention of printing secured the extensive distribution of sacred songs in the form of tracts and books, so that the people could be fully supplied with material for their praise. Previous to the fifteenth century the world depended for its supply of reading matter upon the pens of the monks; hence books were exceedingly scarce and commanded exorbitant prices. Private libraries were almost unknown, and the few books possessed by the colleges and cathedrals scarcely merited the name of library. The length of time required for the transcription of manuscripts, and the cost of securing and preparing the materials for the work, rendered the purchase of books almost impossible to all save the wealthy. The invention of printing changed this condition of affairs. Books were multiplied and sold at a reasonable price; the people everywhere, by the beginning of the sixteenth century, were possessing Bibles and Psalm-books for themselves, and soon learned to read and sing from them with facility. The writings of Luther, the sacred poetry of Hans Sachs, the Psalms of Marot, Beza and others were struck off and sold by the thousands. Printing presses could not supply the demands that came in from all parts of France and the Netherlands for the new French songs. Ten thousand copies were issued in the first edition of the Genevan Psalm-book, and yet edition followed edition with wonderful rapidity. Through Germany, Holland, Prussia and other of the German States, the little primer of Luther containing his Psalms and Hymns entered nearly every family and carried their sentiments into the hearts of multitudes. This diffusion of the Psalms of the Bible was one of the chief elements in the success of the Reformation.

It was the distribution of the Psalms among the masses that laid the foundation for a full restoration of congregational singing.   In the homes of the Reformed were heard the sweet melody of sacred music set to evangelical sentiments of Reformation songs; in the congregation the voices of men, women and children mingled in the praise; and in the vast conventicles that met in the open air and numbered thousands of worshipers, the music that bore up in the clear heavens the joy of redeemed souls, resembled the noise of the sea when agitated in a mighty tempest.   The world in the Reformation witnessed to an extent never known before, and never, probably, to be known again till the millennium dawn, an enthusiasm of praise.   The early ages were to be more than renewed, when from the field, the workshop, the vineyards, from off the bosoms of generous streams, from the crowded ranks of war, from the persecuted in deserts and dens, as well as from the family fireside and the great congregation, the strains of the sweet Psalmist of Judah were to pour forth, in a music rude, perhaps, to a skillful ear, but loud, sincere and powerful with an impartial God.   Even the enemies of the cross, the voluptuous, the profane, caught the inspiration of God's freed people, and purchased and sang their Psalms and Hymns; kings and queens, the counts and nobles in the courts of royalty were affected amid the musical contagion, and unintentionally sanctioned and promoted a purified and holy Psalmody.   Thus did God literally cause the wrath of man to praise him.

In accounting for the character and success of the Reformation Psalmody, much credit must be given to the celebrated Troubadours and their kindred bands.   Those bards of the Middle Ages that are commonly known as the Troubadours, took their rise in the twelfth century; though they were preceded by poets and minstrels for perhaps many centuries before.   We read of the Celtic bards at a very early date; there were Troubadours in Normandy one hundred years before those of the South of France, who composed romances in rhyme and sang them to the music of their harps at festival solemnities.   Previous to the twelfth century and during the reign of the provincial bards, the western part of Europe was both amused and entertained by bands of jongleurs, a class of men who invented different kinds of poetry, and sang their poems to the accompaniment of various instruments. These jongleurs were attached to the courts of kings and princes and noblemen, whose glorious exploits they turned into verse and sang to their harps or violins. When these minstrels began a roving life, they traveled mostly on foot, with their instruments suspended round their necks, while troops of women, dancers and mountebanks followed in their train.

The Troubadours proper claim an important place in history by virtue of the influence they exerted in the development of refinement in social manners, civilization and religion. They arose in France, the birthplace of chivalry, and are sometimes called the Provencal poets, because of their inhabiting Provence in the southern part of France. These Troubadours were to a very great extent the poets of love. Love was their inspiration, their theme, the business of their lives. Though the sentiments of their poems seem idle and foolish in a more learned and dignified age than that in which they lived, yet the language and style of their compositions were the finest of their day; and poetry for many a century since has resorted for some of its most finished expressions to the vapid songs of Provence. The poems of the Troubadours were composed in the form of rhyme, and were cast in almost every variety of metre, from two to twelve syllables. These minstrels like the jongleurs were the guests of royalty. The honorable and the wealthy competed in doing them honor. They received a welcome in the most refined courts and circles of Europe, and sometimes even aspired to link their life-fortune to ladies of a nobler birth than their own.

The Troubadours were undoubtedly "the first product of Christian civilization;" the earliest faint glimmerings of a coming Reformation. Among them were men of noble characters, who mourned over the corruption of society and the Church. Poems were composed and sung in which vice in all its forms was attacked; princes were not spared in their fearless criticisms, and Rome herself received from them some of her earliest wounds.

Sometimes the themes of the Troubadours were drawn from the Scriptures; more frequently they were afforded from the lives and adventures of distinguished patrons, and from the heroic deeds of the crusades.

Although the Troubadours had ceased as a distinct band many years before the Reformation, yet they were succeeded by the Minne-singers, Flagellants and others, who roved in bands of thousands often exciting the minds of men, and continuing till the outbreak of the reform itself.

These minstrel bands were educating society for the success of a nobler and more soul-inspiring Psalmody. Wherever they went the spirit of song was awakened, the masses of society honored those who were the guests of their rulers, and were ambitious to imitate and join them. Western Europe became a country of musicians; and to this day those parts of Italy, Spain, France and Germany, which were the homes of the Troubadours and their successors, are renowned in the records of music and song.

Carlyle thus speaks of the age immediately preceding the Reformation: "Then truly was the time of singing come, for princes and prelates, emperors and squires, the wise and the simple, men, women and children all sang and rhymed, or delighted in hearing it done. It was a universal noise of song, as if the Spring of mankind had arrived, and warblings from every sprig—not, indeed, without infinite twitterings also, which, except their gladness, had no music—were bidding it welcome. This was the Swabian era, justly reckoned, not only superior to all preceding eras, but properly the first era of German literature. Poetry at length found a home in the life of men; and every pure soul was inspired by it and in words, or, still better, in actions strove to give it utterance. 'Believers,' says Tieck, 'sang of faith; lovers of love; knights described knightly actions and battle, and living, believing knights were their chief audience.'"

When the Bohemian Reformers of the fifteenth century, and those of Germany and Geneva, in the sixteenth, looked abroad for the agencies of their success in sacred Psalmody, they found that the mediæval bards had prepared the way for them.

The songs of the Troubadours provided the rhyme and the metres for the moulding of their translations from the Bible, or for the composition of their own inspiration; the metres and rhyme appropriated, the tunes and melodies of those traveling poets were found convenient; and when, through the help of the press, these divine songs were cast upon the world, they found communities already skilled in music and familiar with the very tunes to which they were to be sung. Thus was God for centuries preparing for a great renovation in his Church.

The history of the Psalms and Psalm-singing among the Reformers begins properly as early as the twelfth century. Along the northern portions of Spain and Italy; throughout Southern France; among the Alps; in the country on both sides of the Rhine, and, at a later period, in Germany, Flanders, Switzerland and Austria, lived the Waldenses, a class who have gained an enviable notoriety in the history of the Church, for the purity of their doctrines and for their opposition to the crimes and follies of the Catholic Church. The Christians of the Middle Ages were the successors of the Cathari, or Puritans, who flourished some centuries before. The chief apostle of the Waldenses was Peter Waldo, who has also the reputation of founding and affording the name for this sect. Waldo was born about the beginning of the twelfth century, and is known first as a rich merchant of Lyons; but, becoming a convert to the true faith, he distinguished himself as an opponent of the dogmas and vices of the Roman clergy. According to Milner, the Christian world in the West is indebted to this bard, or pastor of the Waldenses for the first translation of the Bible into a modern tongue after the time that Latin had ceased to be a living language. An account of the doctrines, discipline and persecutions of this remarkable people may be found in the records of all of the church historians. After the rise of the Hussites, the Waldensian Christians retired from Germany, France, Italy and settled in the valleys of Piedmont and Savoy, where their descendants, with many of their ancient forms, and much of their primitive piety, may still be found. The historians who have written concerning the

Waldenses give us little more than the fact that they were
Psalm-singers.   When Waldo translated the Psalms with the
rest of the Bible into the French tongue, it is probable that
his followers at once adopted them in their Psalmody and
chanted them after the manner of the Romish Church.   It is
certain that in the year 1179 there was among this people a
French version of the Psalms, with a gloss accompanying
it; for Walter Mapos, a chaplain to Henry II., informs us
that during the Council of Lateran, held in 1179, the Waldenses presented to Pope Alexander III., "a book containing the text of the Psalms, with a gloss; and the greater part
of the books of both Laws"—the Mosaic Law and the Gospel.   Owing to the poverty of the Waldenses, and the high
prices of manuscripts of the Scriptures, but few Psalm-books
could be possessed by the people, but this difficulty was to a
remarkable degree balanced by their efforts to commit and
retain in their memories what they might hear read by their
pastors.   Reinerius, a Roman Catholic writer, states that
he heard a peasant recite the whole book of Job by heart,
and that he had heard of many others who could so repeat
the New Testament.   It was required, as a part of the requi-
site attainment of young men to the place of pastors, that
they should memorize portions of the Scriptures, among
which were the Psalms.   "They are to learn by heart all
the chapters of St. Matthew and St. John, all the canonical
Epistles, and a good part of the writings of Solomon, David
and the Prophets."
An intimation that the singing of the Psalms was a part
of the public and private worship of the Waldenses is given
by De Thou, one of their enemies.   In a description he gives
of the stony valley of Dauphiny, where many of these Protestants resided, he says of the people: "Their clothing is
of the skins of sheep; they have no linen.   They inhabit
seven villages ; their houses are constructed of flint stone,
with a flat roof covered with mud, which being spoiled or
loosened by the rain, they smooth again with a roller.   In
these they live with their cattle, separated from them, however, by a fence; they have besides, two caves set apart for
particular purposes, in one of which they conceal their cattle,

in the other themselves when hunted by their enemies. They live on milk and venison, being by constant practice excellent marksmen. Poor, as they are, they are content, and live separate from the rest of mankind. One thing is astonishing, that persons externally so savage and rude should have so much moral cultivation. They can all read and write. They understand French, so far as is needful for understanding the Bible, and *the singing of Psalms.* You can scarce find a boy among them who cannot give you an intelligible account of the faith which they profess; in this, indeed, they resemble their brethren of the other villages; they pay tribute with a good conscience, and the obligation of this duty is peculiarly noted in the confession of the faith. If by reason of the civil wars they are prevented from doing this, they carefully set apart the sum, and at the first opportunity pay it to the king's tax-gatherers."

A late writer says of the Waldensian Psalm-singing: "This was not only a part of their worship, but also a part of their recreation from labor, and their solace at work. The women carrying their milk from the pasturage, and the laborer in the field, the shepherd on the mountain side and the mechanic in his workshop cheered themselves by singing the Psalms of David. They committed them to memory in French and sang them without a book, and were so noted for Psalm-singing that for any one to be found singing Psalms, was taken for good proof that he was a Vaudois. Upon their return under Henry Arnaud, after the battle of Salabertraud, 'they had the infinite satisfaction of finding their church at Prali standing.' They removed everything that savored of Romish idolatry, and sang the Seventy-fourth Psalm:

'Oh! God, why art thou absent from us so long.'

Monsieur Arnaud then mounted a bench in the doorway, that he might be audible to those within and without the church, and after the One hundred and twenty-ninth Psalm had been sung, preached in exposition of some of the verses of that Psalm. It is worthy of remark that the church in which God granted to the Vaudois to perform service on their return, was formerly served by Monsieur Liedet, who being detected in singing Psalms under a rock, was, therefore, hung on a gibbet at St. Michael, near Lucerne. To this day, the valleys of the Vaudois echo these songs of Zion in the ear of the traveler."

Dr. Henderson, in an account of a tour that he made, in 1844, through the valleys of the Piedmont, bears testimony to the fact that the Waldenses still sing the inspired Psalms. He describes the first religious service he attended at Angrognd thus: "It was conducted as follows: The school regent, at the desk below the pulpit, read three chapters of the New Testament with the practical remarks of Ostervald's French Bible on the passage, all the services being conducted in that language. He next read the decalogue, and our Saviour's summary of the Law. The minister then offered from the pulpit a short confession of sins, *and gave out some verses of a Psalm, which were sung by all the people from musical note-books, and while sitting.*"

The same traveler quotes a passage from Jerome as applicable, with scarcely any abatement, to the Waldenses or Vaudois of the present century: "In every direction where there is a sound of human voices, it is the voice of psalmody. If the ploughman is guiding his plough, his song is Hallelujah! If it be the shepherd tending his flock, the reaper gathering his corn, or the vine-dresser pruning the tendrils, his chant is the same; it is some song of David that he sings. Hence all poetry is sacred poetry, and every feeling of the heart finds utterance in the language of the Psalmist."

Passing from the valleys of Southern France, into Bohemia, we meet with the successors of the early Vaudois, under the denomination of Hussites. These Christians began to flourish fully two hundred and forty years after the days of Waldo. Though their doctrines varied in some particulars from the Waldenses, yet they owed their rise to the teachings of the Swiss and Piedmontes emigrants, who settled in Bohemia, and peddled among the inhabitants their principles as well as their wares. The Hussites were not pre-eminent for their Psalm-singing. With them began that general use of hymns, which from that day to this, has chiefly characterized the German churches. The author of

the "Encyclopedia of Music" observes of the disciples of
Huss, Wickliff, and Jerome, that they were "celebrated
psalm-singers." A similar statement is made by the author
of "Primitive Psalms." But the term *Psalm* has been so
frequently used both to designate the songs of the Psalter
and the hymns of uninspired poets, that but little can be
known of the proportion the Psalms held in the Psalmody
of the Bohemian worshipers. That the Hussites had the
Psalms and sang them, at least to a limited extent, is certain ;
but, aside from the mere fact, little is known. Bohemia
presents us with one item of interest. It is here we find the
first Psalmist of Reformation times, whose metrical rendering of the Psalter was prepared for the use of the church.
This Psalmist was no other than John Huss, the apostle of
Bohemia. From Rees' Encyclopedia we learn that this
eminent Reformer rendered the Psalms into German metre
and had them published as early as the beginning of the
fifteenth century. Of this version no history has been preserved, but that it formed a part of the Psalmody of the
Hussites there is no reason to doubt.

The first Psalmist of the Reformation of whose version
we have any definite knowledge was Martin Luther.
Luther was a poet as well as a theologian. Soon after his
fifteenth year, he composed Latin verses, "which alike
surprised and gratified his instructors." These early exercises under the inspiration of the poetic muse, instead of
being merely the effusions of a susceptible age, were dis-
ciplining the youthful rhymer for a wider sphere of useful-
ness. Germany will ever remember her great Reformer as
the chief of her sacred poets. His genius gave his country
songs that ever since his day have been administering comfort
and encouragement in hours of trial. Many of them are
yet, three centuries from the age of his personal sojourn on
earth, the household words of German Christians.

From the moment of his gaining access to the old Latin
Bible in his Monastery, Luther was a special admirer of the
Psalms. These formed the basis of some of his earliest ex-
positions of the Scripture.

Luther had some favorite Psalms from which he derived

especial benefit. Of the One hundred and tenth he said, it "is very fine. It describes the kingdom and priesthood of Jesus Christ and declares him to be King of all things, and the intercessor for all men, to whom all things have been remitted by the Father and who has compassion on all. 'Tis a noble Psalm: if I were well I would endeavor to make a commentary on it."

"The Second Psalm," said he, "is one of the best Psalms. I love that Psalm with my heart. It strikes and flashes valiantly among kings, princes, councellors, judges, etc. If what this Psalm says be true, then are the allegations and arms of the papists stark lies and folly. If I were as our Lord God, and had committed the government to my son, as he has to his Son, and these vile people were as disobedient as they now be, I would knock the world in pieces."

He thus compliments the "Sweet Psalmist:" "Neither Cicero nor Virgil, nor Demosthenes, is to be compared with David in point of eloquence, as we see in the One hundred and nineteenth Psalm, which he divides into two and twenty parts, each composed of eight verses and yet all having but one thought—the law of God. He had great gifts and was highly favored of God. I hold that God suffered him to fall so horribly lest he should become too haughty and proud." Of those words in the Third Psalm : "I lay me down and sleep ; I wake ; for the Lord sustaineth me," he was so fond, that he engaged the famous composer, Lewis Leufel, to put music to them. When he would find Melancthon depressed in spirit over approaching troubles, he would say cheerfully to him, "Come let us sing the Forty-sixth Psalm, and let earth and hell do their most."

In the year 1526 Luther published an exposition of certain Psalms. This volume was dedicated to Mary of Austria, the relict of Lewis, King of Hungary, who was drowned in his flight from Solyman, who had defeated him on the plains of Mohacz. This princess was the sister of Charles V. and of Ferdinand ; and the Reformer by his dedicating his book to her, no doubt hoped to promote the Reformation by gaining her to the Protestant religion. Whether or not it was Luther's comments and dedicatory

preface that conciliated Mary's favor, certain it is that she
acted with prudence and moderation when administering the
government in the Low Countries, and sought to warn
Charles against the wiles of the Catholic clergy.

In 1524 Luther announced his intention of having the
Psalms versified for the use of the German churches. His
design at the time was carried out only to a very limited extent. A small primer was issued, having but three sheets,
and containing only eight selections of Psalms and Hymns,
and three melodies. The melody then set to the Eleventh
Psalm may still be found in the German choral books.

According to Milner, "Luther, a short time before he
ventured to administer the Lord's Supper in the German
tongue, had had the precaution to compose and print a very
useful little book, containing thirty-eight German Hymns,
with their appropriate tunes, for the express purpose of conveying and fixing in the memories of the common people
a deal of religious instruction in a very concise and agreeable
manner. The subjects were: parts of the Catechism; leading articles of belief; prayers and thanksgiving; in fact,
the book was a summary of Christian doctrine expressed
in very neat and elegant German metre, and so well
managed, that the harmony and modulation of the voice
agreed with the words and sentiments, and tended to raise
the corresponding affection in the minds of the singers. On
this account the author has been called the true Orpheus of
Germany; and to his praise it is added, that he applied his
knowledge of musical numbers and harmonies to the excita-
tion of the most pious and fervid emotions in the soul."

Some of the versifications in this sacred song book, we
are assured, were metrical Psalms, and of Luther's own
composing; but other than this does not appear. Aside
from those compositions of Luther's, that are commonly
classed among his Psalms, are others that are merely very
fine paraphrases upon some parts of certain Psalms. His
celebrated "Eine feste Burg ist unser Gott," which has
been termed the Marseilles Hymn of the Reformation, is a
paraphrase of the Forty-sixth Psalm. It is said that he
composed it but a short time before going to Worms; and

that as he approached that city on the memorable 10th of April, he rose in his chariot and sang it with a cheerful voice.

When he had recovered, on a certain occasion from a fainting fit, induced by the intensity of spiritual conflict, he composed a paraphrase of the One hundred and thirtieth Psalm. When his dead body was borne through Halle to its last resting place at Wittenberg, his countrymen followed it in throngs, and when it was placed in the church at that place the people gathered about it and amid tears and sobs sang that Psalm beside it.

There were also paraphrases of the Twelfth, Sixty-seventh and One hundred and twenty-fourth Psalms.

As Luther designed the translation of the whole book of Psalms, those which he did not himself versify, he committed to Spalatin and Doezy. To Spalatin he wrote : " We intend, after the example of the prophets and primitive fathers to turn the Psalms for spiritual singing into the vulgar tongue for the common people, so that the word of God may remain among the people even in singing. Upon this account we seek some poets, and as you possess the copiousness and elegance of the German, which you have greatly cultivated. I would request your assistance in this business, in translating some of the Psalms into German verse according to the enclosed example. My wish is to avoid all difficult and courtly terms, and to use the simplest and most common phrases, so that they are fit and proper for the edification of the lowest among the people. Let the sense be clear and as close as possible to the original. To preserve the sense where you cannot render word for word, it may be right to use such a phrase as will most perfectly convey the idea. I confess I am not sufficiently qualified myself, and therefore would request you to try how near you can approach to Heman, Asaph and Jeduthan."

This version of the Psalms was completed, and Luther lived to see it exceedingly popular. Luther sang these Psalms himself and commended them to others—"let them," he says to his friends, "avoid solitariness, keeping always in good company, sing the Psalms and converse upon the

Holy Scriptures.'' ''Every village school-boy among the Protestants was presently employed to get them by heart, and help to sing them on Sunday.'' In the army, as well as in the peaceful walks of life, they resounded the praise of God. It was the ''Eine feste Burg ist unser Gott'' that Gustavus Adolphus, the pious king of Sweden, took for his battle hymn, and which he had his army sing on the morning of the battle of Lutzen, Nov. 6, 1632.

Such was the popularity of the German Psalms, that they were translated into the Hebrew, Greek, Latin, Bohemian, English and other languages.

Of the influence of these Psalms and hymns of Luther, the Jesuit Adam Contzen bore testimony : ''The hymns of Luther have ruined more souls than all his writings and sermons. And hence the rulers of the church must also employ that as a medicine which the deceivers have invented as a destroyer.'' In preparing a hymn-book for themselves, the papists appropriated many of Luther's compositions, so altered as to suit their views. The Papal hymn-book published at Mentz in 1679, contained many of Luther's songs. Luther's '' Eine feste burg '' is here given :

EINE FESTE BURG IST UNSER GOTT.

A Paraphrase of Psalm 46 : 1.

MARTIN LUTHER.

God is our fortress strong and high,
 A sure defense and weapon ;
His powerful aid is ever nigh
 Whate'er distress may happen.

The old and evil foe
 Would fain bring us low
With great craft and might :
 Full armed for the fight,
On earth none can him liken.

Our feeble might achieveth naught,
 Our struggle soon but feigned
By him alone the work is wrought
 Whom God himself ordained.

Dost thou ask the same?
 The Christ is the same,
The Lord of Sabaoth ;
 There is no other God ;
'Tis he the field hath taken.

And were the world of devils full
　All threatening to devour us,
We fear not ; true and dutiful
　They cannot overpower us.

Prince of this world in vain,
　His darts round may rain,
He no harm can us do ;
　His arts must perish too,
A little word can slay them.

That word of his shall sure remain,
　To man no praise is given ;
He's with us on the battle plain,
　His spirit aids from heaven.

Then perish our estate,
　Wife, child—by their hate,
On them be the sin ;
　Naught from us can they win,
We share his glorious empire.

In 1573, the Psalms were rendered in German verse by Ambrose Lobwasser, professor of Jurisprudence in Königsberg. In his translation he imitated the Genevan version of Marot, and, though his Psalms had little merit, they were for a long time used exclusively in some of the German churches. A new edition of his Psalms was issued in 1612 by Maurice of Hessen, with which were printed some austere melodies for the use of German Christians. The influence of many of the early German Psalms and Hymns is still felt among the German Christians of the old and the new world. The impress of them still remains. Wherever you meet the German Christian, you find him charged with these noble and evangelical compositions. Even the emigrant is sure, if a disciple, to carry across the sea in his blouse or wallet, his black-covered hymn-book.

In this country, beside the original selections from the German versification of the Psalms, the Lutheran Church has included in its book of praise, Psalms from the pens of Watts, Tate and Brady, Joseph Addison, Charles Wesley, James Montgomery, Timothy Dwight, John Mason, Henry Francis Lyte, Hariet Auber and James Merrick; so that this large and influential body of worshipers, now, as in the age of the Reformation, gives David's Psalms a respectable place in the material of its praise.

From Germany, the Reformation passed toward the North, and established its supremacy there, while the doctrines of the Swiss and German Reformers held sway over the more southern countries.   In Prussia, Sweden, Norway, Denmark, Livonia, and neighboring states, the Lutheran Liturgy was either adopted as a whole, or made the basis of new liturgies for the regulation of religious worship.   In all these countries the Psalms and Hymns of the German poets were sung, and exerted the same powerful influence in promoting the Reformation there as in Germany.   In lower Germany, the historian, Kurtz, mentions particularly the surprisingly potent influence of Luther's Psalms and Hymns.

In most of these countries, native poets employed their talents in versifying the Psalms in their own native tongues, but of their versions little is known.

In the sixteenth century, Gyllenhjelm was author of the "Psalter in Rhyme" in the Swedish.

In Russia, the "Psalms sung in the Churches" were printed at Nilna in 1623.

It may be added here that the best hymns of Germany in the earliest and brightest era of her hymnology were modeled after the Psalms, and bear evidence of their divine utterances having inspired the pens that gave them to the Church. Especially numerous are those which express trust in God in trial or conflict; which speak of Him like the old Hebrew Psalms, as a rock, a fortress, and a deliverer—they are songs to march to, reviving the fainting strength after many an hour of weary journeying; blasts of the priest's trumpets before which many a stronghold has fallen; chants of trust and triumph, which must often have reverberated from the very gates of heaven as they accompanied the departing spirit thither and mingled with the new song of the great multitude inside.

The majestic hymn of John Gramann, "Now praise the Lord, my soul," was modeled after Psalm One hundred and third; and Lobwasser's, "My hope doth stand in God alone," after Psalm Thirty-seven.   Thus we are indebted, says Tholuck in the introduction to his commentary on the Psalms, to the Psalms as models, not only for hymns sung by the people, but for choral songs in general.

CHAPTER VI.

The Psalms in the Swiss and French Reformation.

Modern Calvinism can regard with pride the place of its birth—Switzerland. Though crowded by its powerful neighbors into a narrow place by the Alps, it has ever been the home of a free, brave and patriotic race. To believe in special providences, God has evidently, from the earliest ages, educated the Swiss for giving origin to an independent church. From a native love for freedom, and long struggles to maintain their independence, where, in Reformation times, a fitter refuge for one, radical in his opposition to a tyrannical hierarchy, than the land of the Swiss! When Calvin was rejected by France, he was welcomed to Geneva, where he found an element already congenial to his rigid, yet free principles. Before the visit of that Reformer, Switzerland had begun a church, distinguished by its radicalism. Through the influence of Farel and Viret, the Presbyterianism of the Alps had been saved from that conservatism toward Popery that characterized the German and English establishments, and which to-day by its natural fruits, is disturbing the Lutheran and Episcopal communions. Calvin only promoted, unfolded and established the principles that now bear his name.

With the Reformation of Geneva, that in France, the Netherlands, and Scotland were intimately connected. Under Calvin, Geneva became the metropolis of the Reformed churches. Its form of government, its creed, its liturgy, the principle of its Psalmody, became the model for the Huguenots, the Walloons, and the Scotch. The Theological School on the banks of the Rhone, became the resort of the learned men from many lands, where primitive principles were imbibed and thence carried everywhere.

In its Psalmody the Presbyterian Church of the Reformation, differed in one important respect from that of the German Lutheran Church; its songs were modeled almost exclusively after the Psalms and spiritual songs of the Scriptures. As has been already remarked, human composition had no prominent place in its worship. Hymns, in exceptional cases, may have been used, but the Psalm-book of Geneva, and its kindred churches, was inspired. Of its inspired songs, the Psalms held the principal place. The Paraphrases were few in number, nor was there in Switzerland and France the same effort as in Scotland at a later date, to multiply them. Until the power of the Huguenots was broken, and the Calvinistic theory had lost much of its influence in France and the Netherlands, the Psalms continued almost the sole praise of the Church.

The Presbyterian churches of the Reformation, in selecting the material of their Psalmody from the Bible, aimed to conform their metrical translations as closely as possible to the expression and sense of the original. The Scriptures were the sole rule of faith and practice, and to depart from them unnecessarily, was sacrilege.

The ordinance of singing praise was held in the highest respect among the Genevan Reformers. Any trifling as to the matter or form of praise was severely punished. From the registers of the Genevan Council and Consistory, we learn that a man was banished from the city for remarking, "Il chante un beau Psaume" (He chants a good Psalm), when he heard an ass bray. The same penalty was inflicted upon another, who, on presenting to his bride an account book, said, "Tuez, madame, voci votre, meilleur Psaume" (Sing, madam, with your voice, the best Psalm).

The history of Psalmody in the Calvinistic churches of the continent begins properly with Zwingle. Before Calvin came to Geneva, this Reformer had introduced metrical Psalmody into Switzerland. What the matter of praise was can only be conjectured. At an early date in the Reformation, the Psalms had been translated into the French, which was the language of parts of Switzerland, and may have been chanted by the Swiss, as by the Waldenses. The probability is that Zwingle and his followers imitated the Christians of Bohemia, with whom they seem to have held friendly intercourse, and so adopted their hymns, and the Psalms versified by Huss.

According to Kurtz the adoption of Psalmody into the worship of the Reformed churches of the French persuasion, was effected chiefly by John Zwick, a clergyman in Constance. In 1530 he published a small hymn-book, with versions of some Psalms, adapted to Lutheran tunes. Of the character of this hymn-book we know nothing.

However, it is evident, that until the days of Calvin's residence in Geneva, the Psalmody of the Swiss Church had been informal. To Calvin himself belongs the credit of reducing that Psalmody to a system, and of giving to it a character that distinguished it for more than a century.

Calvin was a great admirer of the Psalms. While he was yet at Orleans, in the study of the law under Pierre de l'Etoile, his attention was especially turned to this book of God's word, and his private opinion of it he has left in the preface of his Commentary on the Psalms. Says he: "Not without good grounds am I wont to call this book an anatomy of all parts of the soul, since no one can experience emotions, whose portrait he could not behold reflected in its mirror. Yes. the Holy Spirit has there depicted in the most vivid manner every species of pain, affliction, fear, doubt, hope, care, anxiety and turbulent emotion through which the hearts of men are chased. Other portions of the Scriptures contain commandments whose transmission the Lord enjoined upon his servants; but in the Psalms, the Prophets communing with God and uncovering their most inmost feelings, call and urge every reader to self-examination to such a degree, that of the numerous infirmities to which we are liable, and of the many failings which oppress us, not one remains concealed. How great and rare again for the human heart to be thus driven out of all its hiding places, liberated from hypocrisy (that most fearful of vices) and exposed to the light. Lastly, if calling on God is the surest means of our salvation—if better and more reliable directions for it than those contained in the Book of Psalms, are not to be obtained, then everyone who reads this book has attained to an essential part of the Divine doctrine. Earnest prayer originates in our sense of need; afterwards in our faith in the Divine promises. The reader of the Psalms finds himself both aroused to feel his misery, and exhorted to seek for its remedy. The Psalter unfolds every encouragement to prayer. It is not merely confined to promises, but men are introduced who, on the one hand invited by God, and on the other hindered by the flesh, take courage in prayer: if therefore, we are beset by doubt and scruple, here we may learn to combat, till the disenthralled spirit rises anew to God. And more than this, we may learn prayerfully to struggle through hesitation, fear and faint-heartedness, till comfort be attained. For, be it remembered, that though unbelief keeps the door shut to our prayers, we must not desist when in our wavering we are being tossed to and fro, but persevere until faith mounts victoriously from her struggles. Again the Psalms inspire us with the most desirable of all things, in not only teaching us to approach God in confidence, but to openly unbare before him all those failings which a false sense of shame otherwise forbids us to own. They furnish, moreover, the clearest directions how we may render to God that sacrifice of praise which he declares as most acceptable to him. You cannot read anywhere more glorious praises of God's peculiar grace towards his church or of his works; you cannot find anywhere such an enumeration of man's deliverances or praises for the glorious proofs of his fatherly care for us, or a more perfect representation to praise him becomingly, or more fervent exhortations to the discharge of that holy duty. But however rich the book may prove in all these respects to fit us for a holy, pious, and just life, its chief lesson is how we are to bear the cross, and to give the true evidence of our obedience, by parting with our affections, to submit ourselves to God, to suffer our lives to be entirely guided by his will, so that the bitterest trial, because he sends it, seems sweet to us. Finally, not only is the goodness of God praised in general terms to secure our perfect resignation to him, and to expect his aid in every time of need, but the free forgiveness of our sins, which alone can effect our peace of conscience and reconciliation to

God, are in particular so strongly recommended, that there is nothing wanting to the knowledge of eternal life.''

The idea of a special versification of the Psalms for the worship of the Reformed Church was made to Calvin by Zwingle. Before moving in the matter, Calvin consulted Luther, and it was during this consultation that the Psalms of Marot made their appearance.

Clement Marot was a Frenchman, and was born at Cahors, in Querci, near Toulouse, in 1495. Like his father, Jean Marot, he was valet de Chambre to Francis I ; and also page to Margaret of France, wife of the duke of Alencon. In 1521 he accompanied the duke in the Italian campaign, and was wounded and made prisoner in the battle of Pavia. Gaining his freedom, he returned to Paris, but being suspected for complicity with the colonists, he was again imprisoned. Being brought before the Lieutenant-criminel, he was reproached on account of his former irreligion and the licentiousness of his writings, but gained no more by his earnest solicitations than to be removed from the miserable prison of Chatelet to that of Chartres. It was while incarcerated in Chartres that he composed his Enfer and revised his Roman de la Rose. When Francis I returned from his captivity in Spain, Marot was set free, A. D. 1526. After this he returned to the court of the Queen of Navarre ; then to that of the Duchess of Ferrara and in 1536 returned to Paris. But having publicly avowed himself a disciple of Calvin, he fled from persecution, and resided at Geneva. Quitting Geneva, he went to Lyons, where he is said to have renounced Calvinism. After engaging in another campaign under Francis I, in his Italian wars, he returned to Piedmont, and died at Turin in 1544, aged 50 years.

Marot seems to have led a licentious life in his earlier years, and there is little probability that he was a Christian, while espousing the doctrines of Geneva. He was one of those free spirits that opposed popery because of its tyranny; and enlisted his sympathies in the cause of Reformers more because of their enmity to the Hierarchy than from any convictions of his own sins. His renunciation of the reformed cause shows his vascillating disposition. But God had chosen him as an important instrument for promoting the true religion. For the part of a poet to which God had called him, he was well fitted.

Clement Marot was one of France's best poets. His ballads, fables, pastorals, elegies, epigrams were extremely popular. His verses are filled with natural beauties La Fontaine acknowleged himself his disciple and contributed greatly to restore to credit the works of this ancient poet.

On his return to Paris from his residence in the court of the Duchess of Ferrara, he was persuaded by Vatablus, professor of Hebrew in the University of Paris, to undertake the rendering of David's Psalms into French verse. In his attempt he was assisted by Francis Melin de S. Gelays, and other learned men, whose prose translations of the Psalms formed the model of his poetical version. Before leaving Paris on account of his Calvinism he had versified thirty of the Psalms. These thirty were printed in Paris and were dedicated to Francis I. After removing to Geneva, Marot, with the encouragement and aid of Calvin, completed twenty more Psalms. These twenty, with the thirty of the Paris edition, and eight others, the author or authors of which are not known, were printed at Rome, in 1542, by the command of the Pope, and under the supervision of Theodore Drust, a German, "printer in order to his holiness." This edition was printed in the Gothic character, in octavo, and was without the name of either the printer or place of printing. Although sanctioned by the highest authority of the Catholic church, this version was censured by the faculty of divinity in the Paris Theological College, who were afterward instrumental in the persecution of Marot, for his efforts in versifying the Psalms.

In 1543, the version printed in Rome, was issued at Geneva, and no doubt at the instance of Calvin, for it contained a preface written by him, and dated Jan. 10, 1543. With the Geneva edition was printed an agreement with the printers whereby they were to furnish a certain sum for the relief of the poor refugees at Geneva. Marot's Psalms, which were cast in the same mould as his ballads and roundeaux, constituted the Psalmody of the Reformed

Church, until Theodore Beza furnished the remaining Psalms in popular verse.

Nothing more can be gathered concerning the Psalms versified by Beza than that they were translated in imitation of Marot's; took their place with those of that great poet in the Psalmody of the times and were bound up with his in the Genevan Catechism in 1553, or, according to Kurtz, in 1555.

The dedication of Marot's first Psalms to Francis I, was made on account of the satisfaction that sovereign had expressed when some of them were presented for condemnation by the Sorbonne doctors. The following is the poet's royal epigram:—

"Since, O Sire, it is your pleasure that I pursue the royal work of the Psalms which I have begun; and since all those who love God desire the same, I reckon I have a valid license to proceed in it. Wherefore let whoever pleases take offense at it, for they who cannot be reconciled to a design of such important use ought to know, if they are not sensible of it already, that while I do your majesty a pleasure, I am glad, however much I do offend such people."

On the opposite side of the same leaf that contained the dedication, began an address to the ladies of France, in which the poet declared his design to add to the happiness of his fair readers by giving them divine songs in place of their amorous ditties; to banish from the world the foolish and fickle Cupid; to inspire all hearts with a passion in which is no torment, and fill all homes with the praises of Jehovah. This address concludes thus:—

"Thrice happy they who may behold
And listen in this age of gold!
As by the plow the laborer strays,
And carmen wend the public ways,
And tradesmen in their shops shall swell,
The voice of Psalm or Canticle,
Singing to solace toil again
From woods shall come a sweeter strain;
Shepherd and shepherdess shall vie
In many a tender Psalmody;
And the Creator's name prolong
As rock and stream return the song.
Begin then, ladies fair, begin
The age renewed that knows no sin!
And with light hearts that want no wing,
Sing from the holy song-book, sing."

The first Psalms of Marot, coming from one who at the time, was not suspected for any complicity with the Reformed, and being issued simply as rhyming ballads and not as sacred songs for sacred purposes, were taken up by the populace and sung by Reformed, Catholic and Skeptic alike. Surpassing any of this famous poet's former productions, his Psalms gained a celebrity and possessed a circulation far beyond any of his madrigals and sonnets. His remaining twenty and those soon afterward composed by Beza were equally popular. Psalm singing at this time was carried almost to the point of frenzy. The demand for the new songs swept like wild-fire over France, so that in a short time the printers could not supply the demand. Edition after edition was issued, but still the cry was for more. The Psalms were sung in all parts of the country, by men of all trades, and all classes, and became "one of the chief ingredients in the happiness of social life." Especially in the vineyards of Provence, in the market-boats of the Loire and the Rhone, and among the weavers of Flanders, were the melodies of these inspired songs heard, as they were sung to the music of the lute, violin and guitar. The Catholics might be seen mingling with the multitude, with their Psalm-books in their hands, entering heartily into the popular excitement. Even the Catholic clergy participated in the enthusiasm; nor was their fever abated until it was discovered that the Psalms were being sung in the private and public worship of the Protestants.

The Psalms of Marot and Beza supplied the want of Christian families for sacred songs, and it was not long until God's praise was sung in the homes of His people and through the sentiments of his own ancient servants. No gentlemen professing the Reformed religion would sit down at his table without praising God by singing. Yea, it was a special part of morning and evening worship in their several houses to sing God's praises. When the Catholics were forbidden longer to engage in the National pastime, Psalm-singing came to be regarded as a badge of what the French Papists called Lutheranism, and to be found singing a Psalm of Marot or Beza was considered sufficient warrant for the infliction of the penalty pronounced on all heretics.

The popular rage for Psalm-singing was not confined to the lower ranks of society in France, but entered and infected the Palace of Royalty itself. It was a common thing in the court of Francis I, for the King and Queen with their nobles, to refresh themselves with metrical Psalms. It was a fashion in the royal circle for each one to select a favorite Psalm, and sing it especially. A favorite Psalm of Catharine de Medicis was:—

> To thee, O Lord, my cries ascend,
>   O haste to my relief,
> And with accustomed pity hear
>   The accents of my grief.
> Instead of offering, let my prayer
>   Like morning incense rise;
> My uplifted hands supply the place
>   Of evening sacrifice.

Anthony, King of Navarre, chose "Revenge moy, preu le querelle,"—"Stand up, O Lord, to revenge my quarrel." Diane de Poictiers, the favorite of Henry II, chose "Du fond de ma pensie,"—"From the depths of my heart have I cried unto thee." The Queen sang:—

> Ne vucilles pas, O, sire,
> Me reprendre en tonire.

"Rebuke me not in thine indignation."

Henry II, while yet Dauphin, was a great hunter, and chose, appropriate to his favorite recreation, "Ainsi qu'on oit le cerf bruire,"—"As the heart panteth after the water brooks." King Henry continued to solace himself by singing the Psalms till the day of his death. This we learn from a letter written to Catharine de Medicis by a gentleman subscribing himself Villeinadon: "but if any person loved them (the Psalms) dearly, and commonly sang them and caused to be sung, it was the late King Henry, who loved them so well that good men blessed God for it; and his minions and his mistress feigned so great a love for them that they were want to say, "Sir, shall not this be mine, give me that if you please?" insomuch that the good King had much to do to please every one's fancy, according to his desire. Nevertheless he kept for himself the following Psalm, as you remember:—

> The man is blessed, who fears the Lord,
>   Nor only worship pays,
> But keeps his steps composed with care
>   To his appointed ways, etc.

He himself made a tune to this Psalm—which was very good and pleasant—and caused it to be sung so often that he plainly showed he had an earnest desire to be that blessed man whom David describes in the said Psalm, and to see you become the fertile vine therein mentioned. This was when he was recovering from his sickness at Angoulesme, which I found so much abated that he began to sing the said Psalm with lutes, violins, spinnets and flutes attending with voices."

It was during the reign of Henry that Paris was thrown into a ferment by the students of the university of that city. The most frequented promenade at this time in Paris was the Pre-aux-clercs, situated where a part of the Fauburg Saint Germain is at present. The students belonging to the university were, generally, friendly to the Calvinistic religion, and many of them not only made a profession of it, but publicly defended it. A custom of the students for years had been to assemble for recreation and amusement in the Pre-aux-clercs; but the monks of the Abbey of St. Victor, on one occasion, refusing them the liberty they had long enjoyed, the opposing parties fell to wrangling, and finally came to blows. The students being the stronger, carried their point and the monks resigned to them the public promenade. From this time the Pre-aux-clercs became the rendezvous of the Protestants, who would meet there on the summer evenings and sing their favorite Psalms. The multitudes who were accustomed to assemble here to participate in the popular games, at first laughed at the Psalmody of the Christians. But the number of the Psalm-singers increasing and their melodies growing in their fervor, the players left their sports, and gathered about the Huguenots, some to listen, and many to engage in the music. So popular did this summer-evening Psalm-singing become, that hundreds of the citizens of Paris resorted to the Pre-aux-clercs as to an entertainment. Even the nobles were present and participated. Anthony de Bourbon and

Jane de Albert were among the habitues of the promenade on these occasions. Theodore Beza thus speaks of the assembly of Protestants at the Pre-aux-clercs:—" Thus the assembly multiplied daily at Paris, where it happened that some being in the place called Pre-aux-clercs, a public place of the university, began to sing Psalms, which being heard, a great many of those who were walking or playing at divers games, joined the company that was singing, some for the novelty of it, and some to bear part in the music. This continued for some days in a very great assembly, where were present the King of Navarre himself with many lords and gentlemen, both of France and other nations, who fell a singing. And though in a great multitude there is frequently much confusion, yet there was such a harmony and devotion, that every one present was ravished with it; even those who could not sing, nay the most ignorant, got upon the walls round about, to hear the singing, and declared that it was ill-done to forbid so good a thing."

Thus were the Psalms carried among the multitudes, where they became one of the prime agencies in promoting the progress of pure Christianity. By these songs, the truths of God's word were disseminated with a rapidity not equalled even by the preaching of evangelists and teachers. Their melody was heard in many a nook and corner of Catholicism and infidelity, where the voice of the Reformed clergy was never heard. Hence it was that when the Reformation began to appear in France and Switzerland as in Germany, thousands were found infected where there was the least suspicion of heresy. The whole French court seemed Calvinistic; mass was forgotten, meat served during Lent, the authority of Bishop and Pope despised, and, under the toleration of Catharine de Medicis, the Reformed clergy proclaimed their principles in the royal palace, crowds composing their assembly, while a poor Jacobin who preached the Lent sermons at Fontainbleau, had no audience. " Heresy, says an eminent Jesuit, was seen to enter the palace of the most Christian King; and it may be said that there it exercised complete sway."

That the influence of the Psalms for reform, and the

introduction of them into the services of the Swiss and
Huguenot Churches would call forth bitter persecution from
a Church whose mightiest argument has always been the
sword and the guillotine, was to be expected.   A fervor, the
natural offspring of inspired truth, could not awaken a kindred fervor in the hearts of men whose power was secure
only in a popular ignorance of the word of God, but
aroused resistance, such as, failing in accomplishing its
object by denunciations and decrees, ended in that grand
consummation of tyranny, the blood of St. Bartholomew's
day.

At an early stage of the Psalm-singing in France, the
Catholic clergy proclaimed Marot a heretic and forced him
to flee to Geneva for refuge.   When individual denunciation
failed, an attempt was made to secure a public prohibition
from the king.   But Francis I, as we have seen, paid no
attention at first to the entreaties of the Sorbonne doctors,
but complimented Marot for what he had already done and
urged him to complete the versification of the entire book of
Psalms.   He did more than this : he made a request of the
poet that he should send a copy of his Psalms to Charles V,
then emperor of Germany and Spain.   Marot complied with
this request and was gratified and encouraged by a letter
from Charles, in which he presented him with two hundred
Spanish pistols, expressed himself satisfied with the Psalms
already versified, and pressed on him the importance of com-
pleting the version, requesting him especially to send as soon
as possible, a metrical version of Psalm 105th—"Con-
fitemini Domino quoniam bonus," as it is called in the
Latin—because he was particularly fond of it.   But evil
councils prevailed.   The Nuncio of the Pope complained to
the King of the novelty of the Psalm-singing and warned him
of its pernicious influence and dangerous tendency.   To the
efforts of the Nuncio were added those of the Cardinal de
Lorraine, a man of distinction and influence at the Parisian
court.   The Cardinal, aware of the difficulty of persuading
the King by a personal appeal, undertook to influence him
through the agency of Diane de Poictiers, who was known
as "the lovely patroness" of "the Holy Psalm-book."

Diane was not only a Psalm-singer but a reader of the Bible, both of which were regarded as evidence of Lutheranism. Lorraine began with her by finding fault with the Psalms of David and commending the amatory elegancies of the odes of Horace. Diane consented to surrender the Psalm-book, but retained her Bible because the Queen Catharine de Medicis possessed one. On one occasion, the Cardinal entering her apartment, found the Bible lying upon the table. He immediately crossed himself, smote upon his breast, cast the Book upon the floor, and otherwise so well acted his part, that the fair penitent gave up her Bible, and for the time consented to do penance by saying two masses instead of one.

Through Diane, it is probable that Lorraine gained his point with the King ; a royal prohibition was issued against the Psalms of Marot and Beza. To be found singing a Psalm under any pretext was declared criminal. If any one were discovered in the act, he was to be fined two hundred francs, and to have his Psalm-book taken from him and given to the common hangman to be burned.

The Psalm-singing of the Prè-aux-clercs was brought before Parliament by the clergy, but here, so many of the members were found implicated in the assembling at the promenade, that the summons of Cardinal Bertrand for the assembling of the Parliament were at first unheeded. Here too, however, evil councils at last prevailed and the persecutions of the Huguenots began anew, and continued without interruption till about 1562, when the conference in the Abbey of Poissy, near Paris, was held. An edict of toleration was issued, and for a time the Protestants enjoyed the liberty of worshiping in accordance with their preferences. Soon after the edict of toleration, as we are informed by Bayle, a license was issued by Henry IX to Anthony Vincent, a bookseller of Lyons, for the printing of Marot and Beza's Psalms. The license is in the following terms :

" By a special favor of full power and royal authority, we have given and granted to Anthony Vincent, Bookseller at Lyons, the privilege, leave, license and permission to print, or cause to be printed for the space of ten years next following, all the Psalms of the Prophet David, translated according to the truth of the Hebrew text, turned into French metre, and set to good music, as it is well known, and have been examined by men learned in the Holy Scriptures and in the said languages and also in the art of music."—Dated, Oct. 19, 1561.

The "men learned in the Holy Scriptures" were no other than the Doctors of the Sorbonne, who had so distinguished themselves in former persecutions. That the Sorbonne gave its sanction to the printing of the Psalms, appears from the writings of Jurien, who has produced this sanction in the following words :—"We, Doctors of Divinity, whose names are here subscribed, do certify that in a certain translation of the Psalms presented to us, beginning at the Forty-eighth Psalm, with these words, 'C'est en fatres sainte cite,' and ending with the verse, 'Chante a jamais son Empire,' we have found nothing contrary to our Catholic faith, but everything agreeable to it and the truth of the Hebrew text. In testimony whereof, we have signed this present certificate, Oct. 16, 1561."

After the impression of the Psalms had been made by Anthony, and before they were issued to the public, they were examined and approved by Mr. Josse Schelling, Portionary of St. Nicolas at Brussels, deputed for this end by the council at Brabant.

The Catholic clergy did not confine themselves to the issue of decrees and the execution of penalties under the influence of Cardinal de Lorraine, the odes of Horace, and the obscene poems of Tribullus and Catullus were translated into French verse and introduced into the court at Paris. The Catholic laity were permitted to imitate the Psalm-singers, and so assembled in the streets and sang their hymns and odes while they held before them little images of the Virgin.

As they would pass from street to street, they would invite all the persons whom they would meet to join them in singing, and if any would refuse, they were maltreated, and their complaints, when made to the civil authorities, despised.

The respite following the edict of 1562 did not last long. The persecution broke forth anew, and the blood of France's best citizens again reddened her soil. The Papal party continually denounced the Huguenots, and urged the people in many districts to deeds of violence ; so that the party of the Reform was compelled to organize and arm. The struggle between the opposing forces was fierce, and continued for many years. But the Huguenots, unable to succeed against the powerful forces of the Government, were driven from almost every battle field, and thousands of families were forced into exile. The tale of these persecutions and their consequent horrors form one of the darkest chapters of history. The Massacre of St. Bartholomew on the 24th of August, 1572, was but a representation of the bloody scenes all over France and the Low Countries.

After sixty years of persecution, the Protestants of France were restored to comparative liberty of conscience in their worship, by the celebrated edict of Nantes, promulgated in 1598. But peace under this edict was not long enjoyed. Twelve years after its promulgation, the King who issued it was assassinated, when the elements of discord broke loose with more than usual fury. For nearly a century, the rage of the Catholic Church was constantly exerted in the destruction of the Huguenots, and found a satisfaction in the revocation of the Edict of Nantes by Louis XIV, in October, 1685. This was the death-knell of the Huguenots. Soon Papal indignation was to be allayed because there were no more victims for slaughter ; the inquisition to rest in its work of blood, for there were no more armies of the True Faith to conquer. "Great was the rejoicing of the Jesuits on the revocation of the Edict of Nantes. Rome sprang up with a shout of joy to celebrate the event. Te Deums were sung, processions went from shrine to shrine, and the Pope sent a brief to Louis, conveying to him the congratulations and praises of the Romish Church. Public thanksgivings were held at Paris, in which the people eagerly took part, thus making themselves accomplices in the proscription by the King of their fellow-subjects. The provost and sheriffs had a statute of Louis

erected at the Hotel de Ville, bearing the inscription, 'Ludu-
vico Magno, victori perpetrio, ecclesia ac regum, dignitatis
assertori.' Leseuer was employed to paint the subject for
the gallery at Versailles, and medals were struck commem-
orating the extinction of Protestantism in France."

The Revocation of the Edict of Nantes gave license to
every kind of violence against the Huguenots, and everything that belonged to them. Protestant worship was
everywhere proscribed, both in public and in private ; the
churches were broken down ; pastors were banished ; schools
closed ; parents were forbidden to teach their children ;
personal property was confiscated ; Protestant children
must be baptized by a parish priest, a heavy penalty being
inflicted in case of disobedience ; and the galley and prisons
filled with thousands who preferred suffering to the surrender
of their faith.

It seems almost incredible, the vast numbers of French-
men that fled from their native country to escape these
various persecutions. The highways were crowded with
refugees. From every outlet on the north and the east they
poured in an incessant throng. Prohibitions against self-
banishment were issued ; officers patrolled the high roads
night and day ; heavy penalties were inflicted on those caught
in the act of emigrating, but all to no purpose. The frequented routes were avoided, and the fugitives crossed the
frontier through dense forests, over mountain by-paths,
along trackless wastes, traveling in small parties and by
night. "Women of quality, even sixty and seventy years
of age, who had, so to speak, never placed a foot upon the
ground, except to cross their apartments or stroll in an ave-
nue, traveled to some village which had been indicated by a
guide. Girls of fifteen, of every rank, exposed themselves
to the same hazard. They drew wheelbarrows, they bore
manure, panniers and other burdens. They disfigured their
faces with dyes to embrown their complexion, with oint-
ments or juices that blistered their skins and gave them a
wrinkled aspect. Women and girls were seen to counter-
feit sickness, dumbness, and even insanity. Some went
disguised as men ; and some, too delicate to pass as grown

men, donned the dress of lackeys, and followel on foot through the mud a guide on horseback, who assumed the character of a man of importance. Many of these females reached Rotterdam in their borrowed garments, and, hastening to the foot of the pulpit before they had time to assume a more decent garb, published their repentance of their compulsory signature.''

In all subsequent persecutions, as in that of the days of Marot and Beza, the wrath of the Roman clergy and their followers was exercised against the Psalmody of the Huguenots. The severest restrictions were placed upon its exercise, and many are the incidents that might be related of the courage of the Protestants in clinging to their favorite act of devotion, and the sufferings consequent thereto. Psalm-singing was forbidden in the private dwellings and in the workshops of the Protestants, and spies selected to detect them in its exercise. A common act of devastation with the Catholics was to enter churches, gather the Psalm-books and Bibles into a pile and burn them. An edict was issued in France as late as April 25, 1727, in which the Protestants were required to surrender all their religious books within fifteen days that they might be burned in the presence of the commandants of the respective districts, the penalty for withholding being three years' banishment and a fine of not less than one-third of the entire personal property of the offender. Fearless, amid the terrors of persecution, was a Huguenot pastor who published a defense of the prohibited Psalm-singing, and for it was arrested and driven from the country. There is recorded the noble example of an artisan of Lanquedoc, who persisted in his singing of Psalms notwithstanding the royal prohibition ; and, when the officer presented him with the edict, took it and wrote on it the following words of the Thirty-fourth Psalm:

> " Jamais ne cessarai
> De magnifier le seigneur
> En ma bouche auri son honneur
> Fant que vivant serai,"

Which in the English prose version read, "I will bless the Lord at all times, his praise shall continually be in my mouth.''

One Migault, a schoolmaster, for teaching the Psalms to his pupils, came near losing his life, having saved it only by hasty flight.

The massacre at Vassy, in May of 1563, was ordered by the Duke of Guise, because, as he said, when he commanded the congregation to cease its Psalmody, they defied him and only sang the louder. The following account of this massacre is given by Smiles, in the History of the Huguenots: "On the 1st of May, 1593, they held one of their meetings, at which about twelve hundred persons were present, in a large barn, which served as a church. The day before the Duke of Guise, accompanied by the duchess, his wife, the cardinal of Guise, and about two hundred men, armed with arquebuses and poinards, set out for Vassy. They rested during the night at Dampmarten and next morning marched direct upon the congregation assembled in the barn. The minister, Morel, had only begun his opening prayer when two shots were fired at the persons on the platform. The congregation tried in vain to shut the doors; the followers of the Duke of Guise burst in, and precipitated themselves on the unarmed men, women and children. For an hour they fired, hacked and stabbed among them, the duke coolly watching the carnage. Sixty persons, of both sexes, were left dead on the spot, more than two hundred were severely wounded, and the rest contrived to escape. After the massacre, the duke sent to the local judge, and severely reprimanded him for having permitted the Huguenots of Vassy thus to meet. The judge entrenched himself behind the edict of the king. The duke's eyes flashed with rage, and, striking the hilt of his sword with his hand, he said, "The sharp edge of this will soon cut your edict in pieces." So severe were the restrictions upon the Huguenots that they were not even allowed to go to the grave in peace. Many of the dead bodies, because not permitted a decent burial by the friends of the deceased Protestants, were removed from the dwellings by the hangman and cast into the public sewers.

Among those subjected to this brutal indignity was the body of the distinguished M. de Chenevix. He had been celebrated for his learning and piety, and enjoyed for a time the position of Councillor to the King of Metz. During his illness in 1686, the Catholic curate of the parish forced himself into the presence of the sufferer, demanded his re-cantation, and ordered him to communicate. He positively refused to confess his sins to any but God, and declined to communicate after the popish manner. At his death his body was removed by the executioner, placed on a hurdle, dragged off and cast upon a dunghill. During the night about four hundred of his friends, mostly women, proceeded to the spot where the body lay and secured it for a Christian burial. Wrapping the body in linen, four men bore it aloft on their shoulders and placed it in a grave digged in a gar-den. While the body was being lowered to its resting place the mourning assembly joined in singing the Seventy-ninth Psalm, "Save me, O God, for the waters are come into my soul," etc. From this circumstance it would seem that the custom of Psalm-singing at funerals existed among the French Christians, as among those of the early ages of the New Testament Church.

The Psalms were the constant companions of the wan-dering Huguenots, and often solaced them in their galley sufferings, and consoled them as they were led to the scaffold or the stocks. Editions of the French metrical Psalms were published in the form of small primers, and thousands of them carried concealed about the persons of the Huguenots, ready for use when a convenient opportunity was presented.

M. Fulcrand and M. Rochette, distinguished pastors among the reformed, were carried together to their execu-tion, where they sang from the One hundred and eighteenth Psalm,

"This is the day which the Lord hath made,
We will rejoice and be glad in it," etc.

When the Huguenots were not allowed to assemble in their accustomed places of worship, they met secretly by night in caves, among thick forests, in some lone place by the sea shore, or sheltered by the rocks of neighboring mountains. In the desert were regular gatherings of wor-shipers which were known as the "Churches of the Desert." These churches were organized, had their pastors, elders and deacons, and met and adjourned at stated hours. The meetings were held during the night, and so closely were they concealed that it was only by the most rigid search that they were ever discovered. Here in their night gathering, they sang the Psalms of Marot. As the hour for beginning the services would draw nigh, the pastor would sometimes send out companies, who were ordered to sing a Psalm to direct any of the worshipers who might be delayed and in danger of becoming lost in the darkness. It was from the singing of these guides that the rendezvous of the Huguenots was frequently discovered. These churches of the desert continued in existence down to the period of the French Revolution, when Protestantism was again publicly tolerated in France.

Among those who gathered in the Desert for worship and were celebrated in the wars with the Romish forces, were the Camisards, so called from the character of their dress. This band owed its organization to Jean Cavalier, a native of Languedoc, and born near the close of the seventeenth century. The Camisards were poor Protestants, who had been goaded to desperation by the cruelty of their persecutions; but who, although ignorant of the art of war, were so gallant and determined that they carried on a successful struggle against the arms of France for almost five years. They were without money, but received supplies of food and clothing from the peasants and from the spoils of victory. Their bullets were generally moulded from the church bells that had formerly summoned them on their peaceful Sabbaths to the Lord's house. It was an invariable custom with them to engage in prayer and Psalmody, both when pitching their camps and when beginning their march. If they were successful in their onslaughts, they held religious exercise for the benefit of the peasants who would flock in crowds to their rendezvous. The determination and success of these religious soldiers only prepared the way for greater cruelty. An enemy, whose rage is excited by the exercise of the liberty of conscience in religion, is incapable of admiring the valor of a foe, and so, only devises severer tortures for those resisting. Whole villages of those in sympathy with Cavalier and his band were burned to the ground. The stake and the gibbet streamed with the blood of captives all over Languedoc, while many a straggler from his company was shot like a beast and his body trampled in the dust. The Battle Hymn of these sturdy warriors was the Sixty-eighth Psalm, which they usually sang with one knee on the ground, and when the enemy was making the first onset. Their Psalm began :

> " Que Dieu se montre seulement,
> Et l'on verra dans le moment
> Abandonner la place
> Le camp des ennemis epars,
> Epouvante de toutes parts,
> Fuera devant sa face." *

At the battle of Valde Bane, Jan. 12, 1703, a company of only two hundred Camisards was attacked by the Papal soldiers under Count de Broglie. But the smallness of their numbers, and " the approach of his troops did not move the resolute band, who continued singing a Psalm (the Sixty-eighth) with one knee on the ground until they had received the first volley."

On another occasion, in the diocese of Uzes, when La Jonquiere supposed he had annihilated a company of Camisards, and so ordered his men to charge with the bayonet, he was astonished to see them jump from the ground and rush to the attack, singing their favorite Psalm.

An anonymous writer says the papal troops were often paralyzed by the religious fervor of the Camisards. He mentions a conversation with an officer who declared he could not keep his men under control when they heard the music of the

> "Que Dieu se montre seulement," etc.

A scene at the closing of the Camisard war has been thus described: " When D'Aygaliers and Cavalier were in conference with reference to peace, the divisions of the

---

* " Que Dieu se montre seulement,
  Et onverra fondainement
  Abandoner la place:
  Le cap des ennemis epars,
  Et fes haineux de toutes parts,
  Fuer devant fa face."

The above is quoted from Marot and Beze edition, 1684.—J. C. B.

opposing forces mingled, embraced each other and united in singing Psalms.　When the Camisards in Nismis heard that the struggles were over and that they were to be left to the free exercise of their consciences in worship, the town resounded with the accents of praise and thanksgiving. Psalms were heard in the streets and public places.　The Bishop of Nismis thus alludes to the spectacle : "We have seen Cavalier at our gates ; his interview with the Marshall and M. de Basville ; his submission and his pride ; the boldness of Scelerets, who accompanied him : the concourse of new converts who go to see them ; the Psalms they chant and with which the Vaunage resounds, all this greatly scandalizes and afflicts the Catholics."　On this same occasion, the Catholics became so worried with the endless singing of the Psalms, that they threatened, if it were not for the soldiers, they would cast the Huguenots into the Rhone.

Though the Psalms in 1553 were attached to the catechism of Geneva, and thus became formally a part of the Order of the Reformed Church, yet there is little mention made of Psalms and Psalmody in the records of the synods. Enough, however, remains to convince us that Psalm-singing was not a mere accident, but was regarded as an essential part of religious devotion.

From the Synodicon of John Quick, published in London in 1692, we find the acts of the several French Synods. In the second canon, chapter X of the Discipline, enacted in the National Synod at Paris, 1559, there is the following direction :　"Singing of God's praise being a divine ordinance to be performed in the congregation of the faithful and for that by the use of the Psalms their hearts be comforted and strengthened, everyone shall be advertised to bring with them their Psalm-books into the assemblies ; and such as through contempt of this holy ordinance do forbear the having them, shall be censured, as also those who, in time of singing, both before and after sermon, are not uncovered, as also when the holy sacraments are celebrated."

Previous to 1579 the practice of "lining out the Psalms," as was generally customary in Scotland, seems to have been introduced into the French churches. This not meeting with the favor of the ministry generally, an act forbidding it was passed in the Tenth Synod, held at Figeae in 1579—"Churches that in singing Psalms do first cause each verse to be read, shall be advised to forbear that childish custom, and such as have used themselves to it shall be censured." Twelve years later the act requiring Psalmbooks in church was re-enacted. It is in the records of the Eleventh Synod that met at Vitre : "Forasmuch as there is a notorious contempt of religion visible in all places, yea also in our religious meetings, we advise that notice be given unto all persons to bring with them Psalmbooks into the churches, and that such as contemptuously neglect the doing of it shall be severely censured ; and all Protestant printers are advised not to sunder in their impressions the prayers and catechism from the Psalm-books."

At length the Psalms of Marot and Beza came to be regarded as obsolete and barbarous. Voltaire said of them that as taste improved they inspired disgust, and that which in the reign of Francis I. charmed the court, seemed only suited to please the populace under Louis. Geneva, the first to adopt these Psalms, was the first to abandon them. The revision of them was begun by M. Conrart, and completed by M. da la Bastide. This revision was presented to the pastors and professors of the church at Geneva, who reported favorably on it, and, in 1695, published it. In a short time they abolished the use of the old and adopted the new version in the Genevan church, and issued circular letters to the other churches requesting them to do the same. But, notwithstanding the contemptuous reflection of Voltaire, the Psalms of Marot and Beza remained dear to the people, and to them the new version seemed to lack all charms. Because of the love of the people for the old Psalms, the new ones retained the same number of stanzas, possessed the same quantity of syllables in the verses as in the old, and were adapted to the old-fashioned tunes, many of which are used to this day in France and Switzerland. Yet, with all this, the new version was for many years used by no churches except those in Geneva, Hesse-

Cassel and Neufchatel.   As late as the year 1700 a synod of the Walloon district, assembled at Rotterdam, resolved to retain the old version, providing only for a few changes in some exceptionable words.   One, writing at the time of the proposition to have a new version of the Psalms, says : "We may say of the poems of Marot and Beza what Quintilian said of Ennius—'let us reverence the verses of Ennius as we reverence the groves that are venerable for their great age, and whose old and lopped oaks, though they have little beauty, yet strike us with religious awe.'"

The French and Swiss churches of the present day use almost exclusively human composition in their praise.   The Psalms of Marot are still sung, but chiefly in those districts where dwell the descendents of the Piedmont Christians.

In my possession is a Liturgy in the French, with the Psalms in French metre, as they are still sung in some places on the continent.   The Psalms in this version are printed with the music to which they were to be sung, the words coming immediately under their proper notes.   In this version also are some of the old Psalms that were sung in the sixteenth century.   The longer Psalms are divided by pauses after the ancient method, for resting the voice.   At the end of the Psalms are "Sacred Canticles" from the Scriptures, rendered in rhyme, and set to the same music to which the Psalms were sung.   From Switzerland and France, by missionaries and by the refugees, the French Psalms were carried into many different parts.   As early as 1555 the Genevan church sent two missionaries and fourteen students to Coligny's Colony in Rio Janeiro.   Thus, at least sixty years before the landing of the Pilgrims on Plymouth Rock, and fifty before the Book of Common Prayer was borne to the banks of the James River, the Psalms of Marot and Beza were being sung by the missionaries sent to the Spanish possessions of the far West.

From France the refugees carried their forms of worship and their Psalms into the Netherlands and adjoining countries ; to England, Ireland, America, where they established churches and worshiped in their own language and after their own method. In Great Britain the refugees were so numerous that a great number of churches were organized, where their pastors on the anniversaries of their exile would preach to sorrowing assemblies from the words, "By the rivers of Babylon, there we sat down, yea, we wept when we remembered Zion." Owing to the gradual conformity of the descendents of these exiles to customs and language of their adopted country, the Huguenots diminished rapidly in influence and numbers. In Ireland, a French congregation was organized at Portarlington, which existed still in this present century. The last pastor was Charles de Vignolles, and the French language and French Psalms were employed in worship till 1817, after which time it was discontinued, the French language being an unknown tongue in the neighborhood. Several Huguenot families, led by the nephew of Admiral Duquesne, emigrated to the Cape of Good Hope, while others removed as far from France as Surinam in Dutch Guiana.

According to Weiss there are now in the Cape Colony about four thousand descendents of the Huguenot exiles, residing in what is known as the French Valley. In 1739, the Dutch government proscribed the use of their native tongue, and their language is now the Dutch. "On each parlor table is one of those great folio Bibles which the French Protestants were wont to hand down from father to son, and in which the dates of the births and the names of all the members of the family are invariably inscribed. Clement Marot's Psalms and religious books are often found among them. Night and morning the members of each family assemble for prayer and the reading of the Bible. Every Sunday at sunrise the farmers set out in their rustic vehicles, covered with hides or with coarse cloth, to attend divine service, and at night they return to their peaceful homes. The news of the world takes a long time to reach them. In 1828, when evangelical missionaries told them that religious toleration had existed in France for forty years, the old men shed tears."

Some families of French Protestants settled on Long Island Sound, about twenty-five miles from New York City, and

called their settlement New Rochelle, after the name of their
stronghold in the mother country.   From this point they,
in the early days of their settlement, would come to New
York to attend divine service.   The journey was made by
the men on foot, and by the women and children, in carts.
Arriving at the city they would encamp within the suburbs
until the Sabbath bell would summon them to service in the
old church du Saint Esprit.   Though these Huguenots found
a safe refuge in their new abode, yet "the old longing for
home in Allan Cunningham's ballad—

> ' It's hame and it's hame, hame fain would I be,
>   O hame, hame, hame, to my ain countree,'

clung to their breasts and caused singular melancholy in
some of them.   One old man who went every day down to
the seashore to look and gaze his fill towards the beautiful
cruel land where most of life had been passed, with his face
toward the east, and his eyes strained, as if by force of longing looks he could see the far-distant France, said his morning prayers and sang one of Clement Marot's hymns—there
being an edition of the Psalms of David put into French
Rhyme (Pseaumes de David misen Rime francoise, par Clement Marot et Theodore de Beze) published in as small a form
as possible, in order that the book might be concealed in
their bosoms, if the Huguenots were surprised in their worship while they lived in France."

A colony of French Huguenots also settled in Charleston, South Carolina, where they kept up their services in
French, singing the old Psalms of Marot till about 1840.
Owing to the difficulty of procuring pastors who could
preach to them in French they were compelled to secure ministers of other denominations, which soon led to a revolution
of their liturgy and to the setting aside of the Psalms of
their early service.   In the early history of the Carolina colonies, we find the Psalms of Marot and Beza performing the
office of comforting and supporting amid the horrors of Indian
captivity, as they had often done under the persecutions of
the French Papists.   In the attack on Kingston forty-five
Huguenots were taken captive, one of them being Catharine
Le Fever, wife of Louis Dubois.   After the Indians had

selected her to be burned, and when she was already bound
for the sacrifice to savage hate, she consoled herself and
strengthened her spirit for a terrible death by singing one
of David's Psalms.   So highly delighted were the Indians
with her singing that they delayed her sufferings and by
signs urged her to continue.   When she was engaging in her
song the remainder of the captives united in singing the
Psalm of the Babylonish Captivity.   The indulgence of the
savages, for the sake of these sacred melodies, proved the
safety of the captives; for while the strains of the Jewish
lament were yet rising to heaven Dubois and his followers
broke into the Indian camp and secured their rescue.

CHAPTER VII.

The Psalms in the Netherland Reformation.

Though the Low Countries were the home of many sects, yet the Calvinists were the most numerous; and chiefly gave character to the religion of the land. In all of the Southern provinces, and chiefly in Flanders, the Reformed Church triumphed over all others, being supported by the Huguenots of France, the Genevan Republic, and the Calvinistic part of Germany. The principal actors amid the exciting scenes of the Reformation in the Netherlands were the Gueux, or Beggars, so called from the Guesen penny which they wore about their necks, being a gold or silver coin, one side bearing an effigy of the King, with the inscription, "Trust to the King," and the other having two hands folded together and holding a wallet with the words, "As far as the Beggars Scrip." This penny was subsequently worn by all who took up arms against the King.

The Netherlands were favorably situated for these reformers to promote their cause; and notwithstanding the efforts of the King and the cruelty of the Inquisition, their efforts were attended with overwhelming success. Books and tracts were scattered from many a press in England, France and at Geneva, while many a refugee preacher, trained in the school of Geneva, or aroused to desperation by the persecutions of France, awakened the masses by his earnest and persistent appeals.

At first the meetings of the Protestants were held in secret, but conscious of their increased and rapidly increasing strength, they boldly proceeded to proclaim their profession and their tenets in the eyes of the world, and in defiance of the King and the clergy of Rome. The cities either being refused them, or being regarded as too dangerous for their assembling, these fearless Christians took to the fields and groves, thus giving rise to those famous conventicles of the sixteenth century.   Led by some converted priest or friar, these field worshipers began their operations in western Flanders.   Small audiences at first attended the services, but they rapidly increased until the whole country was in a furor, and thousands of the inhabitants, men, women and children, resorted to the rendezvous of the Protestants.   At Ghent, Aalst, Tournay, Valenciennes, Antwerp, were gathered assemblies of Calvinists varying from 5,000 to 15,000.   Although many were attracted by curiosity, others to add to their sport, yet the great majority came with consciousness of their wrongs and hungering for the truths of God's Word.

These field meetings spread through the Walloon provinces and entered the Northern Netherlands.   In July, 1566, Peter Gabriel, an apostate monk, and a man of singular eloquence, opened the first conventicle in Holland.   In the environs of Amsterdam, The Hague, Harlem, at Ypres, Bruges, all over the Low Countries, other converts carried on the work, until the whole population seemed for a while to have no other employment than to attend the religious assemblies.   Many of the Christians, carried away with their zeal and hatred of popery, turned iconoclasts, and images, altars, pictures and many splendid churches and cathedrals were ruined by their hands.

In the worship of the Calvinistic churches of the Low Countries, and especially in the field meetings, the Psalms were a conspicuous and powerful agency in sustaining the enthusiasm of the people.   In those provinces that spoke the French, the Psalms of Marot in the original dialect were used, and translations speedily made for those parts that used a different language.   Of their influence Morton thus speaks in his History of Poetry: "France and Germany were infatuated with a love for Psalm-singing . . . These energetic hymns of Geneva, under the conduct of the Calvinistic preachers, excited and supported a variety of popular insurrections; they filled the most flourishing cities of the Low Countries with sedition and tumult, and fomented the fury which defaced many of the most beautiful and venerable churches of Flanders."

Motley describes the first field assembly in Holland in the following terms:

"Thus the preaching spread through the Walloon provinces to the north of the Netherlands. Towards the end of July (1566) an apostate monk of singular eloquence, Peter Gabriel by name, was announced to preach at Overcen, near Harlem. This was the first field meeting that had taken place in Holland. The people were wild with enthusiasm : the authorities were beside themselves with apprehension. People from the country flocked into the town by the thousands. The other cities were deserted. Harlem was filled to overflowing. Multitudes encamped upon the ground the night before. The magistrates ordered the gates to be kept closed in the morning till long after the usual hour. It was of no avail. Bolts and bars were but small impediments to enthusiasts who had traveled so many miles on foot or horseback to listen to a sermon. They climbed the walls, swam the moat, and thronged the place of meeting long before the doors had been opened. When they could no longer be kept closed without conflict, for which the magistrates were not prepared, the whole population poured out of the city with a single impulse. Tens of thousands were assembled upon the field. The bulwarks were erected as usual. The guards were posted. The congregation was encamped and arranged in an orderly manner. The women, of whom there were many, were placed next the pulpit, which, upon this occasion, was formed of a couple of spears thrust into the earth, sustaining a cross-piece against which the preacher might lean his back. The services commenced with the singing of a Psalm by the whole vast assemblage. Clement Marot's Psalms, recently translated by Dathenus, were then new and popular. The strains of the monarch minstrel, chanted thus in their homely but nervous mother tongue by a multitude who had but recently learned that all the poetry and rapture of devotion were not irrevocably coffined in a buried language, or immured in the precincts of a church, had never produced a more elevating effect. No anthem from the world-renowned organ in that ancient city ever awakened more lofty emotions than did those ten thousand human voices, ringing from the grassy meadows, in that favored midsummer noon.   When all was silent, the preacher arose, a little, meagre man, who looked as if he might melt away beneath the blazing sunshine of July rather than hold the multitude enchanted four uninterrupted hours by the magic of his tongue.''

It was the usual custom of the iconoclasts to proceed to their work of devastation by singing some Psalm of Marot, or some canticle of Geneva, rendered in rhyme.   The author just quoted from, in speaking of the demolition in the convent at Marchiennes, says: ''A large assemblage of rioters, growing in numbers as they advanced, swept over the province of Tournay after accomplishing the sack of the city churches.   Armed with halbreds, hammers and pitchforks, they carried on the war, day after day, against the images.   At the convent of Marchiennes, considered by contemporaries the most beautiful abbey in all the Netherlands, they halted to sing the Ten Commandments in Marot's verse.   Hardly had the vast chorus finished the precept against graven images,

'' 'Tailler nete feras imaige,'

when the whole mob seemed seized with sudden madness. Without waiting to complete the Psalm they fastened upon the company of marble images, as if they possessed sensibility to feel the blows inflicted.   In an hour they had laid the whole in ruins.''

Another favorite practice of the Calvinists was to express their welcome at the approach of any of the nobles who had joined them, by singing their Psalms.   A single instance may be given—in the reception of the Prince of Orleans at Antwerp.   This city was in a tumult from the preaching and singing of the Protestants.   The keys of the city had been captured, and the people were openly escorting their banished pastors back to their places of worship within the walls.   At the request of the magistrates the Prince of Orange, who was recognized as one of the Gueux, was sent by Margaret of Parma to quell the excitement.   The description of his reception, given by Prescott, could apply to many

such occurring all over the Netherlands : "As he drew near
Antwerp the people flocked out by thousands to welcome
him.   It would seem as if they hailed him as their deliverer,
and every window, verandah and roof was crowded with
spectators as he rode through the gates of the capital.   The
people ran up and down the streets singing Psalms, or shouting 'Vivent les Gueux,' while they thronged round the
prince's horse in so dense a mass that it was scarcely possible
for him to force a passage."

Outside of the gatherings in the fields, and the image-
breaking of the iconoclasts, the history of Psalm-singing is
much the same as in Germany and France.   Being a novelty,
the Psalms became a great favorite with the people, who
sang them both at home in worship, and in their daily toils
in field and workshop.

A singular instance of superstition connected with the
Psalm-singing of the Calvinists in the Low Countries, occurred at Valenciennes during March 1567.   While Egmont
was commanding the Protestant fortifications, the chimes all
through the siege played the music of Marot's Psalms.   On
the fatal morning of March 25th, when the city fell, the
chimes happened to sound forth from every belfry the music
set to the Twenty-second Psalm, "My God, my God, why
hast thou forsaken me."   This was taken by the Christians
as an omen for evil, and so filled them with dismay and has-
tened their downfall.

This Egmont, who led the siege, was at first one of the
most barbarous of the persecutors, but afterward became a
confederate of Orange, and went to the scaffold June 5, 1568,
reading aloud the Fifty-first Psalm, "Have mercy upon me,
O God, according to thy lovingkindness," etc.

When any of the Calvinists were being led by the forces
of the government to prison or to death, it very frequently
happened that the people followed them singing Psalms and
shouting to them words of comfort; and it was not an infre-
quent occurrence for both persecuted and persecutors to be
singing Psalms around the same scaffold, the one in the language of Marot, and the others their Miserere (Fifty-first
Psalm) chanted in the prose.

The Netherlanders engaged in their Psalmody at times with great risk to themselves. The Psalms of Marot were prohibited both from being sung and imported. In 1550 an edict was issued against even the possession of the Psalms and other Calvinistic publications, the penalty being "that such perturbators of the general quiet are to be executed; to wit, the men with the sword, and the women to be buried alive if they *do not* persist in their errors; if they do persist in them, they are to be executed with fire." "Capons or sausages on Good Friday, the Psalms of Marot, the Sermon on the Mount in the vernacular, led to the rack, the gibbet and the stake, but ushered in a war against the Inquisition which lasted for eighty years."

In Antwerp there was a degree of toleration, three places in the city being assigned the Calvinists, "where they might either erect new churches, or convert houses for that purpose, with the restriction, however, that no preacher shall assail the ruling religion from the pulpit, and no Psalms should be sung by them out of the appointed districts."

But the edicts and executions did not stop the purchase and singing of the Psalms. They were smuggled into the country from Geneva and France in bales of merchandise, and sold everywhere by pedlers and hawkers, until "The Psalms of Marot were as current as the drugs of Molucca or the diamonds of Borneo."

The accounts of the versions of the Psalms and of their authors are very meagre. At the beginning of the Reformation in Holland, "The Protestants first sung in their families and private assemblies the Psalms of the noble Lord of Nievelte, which he published in 1540." Of these Psalms nothing more could be gathered than that they were prepared as a substitute for the obscene songs with which the cities of Holland resounded and by which the people were drawn away. Simon Cock, with the imperial license granted at Brussels, in 1539, published the Psalms in the Flemish, the dialect of Flanders, but whether or not they were sung is not known.

About the year 1555 the Psalms were rendered in the Low Dutch by Peter Dathen, or Dathenus. His version was only a translation of the French Psalms by Marot and Beza. The French tunes were also published with it, and the whole accompanied with an address or dedication to the Belgic congregations and their pastors groaning under the cross. Though their author was entirely ignorant of the Hebrew, yet these Psalms were highly extolled, because at that time Dutch poetry was very little cultivated, and came into use wherever that tongue was spoken.

Near the close of the sixteenth century the Psalms were turned into Dutch rhyme by Philip de Marnix, Lord of Sainte Aldegonde, and were designed to pass into public use in the place of the version of Dathenus. But, though a better translation, it was destined to fall short of the mark at which it was aimed. From Bayle we learn that "a good many years ago, some people of Holland were displeased with these loose poetical paraphrases, which varied too much from the text of Scripture, especially with respect to the Psalms of Dathenus, which had been formed upon the French Psalms of Marot and Beza. Among others, Philip de Marnix, Lord of Mount Sainte-Aldegonde, employed himself this way, and composed a new paraphrase in metre, exactly agreeing with the Psalms of Dathenus, in the stanzas, lines, and syllables, for this reason, that it might be sung along with them in the churches, or be easily substituted in their room. But whereas most people had already got the Psalms of Dathenus by heart, the churches did not see how they could conveniently and without giving some offense to the common people introduce any alteration in the public worship."

Melchor Adams observes of the same work: "That work had been printed several times, but was not yet received by the common approbation of the ministers. The reason is:

> Books have their fate succeeding well or ill,
> Just in proportion to the reader's skill."

About the beginning of the seventeenth century, a paraphrase of the Psalms in Dutch rhyme was published by Dirk Rafael Kamphuyzen. His paraphrase of the One hundred and thirty-third Psalm, though far from a close rendering of the original, is a most beautiful piece of composition.   Longfellow saw such beauty in it that he translated it into English.   Two verses are given here :

> If there be one whose thoughts delight to wander
> In pleasure's fields, where love's bright strains meander ;
> If there be one who longs to find
> Where all the purer blisses are enshrined—
> A happy resting place of virtuous worth,
> A blessed paradise on earth :
>
> Let him survey the joy conferring union
> Of brothers who are bound in fond communion,
> And not by force of blood alone,
> But by their mutnal sympathies are known,
> And every heart and every mind relies
> Upon fraternal, kindred ties.

In Poland the Psalms, modeled after those of the Reformed Church of France, were sung among the Pinczovian Protestants, a class that had received their name from Pinckzow, an Italian, and a minister of the Reformed Church.   These Psalms, in Polish metre, were issued about 1563, by Bernard Woiewodka, of Cracow, who had been sent by Prince Nicholas Radzivil, Palatine of Wilna, and had established a printing press at Brest, a royal city of Lithuania.

In Hungary, a version of the Psalms was prepared after the model of Marot's Psalms, and accommodated to the airs published with them.   It was printed at Hanau, 1608, and was bound with a translation of the Heidelberg Catechism, and the Liturgy of the Hungarian churches.

In the same country, the Roman Catholics issued a metrical version of the Psalms.   They were printed at Debrecrin, in 1723, and were sung in the service of the Papal church.

In the Wittemberg library, collected in the last century by Charles, Duke of Wittemberg, are poetical versions of the Psalms in Spanish, Portugese and Italian.   The accounts of the authorship, origin and use of these versions are probably lost.   Yet sufficient remains to lead to the conclusion that the Psalms in metre were sung in all these countries by those who, either secretly or openly, espoused the faith of the Reformation.

Many of the refugees, who fled from the inquisition of Spain and Italy, settled in the Grisons, a mountainous country on the East of Switzerland, where they met with the Swiss forms of worship, and soon conformed to them. The language of the Grisons was a dialect of the Romance or Romanese. Here Biveroni, a native of Spain, and a Protestant refugee, versified the Psalms in the Grisonian dialect and published them in 1505. In 1606, in the same tongue, were published the Psalms and Sacred Hymns by Chiampel.

An incident in the history of Juan Gonzaler, a descendant of Moorish parents, shows that although the supremacy of the *auto-de-fe* prevented the public and widespread singing of the Psalms in Spain, as in Germany, France and the Low Countries, yet there were those there who sang them in their retreats and found comfort in them when led to the stake. This Gonzaler had been suspected of sympathizing with Mohamedanism, and was cast into prison. When liberated he espoused the Protestant cause and preached with great celebrity in Andalusia. For his offense he was apprehended, and led to the scaffold. It was while going to his death, that, "at the door of the Triania, he began to sing the One hundred and ninth Psalm."

In Germany, the melodies to which the Psalms were sung were called chorals and were of the same nature with what at the present day are known as "Psalm tunes." These new melodies were studied and sung especially among the Germans. Musical clubs were organized in Mayence, Colmar and Ulm, which shared largely in the events of the sixteenth century. When priests and nobles were vieing with one another in wickedness, the "cobblers," who could oppose to their manifold forms of vice only decent lives and a virtuous education, were diffusing their sentiments and promoting truth by their sacred songs which they sung to their favorite choral melodies, and which were composed in verses so rugged and uncouth, that "Schustereim"— cobbler's rhyme, has become in Germany a synonym for doggerel. The motive in their organization they sang—

> " By making pious hymns we strive
>   Coarse ballads from the streets to drive,
>   For every night we hear with shame
>   Such songs as we refuse to name ;
>   To silence all those idle lays
>   We meet and sing our Maker's praise."

Such life and vigor did these societies of shoemakers possess that the one at Ulm survived almost to the middle of the nineteenth century.

All of the Reformers were patrons of sacred music, and most of them were skillful performers, both with the voice and on various instruments. Luther gained much celebrity for his musical attainments.

His talent for music very early in life aided him in gaining a livelihood, and in middle life contributed largely toward his comfort and success in the mission to which God had called him.

It was said of the Reformer, while involved in the midst of the excitement to which his preaching gave rise, that he never laid aside his music, but frequently resorted to it for recreation and social entertainment. " When he felt himself fatigued with writing or perceived his head becoming dizzy, and that his ideas did not keep pace with his pen, he took his flute and played some agreeable air on it." Music was in his eyes a divine revelation. " Music," said he, " is one of the noblest arts; its notes give life to the text; it charms away the spirit of sadness, as is seen in the case of Saul." " Music is a delightful, noble gift of God and nearly related to theology. I would not give what little skill in music I possess for something great. The young are continually to be exercised in this art; it makes good and skillful people of them."

It was a frequent custom with Luther to engage in singing sacred songs with his family and friends after meals, and sometimes he would invite his guests to form a choir and unite with him in Psalmody.

An instance of the power of music upon himself occurred while he was a monk at Wittenberg. On one occasion he was so overwhelmed with trouble because of his sins that he shut himself up in his cell for several days and nights—allowed no one to approach him. When Edem-berger, his friend, broke open the door he found Luther lying insensible on the floor and without signs of life. He strived, but in vain, to arouse him. At last some chorister boys, whom he had taken with him, began one of their sweet melodies. Their clear voices acted like a voice from heaven, and the prostrate monk returned to consciousness and gradually to accustomed strength.

Luther gained celebrity as a composer of music. Sir John Pringle, in a letter written in 1769, observed that "the late Mr. Handel, that celebrated musician, told me that Luther had even composed the music of his Psalms and hymns, and which was so excellent that he borrowed from it and inserted whole passages in his oratorios."

By many the Psalm-tune known everywhere as "Old Hundred" is supposed to have been composed by Luther, though others place it among those "most favorite songs of the times," or those "ballad airs as would best suit the meter," which were sung years before the Reformation to romances and licentious songs. Its first publication was with the French version of the Psalms in 1550; in 1562 it appeared in England set to the One hundredth Psalm of Sternhold and Hopkins. At first it appeared in but one part, but was afterward frequently composed in two, three, four and even five parts.

With the first edition of his Psalms Luther published "appropriate tunes." In the preface to this he enforces the duty of church Psalmody, and supports the duty by the examples of David and Paul. "He had subjoined," he says, "suitable tunes to show that the fine arts had by no means been abolished through the preaching of the Gospel; but that in particular the art of music should be employed to the glory of God, though he knew this sentiment was contrary to the romantic ideas of some teachers, who were disposed to allow nothing but what was purely intel-lectual." "They are arranged," he added, "for four voices for no other reason than that I am anxious that young people, who should and must be educated in music and other good arts, should have wherewith to get rid of

their lascivious and carnal songs, and instead of them learn
something salutary and receive that good with pleasure
which to youth is meet."

In preparing the music for his Psalm book Luther consulted Conrad Rupff, conductor of the choir at the Elector's
chapel, with reference to the proper character of choral
music, the scale, &c., "after which he finally arranged the
choral notes himself, selecting the octaves for the Epistles
and the sixths for the Gospel and saying: 'Christ is a kind
master and his words are sweet, wherefore we will adopt
sextum tonum for the Gospels; and because St. Paul is a
serious apostle, therefore we will ordain *octavum tonum* for
his Epistles.' "

These "appropriate tunes" of Luther, as well as his
Psalms and hymns, were speedily taken up and carried over
the whole nation by traveling musicians, singing processions
of school boys and city cornetters.

Within a century from the days of Luther sacred music
in Germany had sadly declined from the simple, but effective,
chorals of the people. The new Italian school had exerted
its influence, until by the middle of the seventeenth century,
as one of Germany's best historians has expressed it, "the
modern style gained a decided preponderance over the antique
method. Musical declamation and expression suited to the
words prevail; rhythmical irregularities and the old churchly
tunes disappear before a regular measure and modern softer
tunes, so that Psalmody becomes wholly alienated from its
original vital element, as popular singing religious concert
music, which contained no reminiscent traces even of the old
church melodies, and despised the form of hymns and
strophes, was more constantly cultivated. The congregation wholly ceased to take part in the singing." The same
author says of the sacred music of the following century,
that it sank "with the hymns of this period to the lowest degree of its existence. The old chorals were re-cast
into modern forms, by which they altogether lost their ancient power and beauty. A multitude of new, unnational
and difficult melodies, in a dry, pedantic style, appeared;
the last trace of the old rhymth disappeared, and tedious,

heavy monotony gained the ascendency, by which all sublimity and freshness were lost.   Preludes and interludes of
a secular character were introduced as substitutes.   An
operatic overture generally introduced the people into the
church; a march or a waltz dismissed them from it.   The
Church ceased to foster and to produce music; the theatre
and concert hall took its place.''

Notwithstanding this, Germany did not lose a taste for
music; she has justly acquired for herself the enviable notoriety of a nation of musicians.   At the present day the culture of this fine art is carried to the highest state, and may
be found in the curriculum of studies even in the insignificant
charity schools.   Capability to teach the knowledge of music,
both vocal and instrumental, is an absolute prerequisite of a
schoolmaster.   Hence it is we always find the rudely-clad
and apparently desolate German immigrant, carrying his
instrument, and charged with some favorite national airs.

In France, at the period of the Reformation, sacred
music assumed the most fantastic forms.   Dances, jigs, op-
eras and merry tunes were set to the Psalms of Marot, while
new airs were composed ''by excellent composers, that
chimed so sweetly that every one desired a new Psalter.''
The first edition of Marot's Psalms was published in Paris
without any melodies; hence the populace, who had been
singing his ballads and roundelays, were compelled to take
''secular tunes such as were easy to play on the violin and
other instruments.''

The Queen sang ''Rebuke me not in thine indignation''
to the air of a fashionable jig; Antony chose for ''Revenge
my quarrel,'' the air of a fashionable dance of Poictou.   The
Psalms rendered by Simon Cock into the Flemish tongue,
and published at Brussels 1539, contained a music selected
from the ballads of his day, each Psalm having printed at
the head of it its own appropriate tune.

These popular and vapid airs were sung to the Psalms
not only in the court and among the populace, but by the
Reformed congregations in their public worship, previous to
the second edition of Marot's version.

Florimod de Remond objected to the music of the Calvinistic Psalms, because, as he said, it was borrowed from vulgar ballads, to which Sieur de Pours replied that, what used to belong to profane songs was now separated from them and was become in a measure sanctified.   "In ancient times," he adds, "things that were of common use, even though taken as plunder, when they were with proper rites separated and sequestered for the service of the sanctuary, were counted holy."

When the Psalms of Marot and Beza appeared together, under the auspices of the Geneva Church, they were all found set to popular tunes.   Ten thousand copies of this version were issued, and the new airs soon became as popular as the old.   These Psalm-tunes were procured under the auspices of Calvin.   The chief musician whom he employed for the production of them was Guillaume de Franc; although it has been said that at least fifty contributors were numbered in the edition that was published at Strasburg in 1545.

The musicians of France vied with one another in preparing music for the Psalms, and in commending themselves through them to the attention and favor of the populace and of royalty.   De Pours observes that Lewis Bourgeois set eighty-three Psalms to music, in four, five and six parts, which were printed at Lyons in 1561.

Of the Psalms and their "appropriate tunes," Mason, in his work on English Church Music, says, "The verses were easy and prosaic enough to be intelligent to the meanest capacity.   The melodies to which they were set rivaled the words in plainness and simplicity.   They who could read the one, could find little difficulty in learning to sing the other."

Godeau, Bishop of Grasse, in the preface to his French Paraphrase of the Psalms, bears honorable testimony to the Psalmody of the Huguenots: "Those whose separation from the Church we deplore, have rendered their version celebrated by the agreeable airs which skillful musicians have composed for them.   To know those sacred songs by heart is amongst them, as it were, a sign of their communion; and to our great shame in great cities, where they are most numerous, the Psalms are continually heard from the mouths of artisans, and in the country from that of laborers, while the Catholics are either silent or sing indecent songs."

That which, in the sacred music of the Reformation tunes, most attracts our notice and admiration is its congregational character. Perhaps never before, certainly never since, has the true idea of public praise been so grandly represented as in those vast congregations whose souls united in the spirit and voices in the melody of heavenly song. There was no trained choir of vocalists, no intonings of the organ to lead or inspire the masses; yet the volume of praise that rose from the thousands in the field meetings of Calvinists in the Netherlands has been represented as so sublime that even the Antiphonics of Primitive Worship and the chanting of the Royal Band of the Jewish Temple would appear insignificant beside it. The command was obeyed in the highest sense: "Let the people praise thee, O God; let all the people praise thee. O let the nations be glad and sing for joy."

CHAPTER VIII.

The Psalms in the English Reformation.

The history of the Psalm-singing of the English people began with the conversion of the British Isles to Christianity. At the close of the sixth century when St. Augustine crossed the English Channel on his mission of conversion, he carried with him the old Italic Psalter, for which he had an especial affection, and which he used in all the offices of the mission church. From that day to this the harp of David has never ceased to be heard in the worship of the English-speaking nations. Of St. Cuthbert, in the seventh century, the Historian Bede has written: "Such was the piety of St. Cuthbert that he forgot to take off his shoes for months together, sometimes the whole year round . . . thus did mankind go reeling through the dark ages, quarreling, drinking, hunting, hawking, singing Psalms, wearing breeches, grinding in mills, eating hot-bread, rocked in cradles, buried in coffins—weak, suffering, sublime. Well might St. Alfred exclaim: 'Maker of all creatures, help now thy miserable mankind !' "

It appears that the teaching of the Psalms to mere children was not an invention of Reformation times by the pious parents of Scotland, for nearly one thousand years before the days of Knox and his fellow reformers, it is given as an evidence of the precocity of Wilfrid that he had memorized the entire Psalter before he was fourteen years old.

At the close of the seventh century the celebrated Aldhelm, a bishop in the English Church, rendered the Psalms into the native tongue of the Anglo-Saxons. It is thought by some that an old Psalm-book preserved at Malmesbury till after the Reformation was the one prepared by this early poet.

Bede, the great historian of the ancient Britons, and the ornament of the age in which he lived, is to be classed in the long list of British Psalmists. His death occurred in the year 735.

One of Bede's frequent exercises from his early youth was the singing of the Psalms. A part of each day was spent in this manner. When he was elected mass-priest at the age of thirty, he became obligated by a law that required this daily exercise—"The mass-priest should at least have his missal, his singing book, his reader; his psalter, his handbook, his penitential and numeral one; he ought to have his officiating garments and to sing from sunrise, with the nine intervals, and nine readings. His sacramental cup should be of gold or silver, or tin, and not of earth, at least not of wood."

When in his last sickness, the Psalms afforded him much comfort. Cuthbert, his pupil, in a description of his closing days, says "he continued cheerful and rejoicing, giving thanks to Almighty God day and night, nay, even every hour till the day of our Lord's ascension. He daily read lessons to us, his scholars; the rest of the day he spent in singing Psalms. The nights he passed without sleep, yet rejoicing and giving thanks, unless when a little slumber intervened. When he awoke, he resumed his accustomed devotions, and, with expanded hands, never ceased returning thanks to God."

Bede claims a place among the Psalmists by a translation of the Psalms into the Anglo-Saxon tongue, concerning which, however, little is known. From a canon of Cuthbert, framed in 747, it appears that Psalm-singing was still, in the eighth century, a duty required among the nuns of the English church. It was ordained that "nunneries be not places of secret rendezvous for pithy talk, junketing, drunkenness and luxury, but habitations for such as live in continence and sobriety, and who read and sing Psalms; but let them spend their time in reading books and singing Psalms, rather than in weaving and working parti-colored, vain-glorious apparel."

One of Cuthbert's canons relating to the practice of Psalmody, gives the following curious argument for singing the Psalms of the Church in an unknown language, "Psalmody is a divine work, a great cure in many cases, for the souls of those who do it in spirit and in mind. But they that sing with the voice, without the inward meaning, may make the sound resemble something, therefore, though a man knows not the Latin words that are sung, yet he may devoutly apply the intention of his own heart to the things which are at present to be asked of God, and fix them there to the best of his power.''

Among the earliest missionaries to Ireland, and the first who instructed the Irish in the use of the Roman letters, was St. Patrick, of the fifth century. In conveying his instruction in spelling and reading, Patrick made use of his Psalter, for which he had unusual partiality. Such was the rapidity with which some of his pupils learned to read, that they were able to peruse the Psalms for themselves in fifteen days. A poem written by Fiac, one of the Irish converts, and a poet of no mean distinction, gives some of the habits of St. Patrick in the practice of Psalmody : ''He daily sang the Apocalypse and hymns ; and the whole Psalter he sang thrice ; he preached and baptized and prayed ; and he incessantly praised God. One of St. Patrick's modes of mortification, as we find related in the same poem, was to stand ''every night in the fountain of Slan, which was never dry, while he sang an hundred Psalms.'' This superstitious practice was not confined to St. Patrick ; St. Neat, the kinsman of Alfred ; St. Chad, and even Aldhelm, were accustomed to chant the Psalms while standing in wells or springs of water.

The Psalmist of the ninth century was Alfred, surnamed the Great. Alfred was born about the year 848, and was made king in 871. Till after he was twelve years old, this sovereign did not know one letter from another; yet such was his thirst for knowledge, and his ambition to attain, that he mastered the Latin language and finally even became a profound scholar for those times, a grammarian, a rhetorician, a philosopher, a historian, a musician, the Prince of Saxon poesy, and an excellent architect and geometrician.'' King Alfred was an earnest friend to his country, and made every effort to secure a just administration of the law, and to diffuse knowledge among his subjects. But the character in which he is represented as having been especially distinguished was that of the Christian.   It is no trifling evidence of the confidence that was placed in his integrity, that he was known in his day as "The Truth Teller."   A daily custom with him was to attend divine service, and in his private devotion was much engaged in the singing and reading of the Psalms.   That he might ever have with him a manual of worship, he made a collection of Psalms and prayers for the offices of the day, and carried it in his bosom.   The last literary work that this monarch undertook was the translation of the Psalms into the Anglo-Saxon, which, however, he did not live to finish.

"This victorious warrior; this sagacious statesman; this friend of distress; this protector against oppression who, in an age of ignorance loved literature and diffused it; who, in an age of superstition could be rationally pious; and in the station of royalty could discern his faults, and convert these into virtues, was called away from the world on the 26th day of October in the year 900 or 901."

The first Anglo-Saxon metrical version of the Psalms has been referred to the twelfth century.   The translation is a close rendering of Jerome's Latin Psalter, known as the French or Gallican.   The author of this Psalm-book is unknown.   A copy of it is preserved in the library of the Corpus Christi College, Cambridge, and revised copies, prepared either by the author or some one near his time, in the Bodleian library, and among the Cotton MSS. at the British Museum.   The fourteenth century presents us with the last Psalmist previous to the dawning days of the Reformation.   This was Richard Rolle, a monk of the St. Augustine order, and a native of Yorkshire.   Rolle was both a commentator and versifier of the Scriptures.   The principal work from his pen was an English version of the Psalms.   Of his undertaking he remarks in a prologue to his version, "In this werke I seek no strannge Ynglys, bot lightest and communist, and swilk that is most like unto the Latyne: so that thai that knawes noght the Latyne be the Ynglys may com to many Latyne words.   In the translacione I felogh the letter als—mekille as I may, and thor I fyne no proper Ynglys I felogh the wit of the wordis, so that thai that shall rede it

them thar not drede errynge.   In the expownyng I felogh
holi doctors.   For it may conen into sum envious manner
bond that knowys not what he suld says, at wille say that I
wist not what I sayd, and so do harme tille him and tille
other.''   The following specimen of this translation has been
selected from the MSS. in the British Museum, and published by Rev. H. H. Baber, in his ''Historical Account of
the Saxon and English versions of the Scriptures.''

TWENTY-THIRD PSALM.

"Our Lord governeth me, and nothyng to me shal wante : stede of
pasture thar he me sette.   In the water of the hetying he me brougte:
my soul he twinyde."
"He ladde me on the stretis of ryghtwisnesse, for his name."
"For win gif I hadi goo in myddil of the shadowe of deeth: I shall
not dreede yueles, for thou art with me."
"Thi geerde and the staf; thei haue coumfortid me.   Thou has
greythid in my syght a bord: agens hem that angryn me."
"Thou fattide myn hend in oyle; and my chalys drunkenyng what
is cleer."
"And thi mercy shal folewe me: in alle the days of my lyf."

Concerning the Psalmody of the English Reformers in
the fourteenth and fifteenth centuries very little is recorded.
That the Wickliffites had their sacred songs, and that these
songs were frequently and enthusiastically sung among them
appears from the very name of reproach that was given them
by their enemies.   They were called "Lollards," a term
borrowed from the German root, loben, "to praise," with
herr "lord"—"praise the Lord"—and given them because
the Wickliff Christians employed themselves in traveling
about from place to place, singing Psalms and hymns. Some
derive the appellation from another German root, signifying
"to sing with a low voice," and which among the Germans
was applied to a person who is continually praising God with
songs to his honor.   The Alexians, or Cellites, were called
Lollards because they sang their songs in public; and made
it their business to sing a dirge as they carried to the grave
those who had died of the plague.
There is a strong probability that the material of Wickliff's praise bore the same character with that of his cotemporary Huss, in Bohemia; and that it comprised principally
the Psalms of the Bible.   As there were frequent intimacies

between Great Britain and the Continent during the whole reign of Edward III., it was just as natural that there should be a conformity between the Psalmody of England and that of Bohemia, as that there should be such conformity between France and Switzerland, or between Germany and Sweden or Bavaria.   As the great reformers of that early date were communicating back and forth over the channel, why may we not suppose that the Psalm-book of Huss was transferred to the English, as the writings of Wickliff were transferred to the Bohemians?   The probability that the Wickliffites had the Psalms among their sacred lyrics is strengthened by the fact that there had been a metrical version of the Psalter in the English dialect almost two centuries previous, and that the copy now preserved in the Bodleian library bears evidence of having been remodeled and improved by a hand of a later date than its author.

When we come down to Great Britain, as it entered and passed through the sunshine of the sixteenth century, probabilities and possibilities are dropped with the night, and we are cheered with what we can greet and convey as facts.

Great Britain, in the age of Luther and Calvin, was no exception to the rule of sacred song, as we have seen it written in the scenes of the continent.   To adopt the language of Warton, "The infectious frenzy of Psalm-singing did not confine itself to France, Germany and the other countries on the continent.   It soon extended itself to Great Britain. The Reformation being then in its incipiency, and at a time when the minds of men were ready for a change, Psalm-singing in its history became parallel to that among the Reformers across the continent.   There will be found this exception, that the popular demand for these songs did not reach the height it did in France.   In Great Britain they did not so successfully insinuate themselves into the royal favor and so fully supplant "ungodly ballads."

In England, as a learned writer observes, when the people began to throw off the yoke of Rome, "men's affections to the work of reform were everywhere measured by the singing or not singing of the translated Psalms."

Psalm-singing began in the reign of Henry the VIII.,

was continued under Edward and Mary, but did not reach its highest stage till the accession of Elizabeth. Although, according to statute 2 and 3 Edward VI., c. 1, §7, the people were allowed in the parish churches " to use openly any Psalm or prayer taken out of the Bible, at any due time, not letting or omitting thereby the service or any part thereof," yet in the regular service of the English church, under Henry, Edward and Mary, the Psalms were little sung only as they were chanted in Coverdale's revised edition of the old Italic Psalter.

By the beginning of Elizabeth's reign, the popular Psalm-singing, under the example set by the Reformers across the channel, was reaching its height, when that Queen giving public permission for its introduction into the churches under her control, there began a series of those enthusiastic gatherings, which we have seen meeting in Germany, France and the Low Countries.

Queen Elizabeth came to the throne in 1558 ; and whatever may have been the truth as to her real sympathy being with the papacy, she was at the time evidently regarded by the Reformers as favorable to their cause, and her accession an omen of its speedy triumph. This appears clearly from the conduct of the German exiles, who, in their retreat, published an English prose translation of the Psalms and dedicated it to Queen Elizabeth. This Psalter is dated 1559, the year following this Queen's accession, and contains the following complimentary address :   " To the most virtuous and noble Queene Elizabeth, Queene of England, France and Ireland," etc. After stating that the preparation of the English translation of the Bible had occupied their attention during their exile, the banished Englishmen add : " When we heard that the Almightie and most merciful God had no less miraculously preferred you to that excellent dignitie, then he had above all men's expectations preserved you from the furie of such as sought your blood ; with most joyful myndes and great diligence we endeavoured ourselves to set foorth and dedicate this most excellent booke of the Psalmes unto your grace as a spiritual token of our service and good will till the rest of the Bible, which,

praysed be God, is in good readinesse, may be accomplished
and presented "—Epistle 3, prefixed to the Booke of
Psalmes, Geneva, 1559, 16 mo.

That Queen Elizabeth permitted and virtually authorized
the introduction of metrical Psalmody into the English
Established churches, we learn from the fifty-three articles
of injunction which she directed to the clergy and laity in
1559.   The injunction with reference to "the encouragement and continuance of the use of singing   *   *   *   *
in divers collegiate, as well as parish churches," contains the
following saving clause in favor of uncathedral and metrical
Psalmody, nevertheless, for the comforting of such as delight
in musick, it may be permitted that in the beginning or at
the end of common prayer, either at morning or evening,
there may be sung a hymn or such like song to the praise of
Almighty God, in the best melody, and musick that may be
devised ; having respect that the sentence of the hymn may
be understood and perceived."

As we learn from Strype, in his Annals of the English
Reformation, advantage was taken of the Queen's permission,
first at St. Antholm's, a small church on Walling street,
London : In the month of September, 1559, began the new
morning prayers at St. Antholm's, London, the bell beginning to ring at 5 o'clock, when a Psalm was sung after the
Genevan fashion, "all the congregation, men, women and
boys singing together."

From this church Psalm-singing spread rapidly
throughout the parishes, and soon became so popular that
multitudes were attracted to the churches, where as many as
six thousand voices might at times be heard joining in the
sacred melodies.

The singing of the Psalms was not wholly confined to
the churches.   "Adapting them to popular tunes and jigs,"
which one of them said 'were too good for the devil,' the
people sang the new songs in their homes, and at their
employments, as in the primitive church.   The Psalms were
common at 'Mayor's' dinners and city feasts ; soldiers sang
them when on the march, or when at parade ; few houses,
which had their windows fronting the streets, but had their

evening Psalms ; for a story has come down to us that the hypocritical brotherhood did not always care to sing without being heard."

There is evidence that the infection of Psalm-singing even reached the Cathedrals of the English church, and affected the dignitaries as well as the populace. At the convocation of the clergy of the establishment held at the Cathedral of St. Paul, in January of 1582, and in the presence of Archbishop Grindal and other Bishops, we find that the hymn "Veni Creator," and the Psalm, "Beatus Vir," were sung "in sermone vulgari"—in the vulgar tongue. As there was no prose translation of the "hymn" sung, it must have been the metrical translation of it found in the "form of ordering priests" in the first and second Liturgies of King Edward VI. The Psalm in the vulgar tongue must have been the first Psalm of Sternhold, to which the words "Beatus Vir" were prefixed in the old English translation, and as they are still prefixed in imitation of the Psalm in the Latin Vulgate. So that, although Warton denies that metrical Psalm-singing had the proper authority from the Powers of the church, yet it had plain permission, and the public example of the dignitaries, which, with the people, was as good authority as a written license.

Of the zest with which the Psalms were sung in the reign of Queen Elizabeth, says Burney in his History of Music: "In England in the reign of Queen Mary, the Psalms were sung soto voce; but after the accession of Queen Elizabeth, like orgies they were roared aloud in almost every street, as well as in the churches throughout the kingdom."

Dr. Jewel, Bishop of Salisbury, in a letter to Peter Martyr, dated March 5, 1560, thus speaks of Psalm-singing at that date: "Religion is now somewhat more established than it was. The people are everywhere inclined to the better part. The practice of joining in church music has much conduced to this. For as soon as they had once commenced singing in public in only one little church in London (St. Antholm's, Walling St.) immediately not only the churches in the neighborhood, but even the towns far dis-

tant began to vie with each other in the same practice.
You may now sometimes see at St. Paul's Cross, after service, six thousand persons, old and young, of both sexes,
all singing together and praising God."

These meetings at St. Paul's Cross were led by a
Frenchman, who carried on the Psalmody after the fashion
of that on the continent, as we learn from the following en-
tries by Strype:

"1559-60, March the 3d.—Mr. Veron, a Frenchman
by birth, preached at St. Paul's Cross in his rochet and chi-
mere; the mayor and aldermen present, and a great auditory.
And after a sermon a Psalm was sung (which was common
in the Reformed churches abroad) wherein the people also
joined their voices."

"1559-60, March the 17th.—Mr. Veron, a Frenchman
by birth, preached at St. Paul's Cross, before the mayor and
aldermen, and after sermon they sang, all in common, a
Psalm in metre, as it seems now frequently done, the custom having been brought from abroad by the exiles."

The earliest versification of the Psalms into English
metre in the sixteenth century was that known as "Bishop
Coverdale's Version of the Psalms." Miles Coverdale was
a native of Yorkshire, England, and had his birth about the
year 1486. At first he was a worshiper in the Roman
Church, and a monk of the order of St. Augustine. But
becoming a convert to the principles of the Reformation, he,
in 1535, while an exile for his faith, gave to Great Britain
the first English translation of the whole Bible.

The motive of Coverdale in preparing his metrical
Psalms was not that they might be sung either in public or
private worship, for he was then a Bishop in the English
Church, which confined its use of the Psalms in song to the
prose translation; but that they might be substituted for the
vulgar ballads of the day that were sung by both the nobles
and the people.

With this intention he published in 1539 his "Ghostly
Psalms and Spiritual Songs, Drawn Out of the Holy Scriptures."

The work began with the author's address to his book:

"Go lytle boke, get the acquaintaunce
    Amonge the lovers of God's worde
Geve them occasyon the same to avaunce
    And to make theyr songes of the Lorde

That they may thrust under the borde
    All other balettes of fylthynes
And that we all with one accorde
    May geve ensample of goodlynes

Go lytle boke among mens chyldren
    And get the to theyre compayne
Teach them to synge ye commaundements ten
    And other balettes of God's glorye

    Be not ashamed I warande the
Though thou be rude in in songe and ryme
    Thou shalt to youth some occasyon be
    In godly sports to pass theyr tyme."

Bishop Coverdale's version contained the versification of only thirteen of David's Psalms.

To aid in carrying out his design for displacing the "ungodlie ballates" he conformed his Psalms to the metres of these ballads, and published with the first verse of each Psalm the musical notes to which that Psalm was to be sung.

Coverdale's Psalms never accomplished the end designed for them by their author. The ungodly songs that had corrupted the court and the people continued, and the Psalm-book was included among those books that Henry VIII. prohibited being possessed by the people.

Quite a number of contributions to metrical psalmody bear date during the reign of Edward VI., which terminated in 1553.

The first after the Psalms of Coverdale was probably that of "the ryghte vertuouse Lady Elizabeth, daughter of our late soveragne Henry the VIII.," who afterward succeeded Mary in the throne of the British dominions. This Psalm was the Fourteenth, "aptelie translated into Englyshe," and was published in 1548.

In her translation the Queen followed the Latin Vulgate, as is seen from her including the interpolation found in Vulgate version of the Fourteenth Psalm, the origin of which is accounted for by Dr. Alexander:

"The Septuagint version of these words (Ps. xiv. 3) is quoted by Paul in Rom. iii., 12, as a part of his scriptural description of human depravity, the rest of which is taken from Ps. v. 10, x. 7., xxxvi. 2, cxl. 4, Isaiah lix. 7, 8. Under the false impression that he meant to quote a single passage, some early Christian copyist appears to have introduced the whole into the Septuagint version of this Psalm, where it is still found in the Codex Vaticanus, as well as in the Vulgate, and even in one or two Hebrew MSS. of later date. The interpolation is also retained in the Anglican Psalter."

During this reign, William Hunnis, gentleman of the chapel under Edward VI., and afterward chapel master to Queen Elizabeth, versified the seven Penitential Psalms under the title, "Seven Sobs of a Sorrowful Soul for Sin," and dedicated them to Frances, countess of Sussex, foundress of Sydney-Sussex College, at Sussex. Hunnis is thought also to have been the author of certain Psalms published in 1550 in London, and entitled "Certayne Psalms in English metre," but there is evidence leading to the supposition that these and his seven Penitential Psalms were identical. Hunnis also published meditations in "Certaine Psalms."

1549. In this year Sir Thos. Wyatt published the seven Penitential Psalms (and as some suppose, the whole Psalter) in English metre, with the title, "Certayne Psalms chosen out of the Psalter of David, commonly called the vij. Penitentiall Psalmes, drawen into English metre by Sir Thomas Wyatt, Knight, whereunto is added a Prologue of the auctore before every Psalm, very pleasant and profettable to the godly reader. Imprinted at London, in Paules Churchyarde at the sygne of three starres by Thomas Randall, and John Harrington, cum priviligis ad imprimendum solum. Md. xlix."

These Psalms were reprinted by Bishop Percy with his ill-fated impression of Surrey's Poems, which was burned in 1808, in the destruction by fire, of the warehouse of John Nichol. To these Psalms of Wyatt, Lord Surrey refers in one of his sonnets:

" The Great Macedon, that out of Persie chased
Darius, of whose huge power all Asia rang,
In the riche ark Dan Homer's rimes he placed,
Who fained gestes of heathen princes song.
What holy grave, what worthy sepulchre,
Lo, Wyatt's Psalms should Christians then purchase?

Where he doth paint the lively faith and pure:
The steadfast hope, the sweet return of grace,
Of just David by perfite penitence.''

The few Psalms that Surrey himself rendered into verse were published in London about 1567.

1549. Sir Thomas Smith, Secretary to Edward VI., while a prisoner in the Tower, turned eleven of the Psalms into English metre, which were published the same year.

1549. ''Psalter of David newely translated into English metre in such sorte that it may the more decently and wyth more delygte of the minde be reade and songe of al men. Translated and imprinted by Robert Crowley.''

This was the first entire versification of the Psalms into the English of which we have any definite knowledge. With it were published certain Latin hymns; but the version never came to be esteemed.

1549. In this year were published by E. Whitchurch, ''All such Psalms of David as Thomas Sternhold, late grome of the Kynges Majesties Roobes, did in his lifetime drawe into English metre.''

Thomas Sternhold, according to one authority, was born in Hampshire; according to a second, at Southampton; according to a third, at Aure, a parish about twelve miles from Gloucester. Having passed some time at Oxford, he went to London to serve as groom of the robes of King Henry VIII., who bequeathed him a legacy of one hundred marks. When Edward VI. came to the throne he was continued in the privie chamber.

He was a firm friend to the Reformation, and a man of sincere piety. His death occurred in 1549. Sternhold versified his Psalms with reference to the same end proposed by Coverdale, in England, and Marot in France, that the use of the lascivious songs among the courtiers might be checked; but in this he was disappointed.

Authorities differ as to the number of Psalms turned into metre by Sternhold. Some state that an edition was published earlier than 1549, and contained only nineteen Psalms. Warton in his history, and Townley in his ''Biblical Literature,'' give him credit for fifty-one Psalms in all. By other authorities he versified forty Psalms, and by others forty-four. That opinion, however, which has been accepted by most historians is, that only thirty-seven belonged to him. These were the 1-17; 19-21; 25, 28, 29, 32, 34, 41, 43, 44, 49, 63, 68, 73, 78, 103, 120, 123, 128. According to T. H. Horne, the edition of Sternhold published by Whitchurch in 1549 contained only a portion of his renderings; and that the whole thirty-seven were not published till afterward. In 1551 appeared an edition containing thirty-seven from Sternhold and seven from John Hopkins. These were the 30th, 33d, 42d, 52d, 79th, 82d, 146th.

Of John Hopkins, the successor of Sternhold, biographical history says but little. He was admitted at Oxford in 1544, and is supposed afterward to have served as a minister at Suffolk. He was still living in 1556. By Warton he was considered a better poet than Sternhold. Altogether, fifty-eight Psalms are ascribed to him.

To complete the volume of Psalms that came into use in the English Church, and was bound up with its Liturgy, it is necessary to follow the English exiles, who had fled under the persecutions of Mary. In the language of a recent report of a committee appointed by the Free Church of Scotland, "The next onward step is peculiarly interesting, as our own Knox comes into view in relation to it. It is the reign of Mary of England. A congregation of Protestant refugees from that country is found at Frankfort-on-the-Main. Knox is chosen pastor, and takes a chief part in drawing up a book of Church order. But dissensions arise between the adherents of the English Liturgy and Whittingham and others who concur with Knox. The latter party retire to Geneva in 1555, and there form a distinct church. The Book of Order is completed and published, and Knox, though absent for a time, is continued as their pastor. Materials for praise are sought as part of said Book of Order; and for this purpose the forty-four Psalms (the thirty-seven of Sternhold and seven of Hopkins) already mentioned, are adopted, but after very considerable alterations, these being intended, as stated in the preface, to bring them to closer conformity with the Hebrew. Seven Psalms are added by Whittingham, a tune is attached to each of the fifty-one Psalms, the collection is published along with the

Book of Order in 1556. Sometime afterwards nine Psalms by Whittingham and two by Pullain were added, and in 1561, the work, so far as it may be considered a Genevan publication, reached its final stage by the addition of twenty-five Psalms from the pen of William Kethe, a native of Scotland. Amongst these last, there falls to be ranked the well-known One hundredth Psalm in long metre, which is often erroneously ascribed to Hopkins.''

An edition had been published in 1560, containing sixty-seven Psalms, with the Hymns, Benedictus, Magnificat and Nunc Dimittis, in metre. The edition of 1561, beside the eighty-seven Psalms, had the song of Simeon, the Ten Commandments and the other spiritual songs found in later publications. In 1563 appeared the entire one hundred and fifty Psalms, which were entitled ''The whole Boke of Psalms collected into English metre by Thomas Sternhold, J. Hopkins and others; conferred with the Ebrue, with apt notes to sing them with all. Faithfully perused and allowed, according to the order appointed in the Queenes Majesties injunctions, very mete to be used by all sorts of people privately for their solace and comfort, laying apart all ungodly songs and ballades, which tend only to the nourishing of vice and corrupting of youth. Imprinted at London by John Day, dwelling over Aldersgate, benethe Saint Martins. Cum gratia et privilegia Regie Majestatis per septennium an 1563.''

In all the editions of this version, which is commonly known as the ''old version,'' the authorship of the several Psalms is designated by the initial letters of the authors' names—L. S., J. H., W. W., N., W. K., L. C. (or I. C., as it is in some editions). In the same year with the publication of the complete Psalm-book, and again in 1565, Day printed an edition with the music, in parts, viz.: ''The whole Psalmes in fourt partes (Tenor, Contra-Tenor, Medius and Bassus), which may be song to al musical instruments, set forth for the encrease of vertue, and abolyshing of other vayne and triflyng ballades.''

The completed version of Sternhold, Hopkins and others, did not immediately come into use in the English churches. Until 1548 the Psalms were chanted in the Latin prose, but in this year appeared a prose version in the English tongue bearing the title, "The Psalter or Psalmes of David after the translation of the Great Bible, poincted as it should be song in the churches." This version was adopted by the Establishment, and was for many years the principal basis of praise. By the use of the metrical version of Sternhold and others, beginning at St. Antholms, the prose rendering, and with it the chant, passed into rapid decline. Some idea of the decreasing interest in the prose translation and the increasing interest in that in metre may be inferred from the fact that during the first two years of Elizabeth's reign six distinct editions in prose were published, while only two editions appeared in the last ten years of her power; yet during the latter period there were issued twenty-five editions of Sternhold's Psalms. In the reign of James I., extending over twenty-two years, only four editions of the prose Psalter are recorded, the metrical editions in the same period numbering over sixty. After the appearance of the "Old Version," the Common Metre, known in classical literature as the iambic stanza, 8s and 6s, became almost universal. All of Cowley's Psalms and several of Sternhold's were of this metre.

The "Old Version" was continued in England almost till the time of the Restoration. During the protectorate of Cromwell attempts were made to have the versions of Barton and Rous introduced into the English Episcopal Church, but without success. One of the best evidences of the popularity of these rudely-constructed Psalms is the great number of editions that were issued, even after the authorizing of the "New Version" of Tate and Brady. Previous to the beginning of the seventeenth century there were seventy-four editions; in the seventeenth century there were two hundred and thirty-five editions. "In 1868," Alice Earle tells us in her "Sabbath in Puritan New England," "six hundred and one editions were known." "Among other editions," she adds, "this version had in the time of Charles II., two in short hand, one printed by 'Thos. Cockerill at the Three Legs and Bible in the Poultry.' Two copies of these editions are in the British Museum. They are tiny little 64-mos, of which half a dozen could be laid side by side on the palm of the hand.''

At the present day this version is still in authorized use in the United Church of England and Ireland. It is not often met with in the latter country, but in the country parishes of England it is frequently in use.

In the old register of the town of Ipswich is positive evidence that Sternhold's and Hopkins' version was in use in some of the early New England settlements. An edition was printed in Cambridge, Mass., in 1693, a fact which leads Alice Earle to remark: ''To thus publish the work of the English Psalmists in the very teeth of the popularity of 'the Bay Psalm-Book' is to me a proof that Sternhold and Hopkins' version was employed far more extensively in the colonial churches and homes than we now have records of, and than many of our church historians now fancy.''

Few works that have ever come from the press have met with such extremes of popular favor and personal ridicule as have these old English Psalms.

Thus Phillips refers to them:

> "Singing with woful noise
> Like a cracked Saint's bell jarring in the steeple,
> Tom Sternhold's wretched prick-son for the people."

An English courtier and poet wrote:

> "Sternhold and Hopkins had great qualms
> When they translated David's Psalms."

Even the great and good Wesley could not pass this old version without the sneer: '' When it is seasonable to sing praises to God we do it, not in the scandalous doggerel of Hopkins and Sternhold, but in Psalms and hymns which are both sense and poetry such as would provoke a critic to turn Christian rather than a Christian to turn critic.''

The following criticisms upon the '' Old Version '' are added to show the estimation in which it was held among eminent critics:

> "Its rudeness has become even proverbial. The verse is very incorrect, the sense not always clear, and the expression sometimes exceedingly vulgar. And yet even in this version there are a few stanzas, particularly in the Eighteenth and One hundred and third Psalms, which no true poet would undertake to improve."—Dr. Beattie.

As specimens of the rudeness and vulgarity alluded to by Dr. Beattie the following verses have been selected:

Ps. 78 : 46.

"Nor how he did commit their fruits
Unto the caterpillar;
And all the labor of their hands,
He gave to the grasshopper."

Ps. 74: 12.

"Why dost thou draw thy hand aback,
And hide it in thy lap?
Oh pluck it out and be not slack
To give thy foes a rap."

"The merit of faithful adherence to the original has been claimed for this version, and need not be denied; but it is the resemblance which the dead bear to the living, and to hold such a version forth (which some learned men have lately done) as a model of standard Psalmody for the use of Christian congregations in the nineteenth century, surely betrays an affectation of singularity or a deplorable defect of taste."— James Montgomery, of Sheffield.

"They wonder I would make use of this version which they think is poor, flat stuff; the poetry is miserable, and the language low and base. To which I answer, they had a scrupulous regard for the very words of Scripture, and to these they adhered closely and strictly, so much as to render the versification not equal to Mr. Pope. I grant it is not always smooth; it is only here and there brilliant. But what is a thousand times more valuable, it is generally the sentiment of the Holy Spirit. That is very rarely lost. And this should silence every objection—it is the Word of God; moreover the version comes nearer the Scotch, of which I have made use, when it appeared to me better expressed than the English."—Romaine.

"Perhaps one of the most faultless in this respect (literalness) is an almost obsolete one in our language, viz., that by Sternhold and Hopkins. Because of its uncouth form this version has been unjustly vilified, while others, by far its inferiors, have been unreasonably extolled. The authors of this version, for it is taken directly from the Hebrew text, have sacrificed everything to the literal sense and meaning."—Adam Clark.

They (Christians) may receive much assistance from a work which the ignorance of modern refinement would take out of their hands. I speak of the old singing Psalms, a metrical version of Sternhold and Hopkins. This is not what I believe it is now generally supposed to be, nothing better than an awkward versification of a former English translation; it is an original translation from the Hebrew text, earlier by many years than the prose translation in the Bible; and of all that are in any degree paraphrastic, as all in verse in some degree must be, it is the best and most exact we have to put into the hands of the common people. The authors of this version considered the verse merely as a contrivance to assist the memory. They were little studious of the harmony of their numbers, or the elegance of their diction, but they were solicitous to give the full and precise sense of the sacred text according to the best of their judgment, and their judgment, with the exception of some few passages, was very good; and at the same time that they adhered scrupulously to the letter, they contrived to express it in such terms as, like the original, might point clearly to the spiritual meaning."—Bishop Horsely.

After the period of the publication of Sternhold's Psalms the versions of the Psalms became so numerous that mention can be made of those only that possess historic interest.

1557.   This year Archbishop Parker finished and had published the whole book of Psalms, entitled "The whole Psalter translated into English metre, which contayneth an hundred and fifty Psalms. Imprinted at London by John Daye, dwelling over Aldergate, beneath St. Martyn's. Cum privilegis. Per discennium."

Parker's version of the Psalms was prepared while he was in privacy from the tyranny of Queen Mary.   It contained the following apology for turning the Scripture into rhyme:

> " The Psalmist stayde with tuned songe
> The rage of myndes agast,
> As David did with harpe among
> To Saul in Fury cast.
> With golden stringes such harmonie
> His harpe so sweet did wrest
> That he relieved his phrenesie
> Whom wicked spirits possest."

This rare book was divided into three quinguagenes, or parts of fifty Psalms each, with the argument of each Psalm in metre placed before it, and, at the end of it a suitable collect full of devotion and piety.

This version, though it never came into use, was prepared with reference to being sung in public.   For this purpose, eight tunes were added to the book with this notice of them:

"THE NATURE OF THE EYGHT TUNES."

> " The first is meek, devout to see,
> The second sad, in majesty:
> The third doth rage, and roughly brayth,
> The fourth doth fawne and flatly playth:
> The fifth deligth, and laugheth the more,
> The sixth bewayleth, it weipeth full sore:
> The seventh tredeth stoute in froward race,
> The eyghte goeth milde in modest pace."

Even Lord Bacon, born 1561, spent part of his long, dark evenings in versifying the Psalms. He published seven and dedicated them to his friend George Herbert. Of his Psalms, it has been said, the "fine gold of David is so thoroughly melted down with the refined silver of Bacon, that the mixture shows nothing of alloy, but a metal greater in bulk and differing in show from either of the component elements, yet exhibiting at the same time a lustre wholly derived from the more precious of them." Aubrey declared Lord Bacon to have been a good poet, but that in his Psalms, his piety is more to be commended than his poetry.

Holland, in his "Psalmists of Britain," gives account of over one hundred and fifty persons who versified either a part or all of the Psalms by the close of the seventeenth century. Among others are the names of John Milton and Richard Baxter. Baxter's paraphrase was published in 1692. Many of these versions are said to have been curious specimens of literature. Some were composed at a time when classical studies had become fashionable, and so exhibit an effort to introduce classic metres and classic terms and phrases into the versification.

In the Second Psalm Stranghurst has the following lines:

" He skorns their mocking, that dwells in blessed Olympus:
And at their brainsick trumperie follye flireth."

Fraunce has displayed his classic taste in the Eighth Psalm thus:

" O Prince all-puysant, O King almightey ruling,
How wondrous be thy workes, and how strange are thy proceedings?
Thou hast thy great name with moste greate glory reposed,
Over, above those lamps, bright burning lamps of Olympus."

The version of George Withers and that of George Sandys were both privileged royally to be used in the English churches. After Sandys returned from a tour through the Holy Land, he was employed in the government of the colony of Virginia, where he held the post of Treasurer to the company. It is said that his Psalms were composed by the banks of the James river. His Psalms were published in England in 1638.

The Metamorphosis of Ovid by Sandys was the first literary production ever published in America, having been issued in 1626. Sandys was pronounced by Dryden, the best versifier of the age. Of his Psalms, Montgomery says they are "incomparably the most poetical in the English language." They were one of the few books with which Charles I. solaced himself in his captivity in Carisbrook Castle. A selection from Sandys is given as follows :

PSALM XXIX. GEORGE SANDYS.

Ye that are of princely birth !
Praise the Lord of Heaven and Earth ;
Glory give ; His power proclaim ;
Praise and magnify His name.
Worship in the beauty, bless,
Beauty of His Holiness.
From the dark and showery cloud,
On the floods that roared aloud.
Hark ! His voice with terror breaks,
God—our God – in Thunder speaks !
Powerful in His voice on high,
Full of power and majesty.
Lofty cedars overthrown,
Cedars of deep Lebanon.
Calf-like skipping on the ground,
Lebanon and Sirion bound,
Like a youthful unicorn ;
Labouring clouds with lightning torn.
At his voice the desert shakes ;
Kadish ! Thy vast desert quakes.
Trembling hinds then calve for fear ;
Shady forests bare appear.
His renown by every tongue,
Through His Holy Temple sung ;
He the raging floods restrains ;
He a King forever reigns.
God his people shall increase,
Arm with strength, and bless with peace.

Almost one hundred and fifty years after the first appearance of Sternhold's Psalms, appeared the version that subsequently supplanted the "Old version," and came to be known, by way of distinction, as the "New version." This was the version of Tate and Brady.

The Psalter of these joint authors appeared with the title: " A new version of the Psalms of David, fitted to tunes used in churches. By Nanum Tate and Nicholas Brady. London, 1696." A specimen of these Psalms was printed for the company of stationers in 1695, under the title: "An essay of a new version of the Psalms of David, consisting of the first twenty; fitted to tunes used in churches."

This new version was introduced to the public under the sanction of an order in privy council, by King William III., dated December 3, 1696. Though this sanction had no legal authority after the decease of William, yet it continued to be printed in all subsequent editions. By the order of the privy council it was declared "that the said new version of the Psalms in English metre be, and the same hereby is, allowed and permitted to be used in all such chapels, churches and congregations, as shall think fit to receive them." In 1698, a second edition of the new version was printed, corrected and improved. In the same year appeared "a brief and full account of Mr. Tate and Mr. Brady's new version of the Psalms; by a True Son of the Church of England." From it, as quoted by T. H. Horne, we learn that the undertaking originated between Tate and Brady themselves—"in a little time it was communicated and as speedily received and nourished by persons of the highest rank and principal authorities in the nation in the Church and State. * * * When the work was finished and had passed the censure of His Grace, the Archbishop (Dr. Tillotson), and several more of his brethren, the Rt. Rev. Prelates, a petition was presented to His Majesty (William III.) in council, for allowing the liberty of public reception of it in all churches, chapels and congregations. For the perfection of their Psalms, the translators invited "all their friends, both in city and country, to supervise and correct what was amiss." The Bishops and the translators' friends having made their corrections, and the version having gained public approbation by His Majesty's royal indulgence, the new version was used first in the churches of London, and its vicinity, principally through the recommendation of Bishop Compton; and subsequently was gradually adopted in all England through the recommendation of Archbishop of York, and others. At the first, though the new version was patronized by William and his court, the villages were slow in adopting it.   The masses of the communities were familiar with the "old version," and so clung tenaciously to it.   Like Hannah Moore's Squire,

> " They thought 'twould show a falling state
> If Sternhold should give way to Tate."

Notwithstanding the opposition of many critics, among whom was the well-known Dr. Beveridge, the "new version" at length took the place of the old, and is now used in most of the Episcopal churches in England, Ireland, Scotland and the British colonies.

Of the new version, Bishop Compton said in 1698: " I find it a work done with so much judgment and ingenuity that I am persuaded it may take off that unhappy objection that has hitherto lain against the singing Psalms, and dispose that part of divine service to much more devotion.   And I do heartily recommend the use of this version to all my brethren within my diocese."

Drake, in his "Harp of Judah," says of this version, " The prevailing defect is that of tameness and monotony of execution, though there are a few beautiful exceptions to this censure."

" The rude English version of the Psalms by Sternhold and Hopkins was superseded by that of Tate and Brady—a sacrifice of rugged strength to insipid smoothness and inflated verbosity.   Milton's attempts at translation only show that his strong arm could not bend the bow of Ulysses. The Scottish version, though in reality the work of an English Puritan, has, with all its roughness and dissonance, preserved more of the vital spirit, the rich, pure aroma of the Hebrew original."—British Encyclopædia.

The third great epoch in the Psalmody of England began with the publication of the Psalms and Hymns of Dr. Isaac Watts, soon after the opening of the eighteenth century.

His first renderings of the Psalms were made previous to 1707, as the addition of Hymns used in that year contained fourteen or fifteen Psalms.   In the edition of 1709 these were omitted, as the Doctor had formed the idea of versifying the entire Psalter.   His whole Psalm-book was published with his Hymns in 1719, the entire volume containing six hundred and ninety-eight pieces.

The origin of Dr. Watts' design for composing his

Psalms and Hymns for the Church arose from a dislike he had contracted for the Psalms and Psalm-singing in the old Dissenting meeting house, where he had become a member under Rev. Thomas Rowe, about 1693. Of this, the Rev. John Morgan, of Romsey, Hampshire, Eng., says, "The occasion of the Doctor's hymns was this, as I heard the account from his fellow-laborer and colleague, Mr. Price, in whose family I dwelt fifty years ago. The hymns which were sung at the Dissenting meeting-house at Southampton were so little to the taste of Mr. Watts, that he could not forbear complaining of them to his father. The father bade him try what he could do to mend the matter. He did so, and had such success in his first essay that a second hymn was earnestly desired of him, and then a third and fourth, etc., till in process of time there was such a number of them as to make up a volume."

In a letter to Cotton Mather, of England, Dr. Watts stated, "It is not a translation of David I pretend, but an imitation of him so nearly in Christian hymns that the Jewish Psalmist may plainly appear, yet leave his Judaism behind."

Whatever may be said of the propriety or impropriety of this scheme of Dr. Watts, in undertaking his imitations of the Psalms, it can certainly claim originality. In England, Watts' Psalms and Hymns are extensively used by the churches descending from the early Puritans. In the Hymn-book of the United Presbyterian Church of Scotland and Ireland are seventy selections from Dr. Watts, and a single representative among the five hymns that have long been bound up with the Psalm-book of the Secession Scottish Church.

Out of twelve hundred and ninety hymns in the old Sabbath School Hymn-book, published in the United States, two hundred and fifty-four are from Watts; of thirteen hundred and seventy-four, in the Plymouth collection, two hundred and eighteen are from Watts; in the Songs of the Sanctuary, by Dr. C. S. Robinson, Watts has five hundred and fourteen out of twelve hundred and ninety-three; in the Baptist collection, three hundred and one of the eleven hundred and eighty, are from Watts.   Even in the Hymn-book of the Unitarian body, Watts takes the lead of all authors.   A recent writer in an English magazine, after an examination of seven hundred and fifty Hymn-books, ascribes to Dr. Watts the authorship of two-fifths of all the Hymns used in the English-speaking churches.

The criticisms of Dr. Watts' Psalms and Hymns would, in themselves, fill a volume.   The following will represent the views of those who were favorable and those adverse to their use in the Christian Church :

A century and a half have nearly passed since the publication of Dr. Watts' Psalms and Hymns ; yet nothing has appeared to dim their luster, as yet, nothing threatens to supersede them with their doctrinal fullness, their sacred fervor, their lyric grandeur, they stand alone, over-topping all their fellows.   *   *   *   To elevate to poetic altitudes every truth in Christian experience and revealed religion, needs the strength and sweep of an eagle's wing ; and this is what Isaac Watts has done. He has taken almost every topic which exercises the understanding and heart of the believer, and has not only given it a devotional aspect, but has wedded it to immortal numbers ; and, whilst there is little to which he has not shown himself equal, there is nothing which he has done for mere effect.   They are naturalized through all the Anglo-Saxon world, and next to Scripture itself, are the great vehicle of thought and feeling *   *   *   A climbing boy was once heard singing in a chimney,

> ' The sorrows of the mind
>   Be banished from this place,
> Religion never was designed
>   To make our pleasure less ;'

and, like King David's own Psalter, the same stanzas which cheered the poor sweep in the chimney, and melted to tears the Northumberland peasant, have roused the devotion or uttered the raptures of ten thousand worshipers ; and there is many a reader who, in his experience, can imagine the sensation which he shared in singing, when the heart of some solemn assembly was uplifted as one man :

> ' Come, let us join one cheerful song ;' or,
> ' Jesus shall reign where'er the sun.''
> —" North British Review " of August, 1857.)

" In his Psalms and Hymns (for they must be classed together), he has embraced a compass and variety of subjects, which include and illustrate every truth of revelation, throw light upon every secret move-ment of the human heart, whether of sin, nature or grace ; and describe every kind of trial, temptation, conflict, doubt, fear and grief, as well as the faith, hope, charity, the love of joy, peace, labor and patience of the Christian in all stages of his course on earth ; together with the

terrors of the Lord, the glories of the Redeemer, and comforts of the
Holy Spirit to urge, allure and strengthen him by the way. * * * *
Dr. Watts' Hymns are full of the glorious Gospel of the blessed God;
his themes, therefore, are as much more illustrious than those of the
son of Jesse, who only knew the honor and glory of Jehovah, as he
had seen them in the sanctuary, which was but the shadow of the New
Testament Church, as the face of Moses, holding communion with God,
was brighter than the veil he cast over it, when conversing with his
countrymen."—James Montgomery.

" We freely confess that, for ourselves, we consider the paraphrase
of the Psalms by Dr. Watts the most defective part of our Psalmody;
and only more and more marvel that such a miserable attempt should
have acquired so much reputation."—Dr. R. J. Breckenridge.

"Dr. Watts has attempted professedly to improve upon the sentiment of the very matter and order, and by various omissions and ad-
ditions, to fit the Psalms for Christian worship. This is unfair. If
Pope had taken the same license with the poems of Homer, all the
amateurs of Greek poetry in the world would have cried, shame on the
presumptious intruder ! But it is a pious and zealous Christian that has
taken this liberty with the songs of Zion, and almost the whole church
acquiesces in it. What would we think of the French poet, who, pro-
posing to enrich French literature with a version of the masterpiece of
the English muse, should mangle and transpose the torn limbs of the
Paradise Lost, until Milton himself might meet his first-born on the
highway and not recognize it? And must this literary butchery be
tolerated because forsooth the victim is the inspired Psalmist? Why
should the heaven-taught Bard be misrepresented thus? Let us
rather have the songs of inspiration as God inspired them and as nearly
as possible and consistent with the laws of English versification. God's
order of thought is doubtless the best for his Church. If any one thinks
he can write better spiritual songs than the sweet singer of Israel, let
him do it, but let him not dress the savory meat which God hath prepared until all the substance and savour are gone and then present it to
us as an imitation of David's Psalms."—George Junkin, D. D.

In 1846, a cenotaph to the memory of Dr. Watts was
erected at Abney Park Cemetery—a full length figure of
Dr. Watts in his ecclesiastical costume, nine feet in height,
and standing on a pedestal of purest Portland stone, thirteen
feet high and six feet square. In his left hand he is holding
a book and two others are open on a seat on his right side.

On the side facing Abney Chapel, is the following inscription:

In Memory of
Isaac Watts, D. D.

In testimony of the high and lasting esteem in which his character and his writings were held in the great Christian community by whom the English language is spoken. Of his Psalms and hymns it may be predicted in his own words:

"Ages unborn will make his songs
The joy and labor of their tongues."

He was born at Southampton July 17, 1674,
and died November 25, 1748,
After a residence of thirty-six years in the mansion of
Sir Thos. Abney, Bart, then standing on these
grounds.
Erected by public subscription.
E. W. Bailey, R. A.

In the eighteenth century many of the Psalms were versified by the three Wesleys—the father and two sons. But as they did not publish their Psalms separately from their hymns, they can scarcely be said to have a place among the Psalmists.   The following testimonial to David's Psalms by the elder Wesley will be found to possess interest:

1. "Has David's Christ to come foreshadowed?
    Can Christians then aspire
  To mend the harmony that flowed
    From his poetic lyre?

2. How curious are their wits and vain
    Their erring zeal, how bold,
  Who durst with meaner dross profane
    His purity of God!

3. His Psalms unchanged the saints employ,
    Unchanged our God applies;
  They suit the apostles in their joy,
    The Saviour when he dies.

4. Let David's prose unaltered lays
    Transmit through ages down
  To thee, O David's Son! our praise!
    To thee, O David's Son!

5. Till judgment calls the seraph throng
    To join the human choir,
  And God who gave the ancient one
    The new one to inspire.

Joseph Addison, so well known by his literary labors, planned a paraphrastic version of the Psalms in the early part of the eighteenth century, a plan that was never fully carried out.

From his pen came that beautiful rendering of the
Twenty-third Psalm, beginning:

"The Lord my pasture shall prepare."

To him also belongs that piece of poetry which many a
school boy has declaimed, and which is only a paraphrase of
the Nineteenth Psalm:

"The spacious firmament on high
With all the blue ethereal sky," etc.

This latter paraphrase, with the hymns of the same
author beginning:

"When all thy mercies, O my God,"

and

"When rising from the bed of death,"

compose three of the five hymns of the Scottish Psalm-book.

Of the many other versifyers of the Psalms in the
last and in the present centuries, the name of James Montgomery may well be added here. Montgomery is known
principally by his hymns, but his beautiful renderings of
some of the Psalms have contributed much in gaining him
the reputation of being one of England's most popular sacred poets. His versions the author calls "imitations,"
having modeled them after the design of Dr. Watts, yet do
they carry with them the idea of the original, and so impress the reader with the fact of their having sprung from
the rich fountain of God's Word. These "imitations"
were sixty-seven in number, and were printed in 1822 under the title "Songs of Zion."

Even Lord Byron turned aside from his other poetic
inspirations long enough to have his muse sing for us his incomparably beautiful rendering of Psalm One hundred and
thirty seven:

"In the valley of waters we wept o'er the day
When the host of the stranger made Salem his prey;
And our heads on our bosoms all droopingly lay,
And our hearts were so full of the land far away.

"The song they demanded in vain—it lay still
In our souls as the wind that hath died on the hill.
They called for the harp, but our blood they would spill
Ere our right hands shall teach them one tone of their skill.

"All stringlessly hung on the willow's sad tree,
As dead as her dead leaf those mute harps must be.
Our hands may be fettered, our tears still are free,
For our God and our glory, and Sion for thee."

CHAPTER IX.

THE PSALMS IN THE SCOTTISH REFORMED CHURCH.

Scotland can claim but little notice from her versifiers of the Psalms. The sacred poets who furnished her songs were mostly of foreign birth. Yet in a history of the Psalms no people, next to the Jews, can hold a more prominent place than the Scotch. Psalm-singing has been a vital element in their entire history from the days of the Culdees to the present moment, and the zeal and prejudice that yet remain for it, bid fair for continuing David as the perpetual sovereign of her sacred melodies.

In Scotch history we look in vain for even a fraction of that enthusiasm of Psalmody that awakened the continent of Europe at the middle of the sixteenth century. Enthusiasm is not a trait in the Scotch character. A Scotchman is a model of religious dignity; and extreme devotion is in his case marked with extreme reserve. The Psalm-singing of France and the Low Countries could not fully repeat itself among the Highlands, where impulse had settled within the impassable boundary of propriety. Still none, more than the Scotch, were true to all the essential principles of the Reformation. They believed, with the Calvinists of Switzerland and France, that all worship should be conformed rigidly to the Word of God, and the practices of the primitive disciples. With this fundamental of Calvinism, they without hesitation embraced the Genevan basis of praise—the Psalms of the Bible; and when the Psalms became the material of sacred song for one Scotchman, they became the medium of praise for all Scotchmen, in all times.

In France, Switzerland and the Netherlands, the fervor of Psalm-singing gradually died away, and the Psalms themselves were laid aside; but in Scotland are heard the same inspired strains, and in the same solemn yet devout utterance as of three hundred years ago. And in America, the only denominations that pretend to adopt a full and faithful rendering of the Psalms are those in which predominate the element from the Highlands of Scotland and North Ireland.

For the history of Scotch Psalmody we must leave the streets and highways and go into the religious assemblies and into the houses of the inhabitants. Sometimes when persecution was abroad in the land, these assemblies were gathered amid the friendly forests, or under the shades of mountain rocks; but whether in the home sanctuary, or in these retreats, might ever be heard the slow yet earnest singing of David's Psalms. There is scarcely a den or a forest in all the Highlands which some faithful band has not sanctified by singing God's praise in the songs of his early Church.

In Blackburn's memoirs is given a description of a Covenanter communion in 1674, and a reference to their Psalmody: "The tables were served by some gentlemen and persons of the greatest deportment. None were admitted without tokens as usual, which were distributed on Saturday, but only to such as were known to some of the ministers or persons of trust, to be free from public scandals. All the regular forms were gone through; the communicants entered at one end of the table and returned at the other, a way being kept clear to take their seats on the hill's sides. The communion was peaceably concluded, all the people heartily offering up their gratitude, and singing rose to the Rock of their salvation. It was pleasant, as the night fell, to hear their melody swelling in full unison along the hill, the whole congregation joining with one accord and praising God with voice of Psalms."

The tune most frequently used on such occasions was the well-known "Martyrs," which, in some parts of Scotland has been perpetuated in the rude rhyme:

"This was the tune the Martyrs sang,
When they were gaen to die,
When at the gallows tree they stood
Their God to glorify."

A distinguishing feature of Scotch religion has been that of family worship, in which, morning and evening, the Psalms were sung, the Bible read, and prayer offered.

In the seventeenth century, observes a writer, "you could not for a great part of the country have lodged in a family where the Lord was not worshiped in reading Scripture, singing Psalms, and prayers."

This prevalence of family worship has not passed unnoticed by the author of "Cotter's Saturday Night," who in his picture of a Scotchman's after-supper fireside, says:

> "The cheerfu' supper done, wi' serious face,
> They round the ingle* form a circle wide.
> The Sire turns o'er with patriarchal grace
> The big Ha' Bible, once his father's pride:
> His bonnet rev'rently is laid aside,
> His lyart haffets wearin' thin and bare,
> Those streams that once did sweet in Zion glide,
> He wales† a portion with judicious care,
> And 'Let us worship God,' he says with solemn air.

> " They chant their artless notes in simple guise ;
> They time their hearts, by far the noblest aim,
> Perhaps Dundee's wild, warbling measures rise;
> Or plaintive Martyr's worthy o' the name;
> Or Noble Elgin beets the heav'nward flame;
> The sweetest far o' Scotia's holy lays;
> Compared with these, Italian trills are tame,
> The tickled ears no heartfelt raptures raise,
> Nae unison hae they with our Creator's praise."

In the Scotch families every child was taught to commit the Psalms to memory; and many a time, when a son or daughter was given away in marriage, the solemnities were not thought complete till the whole household and guests would join in the Psalm:

> " O what a happy thing it is,
> And joyful for to see,
> Brethren to dwell together in
> Friendship and unity."

In both the Scotch and English armies Psalmody was customary in most of the regiments; and sometimes when these armies of the two nationalities were lying encamped near each other, awaiting the conflict, there might be heard a melody of the same Psalm sung to the same tune. It has been remarked that in the war between England and Scotland, in the days of King Charles, when the English soldiers " saw the written Covenant floating on the Scotch banner, and beheld at sunrise, the whole camp ringing with Psalm-singing and prayers, they cursed the impious war in which they were engaged, and felt they were fighting against their brethren and their God."

A Presbyterian camp in those days must have presented an interesting scene. "Had you lent your ear," says Baillie, "and heard in the tents the sound of some singing Psalms, some praying, some reading the Scriptures, you would have been refreshed. I found the favor of God shining upon me ; and a sweet, meek, humble, yet strong and vehement spirit, leading me all along."

Of the same occasion referred to by Baillie, Livingston, a chaplain, remarks : " It is refreshful to remark that after we came to our quarters at night, there was nothing to be heard through the whole army but singing of Psalms, prayer, and reading of Scripture by the soldiers in their several tents."

An incident connected with the burial of Hampden, one of the Roundheads, who was killed on Chalgrave field in one of the battles with the soldiers of Charles, will illustrate the devotion of the soldiery and their customs of Psalmody in the sixteenth and seventeenth centuries. When Hampden was carried to his grave, his comrades in war followed in procession, with arms reversed, their heads uncovered, singing as they marched, the Ninetieth Psalm from the version of Sternhold and Hopkins :

"Thou, Lord, hast been our sure defense,
    Our place of ease and rest,
In all times past, yea, so long since
    As cannot be exprest.

*   *   *   *   *   *   *   *   *

Thou grindest man through grief and pain
    To dust, or clay, and then,
Thou unto them dost say again,
    Return ye sons of men," etc.

Returning from the burial, the mourners again sang the Forty-third Psalm :

Judge and avenge my cause, O Lord,
    From them that evil be,
From wicked and deceitful men,
    O Lord deliver me.

> For of my strength, thou art the God,
> Why put'st thou me thee fro ;
> And why walk I so heavily,
> Oppressed with my foe.''

The author of "Helen of the Glen," thus alludes to
the devotion of the Scotch soldiers under Cameron, in the
bloody days of Claverhouse :

> "The lyart veteran heard the word of God
> By Cameron thundered, or by Renwick poured
> In gentle streams ; then rose the song ; the loud
> Acclaim of praise ; the wheeling plover ceased
> Her plaint ; the solitary place was glad,
> And on the distant cavins, the watcher's ear
> Caught doubtfully, at times, the breeze-borne note.''

The Scotch, like the Christians in the days of Julian
the Apostate, sometimes made use of their Psalms to irritate
their foes. It is related of a Scotch minister that he
preached " boldly before King Charles, December 16, 1646,
at Newcastle, and after his sermon, called for the Fifty-
second Psalm, which began,

> "Why dost thou, tyrant, boast thyself,
> Thy wicked works to praise.''

His Majesty thereupon stood up and called for the Fifty-
sixth Psalm, which begins,

> " Have mercy, Lord, on me I pray,
> For men would me devour.''

The people waived the minister's Psalm and sung that
which the King called for.''

The use of metrical Psalms, within the period of the
Reformation, must have begun in Scotland, almost as early
as in the Continent. This appears from a document drawn
up by the English Exiles at Frankfort in 1550, in which it
is stated that " the people do singe a Psalme in meeter, in a
plain tune, as was, and is accustomed in the French, Dutch,
Italian, Spanish and Scottische churches.''

Dalzell, in his " Cursory Remarks," states that there
was a Scotch version early. The two lines quoted from
Wishart by Knox, answer to the beginning of the second
stanza of the Fifty-first Psalm inserted among Scottish
poems of the sixteenth century. The first distinct record of

the existence of metrical Psalms and of Psalm-singing among the Scotch is in connection with the apprehension of the Martyr Wishart in 1544. The night in which he was arrested he was spending in the house of the Laird of Orm-istown ; the account of his devotional conduct there, and of his calling for the singing of a Psalm, is thus given in the quaint language of that early day : "Maister George, having to accumpanie him, the Laird of Ormistown, Johne Sandielands, of Calder Younger, the Laird of Brounstown and utheris, with thair servands, past upoun their Fute (for it was a vehement Frost) to Ormistown. Efter supper he held a comfortabill Purpois of the Deith of Godis chosen children, and merrilie said, me thinks that I desyer eirnestlie to sleep ; and thairwith he said we'll sing ane Psalme ; and sae he appointed the fyftie ane Psalme, quhilk was put in Scotis meiter and began thus : ' Have mercy one me now, guide Lord,' etc."

According to Coverdale this Psalm was one of the "Dundee Psalms," composed by the brothers John and Robert Wedderburn, of Dundee.

Of the Wedderburn family, but little is known ; the father was a merchant of Dundee, and the three brothers, John, Robert and James, were friends to the Reformation.

From an "original copie" of the Dundee Psalms, printed in 1621 and now in the Advocates' Library in Edin-burgh, we learn that only twenty Psalms were versified by John and Robert Wedderburn. With the Psalms were published a number of doctrinal and devotional pieces, also some satirical poems on the papacy. These Psalms and Spiritual Songs were published without tunes, but in metres evidently suited for the music of the continent. John Wed-derburn had spent some time in Germany under the in-struction of Luther and Melancthon, from whom he learned not only the principles of the Reformation, but of the Ger-man Psalmody, and it was what he carried with him from his visit that no doubt influenced him in determining the metres of his Psalms. In the Dundee Psalms were nine di-versities of metres, but scarcely an instance of the common metre.

PSALM LI.—MISERERE MEI, DEUS.

Sung by Wishart in the Castle of Ornuston on the night before his apprehension.

"DUNDEE PSALM-BOOK."

Have mercie on me, God of might,
  Of mercie, Lord and King;
For thy mercie is set full right
  About all eirdly thing;
Therefore I cry baith day and night
  And with my hert sall sing,
To thy mercie with thee will I go.

    Et secundum multitudinem;
Gude Lord, I knaw my wickedness,
  Contrair to thy command,
Rebelland ay with cruelnes
  And led me in ane band
Lo satham quha is merciles;
  Zit Lord, heir my cry and
To thy mercie with thee will I go.

Quhat king can tell the multitude,
  Lord, if thy greit mercie
Sen sinners hes thy celsitude
  Resisted cruellie?
Zit na sinner will thou seclude,
  That this will cry to thee,
To thy mercie with thee will I go.

    Tibi soli peccavi;
Only to thee did I offend,
  And me kill euill hes done,
Throw quhilks appeirandly defense
  To me is nane aboue;
Thus men will judge thy just vengeance
  Hes put me from thy throne,
Zit to thy mercie with thee will I go.

The most illustrious of all the Scotch Psalmists was George Buchanan. Buchanan began the rendering of the Psalms into Latin verse while in his prison cell at Coimbra, in Portugal, 1548. Knox says of him:

"Mr. Geo. Buchanan remains alive to this day, in the year of God 1566 years, to the glory of God, to the great honour of this natioun, and to the comfort of thame that delyte in letters and vertew. That singulare work of David's Psalms in Latin metere and poesie, besyde many other, can witness the rare graces of God gevin to that man."

The first complete edition of Buchanan's Psalms was published by his nephew, Alexander Morrison, the date being omitted. A second edition appeared in 1566. Another in 1567, entitled Paraphrasis Psalmorum Davidis Poetica.

Buchanan's Psalms have called forth high encomiums from the best critics, a few of which inserted may exhibit the estimation in which they have already been held by those familiar with the Latin tongue:

"His immortal paraphrase of the Psalms doth show that neither the constraint of limited matter, the darkness of expression nor the frequent return of the same or like phrases could confuse or exhaust that vast genius."—Crawford's History of the House of Este.

"His masterpiece is his paraphrase upon the Psalms, in which he outdid the most famous poets among the French and Italians."—Leissier.

"Buchanan executed this translation with such inimitable sweetness and elegancy that this version of the Psalms will be esteemed as long as the world endures, or men have any relish for poetry."—Mackenzie.

"It is generally admitted that to Scotland belongs the honor of having produced the best Latin version of the Book of Psalms. At a time when literature was far from common in Europe, Buchanan, then a prisoner in a foreign land, produced a work which has immortalized his name. . . . There are twenty-nine different kinds of measure in the work, in all of which he shows how completely he was master of the varied metres of Latin verse. In many of the Psalms he has succeeded to admiration."—Orme.

Though other Latin versifiers obtained considerable commendation for their efforts, Buchanan still held the principal place in the estimation of Scotch critics. Before the close of the century in which he was born, his Psalms had been included as part of the education given in the High Schools of Scotland. This appears from the minutes of the town council of Edinburgh, of July 21, 1598, which contain the earliest regulations of the High School of that city. The record runs, " The first class and regent thairof sall teache the first and second rudiments of Dumbar with the Colloques of Corderius; and on Sonday Cathechesis Palatinatus. The second regent sall teache the rules of the first part of Pelisso with Cicerois familiar epistilles. The third regent sall teache the second part of Pelisso with the supplement of Erasmus Sintaxis Terence, the Metamorphosis of Ouid with Buquhannanis Psalms on Sonday. The ferd sall teache the third part of Pelisso with Buquhannanis Prosodia . . . and the heroick Psalmes of Buquhannanis on Sonday."

In those early days, while the Latin was yet a living

language among the educated, Buchanan's Psalms were studied with all the zeal and pleasure with which the antiquarian now pours over Homer, or the poet over Paradise Lost. They frequently afforded to the persecuted and the banished that comfort and pastime afterward afforded the Scotch Covenanters by their English versions. So highly were they prized by Sir Patrick Hume, that he committed them to memory; and, while he was self-incarcerated in a subterranean vault in Polwarth churchyard, a refugee from persecution, and without light to cheer the gloom of his sepulchral retreat, he nerved himself and sustained his courage by these Latin lyrics of the Scotch Bard. So thoroughly were they impressed upon his memory, that he could at the day of his death repeat every Psalm without so much as missing a word.

Buchanan's Psalms were among the earliest poetic compositions that inspired the muse of Dr. Isaac Watts. While yet a school-boy, he studied them with admiration, and through them contracted a love for the Psalms themselves that afterwards led to his own imitations.

The high-sounding lyrics of Casimir Sarbiewski seem to have borrowed their inspiration from the same source. Casimir has left the following tribute to the genius of Buchanan:

> " See from the Caledonian shore,
>   With blooming laurels covered o'er,
>   Buchanan march along !
>   Hail honored heir of David's lyre,
>   Thou full-grown image of thy Sire,
>   And hail thy matchless song !"

For the pastime of those who still preserve a knowledge of the Latin they learned at college, a selection from Buchanan is here appended.

PSALM XXIII.

GEORGE BUCHANAN.

Quid frustra rabidi me petitis canes?
Livor propositum cur premis improbum?
Sicut pastor ovem, me dominus regit;
 Nil decrit penitus mihi.

Per campi vividis initia pabula,
Que veris teneri pingit amœnitas,
Nunc pascor placide; nunc saturum latus
    Fessus molliter explico.

Puræ rivus aquæ leniter astrepens
Membris restituit robora lanquidis,
Et blando recreat somite spiritus
    Solis sub pace torrida.

Saltus quum peteret meus vaga devios,
Errorum teneras illecebras sequens,
Retraxit miserans denero me bonus
    Pastor justitiæ in viam.

Nec si per trepidas luctifica manu
Intentet tenebras mors mihi vulnera,
Formidem duce te pergere; me pledo
    Securum facies tuo.

Tu mensas epulis accumulas, merum
Tu plenis pateris sufficis, et caput
Unguento exhilaras: conficit æmulos,
    Dum spectant, dolor anxius.

Me nunquam bonitas destituet tua
Prosususque bonis perpetuo favor;
Et non sollicitæ longa domi tuæ
    Vitæ tempora transfigam.

In Scotland the Psalms of the Wedderburn brothers
were sung in the congregations and private families till they
were supplemented by the version commonly known as
that of Sternhold and Hopkins.   This substitution of the
English renderings must have taken place to a certain extent previous to the year 1555, for in this year Elizabeth
Adamson, on her death bed, sang a Psalm which has been
identified as one of Sternhold's.   The versions sung at this
early date must have been from the edition of 1551, which
contained the thirty-seven of Sternhold and the seven of
John Hopkins.   It is probable that the Scotch immediately
adopted the first issue of Sternhold in 1549, which may be
taken as the date at which began the decline of the Dundee
Psalms.

When the Genevan edition, containing eighty-seven
Psalms, was published, it, with the Book of Order, was immediately adopted by the Scotch Church.   From Calderwood we learn that "before the Confession of Faith was
formed (1560) and ratified in Parliament, and the Book of

Discipline contrived, the Reformed Kirk within the realme had that book, which was prefixed to the Psalms in meeter, for their direction in discipline, the Book of Common Order or the Order of Geneva; whereby is meant the Order of the English Kirk of Geneva where Mr. Knox had been some time minister.''

The first Book of Discipline, adopted by the Church of Scotland at its first Assembly in 1560, makes express mention of ''Our Book of Common Order'' having been used in some of our churches previous to that period.

At the meeting of the second Scotch Assembly, which was held in 1561, the attention of the delegates was turned to the preparation of a new Psalter.   This action was called forth by the English Church binding up, with the Book of Common Prayer, the Genevan edition of the Psalms, published in 1561.   The Scottish Reformers had little relish for the Liturgy of a semi-papal body thrusting itself into their families and worshiping assemblies through its association with their metrical Psalms, and so determined to have their Psalter issued to suit themselves.

The pieliminary steps toward an Edinburgh edition of Sternhold and Hopkins were taken in 1561.   In December of this year ''the kirk lent Robert Lepruik or Lekprevic, printer, twa hundred pounds (Scots) to help to buy irons, ink and paper, and to fee craftsmen to print the Psalms.'' In 1564 the work was completed, and was published by Lepruik with the title: ''The forme of prayers and ministration of the sacraments, etc., used in the English Church of Geneva, approved and received by the Church of Scotland.   Whereunto that was in the former Bookes are added sondrie other prayers, with the whole Psalms of David in English metre.''

The Scotch, in preparing their Psalm-book, acted independently of the English Church.   Instead of accepting the work of Sternhold, Hopkins and others, as it was issued and used in England, they proceeded to make such modifications as would best suit their peculiar tastes.   The eighty-seven Psalms published by the Genevan exiles were retained entire.   Of the new Psalms composed by Hopkins, &c., and adopted in England, forty-two were selected, but not adopted till after numerous, and, in many instances, very extensive alterations were made. The work was completed by selecting twenty-one Psalms of Scotch origin by Robert Pont and John Craig, the colleague of Knox. The Psalms in which the Scottish version differed from the English numbered forty-one, besides numerous variations in words, lines and entire verses.

In this edition Scotland claims only thirty-six—some say forty-six—those by Kethe, who spent most of his life in England, being included. Thus was Scotland indebted principally to England for her first regularly authorized Psalm-book. Dr. Lee observes of this and all other versions prepared for the use of the Scottish Church previous to 1640, that "all the editions of the Psalms printed for the use of the Church of Scotland before 1640, with the exception of King James', were in general taken from the version by Thomas Sternhold and other English authors, not above one-tenth of the number having been versified by divines of the Church of Scotland."

The versifyers, who were connected with the history of the Scotch Psalm-book, but not with that of England, were Robert Pont, and John Craig, the former of whom versified six Psalms, and the latter fifteen.

In December of 1564, when the Scottish Psalter was completed, the General Assembly, to further the matter of Psalmody, ordained "That everie minister, exorter and reader shall have one of the Psalme Bookes latelie printed in Edinburgh, and use the order therein contained in prayers, marriage and ministration of the Sacraments."

Ten years later, in 1574, the Scotch Parliament enacted "That all gentlemen, house holders, and others worth three hundred marks, of yearly rent, and every yeoman and burgess with five hundred pounds, should have a Bible and Psalm-booke in vulgar language in thair hous for the better instruction of thame selffis and yair families in the knowledge of God, under pain of ten pounds."

In January, 1580, His Majesty, King of Scotland, appointed "Johne Williamson Burgess of Edr., his general sercheour throuchout ye haill boundis of this his hienes realme to that effect," giving him power to visit the houses of such as are described in the act of Parliament, "and to requyre the sicht of thair Bybill and Psalm-buik gif thai ony hane to be markit with their owin name of the said John or his deputtis hand wryte, for eschewing of fraudful and deceavabill dealing in that behalf ; and if they have none to exact the penalty."—Record of Privy seal, vol. 46, fol. 129.

The Scottish Psalter of 1564 continued in authorized use in Scotland till the adoption of what is commonly called Rouse's version in 1650.

Several editions of the Scotch Psalm-book were published in Holland for the benefit of the Scotch congregations in that country, and it continued to be used as the only version there until some years after the adoption of the new version in Scotland.

For a period of almost forty years, the Scottish Kirk seems to have paid no further attention to the modifying of her Psalmody. The old version had gradually grown dear to the people, and there appeared to be no need for a change. About the close of the sixteenth century, however, certain errors in the translations and vulgarisms in the metrical forms of the authorized Psalms began to be criticised ; soon followed the conviction that the old was not what it should be, and a revision was finally proposed. Measures to procure this revision were taken in 1601, by the appointment of Robert Pont to perform the task. This appears from a record made by Calderwood. "In the last session it was meaned by sundrie of the brethren that there are sundrie errours in the vulgar translation of the Bible and of the Psalms in meeter, which required correcting ; also, that there were sundrie prayers in the Psalme Book that were not convenient for the time. It was therefore concluded that for translation of the Bible, every one of the Brethren, who had greatest skill in the languages, employ their travels in sundrie parts of the vulgar translation of the Bible, which need to be amended and to confer the same together at the next Assemblie. As for the translation of the Psalms in meeter, it was ordained that the same be revised by Mr.

Robert Pont and that his travels be revised at the next Assemblie." The movement for a revision of both the Bible and the Psalm-book was made by King James I.; a fact which alone may have influenced the Assembly to appoint the revision on that occasion. The King at that time is said to have proposed not only a correction of the old version, but the formation of a new one.

As no further notice is taken of the action of the Assembly of 1601, it is presumed that the matter of revision was quietly dropped.

The proposition of James I. for a new version of the Psalms was probably a step towards his assuming himself the dignity of a Psalmist; James did, after his accession to the throne, undertake a version of the Psalms, and had proceeded as far as the Thirty-first by 1625, when he was interrupted in his work by death.

Calderwood thus speaks of the undertaking of the King in connection with the mention of his conduct in the Assembly of 1600:

"A proposition was made for a new translation of the Bible, and the correcting of the Psalms in metre. His Majesty did urge it earnestly, and with many other reasons did persuade the undertaking of the work; showing the necessity and the profit of it, and what glory the performance thereof would bring to this church. When speaking of the necessity he did mention sundry escapes in the common translation (of the Bible), and made it seem that he was no less conversant in the Scriptures than they whose profession it was. When speaking of the Psalms he did recite whole verses of the same, showing both the faults of the metre and the discrepancies of the text. It was the joy of all who were present, and bred not little admiration in the whole Assembly, who, approving the motion, did recommend the translation (of the Bible) to such of the brethren who were most skilled in the languages, and the revising of the Psalms to Mr. Robert Pont. But nothing was done in the one or the other. Yet did not the King let his intention fall to the ground. The perfecting of the Psalms he made his own labor, and at such hours as he could spare from the public cares went through a number of them, commending the rest to a faithful learned servant, who hath therein answered His Majesty's expectation."

The "faithful learned servant" was William Alexander, afterward Earl of Sterling, who completed the version which James had begun, and remodeled those of James himself. This version was presented to the world in 1630 or 1631, as the veritable production of King James, and so

was known as the Royal Psalter.   Of it Beattie remarks:
" The work does honor to the learned Monarch.   It is not
free from the Northern idiom, but the style seems to me to
be superior to every other Scotch writer of that age, Haw-
thorunden excepted.   There are in it many good stanzas,
most of which have been adopted by the compilers of the
version now authorized in Scotland, whereof this of King
James is indeed the groundwork.   Nay these compilers have
not always equaled the Royal versifier, where they intended,
no doubt, to excel him.   I shall give one example.   The
third verse of the Fiftieth Psalm stands thus in our version :

> ' Our God shall come and shall no more
>   Be silent, but speak out ;
> Before him fire shall waste, great storms
>   Shall compass him about.'

James has the advantage both in arrangement of the
words and in the harmony :

> ' Our God shall come and shall not then
>   Keep silence any more ;
> A fire before him shall consume,
> Great storms about him roar.' "

Of the same production, Row remarks : " There were
some expressions so poetical and so far from the language
of Canaan, that all who had any religion did dislike them,
such as calling the sun, ' the Lord of Light,' and the moon,
' The Pale Ladie of the Night.' "

When Charles I. succeeded James in the government of
Great Britain, he did everything in his power to carry out
the scheme of his father for fixing upon the Scotch the
episcopacy of England.   Among his many misguided innovations was his attempt to substitute the Royal Psalter of
James for the old version of the Scotch Assembly.

According to Row : " In the year 1634, there was a report that the
King would have the Psalms of David as they were translated and paraphrased by King James, his father, received and sung in all the Kirks of
Scotland.   Some of the books were delivered to Presbyteries that ministers might advise concerning the goodness or badness of the translation, and report their judgments, not to the General Assembly, for that
great bulwark of our church was now demolished, but to the diocesan
assemblies.   Yet the matter was laid aside for some time."

However, though the new Psalter was the production of
a Scotch King, and was modeled after the old version in the

matter of metres, yet the movement of Charles only excited
the contempt of the Scotch. Says Calderwood: "The
people are acquainted with the old metaphrase more than
any book in Scripture ; yea some sing all on the most part
without a buik, and some that cannot read sing some
Psalms."

In 1636, a new and revised edition of the Royal Psalter
was published, when Charles again urged the adoption of it
by the Kirk of Scotland. "Finding it to be exactly and
truly done," he allowed "it to be sung in all churches of
his dominions," and gave the special direction with regard
to Scotland, that "no other Psalms of any edition whatever
be printed hereafter within that Kingdom, or imported
thither from any forrayne parts."

That he might better carry out his design, Charles had
the Royal Psalter bound up with a Liturgy prepared by the
Scotch Bishops, with the assistance of Archbishop Laud.
But this act only outraged the feelings and prejudices of the
Scotch, and cast a deeper odium upon Charles and his father's
Psalm-book. The following note, made in a copy of this
Liturgy or Service Book, which has been preserved in the
library of the University of Glasgow, will show something
of the estimate placed upon it, and of the bitter feeling
awakened by it. The signature is that of Alexander Block-
head, said to be genuine :

> "This is the book called the Service-book, that was pressed upon the
> Kirk of Scotland by the Prelates of that tyme (1637) ; a book full of
> errors, and may be called 'The Masse in English.' The reason I kept
> it undestroyed is, that all generations following may take heed of
> Novacions in the Kirk, and praise God for our preservation. (Signed)
> Alexander Blockhead."

When the service under the new Liturgy was first read
in the great Cathedral of Edinburgh, the audience was
mostly composed of women, who shouted as the Dean began
his exercises, that "the mass was entered and Baal was in
the church." Some of them upbraided the presiding clergyman with opprobrious epithets, while one found no better
expression of her contempt than to hurl a stool at his head.
"Ane godly woman, when she heard a young man behind
her sounding forth Amen to that newly composed comedie,

quickly turned her round about, and after she had warmed both his cheeks with the weight of her hands, she then shot against him the thunderbolt of her zeal : 'False thief, is there na either pairt of the churche to sing mess in but thou must sing it at my lugge."

In the commotions of 1638, when the Scotch banded themselves in a covenant for the maintenance of their religious liberties, the Psalm-book of Charles, with the Service Book of Laud and the Scotch Bishops, went down. An incident connected with the effort of Charles to conciliate those whom he had attempted to ruin, will show the persistence with which he and his priesthood sought to carry out their measures. At one time, when twenty thousand Covenanters, were assembled at Edinburgh to observe a Fast, Charles sent the Marquis of Hamilton to cajole and flatter them into terms. As these twenty thousand Covenanters went to meet the Marquis, seven hundred priests, who accompanied him, placed themselves upon an eminence and sang Psalms from the Royal Psalter, as the commissioner passed along.

But neither force nor flattery would avail, and to the proposition that they should dissolve their league, the Scotch replied, " that they would sooner renounce their baptism than their covenant."

Although the Scottish Church did not choose to accept of the Royal Psalter as a substitute for its old version, yet there were many of the leading Scotch minds that were impressed with the necessity for securing a new and improved Psalm-book. This same conviction was participated in by the Puritans of England. This dissatisfaction finally culminated in a series of efforts that gave to us the version commonly known as "Rous' Version of the Psalms of David."

For the incipient movements in the history of this version, we must come down in our narrative to the convocation of the Westminster Assembly of Divines. This Assembly, the offspring both of religious controversy and of the desire of the Scottish and English Christians for a closer union in the bonds of their faith, was convened by Parliament in an ordinance issued June 12, 1643. In the calling of the Assembly there does not seem to have been any reference to the subject of a new version of the Psalms. The agitation that gave origin to that great body had reference chiefly to the more important features of faith and worship. But as the Christians of both England and Scotland felt the need of an improvement in their sacred songs, no better opportunity for securing uniformity in the choice of a new Psalm-book could be presented than that convocation of Divines.

The two versions that were especially prominent before the Westminster Assembly were those of William Barton and Francis Rous or Rouse. Barton's Psalms were first printed in 1644, and upon his own petition were introduced to the notice of Parliament and the Westminster Assembly in October 1645, as appears from the Journals of the House of Lords, under date of Oct. 7, 1645: "Upon the humble petition of William Barton, Measter of Arts, read this day in the House: It is ordered, etc., That two Books of David's Psalms composed in English metre by the petitioner, and presented to their Lordships, are hereby referred to the Assembly of Divines to be read over, and judged by them; and the result of their judgments thereupon returned to this House, that such further direction may be given touching the same, as shall be meet."

Several editions of Barton's Psalms were published between 1644 and 1682. The edition of 1645 contained the license of Cromwell as Protector. In his later editions Barton amended many of his Psalms in accordance with criticisms made upon them, and added "many fresh metres." In the preface to the edition of 1654 appeared the following statement with reference to the Psalm-book that had been prepared and adopted by the Scotch Kirk: "The sects of late have put forth a Psalm-book, most-what composed out of mine, and Mr. Rous his, but it did not give full satisfaction, for somebody hath been at charge to put forth a new version of mine, and printed some thousands of mine in Holland, as it is reported; but whether they were printed there or no, I am in doubt; for I am sure that fifteen hundred of my books were heretofore printed by stealth in England and carried over to Ireland." In the versions published between 1682 and 1705 Mr. Barton's Psalms appeared "as he left it finished in his lifetime."

The successful competitor before the Westminster Assembly in the matter of Psalmody was Francis Rous, one of the most prominent Englishmen of the time, a great scholar, and several times a member of Parliament. "He was a learned and religious man, fearless in his opposition to error and zealous for everything which he conceived to be for the interest of the Gospel. During the latter years of his life he enjoyed the high satisfaction of seeing his version of the Psalms in very general use in England, and of knowing it to be universally adopted by the Church of Scotland, and that the pious people of an entire kingdom were daily employing his strains in both their public and domestic worship." It was during the twelve years previous to 1640, in which the Parliament was not permitted to assemble, that Mr. Rous turned his attention to the versifying of the Psalms. His version is supposed, by a writer in Wood's Athenæ Oxonienses, to have been first put in print in 1641. Copies of this edition are very scarce. Dr. Cotton says he never met with but one copy of it in all the libraries he had seen, and that was in possession of Dr. Bliss, of Oxford.

The edition that was recommended for the consideration of the Westminster Assembly was printed in 1643, and bore the title: "The Psalmes of David in English meeter, set forth by Francis Rous. April 17, 1643. It is this day ordered by the Committee of the House of Commons in Parliament for printing, that this Book, entitled The Psalmes of David, &c., (according to the desires of many reverend ministers) be published for the generall use. And for the true correcting of it, be published by these the Author shall appoint.

"I do appoint Philip Nevill and Peter Whateley to print these Psalms. FRANCIS ROUS.

"London: Printed by James Young, for Philip Nevill, at the signe of the Gun in Ivie-lane, 1643."

In this volume were 312 pages and twelve leaves not paged of "Psalmes of harder and lesse usuall Tunes corrected, and the tunes not altered," along with "A Table of the Psalmes."

In 1646 Mr. Rous published an edition, revised and

corrected in accordance with the criticisms made and the changes recommended by the various committees of the Westminster Assembly. This edition was printed by Miles Fletcher for the Company of Stationers, and contained 255 pages of 12mo.

Mr. Rous in the preface to his Psalms thus refers to the undertaking of his versification: "Apprehending many years past that a forme wholly new would not please many, who are fastened to things usual and accustomed, I assaied only to change some pieces of the usual version, even such as seemed to call aloud and, as it were, undeniably for a change. These being seen, it was desired that they should be increased, which being done they are hereby subjoined."

The subject of a new version of the Psalms was first brought before the Assembly by an order from the House of Commons, bearing date of "20 Novembris, 1643," yet the new Psalm book was not reported completed till Nov. 14, 1645. This report was made to the House of Commons, and is thus referred to in the Journals of that body: "The House being informed that some of the Assembly of Divines were at the door, they were called in, and Mr. Wilson acquainted the House that, according to a former order of this House, they had perused the Psalms set out by Mr. Rous; and as they are now altered and amended do conceive they may be useful to the Church." Upon the receipt of this report the House immediately resolved, "That this Book of Psalms, set forth by Mr. Rous, and perused by the Assembly ot Divines, be forthwith printed."

Speaking of this Psalter, Baillie, in a letter dated Nov. 25, 1645, remarks: "The Psalms are perfyted: the best without all doubt that ever yet were extant. They are on the presse; but not to be perused till they be sent to yow, and your animadversions returned hither, which we wish were so soon as might be."

Under date of 22d Nov., 1643, appears the following: "The first thing done this morning was, that Sir Benjamin Rudyard got an order from the House of Commons wherein they require our advice whether Mr. Rous's Psalms may not be sung in churches; and this being debated, it was referred to the three committees to take every one—fifty Psalms."

When the communication of the House of Commons appeared, a committee was appointed by the Assembly "to consider these Psalms." The Scotch Commissioners were not prepared to take part in this action, owing to their not having received the opinion and direction of the Church at home. In May, 1644, they wrote home as follows:

"There was also presented to the Assembly a new paraphrase of the Psalms in English metre, which was well liked and commended by some members of the Assembly. But, because we conceived that one Psalm-book in all the three kingdoms was a point of uniformity much to be desired, we took the boldness (although we had no such express and particular commission) to oppose the present allowing thereof, till the Kirk of Scotland should be acquainted with it ; and therefore we have now sent an essay thereof in some Psalms."

Although the Scottish Kirk soon after this date gave its permission to its commissioners to take part in the movement for a new Psalter, yet the matter progressed very tardily. Something of the impatience of the delegates at the delay will appear from the following notices of Principal Baillie:

To Lord Lauderdale he wrote, June 17th, 1645, "You have here also the last fifty of Mr. Rous's Psalmes. They would be sent to Edinburgh to the committee for the Psalmes. Mr. Andrew Kerr will deliver them. When your Lordship goes hither, you would stirr up that committee to dilligence, for if once their animadversions were come up, I believe the book would quickly be printed and practiced here."

The House of Lords does not seem to have given its final sanction to the publication of Rous's version till some time in 1647, as we learn from the letter of Baillie, bearing date of Jan. 26, 1647.

In the efforts of the Westminster Assembly, we see prominent the same determination manifested in France, Holland and Scotland at an earlier date to sanction no version of the Psalms that was not closely conformed to the "original text." The versions of Boyd and Barton were both refused because of the liberties taken in their translation. Rous's Psalms became the basis of the Assembly's work because it was "so closely framed according to the original text." As close as Rous's translations were, the Assembly of Divines could not express its final approbation of the whole volume, until it presented the modifications of two years' deliberation.

Baillie, in his letters, frequently expresses what was the desire of the majority in the Assembly. In a letter to Rowallan in 1645, when one hundred of the Psalms had been completed, he says they were "sent down to the Commissionersof our Generall Assemblie, to be mended in every thing which the Committee appointed there for that end shall find to have need of amendment; the fifty that remain will soon follow. It is our earnest desyre that the Psalter might at this time be put in such a frame that we need not to be troubled hereafter with any new translation thereof."

To Robert Douglass he writes, in the same year, of his fears that there were too few anxious to join in the work of correcting the Psalter, and adds, "This my feare hes made me bold to intreat you, both for the zeal you have to the puritie of that translation and to the honor of the Church, to bestow much of your time as convenientlie you may upon that very necessar service. These lines are likely to go up to God from many millions of tongues, for many generations; it wore a pity but all possible diligence were used to have them framed so well as might be."

Though the Psalms of Rous, as they passed the Assembly at Westminster, are pronounced by the Scotch Commissioners most perfect, and though the Committee of the Scottish Assembly sat in judgment on them as they were sent to them, from time to time, by their delegates at London, yet the Scottish Kirk was not content to finally adopt them until they had passed through a new series of "animadversions," and so had really lost their character as the real versions of Francis Rous. According to Baillie, "they dismissed from Rous' version every extraneous composition. The Assembly were determined to keep not only to the sense, but as far as possible to the very words of the sacred text."

After more than seven years of revising and re-revising, of correctings and re-correctings; after passing through

Committees and Presbyteries and Assemblies, the version that was originally the production of Rous, came forth in the form in which it was to be sung in the Psalm-singing Churches for two hundred years.   This new paraphrase, a compilation from the old version of Sternhold and Hopkins, the version of King James, those of Boyd, Barton, Rous, and probably of others, was printed with the title: "The Psalms of David in Meeter: Newly translated and diligently compared with the Original Text and former Translations; More plain, smooth and agreeable to the Text than any heretofore. Allowed by the authority of the General Assembly of the Kirk of Scotland, and appointed to be sung in Congregations and Families.   Edinburgh.   Printed by Evan Tyler, Printer to the King's Most Excellent Majesty, 1650."   With the Psalms were also printed the Acts of the General Assembly, Aug. 6th, of the Assembly's Commission, 23d Nov., 1649, and of the Committee of Estates, 8th January, 1650, authorizing the version to be used from May 1, 1650.

While engaged in the preparation of this version of the Psalms, it was the fond hope of the Scotch that it would be adopted by the Presbyterians and Independents of England, and that the desired uniformity in praise would be thus secured; but in this they were disappointed, owing to the desire of many English divines to use whatsoever Psalter they might wish.   Of this Baillie complains in a letter written as early as 1646.   To William Spang he observes: "Our long labour on the Psalmes, when readie to be put into practice, are lyke, by a faction, to be altogether stiflled; they will have a libertie to take what Psalter they will."

In Scotland, when the new paraphrase was almost completed, there arose a doubt in the minds of some whether the version of Rous, even as amended, should be received, owing to that author having joined what were then termed the Sectaries of England.   Among those entertaining scruples on this point was Baillie, who writes in September of 1649:   "I think at last we shall get a new Psalter.   I have furthered that work ever with my best wishes; but the scruple now aryses of it in my mind, the first author of the translation, Mr. Rous, my good friend, has complyed with the Sectaries, and is a member of their republick; how a Psalter of his framing, albeit with much variation, shall be receaved by our church, I do not know; yet it is needful we have one, and a better in haste we cannot have." The apprehensions of Baillie as to division in the Assembly were not realized, and the new version passed without difficulty.

This new Paraphrase, which may well be termed "Rous' version," owing to his versification having been the basis of the Assembly's work, has now been in use for over two hundred years, having possessed an unrivaled reign longer than any other metrical version since the beginning of the Reformation.

Its merits and demerits have been variously canvassed; by friends it has been extolled beyond what it really deserves, by enemies charged with follies that it does not possess.

It may be said in its praise that at the time of its completion it constituted the best metrical translation of the Psalms that had ever been published. Its close adherence to the original text has not, even to this day, been surpassed. Accepting the opinions of good and unprejudiced critics the assertion may be ventured that while the Old Testament would lose in grandeur and in sublime diction, it would not sacrifice any of its ideas and inspiration by a substitution of Rous' metrical version of the Psalms for King James' prose translation. These Psalms are, as far as a translation can well be, the very utterances the Spirit dictated to the Psalmists in the days of old.

That this close adherence to the original has been obtained at a sacrifice, and in some instances a complete sacrifice, of poetic merit, no reasonable man can deny. When these Psalms compete with other more recent versions, or with the popular hymns of the day for the awards of modern taste and of latter day poetic refinement, they fall far in the background. There are portions of them that may have been appreciated two hundred years ago, but which now are read or sung with a smile.

Such constructions as:

> "The na-ti-ons of Ca-na-an
> By his Almighty hand,
> Before their face he did expel
> Out of their native land."—Ps. 78: 55.

Or

> "A man was famous and was had
> In estima-ti-on
> According as he lifted up
> His axe thick trees upon;

> "But all at once with axes now
> And hammers they go to
> And down the carved work thereof
> They break and quite undo."—Ps. 74: 5, 6.

Or

> "Do to them as to Midian;
> Jabin at Kison strand,
> And Sis'ra; which at Endor fell
> As dung to fat the land."—Ps. 83: 9, 10.

are so rude and so unpoetical that even their literalness will not make atonement.

Yet there are, beyond a doubt, entire Psalms, and parts of almost all the versifications, that the criticism of the musician or rhetorician can not depreciate in the estimation of their friends. They have in them so much of the divine power, and are so completely interwoven with our early and later religious experience, that, like all works of real worth, they have outlived, and should ever outlive, the complaints of the learned.

It seems almost like profanity to a life-long Psalm-singer to criticize the time-honored Twenty-third Psalm:

> "The Lord's my shepherd, I'll not want,
> He makes me down to lie
> In pastures green; he leadeth me
> The quiet waters by."

Who that has had his heart warmed by the tender mercies of God can find a fitter expression for his affections than in the One hundred and sixteenth Psalm?

> "I love the Lord because my voice
> And prayers he did hear.
> I while I live will call on him
> Who bowed to me his ear," &c.

The Twenty-seventh could not be improved as a battle
song when we contend either against our spiritual or temporal foes:

> " The Lord's my life and saving health;
>   Who shall make me dismayed ?
>   My Life's strength is the Lord; of whom
>   Then shall I be afraid ?"

The First, Second, Sixth, L. M.; Eighteenth, Twenty-
second, Twenty-third, Twenty-fourth, Ninetieth, One hundredth, L. M.; One hundred and twenty-first and many
others contain, either throughout or in parts, elements that
might be comprised in the forming of a perfect Psalm-book;
and it is a matter of surprise that compilers in hymnology
who have gathered from so many sources, both ancient and
modern, have found little worthy of culling out of the old
Psalms that have stood the wear and tear of two centuries.

The Scotch version of 1650 formed the staple of praise
among the Covenanters in some of their most terrible persecutions, and ever since it has contained the only authorized
Psalms of the dissenting churches of Scotland and Ireland.
Soon after its first publication, it was extensively adopted
among the English Presbyterians and Independents. In
1673, an edition was published in England with a preface
written by the celebrated Dr. Owen. This preface is as
follows :

"Surely, singing of Psalms is a duty of such comfort and profit, that
it needeth not our recommendation ; the new nature is instead of all ar-
guments, which cannot be without this Scriptural solace. Our devotion
is best secured, where the matter and the words are of immediately
divine inspiration ; and to us, David's Psalms seem plainly intended by
those terms of psalms, and hymns, and spiritual songs, which the apostle
useth. Eph. 5, 19; Col. 3, 16. But it is meet that these divine compositions should be represented to us in a fit translation, lest we want David
in David ; while his holy ecstacies are delivered in a flat and bold expression. The translation which is now put into thy hand, cometh
nearest to the original of any that we have seen, and runneth with such
fluent sweetness, that we thought it fit to recommend it to thy Christian
acceptance ; some of us having used it already, with great comfort and
satisfaction."

These Psalms were also sung by some of the Baptist
congregations, toward the close of the seventeenth century,
and have even been adopted by the Irish Unitarians at Ulster.

In America, they formed the sole praise of the present Presbyteran churches, until after the Revolution, when in some of the bodies they were superceded by the paraphrase of Isaac Watts. In the Covenanter churches, the United Presbyterian church, and the Associate Reformed Presbyterian church of the South, they are still the substance of praise.

It was the One hundred and seventeenth Psalm of this version that the soldiers of Cromwell sang at the Battle of Dunbar, September 3, 1650. After the routing of the Scotch army, and while the cavalry was collecting for the chase, Cromwell halted his forces at the foot of Doon's hill, where they sang to the tune of Bangor, or some still higher score, and rolled it strong and great against the sky,

> " O give ye praise unto the Lord,
> All nations that be ;
> Likewise, ye people all, accord
> His name to magnify.
> For great to us-ward ever are
> His loving-kindnesses ;
> His truth endures forevermore,
> The Lord, O do ye bless."

At the battle of Drumclog, in June, 1679, this old version afforded the martial song of the Scotch soldiers. "As Claverhouse descended from the opposite side of the mountain, the women, children and old men retired to the rising in the rear of our hosts." The aged men walked with their bonnets in their hands, and their grey locks waved in the breeze. They sang a cheering Psalm. The music was that of the well-known tune of "The Martyrs," and the sentiment breathed defiance. The music floated down on the wind. Our men gave three cheers as they fell into rank. As they marched out, the army "sang the following verses of a Psalm":

> "Their arrows of the bow he brake,
> The shield, the sword, the war.
> More glorious thou than hills of prey,
> More excellent art far.
> Those that were stout of heart are spoiled,
> They slept their sleep outright.
> And none of these their hands did find
> That were the men of might."

Among the many criticisms of Rous' version, the following have been selected :

Some allowance must be made for early impressions ; but at a maturer period of life, after looking at various metrical versions of the Psalms, I am well satisfied that the version used in Scotland is, upon the whole, the best, and that it is in vain to think of having a better. It has, in general, a simplicity and unction of sacred poetry, and in many places its transfusion is admirable.—Boswell, Biographer of Dr. Johnson.

McChene was such an admirer of this version that he gave it as his opinion "that it should be read or sung through at least once a year. It is truly an admirable translation from the Hebrew, and is frequently more correct than the prose version."

Said Rufus Choate—"An uncommon pith and gnarled vigor of sentiment lies in that old version ; I prefer it to Watts."

It may be noticed here that the Doxology that had been printed in some of the editions of the old Scotch Psalter, and which was widely used in Scotland and England, was dropped in the Westminster Assembly. Baillie thus refers to the omission of it :

About the conclusion of the Psalms we had no debate with them ; without scruple, Independents and all sang it, so far as I know, when it was printed at the end of the Second or Third Psalm. But in the new translation of the Psalms, resolving to keep punctuallie to the original text, without any addition, we and they were content to omit that whereupon we saw both the Popish and Prelaticall parties did so much dote, as to put it to the end of the most of their lessons, and all of their Psalms."

Soon after the publication of the first authorized Scottish Psalm-book, the Psalms were translated into metre in the Gælic, the language of the Highlanders.

In 1781 the General Assembly of Scotland gave its approval to a full version of the Psalms in Gælic metre, by John Smith. In 1783 the Synod of Argyle revised and examined this version, and returned it to Mr. Smith that he might prepare it for the press, with the corrections suggested by the Synod. This version, as then published, is still in use among those countries in Scotland where the native Highland language is spoken, and among many of the Gælic settlements in the Canadas and the United States. The title to this version was: "Sailm Dhaibhidh Maille Ri Laoidhean o'n Scrioptur Naomha chum rhi air an seinn ann

an aora' dhia.   Air an leasachadh agus air an cur amach do
reir seolaidh, iartais, agus ughdarais seanaidh earraghaeil.
Le I. Smith, D. D.   Dun-eiden: Air son W. Andersan,
sruileadh, 1805."   This version is a translation of Rous'
Psalms.   A selection is here given:

SALM 1.   Le I. Smith, D. D., 567.

Gælic Edition of 1805.

'SBEANNUICHT an duine sin nach gluais
  An comhairle nan daoi,
An slighe fhiar nam peacach baoth,
  'Na sheasamh fos nach bi;
An cathair fanoid luchd an spors
  Nach togair suidh' gu brath.

2. Ach gam bheil toil do naomh-reachd, Dhe,
    Ga smaointeach' oidhch' is la.

3. Mair ur-chrann uaine bithidh e,
    Aig uisge seimh a' fas,
  A bheir 'na aimsir toradh trom,
    Gun duille chall no blath.
  Soirbhichibd leis gach ni d'an dean:

4.   Ni h-amhluidh sin a bhios
  Na daoine peacach, ach mar mholl
    Air fhuadachadh le gaoith.

5. Fan aobhar sin cha seas a suas
    Na h-aingidh anns a' bhreith,
  No peacaich ann an comunn naomh
    Nam fireanach air leth
  Oir's fiosrach dia air slighe ghloin
    Nam foreanach air fad:
  Ach shlighe fhiar nam peacach baoth,
    Di-mhilltear i gu grad.

The Psalms were also translated into the native language of the Welsh, but at what period this first occurred
does not appear.   As early as 1603 a Welsh metrical version was prepared by the celebrated bard and navigator,
William Myddleton, and was printed in London by Simon
Stafford and Thomas Salisbury.   About the beginning of
the same century Rev. Edmund Prys, Arch-Deacon of Meri-
noth, versified the Psalms in the Welsh dialect.   His version
was subsequently revised by Rev. Peter Williams, and is
now in use throughout the principality of Wales.

In conformity with an act of the Scotch Assembly, passed in 1690, the Synod of Argyle undertook and completed a version of the Psalms in the Irish language. This version was introduced to the Christians worshiping in that tongue by a recommendation of the Assembly in 1694: "It is recommended to all congregations and families who worship God in the Irish language, to make use therein of the paraphrase of the Psalms in Irish metre, approven and emitted by the Synod of Argyle, conform to the act of the General Assembly 1690; and that where preaching and prayer are used in Irish, the singing of the Psalms at the same diet in a different language be forborne thereafter, as an incongruous way of worshiping God."

In 1761 a metrical version of twenty-eight Psalms was executed in the Manx language, spoken in the Isle of Man, by Revs. Robert Radcliffe and Matthias Curgey, residents of that isle.

In 1836 there appeared another version of the Psalms in the Erse or native Irish tongue, prepared by Dr. McLeod, Rev. H. H. Beamish, Thaddeus Connettan and David Murphy. This version was published in London.

CHAPTER X.

THE PSALMS IN THE AMERICAN COLONIES.

The Psalmody of the Puritans in old England, and that of the sects into which they subsequently divided, has always been somewhat confused. At no time even since the separation from the Episcopacy, had there been any special version of the Psalms adopted to the exclusion of all others. Congregations and families seem to have been left to employ such versifications as their own tastes dictated. Before the Non-conformists had withdrawn from the Establishment, but while they were in many places holding meetings by themselves, the Psalms used were those of Sternhold and Hopkins, as they had been allowed in the churches of England. This version continued among them, as well as among the adherents of the Episcopacy, until some time after the meeting of the Westminster Assembly; in a few instances, indeed, until in the last century.

In addition to this version, others seem to have had a limited use in the Puritan congregations from time to time. The editions of Merrick and Sandys were authorized by the English Parliament, and found a few patrons. When Barton's Psalms were issued and allowed by the English authorities, they were extensively adopted among the Presbyterians and Independents, and continued in use for a period of more than fifty years. The license of Oliver Cromwell did much to introduce them to public favor.

The version of the Westminster Assembly, by Francis Rous, had its friends who exerted their influence towards its adoption in the families and congregations of the Presbyterian churches. It was this version that some refugees, about the close of the seventeenth century, took with them over to Holland, and it was from this that they sang, as a song of gratitude after narrowly escaping shipwreck off the coasts of Norway:

> " O that the Lord to men would give
> Praise for his goodness then," etc.

As we have already seen, the version adopted by the Scotch Kirk, in 1650, was published in England and passed into use among some of the most prominent non-conformist churches.   This version is still in use in some of the English Presbyterian churches.

When the imitations and hymns of Dr. Watts were published, they gradually worked their way among the descendants of the early Puritans of England, and are now, in most cases, the principal Psalmody of their congregations.

To the Puritans of England we are indebted for the religious carols, which almost two centuries ago were common among those embracing that peculiar faith.   Finding the Catholic custom of carol-singing so deeply rooted as to not be easily destroyed, they endeavored to divert the affections of communities into a channel more consistent with their views.   For this purpose the Psalms of Sternhold and Hopkins were put into a form for carol singing.   A duodecimo volume appeared under the title, "Psalms, or Songs of Zion, turned into language and set to Tunes of a strange land, by W. S. (William Slatyr), intended for Christmas carols and fitted to divers of the most noted and common tunes everywhere familiarly used and known.

The Puritans in Holland, from whom came our Plymouth colonists, adopted the Psalms of Henry Ainsworth, their pastor, early in the sixteenth century.   Mr. Ainsworth has been represented as a man of great learning and of exemplary piety.   For his knowledge of the Hebrew language, he was widely distinguished.   Some of the dignitaries of the University of Leyden remarked, that in this respect he had but few superiors in Europe.   He was the author of a work entitled " An Arrow Against Idolatry," and of a superior commentary on the Books of Moses.   " In a word, the times and place in which he lived were not worthy of such a man."

The Psalms of Ainsworth were published in Amsterdam in 1612, with the title, " The Book of Psalms; " published both in prose and metre.   With annotation opening, the words and sentences by conference with other Scriptures.   By Henry Ainsworth, Eph. 5: 18, 19.   "Bee yee

filled with the Spirit ; speaking to yourselves in Psalms and
Hymns and Spiritual Songs ; singing and making melodie in
your hearts to the Lord.'' In ''a preface declaring the
reason and use of this booke,'' he says, '' I have interspersed
(Christian Reader) this work, with regard of God's honor,
and comfort of his people ; that his word might dwell in us
richly, in all wisdom ; and that we might teach and ad-
monish ourselves in Psalmes and Hymnes and songs spirituall.
This I have laboured to effect, by setting over into our
tongue the Psalmes in metre, as agreeable to the originall
Hebrew, as are also usuall translations.   For the better discerning thereof, I turned them also into prose, and set these
versions one by another to be the more easily compared.
And because the Psalmes have hard words and phrases, I
have added notes to explain them with brevity, which to me
was as laborious as if I had made a larger commentary.''
The prose and poetry of this version are arranged in parallel
columns, the prose on the left and the poetry on the right.
With his version were also published melodies placed over
the Psalms, to which they were to be sung.   ''The music
was printed in the lozenge or diamond-shaped notes, without
bars, and was in the German choral style.''   This music is
represented as being ''akin'' to the poetry of the Psalms ;
and both ''alike to jargon,'' ''though doubtless to the
Puritans they afforded high gratification, and were the only
tunes and words used for many years after the settlement of
Plymouth.''   These Psalms, with the Confession of Faith
prepared by Ainsworth, immediately became parts of the
system of faith and worship among the Refugee Brownists.

   In eight years after the publication of these Psalms we
find the Puritans leaving Holland, and taking ''a neat edition
of Ainsworth's version of the Psalms'' with them.   In the
account of the departure of the Pilgrims from Holland in
1620, Edward Winslow thus refers to the religious exercises
at Leyden :   ''When the ship was to carry us away, the
brethren that stayed at Leyden, having again solemnly
sought the Lord with and for us, feasted us that were to go,
at our pastor's house, it being large, when we refreshed ourselves, after tears, with singing of Psalms, making joyful

melody in our hearts, as well as with our voice, there being many of the congregation expert in music; and indeed, it was the sweetest melody that ever mine ears heard."

On the 19th of December, in the year 1620, we meet this brave band of worshipers, at the shores of the New World, weary and worn with exposure, but still fresh in their hopes of liberty and in their devotion to God.   It is the Sabbath: and like all the Puritans of their day, they dare not leave their ship, nor make any efforts even for their relief; but spend the holy day in their accustomed religious worship.

Thus it was that the first notes of sacred praise that awoke the slumbering echoes of the New England shores, were those of the old Jewish Psalms.   If there be any glory in it, these songs deserve it.   The harp that presided at the dedication of the Hebrew temples; that bore part in the triumphant returns of the Jews from their captivity; that gave the melodies when the Messiah inaugurated his New Kingdom, and that led the glorious anthems of praise, when Zion put on the beautiful garments of Reform, was well selected, by the God who gave it tone, to preside at the baptism of a new world to the service of civil liberty and of the religion of the Protestant Church.

The Psalms of Ainsworth comprised the whole Psalmody of the New England Puritans, for twenty years after their landing at Plymouth; and along with those of other versions, they were continued in some parts until the close of the seventeenth century.

In the library of the Massachusetts Historical Society may be seen a copy of Ainsworth's Psalms, with the following note written on the blank side of the title page, by "T. Prince. Plymouth, May 1, 1732;" "I have seen an edition of this version (published) in 1618 in quarto; and this version of Ainsworth was sung in Plymouth Colony, and I suppose in the rest of New England, till the New England version was printed in 1646."

In addition Rev. Thomas Symmes, in a work printed at Boston in 1723, informs us: "Furthermore (as is evident from a Psalm Book of Elder Chipmans now in my hands) the church at Plymouth (which was the first church in N. E.) made use of Ainsworth's version of the Psalms until the year 1692. For although our N. E. version of the Psalms was composed by sundry hands, and completed by President Dunster about the year 1640, yet that church did not use it, it seems, till two and fifty years after, but stuck to Ainsworth, and until 1682 their excellent custom was to sing without reading the line."

Though this version has been ridiculed for its lack of taste and true poetic merit, yet, in the olden times of the Republic, "how many glad hearts have rejoiced over these songs of praise, how many sorrowful ones sighed out their complaints in these plaintive notes, that steal sadly yet sweetly on the ear—hearts that now cold in death are laid to rest around that sacred urn, within those walls where they had so often swelled with emotion."

These Psalms were held in as great reverence by the early Puritans as though they had been very models of taste. They were heard everywhere in their homes. The emigrant sang them to wear away the monotony of his travels as he journeyed from one colony to another. Not infrequently were heard whole bands of these sturdy sons of toil, making the forests ring by uniting in the melody of some Psalm, the Indians, as it is said, listening with wonder and admiration. Even the troops, in their marches and in their camps, dispensing with what Puritanism called "the carnal fife and drum," drew their martial songs from the Psalms of David, which they sang in true heroic style to the tunes of Mear and Old Hundred.

It was this old Ainsworth version that Longfellow mentions in "The Courtship of Miles Standish," where, when John Alden came on "The Lover's Errand," he

"Heard as he drew near the door the musical voice of Priscilla
Singing the Hundredth Psalm, the grand old Puritan anthem,
Music that Luther sang to the sacred words of the Psalmist,
Full of the breath of the Lord, consoling and comforting many.
Then as he opened the door, he beheld the form of the maiden
Seated beside the wheel, and the carded wool like a snow-drift
Piled on her knee, her white hands feeding the ravenous spindle,
While with her foot on the treadle she guided the wheel in its motion.
Open wide on her lap lay the well-worn Psalm Book of Ainsworth,

Printed in Amsterdam, the words and music together
Rough-hewn, angular notes, like stones in the walls of a churchyard,
Darkened and overhung by the running vine of the verses,
Such was the book from whose pages she sang the old Puritan anthem.''

The following rendering of the First Psalm is taken from the early version of Ainsworth and given as a specimen of its style and merits:

PSALM 1.

1. O blessed man that doth not in
    The wicked's counsell walk;
    Nor stand in sinners' way; nor sit
    In seat of scornful—*folk*.

2. But setteth in Jehovah's law
    His pleasureful delight;
    And in his law doth meditate,
    By day and eke* by night.

3. And he shall be, like-as a tree,
    By water brooks planted;
    Which in his time shall give his fruit
    His leaf eke shall not fade.

4. And whatsoever he shall doe
    It prosp'rously shall thrive.
    Not so the wicked; but as chaff,
    Which winde away doth—doth drive.

5. Therefore the wicked shall not in
    The judgment stand—upright:
    And in th' assembly of the just,
    Not any sinfull—wight.

6. For, of the just, Iehovah he
    Acknowledgeth the way:
    And way of the ungracious
    Shall utterly—decay.

Ainsworth version was superseded by what is generally known as ''The Bay Psalm-book,'' printed in 1640. The following account of this version is taken from the Magnalia of Mather, book 3, p. 100. ''About the year 1639, the New English Reformers, considering that their churches enjoyed the other ordinances of heaven, in their spiritual purity, were willing that the ordinance of singing Psalms should be restored among them unto a share in that purity. Though they blessed God for the religious endeavor of those who translated the Psalms with the metres usually annexed, at the end of the Bible, yet they beheld in the translation variations of not only the text, but the very sense of the Psalmist, that it was an offense unto them.   Resolving then upon a new translation, the chief divines of the country took each of them a portion to be translated: among whom were Mr. Welds; Mr. Elliot, of Roxbury, and Mr. Mather, of Dorchester.   These, like the rest, were of so different a genius for their poetry, that Mr. Shephard, of Cambridge, on the occasion addressed them to this purpose:

> " You Roxbury Poets keep clear of the crime
> Of missing to give us a very good rhyme.
> And you of Dorchester your verses lengthen,
> And with the text's own word you will these strengthen."

" The Psalms thus turned into metre, were printed at Cambridge in the year 1640.   But afterwards it was thought that a little more art was to be employed upon them; and for that cause they were recommended to Mr. Dunster, who revised and refined this translation ; and with some assistance from one Mr. Richard Lyon, who being sent over by Sir Henry Meldway, as an attendant, with his son, then a student in Harvard Colege, and residing in Mr. Dunster's house—he brought it into the condition wherein our churches ever since have used it."

This work, at first known as "The Bay Psalmist," but afterwards called "The New England Version," was the first book printed in the Colonies, and with the exception of the printing by the Spanish, in Mexico, the first in the whole American Continent.   It bore the title, " The Psalms in metre, Faithfully translated for the Use, Edification, and Comfort of Saints, in publick and private, especially in New England."   Crown 8vo. 300 pages.

This novel and rare book was printed in the house of President Dunster, of Harvard College, upon a printing press, or "printery," which came to this New England settlement as a gift from friends in Holland, and which cost £50.

The type of this Psalm-book is Roman, and is said to abound in typographical errors. The words, "The Preface," are written, the "The" on the left hand page with a period following it, and "Preface" on the right.   Words of one syllable at the end of lines are sometimes divided by a hyphen.   At the top of the left hand page throughout the book the word "Psalm" is spelled properly; but at the head of each right hand page it is closed with the letter e, thus, "Psalme."

In the first edition of The Bay Psalm-book, there were no Spiritual Songs, the Psalms being accompanied only by the original long preface, and "An Admonition to the Reader," filling half a page after the "Finis." The following is the "Admonition":

"The verses of these Psalmes may be reduced to six kindes, the first whereof may be sung in very neare fourty common tunes; as they are collected out of our chief musicians, by Thos. Ravenscroft.

"The second kinde may be sung in three tunes, as Ps. 25, 50 and 67 in our English Psalm-books.

"The third may be sung indifferently, as Ps. the 51, 100 and ten commandments, in our English Psalm-books, which three tunes aforesaid, comprehend almost all this whole book of Psalms, as being tunes most familiar to us.

"The fourth as Ps. 148, of which there are but about five.

"The fifth, as Ps. 112, or the Pater Noster, of which there are but two, viz: 85 and 138.

"The sixth, as Ps. 113, of which but one, viz: 115."

After the publication of the second edition of this version, in 1647, Henry Dunster, president of Harvard College, and Richard Lyon were appointed to revise and improve the Psalms. In 1650 this revised edition was printed with the title: "The Psalms, Hymns and Spiritual Songs of the Old and New Testament, faithfully translated into English Metre, For the Use, Edification, and Comfort of the Saints in publick and private, especially in New England. 2 Tim. 3, 16 and 17. Col. 3: 16. Eph. 5: 18, 19. James 5: 13." 8vo. 308 pages.

For over one hundred years, this revised Bay Psalm-book passed through edition after edition without any alteration whatever. It met with favor, not only in New England, but in the old country. In England, at least eighteen editions were printed, the eighteenth appearing in 1754. In Scotland, it passed through twenty-two editions, the last being issued in 1756. In the latter country, it was bound up with the Bible and imported to this country, in large numbers. In most of these reprints, if not in all of them, the original preface was continued.

In Scotland, as late as 1770, there were congregations of considerable eminence praising God through these New England Psalms.

Says Hood, in his "History of Music in New England," The design of the versifyers of the Bay Psalm-book was to produce a metrical translation nearer to the original than those then in use. In this they succeeded. Theirs was a literal translation. Many similar attempts had been made before, but no one had proved so successful. Their numbers were generally worse, while they had more violations of the text, and this to our Puritan fathers, was the fault of faults. This work, as a faithful translation, was highly esteemed, both in England and Scotland, and was reprinted in each in large and frequent editions. * * * Its faults, as a metrical version, designed to be sung, were many and palpable. But at that day, it had no rivals ; and is it venturing too much to say, that under the same restrictions, it could have few, if any now ? Theirs was indeed a difficult task—a close literal translation, in measure and in rhyme ! We venture the assertion, that no one with those requirements has equaled it. Those who made more pleasing numbers, fell far short of their conformity to the text ; while those who made the smoothest and most desirable numbers, have merely paraphrased, imitated, or drawn their subjects from the Bible. Watts is but a paraphrase. Addison's beautiful samples, in the lines beginning, "The spacious firmament on high," and "The Lord my pasture shall prepare," of what he intended, and of what he could have prepared so ably, namely, a complete metrical version of the Psalms, were but a pre-translation or paraphrase."

The variety in the metres of the Bay Psalm-book was somewhat greater than in previous versions ; though the principal metres were the Long, Common, Short and Tens, the Tens being regular iambics. The length of some of the Psalms extended as far as sixty, seventy, a hundred, and even one hundred and thirty lines ; yet these Psalms, like the shorter ones, were sung through at one time, a full half hour being required for the performance of some of them. The quantity of the lines varied greatly, some containing more, some fewer syllables than the metre required. This defect was remedied by contracting or lengthening a word, as the case might require ; thus,

> " I' th' city of the Lord of Hosts."
>   This is the Lord on whom we had
>   Our expectation;
>   We will rejoice, and will be glad
>   In his salvation."
>   —Hymn of Isaiah, chap. 25.

When the translators of this version were reminded of the rudeness and unpoetic construction of their Psalms, they gave it as their apology, "That God's altar needs not our polishing ; for we have respected rather a plain translation, than to smoothe our verses with the sweetness of any paraphrases, and so have attended to conscience rather than elegance ; fidelity rather than poetry, in transcribing the Hebrew words into English language, and David's poetry into English metre."

The Bay Psalm-book was almost universally adopted in the New England churches. Still in some instances the old one had too firm a hold on the affections of the people to yield. The new version was not adopted in the church at Salem till 1667 ; and then, as will be seen from the records of the First Church, it was only to be used with the old, not to supersede it. " At a church meeting, 4th of fifth month, 1667," or May 4th, "The pastor having formally performed and given reason for the use of the Bay Psalm-book in regard to the difficulty of the tunes, and that we could not sing them so well as formerly and that there was a singularity in our using Ainsworth's tunes ; but especially because we had not the liberty of singing all the Scripture Psalms according to Col. 3, 16. He did not again propound the same, and after several brethren had spoken, there was at last a unanimous consent with respect to the last reason mentioned, that the Bay Psalm-book should be used together with Ainsworth's to supply the defects of it."

About the same time the Ipswich church adopted the Bay Psalm-book, and continued its use almost a century. In the Plymouth church it was not adopted till 1692, fifty-two years after the first edition was printed. The following extracts are from the records of the Plymouth church :

" In 1685, May 17, the Elder stayed the church after the public worship was ended, and moved to sing Psalm One hundred and thirtieth in another translation, because in Mr. Ainsworth's translation, which we sang, the tune was so difficult few could follow it—the church readily consented thereunto.

"June 19, 1692. The pastor stayed the church after meeting and propounded that, seeing many of the Psalms in Mr. Ainsworth's translation, that we now sung, had such difficult tunes that none in the church could set, that the church would consider of some way of accommodation, that we might sing all the Psalms, and left it to their consideration.

August 7. At the conclusion of the Sacrament, the pastor called upon the church to express their judgments about this motion ; the vote was thus : when the tunes are difficult in the translation we use, we will sing the Psalms now used in our neighbor churches in the Bay ; not one brother opposed the conclusion. The Sabbath following, August 14, we began to sing the Psalms in course according to the vote of the church."

During the period of its use in N. E. the Bay Psalm-book passed through at least thirty editions in this country, and including the edition printed in Europe, at least seventy. The twenty-seventh edition may now be seen in the Antiquarian Hall at Worcester, Mass.

Copies of the early issues of the Bay Psalm-book are scarce and very valuable. The American Antiquarian Society owns a copy of the first edition, which it keeps carefully locked in the iron safe in the building of that Society, in Worcester. Up till 1860, five copies of this first edition were in the possession of the Old South Church, of Boston. Two of these copies still remain in the possession of that church, the other three being surrendered to certain gentlemen in Boston for other more modern works bestowed upon the Prince Library.

In the library of Mrs. Carter Brown, of Providence, R. I., is Richard Mather's copy of the Bay Psalm Book. In October, 1876, it was sold at the Library salesroom, Beacon street, Boston, for one thousand and fifty dollars.

A copy may also be seen in the Lenox Library, in New York, for which Cornelius Vanderbilt paid $1,200.

The following rendering of the One hundred and thirty-third Psalm is given as a specimen of the Bay Psalm Book and its style of publication:

PSALM CXXXIII.

A Song of Degrees, of David.

1 How good and sweet to see,
   it's for bretheren to dwell
   together in unitie:

2 It's like choice oyle that fell
    the head upon
  that downe did flow
    the beard unto
      beard of Aron:
  The skirts of his garments
    that unto them went down:

3 Like Hermons dews descent
  Sions mountaines upon,
    for there to be
  the Lords blessing
    life aye lasting
      commandeth he.

In 1718 Dr. Cotton Mather published the "Psalterium Americanum,"—"The Book of Psalms in a translation exactly conformed unto the Original; but all in blank verse; fitted unto it tunes commonly used in the Church."

In the Introduction to this Psalm-book, Dr. Mather speaks of the excellence of the Psalms, and the manner of the translation; and the Psalms themselves are a good metrical version, without injuring the conformity to the original, "for the clink of Rhyme." Of the literalness of the translation he remarks: "For the New Translation of the Psalms, which is here endeavored, an appeal may be with much assurance made, unto all that are masters of the Hebrew Tongue, whether it be not much more agreeable to the Original than the Old one, or than any that has yet been offered to the world. It keeps close to the original; and even when a word of supply is introduced, it is usually a needless compliment unto the case of exactness, to distinguish it at all, as we have done, with an Italic character; for it is really in the Intention and Emphasis of the Original. Yea, the just laws of Translation had not been at all violated if a much greater liberty had been taken for the beating out of the golden and massy Hebrew into a more extended English."

The arrangement of the Psalms in this translation is in the 8s and 6s, or "common metre," as he says, without rhyme. Some of the Psalms were so arranged that Long Metre tunes could be sung to them. This was done by the insertion of two syllables in black letters in the second and fourth lines. By using these, the Psalms could be sung to Long Metre tunes; by omitting them, which could be done without injuring the sense, to Common Metre tunes.

Nine of the Psalms were arranged in this manner. The 136th Psalm was so arranged that by omitting the word or words in brackets, it could be changed from Common to Short metre. This method of arranging the Psalms for tunes of different lengths, was invented by Richard Baxter, who translated the Psalms into English verse.

Each of Mather's Psalms is accompanied with illustrations. "To assist the reader in coming at the vast profit and pleasure which is to be found in this rare part of Christian ascetics, every Psalm is here satellited with illustrations, which are not fetched from the vulgar annotations (whereof still, reader, continue thy esteem and thy improvements). But have the more fine, deep and uncommon thoughts which in a long course of reading and thinking have been brought in the way of the collector. They are golden keys to immense treasures of truth."

The Psalterium Americanum was divided into five books, the first extending to the Forty-second Psalm; the second to the Seventy-third; the third to the Ninetieth; the fourth to the One hundred and seventh, and the fifth to the end. Sixteen pages of hymns, arranged like the Psalms, completed the last volume. Unlike the most of the Psalm-books of his times, this of Mather was published without music, a fact which may partially explain the entire neglect into which this valuable contribution to the literature of the Church fell.

The following selection is from Mather's version of the One hundred and sixteenth Psalm, and will show the manner in which several Psalms were arranged for either Long or Common Metre tunes:

PSALM CXVI.

1. I'm full of Love: It is because‖ [of this] that the ETERNAL God hath hearkened now unto my voice;‖ [and hath] my supplications heard.‖

2. Because that he hath unto me‖ [kindly] inclined His gracious ear; ‖ therefore upon Him I will call ‖ while I have any days [of life.]

3. The cords of Death surrounded me‖ and me the [dreadful] pangs of hell‖ found out; a sad anxiety‖ I found and sighing [heavy] grief.‖

4. But I call upon the Name‖ of the ETERNAL God, [for this]; I pray Thee, O ETERNAL God,‖ Deliver Thou my [sinking soul].‖

5. Most full of tender mercy‖ [forever] is the ETERNAL God: Righteous He is, too, and our God‖ is most compassionate [withall].‖

6. The simple ones th' ETERNAL God‖ takes into [his kind] custody; ‖ I was brought miserably low,‖ and then [it was] He helped me.‖

7. O thou my soul, do thou return‖ where 'tis [alone] thou findest rest; ‖ Because that the ETERNAL God‖ hath well [enough] rewarded thee.‖
8. Because I hou hast from threatening Death‖ [safely] delivered my Soul;‖ my Eye from tears, my foot from fall‖ by a thrust given [unto] me.‖

At the request of the General Association of Connecticut Joel Barlow undertook to revise the Psalms of Watts, and to supply those which that author had omitted.   In 1785 Barlow's improved edition was published and was entitled, "Dr. Watts' Imitations of the Psalms of David, corrected and enlarged, by Joel Barlow, to which is added a collection of Hymns; the whole applied to the state of the Christian Church in general.   Luke xxiv.   'All things must be fulfilled which were written   . . .   in the Psalms concerning me.' Hartford: Printed by Barlow and Babcock, 1785."

This edition of Watts was largely adopted in New England, and was allowed by the Synod of the Presbyterian Church by an act of 1787:   "The Synod did allow and do hereby allow that Dr. Watts' imitation of David's Psalms, as revised by Mr. Barlow, be sung in the churches and families under its care."

A story is told of a local poet who perpetrated an extempore verse upon Barlow.   Oliver Arnold, a cousin of Benedict, was introduced to Joel Barlow in a book store in New Haven.   Barlow asked of the poet a specimen of his off-hand talent, when Arnold, with the knowledge of Barlow's recently-acquired celebrity from his revision of Watts, immediately repeated the following stanza:

> " You've proven yourself a sinful cre'tur;
>   You've murdered Watts and spoilt the metre;
>   You've tried the word of God to alter,
>   And for your pains deserve a halter."

Through a request of the General Association of Connecticut, Dr. Timothy Dwight undertook the task of reviewing Watts' Psalms, and of adding where they were deficient.   About the year 1797 Dr. Dwight began his work, and soon succeeded in presenting a version suited to the state of the American churches.

In 1800 a committee from the Presbyterian Assembly, consisting of Drs. John Rodgers, Jonathan Edwards and

Asa Hillyer, met a similar committee from the Connecticut Association for the purpose of examining the revision and versifications of Dr. Dwight.   This joint committee reported its approval of what had been done, and in 1802 the new edition of Watts was allowed by the Assembly of the Presbyterian Church in the following act: "Whereas, the version of the Psalms made by Dr. Watts has heretofore been allowed in congregations under the care of the General Assembly, it is now thought expedient that the hymns of Dr. Watts be also allowed; and they are hereby accordingly allowed in such congregations as may think it expedient to use them in social and public worship; and whereas the Rev. Dr. Timothy Dwight, by order of the General Association of Connecticut, has revised the version of the Psalms by Dr. Watts, and has versified a number omitted by him, and has also made a selection of hymns from various authors, which, together with the Psalms, were intended to furnish a system of Psalmody for the use of churches and families, which system has been revised and recommended by a joint committee of the General Assembly and the General Association of Connecticut, heretofore appointed, as examined and approved by a committee of this present Assembly; the said system is hereby cheerfully approved in such congregations and families as may think it for edification to adopt and use them."

The One hundred and thirty-seventh Psalm is a popular specimen of Dwight's versification, beginning:

> "I love thy kingdom, Lord,
>   The house of thine abode,
> The church our blest Redeemer saved
>   With his own precious blood."

During the present century there have been several versions of the Psalms presented to the public.   Of these the version of George Burgess and that of Abner Jones do not fall below their predecessors of any age in point of merit. The Psalms of both these authors retain more than is usual in metrical translations, the sublimity of the original text, and that without serious departure from a literal rendering. The version of Abner Jones has had no superior in elegance of diction and in its adaptation to musical purposes. It displays in its author a keen insight into the genius of the Hebrew language and Hebrew poetry, and a poetic taste almost faultless. Mr. Jones made his translation of the Psalms a matter of thought for twenty years. The origin of his work he dates back to his early affection for the Psalter, and for the study of sacred music. His Psalm book contains three hundred and seventy-six versifications, cast into every variety of metre. The First Psalm alone has ten different versions. "The object," says the author, "was to render the Book of Psalms into easy and flowing verse of various measures, evenly rhymed, with uniform accent, divided according to their musical cadences, and comprised in their own limits; in which their peculiar structure in responsive lines should be kept unbroken, the devout and exalted sentiments with which they everywhere abound, expressed in their own familiar and appropriate language, and the graphic imagery by which they are rendered vivid, and preserved entire."

The following from Abner Jones is a charming rendering of the Twenty-third Psalm:

PSALM XXIII.

Jehovah, my Shepherd, with goodness will crown
    And everything needful bestow;
In pastures of verdure will make me lie down,
    And lead me where cool waters flow.

My soul He restores, and in right lays my path,
    To honor His name and His skill;
Thy rod and Thy staff in the dark vale of death,
    Shall comfort and keep me from ill.

My table with bounties Thy hands will keep spread
    In sight of my envious foes;
With oil in abundance anointing my head,
    My cup with its fullness o'erflows.

Such goodness and mercy, so copious and free,
    Shall follow me all of my days;
The house of Jehovah my dwelling shall be,
    My work evermore for His praise.

It is creditable to the missonary zeal of the early Puritans of New England that they were not long in giving the Holy

Scriptures to the Indians in their own native tongue. As early as 1653 the Catechism was prepared in the Indian by John Eliot, and printed in England, at the expense of the corporation. In 1659 a prose version of the Psalms was printed in the same dialect, and in 1663 the whole Bible. That which is of special interest here is the version of the New England Psalm-book, translated into Indian verse, by John Eliot, and published in 1661.

The work was printed by Samuel Green, and was entitled, "Wame Ketoohomæ Uketoohomaongash David." These Psalms were at first bound up with the New Testament, published the same year, but afterwards with the entire version of the Bible. According to Thomas, the Psalms were issued, in some cases, with the Indian Grammar.

Those who have traveled among the Indians tell us they have no proper songs, and know nothing of melody. What tones they have that at all approach to music, are described as barbarous and offensive. Yet they not only seemed to be delighted with the singing of the Colonists, but when the Psalms were translated into their own tongue, their music, according to Dr. Mather, was "most ravishing." No doubt Mr. Eliot instructed them in the art of music and taught them to sing in it the tunes of New England. In the letter of Mather and Walter to Sir William Ashenhurst, is mentioned that "Jonathan George (Indian,) set the tune for the Psalm and carried it out most melodiously."

In 1687, a letter from Dr. Increase Mather to Dr. John Leusden, at Utrecht, says, "The whole congregation of Indians praise God with singing, and some of them are excellent singers."

Experience Mayhew also speaks of the good singing of the Indians. "About two months since, at Little Compton, they came to hear me preach; had you been there to see how well they filled their seats, how powerfully Nishokon prayed, and how melodiously Paquawise set the tune for the Psalm, and carried it out, and how dexterously it was taken up by the others, I am sure you would have been much affected with it."

About the middle of the eighteenth century, Brainerd, another apostle to the Indians, and who lived among the Susquehannas, translated sundry forms of prayer into the Indian tongue. "I also," says he, "translated sundry Psalms into their language, and soon after we were enabled to sing them in the meeting."

In 1787 some Psalms were translated into the Mohawk tongue for the Christian Indians of that tribe. They were printed in London, at the expense of the British Government, and were bound up with the Book of Common Prayer. The Psalms were the 23d, 67th, 100th, 117th and 134th. In addition were the "Gloria Patri," the "Veni Creator," and two hymns on Baptism and the Lord's Supper.

In 1839 a collection of Psalms and Hymns was made for the use of the "Six Nations," and printed at Hamilton, in the Diocese of Toronto, at the expense of the New England Corporation. It contains the five Psalms prepared for the Mohawks, and eighty-one hymns; sixty-eight of which are in Mohawk and English.

The following is from Eliot's Indian Psalms:

PSALM CXVII.

1 Wacenomok Maniz wame
        wutohtimoneunk
    Wacenomokkenaan wame
        miffinninnuog wonk.

2 Ummonaneteaonk miffi
        en kuhhogkanonut
    Wunnomwaonk God michemohtem
        watenomook Maniz.

CHAPTER XI.

The Psalmody of the Scotch and Irish Presbyterian churches of the United States deserves a special notice.

In the latter half of the last century two bodies of the Scotch Dissenters were organized, the Reformed and the Associate Presbyterian. Subsequently—in 1782—these two bodies united to form the Associate Reformed Church. This union instead of consolidating two bodies into one, really produced three, protesters from both of the original parties remaining out of the union and continuing under the names of Associate and Reformed Presbyterians. The Reformed Presbyterian Church subsequently divided into the two parties known as the "Old Side" and the "New Side" Covenanters. In 1858 the Associate and the Associate Reformed Churches united in Pittsburgh, to form the body now known as the United Presbyterian Church.

The emigrants from the Scotch and Irish churches came to America with all the affection of the old country for Psalm-singing and for the Scripture Psalms as the subject-matter of their public and private praise.

The history of Psalms and Psalm-singing in the Dissenting churches differs nothing in most respects from that already given in connection with the Scotch Church. Yet in two respects the aforementioned Churches are peculiar; they excluded the paraphrases from their worship and have adhered exclusively to the Psalms of David, and have undertaken to procure uniformity and prevent innovation in the matter of Psalmody by legislation and discipline.

Whether the American Psalm-singing churches are, or are not extreme in their zeal for the Psalms; whether they, in excluding hymns and imitations from religious worship; or the other American churches, in practically excluding the Psalms in a faithful rendering of the original, from their manual of praise, have departed farther from the principle and practice of the Calvinistic and Presbyterian Reformers, and, indeed, from the custom of the Primitive Church, let those decide who write for controversy.

It may be remarked here that the Psalm-singers themselves have been to some extent responsible for the agitations in the Church concerning her songs, and for the departure of many from the early faith, in that they have not at suitable periods so remodeled their versions of the Psalms as to conform to the innocent and reasonable demands of the age. These versions are the only medium through which the people are to form an appreciation of the Psalter as a book of sacred praise; hence it is to be expected that those who lose their taste for a *version* will in a measure lose their taste for the Psalms themselves. In the passing of a hundred years, the world progresses vastly in poetical and musical attainments, and we cannot expect the mind of to-day to rest content amid what it regards the barbarisms of a century ago. Old orthography, old fashions and old versions must pass away so far as they prove themselves out of harmony with the present. We justly subject ourselves to the charge of eccentricity, in clothing either ourselves or our songs in ancient robes, unless there be a very evident reason for doing so. When the Church adheres to a version for two centuries without a change, she in a measure invites discussion and dissension. Clothe the whole Bible in the garb of some of Rous's or Sternhold and Hopkins' Psalms and the world will soon be demanding a Watts imitation of more books than the one.

It is a reasonable proposition that a version of the Psalms should not he regarded as closed to improvement. As soon as imperfections are plain, let them be remedied; when a proper change is suggested, let it be made. Let a Psalm-book grow up with art and refinement and its growth will be toward perfection. Certainly wise and discreet conformity to the reasonable tastes of the people will secure more than law.

The first enactment in the American church restricting the Psalmody of the church to an inspired basis is that of the Reformed Presbyterian Church of 1774. It is as follows: "Singing God's praise is a part of public, social worship, in which the whole congregation shall join; the Book of Psalms, which are of divine inspiration, is well adapted to the state of the church and of every member in all ages, and these Psalms, to the exclusion of all imitations and uninspired compositions, are to be used in social worship."

The Associate Church, Oct. 25, 1784, approved the following testimony:

"1. We declare that the Psalms of David are proper to be sung in public worshiping assemblies, and in families, and that we believe they were designed for this purpose by the Holy Spirit. Every human composition must be inferior to them as the writings of the best men are inferior to the Word of God.

"2. That imitations of the Psalms of David, which are by many substituted in their place, we reject for the following reasons," &c.

"5. We use, it is true, a poetical version of the Psalms, and it is scarcely, if at all, possible to form a version of this kind as strictly agreeable to the letter of the original as a prose one can be formed. But this defect cannot be remedied by departing still further from the original in an imitation which bears but a faint resemblance to it. We have the original matter and the original order of the matter in the version used by us, and we are not ashamed to prefer this matter to the best sayings of men, and this order to any men ever did or ever will devise."

The testimony of the Associate Reformed Church was approved in 1799. In it are the following declarations on Psalmody:

"1. It is the duty of Christians to praise God publicly by singing of Psalms together in the congregation.

"2. It is the will of God that the sacred songs contained in the Book of Psalms be sung in his worship to the end of the world, and the rich variety and perfect purity of their matter, the blessing of God upon them in every age, and the edification of the church thence arising set the propriety of singing them in a commanding light; nor shall any composures merely human be sung in any of the A. R. churches.

"3. These songs should be sung not barely with the same frame of spirit with which they should be read, but with such an elevation of soul as is suited to praise as a distinct ordinance, and in singing those parts of them that are expressed in ceremonial style, or describe the circumstances of the writers, or of the church in ancient times, we should have an eye on the general principles which are implied in them and which are applicable to individuals or the church in every age.

"4. In singing the voice is to be timeably ordered, but the chief care must be to sing with understanding and with grace in the heart, making melody unto the Lord. No tunes shall be sung in worshiping assemblies but such as are grave and simple; and no new tunes shall be introduced into any of the churches without the knowledge and consent of the church officers, nor even then unless it shall be evident that the introduction of such tunes would be acceptable to the congregation and would promote its real edification.

"6.   No chorus of singers nor alternate singing shall be introduced into any of the churches, because it is the duty of the whole congregation to praise God with united voices.

"8.   That the whole congregation may the more profitably join in the delightful exercise of praise, it is recommended that everyone who can read have a Psalm-Book."

In addition to this the Associate Reformed Church in 1816 passed a resolution permitting the use of a version of the Psalms prepared for the Reformed Dutch Church: "Resolved, That the version of the Book of Psalms in the Old Testament, recently prepared for the use of the Reformed Dutch Church in America, be permitted to be used."

The United Presbyterian Church at its formation in 1858 gave its declaration as follows: "We declare that it is the will of God that the songs contained in the Book of Psalms be sung in his worship, both public and private, to the end of the world; and in singing God's praise these songs should be employed to the exclusion of the devotional compositions of uninspired men."

During the present century many efforts have been made to improve the version of the Scotch Assembly and many proposals to adopt a new one.   As early as 1810 it was felt by some in the A. R. Church that their principles on Psalmody were in peril for the want of an improvement in their Psalm-Book.   In this year a committee made a report to the Synod in which it said there existed a "very critical condition of a large section of their body, arising from the unpopularity of the Psalms. * * * * From Washington northward our present version is the chief obstacle to our prosperity * * and our social praise languishes and is ready to die * * * Either the rising generation will take the reform into their own hands and then there will be no computing the disasters of such a precedent, or our churches will be swept entirely away."

The remedy proposed was a new version of the Psalms. However, but little progress was made in the way of a new version in any of the Psalm-singing Churches until

1859, when the United Presbyterian Church took measures that led to the beginning of a new collection.

A memorial from the First Presbytery of Ohio, asking for an improved version of the Psalms was presented to the General Assembly of the United Presbyterian Church, which met in Xenia, Ohio, May 18, 1859. This was the first General Assembly of the United Presbyterian Church. This Memorial was referred to the Committee on Psalmody. This committee consisted of the Revs. D. R. Kerr, D. D., John G. Smart, R. K. Campbell and Samuel Collins. At a later session of this Assembly the committee presented a report of considerable length, concluding with these resolutions:

1st, That the version of the Book of Psalms now used by the United Presbyterian Church be retained without any change that would affect its integrity.

2d, That to be used in connection with this, it is desirable to have an entirely new version of equal fidelity, and up to the present state of literature and laws of versification.

3d, That a committee of —— be appointed to take charge of this work, and either by selections from versions extant, or the labors of a competent person, endeavor to have such a version in readiness to report to the next Assembly; that in this work they be instructed to make fidelity to the original an object of special attention; and that, as they progress, they publish the results of their labors in the periodicals of the Church.

4th, That this version, when reported to the Assembly, if deemed worthy, shall be overtured to the Presbyteries.

The Assembly appointed as the committee contemplated in the third resolution, the following ministers: The Revs. G. D. Archibald, Thomas Beveridge, D. D., R. D. Harper, Joseph T. Cooper, D. D., Alexander Young, D. D., and David R. Kerr, D. D.

This committee reported to the next General Assembly, which met in Philadelphia, recommending submission to the Presbyteries, for their judgment, a number of the versions prepared by Professor Abner Jones.

The report of the committee was not acceptable to the Assembly, and instead of adopting it they appointed the following committee on the "new and improved version of the Psalms": Drs. Thomas Beveridge, D. R. Kerr and Joseph Clokey, and the Revs. G. D. Archibald and R. B. Ewing. The work of revising the Scotch version and preparing new versions and submitting them in overture to the Presbyteries was continued until the year 1870. The General Assembly of that year, meeting in Pittsburgh, appointed a committee of five to embody such amendments as seemed to be needed, together with the new versions adopted, and publish them in one volume for the use of the Church. Final action was taken by the General Assembly, meeting at Xenia, in 1871, as follows: "Resolved, That the revised edition of the present version of the Psalms and the New Versions published in the same volume, be authorized to be used according to the action of the last Assembly."

The Psalms revised and the new versions approved by that General Assembly are now in use in the United Presbyterian Church, also in the Associate Reformed Presbyterian Church of the South, and some of them are found in Moody and Sankey's "Gospel Songs," in the Christian Endeavor Hymnal, and other hymn-books. In its poetic merits and the adaptation of its sacred songs to the well-known and popular melodies of the times the present Psalm-book of these Psalm-singing Churches is not a particle behind the Book of Praise in any body of worshipers.

Among those early Presbyterians, from which originated the Old School, New School and Cumberland Presbyterian Churches, the version of the Psalms used depended on the direction from which they had emigrated. At least ten or fifteen congregations in colonies of New York and New Jersey were formed by settlers from New England, who brought with them the Bay Psalm-book. In other congregations the predominating element was composed of "dissenters" from Scotland and Ireland, who made choice of the Scotch version; while in a few instances were settlements from Dutchland, where a version after the model of some one used on the continent would be naturally adopted.

In 1729, the General Synod agreed upon its adopting Act, but there was no action taken with reference to making any particular version of the Psalms the authorized basis of praise.

Up to the time of the great American Revolution, the Psalms of David were the almost exclusive sacred songs,

and the old Scotch or Rous's version, the almost exclusive
version of these songs, used in the Presbyterian colonial
churches. "Presbyterian" and "Psalm-singer" were, in
the eyes of the royal troops, during the war, synonymous
terms.

"A house, that had a large family Bible and David's
Psalms in metre in it, was supposed, as a matter of course,
to be tenanted by Rebels. To sing 'Old Rous' was almost
as criminal as to have leveled a loaded musket at a British
grenadier."

On one occasion, while Duffield was preaching to the
soldiers in an orchard on the opposite side of the Bay, from
Staten Island, using the fork of a tree for a pulpit, the
noise of the singing of Psalms gave the enemy the first
notice of their presence and their voice of thanksgiving was
soon substituted by the singing of rifle balls.

That movement which led to the practical exclusion of
a literal rendering of the Psalms from the worship of the
General Assembly Presbyterian Church, did not begin in the
church courts but among the people; and it began among them
only after the young people, having grown up with more
delicate notions of poetry and music, had grown ashamed
of the "old version." Had there been a version that
would have won the esteem of the rising generation by its
poetic attractions, the introduction of Watt's would, at
least, have been very much delayed. As it was, the change
was a slow one, and did not take place without the usual dissensions in such reform movements.

Eaton, in his History of the Presbytery of Erie, observes of the early Psalm-singers in that section: "But there
were almost intolerable prejudices in the minds of the people
against the use of anything but Rous. Some who did not
appear to have much conscience in regard to other things of
greater importance, were here immovable. They could not
sing words of human composition in the Lord's worship.
They were wedded to the rough, jagged lines of Rous and
could as readily be diverted from them as from the Holy
Bible itself. And Synod acted reasonably and well in the
matter, to urge charity, tenderness and forbearance towards

the people. These old Psalms had been hallowed in their minds as being connected with blessed memories of early years, as associated with the family altar, as having been sung by lips voiceless now upon earth, but therefore on the heights of Mount Zion. * * * * When Mr. Riggs took charge of Scrubgrass and Unity churches, they used Rous's version of the Psalms exclusively in divine service. This continued for some time, when the pastor, having scruples against this exclusive use, began to labor in private to prepare the way for a change. He used the version of Watts, together with his Hymns, in social meetings, and occasionally sung one before divine service. When he thought the people were ripe for a change, a vote was taken in Unity Church, when it was directed that one of Rous's Psalms should be sung at the opening of the morning service, and Watts' the remainder of the time. This vote was passed, with but three or four dissenting voices. Accordingly on the next Sabbath, one of Rous's Psalms was sung ; and at the second singing one of Watts' Psalms was announced, and the pastor commenced reading it, when a certain tall, broad-shouldered, brusque-looking man, with Milesian accent to his voice, having looked in vain for the Psalm in his own thin volume, and thinking perhaps that the speech of the Psalm betrayed it, arose from his seat, stepped into the aisle, and addressing the minister, cried out: 'Quut that ;' and receiving no attention from any source, proceeded up the aisle toward the pulpit, crying, 'If you dunno quut that, I'll go up and pull ye doon by the neck.' * * * * In other congregations there were difficulties of a similar kind. But these days passed away. Many, no doubt, left the Presbyterian Church and found a home in other branches of the church, on account of Psalmody, yet peace and harmony on this question at length prevailed.''

In the year 1800, a commission from the Presbytery of Charleston, S. C., appeared before the Assembly, wishing to know the terms under which they might be taken into connection with the General Assembly : but, making the explicit and positive stipulation, that '' they must not be disturbed in their edifying enjoyment of Rous.'' The accession of this Presbytery did not take place till several years after this, owing, it seems, to the approval given to Dr. Dwight's Psalms by the Assembly soon after the commission appeared.

Before me lie the minutes of the Presbyterian Church from 1706 to 1788, comprising the records of the Presbytery of Philadelphia, of the Synod of Philadelphia, of the Synod of New York, and the Synod of Philadelphia and New York. For forty-seven years these minutes are filled with controversies over the Confession of Faith and the Directory for Worship; but there is not a line to show any disaffection with the old Bible Psalms. In 1753, at a meeting of the Synod of New York, appears in the public records the first evidence of the controversy over the use of Dr. Watts' imitation. The congregation of New York complained to the Synod that the session had attempted "to introduce a new version of the Psalms" without the consent of a majority of the congregation.

A committee appointed by Synod visited the disturbed congregation. Among the members of it were the Rev. William Tennent and Aaron Burr. In their report is the following: "As to the third article against the session concerning the new version of the Psalms, the committee cannot think it regular for the ministers and elders to introduce a new version without the express consent and approbation of the majority of the congregation; yet, since Dr. Watts' version is introduced in this church and is well adapted for Christian worship, and received by many congregations both in America and Great Britain, they cannot but judge it best for the well being of the congregation, under the present circumstances, that they be continued." This is the first official recognition of Watts' Psalms by the Presbyterians of America.

A similar controversy took place later in the Second Presbyterian Church of Philadelphia. In 1773, at a meeting of the Synod of Philadelphia and New York, held in Philadelphia, an appeal came from this church from a decision of the Presbytery of Philadelphia allowing the use of Watts' Psalms in that congregation. On a committee ap-

pointed to visit the church appears the name of the celebrated Dr. Witherspoon.   The result in Synod was the
same as in the case of the New York church; the members
were exhorted to keep the peace and allow both Rous and
Watt to be sung.

The Presbyterian Church did not formally become a
hymn-singing church till within the present century. When
the Psalms of Dr. Dwight were reported his 263 Hymns
were reported with them, as also were the Hymns of Dr.
Watt.   The Assembly of 1802 decreed: "They are according hereby allowed in such congregations as may think
it expedient to use them in public and social worship."

For sixty years more in the history of the American
Presbyterian Church the Book of Praise consisted of Psalms
and Hymns.   Up till twenty or thirty years ago the Bible
Psalter was granted a distinct place in the worship of the
church.   Then the Hebrew Psalter dropped out, and now
for a quarter of a century the Presbyterian Church has been
trying an experiment that no religious body, in the line of
the Calvinistic faith, had tried in thirty centuries before it—
that of singing God's praise out of a hymnal where the inspired Psalms have no distinct recognition.   In the hymnal
edited by Dr. Duryea, and published in 1874 by the sanction of the General Assembly of the Presbyterian Church,
there are Psalms, it is true.   Many of Dr. Watts' are in the
collection.   A few are there from the United Presbyterian
Psalter.   But these Psalms are thrown in with the general
mass of 972 sacred songs and all of them called Hymns.
There is nothing left to tell the rising generation that the
kingdom of heaven on earth had ever heard of the Bible
Psalter.   Multitudes who sing out of this collection:

> " The Lord's my Shepherd, I'll not want;
>   He makes me down to lie
> In Pastures green; He leadeth me
>   The quiet waters by."

or,

> " All people that on earth do dwell,
>   Sing to the Lord with cheerful voice.
> Him serve with mirth, his praise forth tell;
>   Come ye before him and rejoice."—

never dream that they are as faithful a rendering of Bible Psalms as the Prose version, and that they have come down to us fragrant with the memories of two hundred and fifty years of Psalm-singing Presbyterianism.

The author of this work—a pastor of more than twenty years in the Presbyterian Church, has witnessed with pain the "Passing" of the Bible Psalms. Since the beginning of her "Hymnal" era our Church has been at sea in the matter of her Psalmody. Her authorization of Hymn-Books means nothing to her congregations. For the first time in her history her authority over her Book of Praise is gone, and the people buy their hymn-books where they please.

The Hymnal of 1874 is already worn out, and the Assembly has sent forth a new one, doubtless to meet the fate of the former one.

The people of the Presbyterian Church, who love what is solid and majestic in their sacred songs, miss something in their modern Hymnals. As an old Psalm-singer, the writer would suggest it is the Bible Psalter we miss. Give us back the old Psalms, dressed in the attractive forms of these modern days, as they can be dressed; and winnow away several hundred of the hymns of our present collection, and the Presbyterian Church will do more to settle her churches in the matter of their Psalmody than will all the decrees of her courts.

It may not be out of place here for the author to suggest to the ministry of his own Church that, whilst they are endeavoring so zealously to maintain that form of doctrine which is given in the Old Confession of Faith, their efforts will prove worthless unless they see that the Psalmody of the Church breathes the same evangelical principles.

Few people read the Confession of Faith, but every week the thoughts and doctrines of our Hymns are sung into our ears and hearts; and the faith which will be held in the future will not be that of your Confession and Creed, but of your Hymnology.

At present, when the hymn-writers and hymn-collectors are so thoroughly imbued with the true doctrines of the Bible, nothing but good can result to the members of the

Church. But a wave of decadence may sweep over the future Church, as it has often done in the past, when we may bitterly regret that we have lost control over the material of our Psalmody.

The history of Hymnology is not without its emphasis upon the caution often given, that the Church should guard her songs of praise with a jealous care. Poetry, when set to popular music and given to the people, exerts a most powerful influence in extending and perpetuating error as well as truth. It was Fletcher, of Saltoun, who is reported to have said, "if he could but make the ballads of a nation, he would care very little who made the religion of it." To whatever age of the New Testament dispensation we turn, we find that the piety and the orthodoxy of the Church seldom rise above the level of the piety and orthodoxy of her hymns—the heart, in a relapse, first corrupting the hymn, and the hymn in turn further corrupting the heart. This has occurred so frequently as to teach us that we shall have secured ourselves against one of the most potent agencies for ecclesiastical corruption only when we put the material of the Church's praise beyond the vacillating influence of the human heart. The very earliest records of Hymnology furnish instances of the corruption of this department of our praise. As early as the second century, in the Eastern Church, Bardesanes and his son Harmonius distinguished themselves by rejecting preaching and composing hymns for disseminating their Gnostic heresies. Bardesanes composed one hundred and fifty mystical hymns in imitation of the inspired Psalter, "in them," says Ephraim Syrus, "presenting to simple souls the cup of poison tempered with seductive sweetness." It was this abuse of the praise of the Church that doubtless called forth the hymns of the earliest hymn-writers Says Bingham, "As for those (hymns) composed by Gregory Nazianzen, Paulinus, Prudentius and other Christian poets, they were not designed for public use in the Church, but only to antidote men against the poison of heresies, or set forth the praises of the martyrs, or recommend the practice of virtue in a private way." Ephraim Syrus, in order the better to secure his purpose against Bardesanes and Harmonius, studied the measures and tunes of these heretics, and employed them in composing orthodox songs.

Paul, of Samosata, like Bardesanes, distributed his errors by composing one hundred and fifty Psalms and circulating them among the people. Arius, the great leader of the Arian controversy, wrote songs for the sea, the mill and the high-way and set them to music, so as to attract men of all trades to his views. These rude chants scattered his errors throughout the whole Church. Chrysostom, on his arrival at Constantinople, found Arian canticles in such great esteem, that he could counteract their influence only by composing orthodox hymns, and allowing the people to parade the streets, in imitation of the Arians, and sing them in their religious processions.

These abuses led the Eastern Church, at a very early period, to be very cautious as to what hymns were introduced into their services. The depredations of the Gnostics, Arians, Apollinarians, Donatists and other sects, led the Council of Laodicea, about the middle of the fifth century to prohibit "all hymns of dangerous tendency and restricting their churches to the Psalter and other canonical songs of Scripture."

The heretical hymns of the Priscillianists, a sect that arose at the close of the fourth century, gave occasion for the decree of the Council of Braga early in the sixth century, "that beyond the Psalms or Scripture canons, no poetical composition should be sung in the Church." And it was probably on account of the dissensions produced by these sects through their poetry, that hymns were not formally sanctioned in the Western Church till the meeting of the Council of Toledo, in A. D. 633.

During the Middle Ages, hymnology degenerated till it became the mere vehicle of conveying the praises of saints and martyrs. God's house was insulted, and the piety of the Church ruined by the outrages under the form of praise.

The corruptions of the Middle Ages made their appearance in the hymns of the Church before there was any evidence of degeneracy in the matter of the creeds. "We need only to study the sacred poetry of the Middle Ages to understand why the Reformation was needed.   One painfully expressive fact meets us at the outset.   Of Mone's "Collection of Latin Hymns of the Middle Ages," in three volumes, one is filled with hymns to God and the angels, one with hymns to the blessed Virgin Mary, and one with hymns to the saints."

As early as 840, A. D., Agobard of Lyons, by birth a Spaniard, came to the Bishop of Lyons to urge the necessity of a reform in the Church Liturgy because of the influence the hymns to the Virgin and the saints was having in disseminating error.

In the thirteenth century, when the Cathari and Waldenses were extending their influence by their preaching and singing, and when the Council of Toulouse had prohibited the Bible being read in the vernacular, the Romish Church introduced among these mountain worshipers legends in rhyme to counteract the influence of the Reformers, knowing the power that error, set to music, would have toward accomplishing its purpose.   The oldest work of this kind is in German, comprising three books of one hundred thousand lines: the first treating of Christ and Mary; the second, of the apostles and other personages of the Bible, and the third, of the saints according to the arrangement of their names in the calendar.   As most of the people could not read, wandering minstrels were wont to scour the country and relate these wonderful stories.

Since the Reformation, Hymnology has not escaped poetic vandalism.   Though the early songs breathed only piety and truth, and so exerted most extensive power in the reform, yet, in after years, the old Hymns were so perverted, and new ones introduced so degenerate, as to operate ruinously upon the faith and fervor of the multitude.   One of the first attempts of German Rationalism was to tone down the energetic force of the old Hymns to make them harmonize with the corruption.   This among the Germans was known as "Gesangbuchs' verwasserung"—Hymn-book watering—and it is to the credit of the people, who still retained a veneration of the name and songs of Luther, and not to the schools and pulpits, that the devotion and virtue of the Reformation were not entirely lost to the worship of the Church in Germany.

Dr. Kurtz, a zealous Lutheran, remarks of this vandalism of the last century : " It was Klopstock who opened the way for the unparalleled Hymn-book vandalism of the period by remodeling twenty-nine old church Hymns. Their numberless successors among the champions of Illumination only made the more thorough havoc both with contents and form. General superintendents, consistorial counsellors, and court-preachers, rivaled each other in preparing and introducing new Hymn-books, with diluted old and still more watery new Hymns. * * * * These are almost entirely of a moral character ; and where a well-meant Hymn of faith appears, it bears not the least comparison with the Hymns of the sixteenth and seventeenth centuries. Abstraction, dogmatic tone and pathos, are the substitutes for the sublimity, inwardness, freshness and nationality of the old Hymns."

This eminent writer might have applied his remarks, to a greater or less extent, to the Hymnology of many other sections of the Church, as well as of Germany and its neighboring countries.

Bearing upon the same caution in the selection and use of material for praise is the action of the Reformed Church of Germany, which at Eberfield in 1859, enacted that "only hymns whose authors are known to be truly regenerate Christians shall be received" in the worship of the congregation.

Two articles are inserted here in the hope that they will receive the attention of the joint Committee on Psalmody referred to in the preface to this work. The first is an article—"The Old Scotch Psalmody"—from the pen of Tayler Lewis, L. L. D.

Early in life Dr. Lewis united with the Reformed Dutch Church, and continued a consistent member of it till his death in 1877. For more than forty years from the time of his becoming Principal of Waterford Academy in 1833, till the day of his death, Dr. Lewis' name was the synonym for the highest order of scholarship. A cotemporary observes

of him : " In classical and Biblical culture he had, perhaps,
no superiors and very few equals in modern times. His
knowledge of language was both extensive and profound.
He seemed to acquire it almost by inspiration. He was a
man, as one of his gifted students has sung,

> " Whose polyglot brain
> Seemed the lore of all ages and lands to contain."

What is here given from Dr. Lewis' pen was a contribution to one of the periodicals of his day, and is interesting
not only on account of its opinion of the old Rous's version
of the Psalms, but of one of the popular and much loved
hymns of the times.

THE OLD SCOTCH PSALMODY.

The subject of hymnology has lately occupied much space in our religious newspapers. There have been Dr. Cuyler's rich criticisms, no
little discussion in respect to Sabbath school poetry, and, withal, something of a spicy controversy on the merits of that popular hymn,
" Nearer, my God, to Thee." Permission, therefore, may reasonably be
asked for a few words on another department, which has either been
wholly ignored or treated with contempt. Reference is had to the old
Scotch Psalmody, still used by some churches in this country, as it is by
all the Presbyterian churches in Scotland. It does not deserve the un-
worthy treatment it has received from some who have styled it " religious doggerel." We are compelled to say this when we think of the
strong Christianity—strong to act and strong to suffer—which has been
nourished by that intensely scriptural style of devotional song which
ignorance and prejudice are so much inclined to undervalue.

In these matters we are much influenced by association. The
writer has some very precious early recollections connected with this
kind of church music, and the peculiar methods of exposition to which
it gave rise. It was the custom to expound the Psalm first selected, and
to an extent almost equal to that of the sermon itself. This would not
be tolerated now, as it was practiced fifty years ago by those old
worthies, the venerable Alexander Proudfit, of Salem, N. Y.; the Rev.
George Mairs, Sr., of Argyle, and Dr. Bullions, of Cambridge. Besides,
it could not be done with our indiscriminate hymnology. There is so
little in it to expound, even in its best effusions; whilst in others the
very attempt would but reveal the thinness and poverty of their ideas
for the soul, though so harmonious to the ear, and so pleasing, sometimes, to an undefined emotional sentimentality. A studied exegesis
would only bring out their tautologies, their platitudes, the barrenness
of their superabounding epithets. It was not so with the Scottish version of the Psalms of David. With all its seeming uncouthness, the
translation it gave was most trustworthy. It was the Scripture itself on
which the expounder was commenting. He could, therefore, safely
proceed upon the hypothesis expressed in the Sacred Word, and often
sung in their devotional service:

" The words of God are words most pure;
They be like silver tried
In earthen furnace, seven times
That hath been purified."

Take a specimen from the One Hundred and third Psalm. It is selected as vividly mingling with some of those early and ineradicable associations:

" Oh thou my soul, bless God the Lord;
And all that in me is
Be stirred up, His holy name
To magnify and bless."

Here there is no redundancy. Here every word is pure, every word
is true, every word has a divine significance. The expounder could
throw his soul into them; the people could confidently follow—getting
into their hearts the rich melody of the thoughts before uttering them
into song. Besides the lessons of gratitude, or the direct practical instruction, there were other ideas, lofty, profound and suggestive. In
the Psalmist's address to his soul there is the wondrous mystery of the
human quality—the inner and the outer man. In the mention of God
and his holy name there is no tautology, no empty parallelism. One
refers to the very being of Deity, the other to everything in nature or in
grace by which God is made known or his glory manifested.

" All thine iniquities who doth
Most graciously forgive ;
Who thy diseases all, and pains,
Doth heal and thee relieve."

God's forgiveness and his healing mercy ; the graciousness of both ; the
bodily a type of the spiritual salvation—such were the topics—not far-
fetched, surely, but a true " opening of the Word," regarded as divinely
given for human study and the intelligent utterance of human praise.
It was a standing rule of exposition that the lower or temporal salvation
spoken of did not exhaust the significance of the language. Its sublime
glow, which even the superficial reader can hardly fail to see, was evidence of something greater there. It was not an arbitrary " double
sense," but a mounting sense, an ever-rising, ever-expanding sense,
having its base on earth, but reaching far above, carrying us ever from
" the tabernacle " to the " Holy Hill," from the earthly temple to that
" House of God" in which healed souls should "dwell for evermore."
" If I may but touch the hem of his garment, I shall be made whole."
The words refer to a temporal evil ; but, if uttered in a right faith, they
embrace the whole essence, the whole " healing virtue " of the great
Christian salvation.

With Bible ever in hand, the people followed their spiritual guide,
as he made every separate verse and word an occasion for directing them
to analogies in every part of the Scripture. It was a method of keeping
the whole Bible ever before them—its historical, its supernatural, its
ritual, its devotional ever in connection with the perceptive and the
doctrinal.

Hence arose a peculiar language, which appears most prominent in
their peculiar Psalmody : The House of God, the People of God, the
Chosen of God, the mighty works of God in his dealings with them.

Under this head there comes up a reminiscence of the Rev. George
Mairs, the elder, and of his manner of expounding the One hundred and
fourteenth Psalm.

> " When Israel out of Egypt went,
>   And did his dwelling change ;
> When Jacob's house went out from those
>   Who were of language strange."

Here, of course, the spiritual interpretation was prominent; the
Egyptian bondage, the spiritual slavery ; the Egyptian dialect of the
world, the new and heavenly speech of the redeemed. But these topics
did not shut out the fair attention due to the historical exegesis and the
poetical sublimities of the passage. They were dwelt upon with all
fidelity, and without any of that fastidiousness with which some might
now regard its strange comparisons or its most daring apostrophe :

> " Like rams the mountains, and like lambs
>   The hills skipped to and fro.
> O Sea, why fled'st thou? Jordan back
>   Why wast thou driven so?"

Some may smile at this. It may be spoiled for them by fantastic
associations, It was not so, however, with the men—most pious, learned
and intelligent men like Erskine, Witherspoon and Chalmers—who
listened to or who taught this exegetical Psalmody. They were at home
in the scriptural figures. They had no need to change rams into fallow
deer or skipping lambs into gazelles, even if that would seem to help its
picturesqueness or its euphony. They were not shocked by the bold
apostrophe, so faithfully versified :

> "O Sea, why fled'st thou? Jordan back
>   Why wast thou driven so?"

The abrupt inversion only gave it the greater power, and prepared the
better for the sublime answer that follows :

> "O ! at the coming of the Lord,
>   Earth, tremble thou with fear."

It is not a tautology, but an attempt to render the Hebrew *hhuli*, de-
noting a convulsive shuddering. It was the awe of Nature at the appearance of her Lord, her shrinking dread of " Him who sitteth on the great
white throne, from whose face the earth and heaven flee away, and there
is found no place for them." It was in this manner that the great Bible
ideas, facts and images were ever kept before the minds of the people.
And thus was there trained up a peculiar class of Bible Christians,
having a knowledge of the Scriptures the like of which is not now
acquired from the best teachings of the modern pulpit.

The rich instruction ended, then " sang they to the Lord, and made
a joyful noise." From young and old went up the strain, borne on the
notes of the quick-ascending " Mear," or the waving " St. Martin's," or
the swelling " Dundee," or in the majestic movements of " Winchester "
and " Old Hundred." Or was it a Psalm of Zion's desolations ; then
did it rise mournfully in the minor modulations of the wailing " Bangor,"
or of the " plaintive Martyrs worthy of the name." To the ear laid
close there might have seemed discords in the tremolo of the old man's

quivering voice, or in the sharp note of the child ; but in its blended fullness it rose smooth and glorious, because beneath it all there lay the deep "fundamental bass," the "music in the heart unto the Lord," as they thus sang his praises "with the spirit and with the understanding."

In this old Scotch version there are doubtless not a few unmusical lines. Its frequent division of ti-on into two syllables, its quaint and sometimes inadmissible inversions may excite our surprise, or even make us smile ; but they are very far from justifying that epithet which has so basely been applied to it. It still challenges respect for its substantial Hebrew strength, its exhibition of the grand Hebrew thought, and as a medium of that Biblical form of praise for which no other can be an adequate substitute. Another feature is its clear objectiveness, or the striking contrast it presents to that extreme subjectiveness which makes much of our most modern hymnology so feeble because so vague. The former has ever some glorious outward object, or idea, drawing the soul out of itself. Even the expression of individual misery, or of individual joy, is connected with some real outward calamity, or some real outward deliverance, driving the soul to earnest prayer or rousing it to rapt thanksgiving. Hence the difference of phraseology and the objective term before alluded to as peculiar to the one species of pious song. The other is characterized either by a wholly subjective rapture, or by a continual moaning, a continual self-questioning about inward frames and feelings. Take for a few examples the hymns beginning :

"I love to steal away."

"Far from the world, O Lord, I flee."

"I am weary of straying, O fain would I rest."

"There is an hour of calm repose."

Very sweet and soothing are such hymns at times. They may be channels, too, of grace; but how different from those more churchly strains which the Scriptures give us; how different, too, from any conception we can form of the hymns that Paul and Silas most probably sang at midnight in the jail of Philippi !

The subjective solitariness, so inconsistently loquacious, often, in its minute recitals, pervades many of the hymns sung as favorites in our churches, but it is very much the same as though each individual worshiper were singing them at home in his own parlor or study. Very tender and touching are they: but there is in them no "communion of saints." They are not in the style of Scripture. They give us none of those great ideas of the people and city of the Most High, which have ever been the accompaniments of a strong Christianity. But listen now to the silver trumpet of Zion in one of her glorious "Songs of Ascension:"

"I joyed when to the House of God
    Go up, they said to me.
Jerusalem, within thy gates
    Our feet shall standing be.

"To Israel's testimony there,
    To God's name thanks to pay;
Let them that love thee and thy peace
    Have still prosperity.

> "Now, for my friends' and brethren's sakes,
>   Peace be in thee, I'll say;
> And for the House of God our Lord
>   I'll seek thy good alway."

Again the divine security of this chosen people—how much better is it expressed than in the feeble plaints with which we might compare it?

> "They in the Lord that firmly trust
>   Shall be like Zion hill,
> Which at no time can be removed,
>   But standeth ever still.

> "As round about Jerusalem
>   The mountains stand alway,
> The Lord his folk doth compass so
>   From henceforth and for aye."

The selfish individual joy and grief lose themselves in these allusions to Zion and her sons. Therefore it is that the best of our hymns, such as

> "I love thy kingdom, Lord,"

have it for chief merit that they are mainly paraphrases of this glorious Scripture language.

But let us make a clearer contrast by means of the popular hymn before alluded to—"Nearer, my God, to Thee." We would not join in the censure that one has pronounced upon it for not having the name of Christ. It may, however, be more justly said that the "nearness to God" is not sufficiently recognized as itself the divine drawing. It is the soul looking to itself, talking to itself, dreaming to itself; the objective dream of Jacob made subjective by being dreamed over again:

> "Darkness comes over me,
>   Daylight all gone!
> Yet in my dreams I'd be
> Nearer, my God, to thee,
>   Nearer to thee."

Very beautiful, very touching; but all from within. Its cross is the soul's sorrow, something borne instead of bearing. This is a Scriptural use of the word, indeed; but it is not the cross of Christ, the objective cross, the great uplifted sign to which all must look who would be healed of the deadly serpent's bite. Equally subjective is the "house of God," built from itself:

> "Out of my stony griefs
>   Bethel I'll raise."

This self-contemplation—or introspection, rather—is carried along even in its lofty soarings:

> "Sun, moon and stars forget,
>   Cleaving the sky."

This was written by a pious as well as a gifted soul. We must, therefore, suppose that there was present to it the mediatorial feeling at least, if not the expressed idea. For without it, surely it would be but an Icarian flight thus to approach, on self-made waxen wings, the burning Sun of Righteousness.

Now turn we to a strain similar in its leading thought, but from that older Psalmody in which the Christian soul will ever find something for all its wants. It is from the once desponding author of the Seventy-third Psalm—the man "whose feet were almost gone, whose steps had well night slipped." He was falling into an abyss of skepticism in respect to the divine providence; he was confounded by the prosperity of evil men, until he learned wisdom by going into the sanctuary of God. Such was his method of approaching the Infinite Help, and this was the way in which a sense of the adored presence affected his soul:

> " Yea, surely it is good for me
>   That I draw near to God.
> In God I trust that all my works
>   I may declare abroad.

> " Thou, with thy counsel, while I live,
>   Wilt me uphold and guide;
> And to the glory afterward
>   Receive me to abide.

> " Whom have I in the heavens high
>   But thee, O Lord, alone?
> And in the earth, whom I desire
>   Besides thee, there is none.

> " My flesh and soul doth faint and fail,
>   But God doth fail me never;
> For of my heart God is the strength,
>   My portion sure forever."

It is the most lowly dependence—a seeking to get hold of the hand that holds us (see Philip. 3:12, in the Greek). This is expressed in another verse, more irregular than the rest, notwithstanding a few slight emendations:

> " Nevertheless, continually,
>   O Lord, I am with thee;
> By my right hand, lest I should fall,
>   Secure thou holdest me."

The question is left with the reader. But the writer would not shrink from expressing the opinion that there is something unsound in that religion which would prefer the popular hymn to the ancient Psalm, even in a rhythmical dress so plain as that which is given in this old Scottish version.

The second article is a Memorial presented to the Presbytery of Detroit by Dr. George Duffield, of Detroit, in 1856. It was read by him and was no doubt the expression of his own sentiments. The Presbytery adopted the Memorial, and it was sent to the General Assembly of the New School Church, which met in New York City that year.

The "Present Collection," to which the Memorial refers, was the "Church Psalmist," which had been prepared by Dr. N. S. Beman, and was recommended by the Assembly of 1843.

The movement which called forth the Memorial from Detroit was that initiated by the New School Assembly of 1855, to purchase the Church Psalmist, that the Assembly might own it and enjoy the profits from its sale. The Memorial expressed the desire of a large number of Presbyterian ministers of that day to have a more faithful rendering of the Psalms of David than they had in Watts' Psalms.

MEMORIAL.

It is not the object of this memorial to disparage the merits of the present collection, or insinuate aught unfavorable to it, or to the extreme care that has been taken to give it poetic excellence according to the taste and views of the distinguished compiler.

So far as lyrical odes were a part of the collection, we doubt not that poetic taste and spiritual piety have been advantageously blended in the present collection, which is especially characterized by the absence of a class of hymns found in many others, by no means sufficiently elevated and dignified, either in conception or language, to be adapted to the purposes of praise to God by a worshiping assembly. Lyrical poetry claims to excite and express emotion, but the emotions appropriate to lyrical song are not all those of which the heart is susceptible and which it is the province of religious worship on different occasions to induce and indulge. Epic, pastoral and didactic poetry all find appropriate place in spiritual song. Some of the Psalms of David furnish admirable specimens of each. This inestimable collection, made by the Spirit of God, possesses a worth and power far beyond anything to be found in Watts' Imitation, or any other collection of sacred songs, the production of uninspired men. These collections have served the purposes of evangelical religion in many important respects; but the numerous changes that have been made in the Psalmody of different evangelical Churches prove that they have not fully met the wants of the members or the purposes of sacred song. The experience of a few years has demonstrated the defectiveness of our own; and the change introduced into it in that portion which purports to be (as Dr. Watts claimed for his) an imitation or paraphrase of the Psalms of David, we think has been an imperfection instead of an improvement. None of them can claim to be translations and but few of them paraphrases of the Psalms of David. There is a depth, a power, an unction, a reach, a grandeur, a comprehensiveness and sublimity in the Psalmody of the Bible which we look for in vain in Watts' Imitation or any other imitators.

We would not wish to see the latter wholly excluded from our collection, for they have become embalmed in the recollections and incorporated with the pious exercises and breathings of many devout worshipers. But we see no reason why they should occupy a prime and conspicuous place, as though they were the Psalms of David or actually do express their identical thoughts. They might much more appropriately be distributed under their respective suitable heads among the hymns or spiritual songs to which they more properly and characteristically belong. The wants and feelings of very many, as well as great and important benefits that cannot be secured by the existing imitations, would be much more directly and efficiently met and gratified by a restoration of the Book of Psalms to its proper place, and, as we think, the design assigned to it by the Spirit of God, as a part and parcel of the acknowledged matter for the Church's praise in her worshiping assemblies.

There is a simplicity, a pathos, a power and grandeur in most if not all of this sacred collection which gives it incalculable value. Its use, we think, is eminently calculated to preserve the purity of doctrine, to promote the power of faith, to exalt the authority of the sacred Scriptures and to secure respect for their inspiration. Its value and importance have been proved abundantly in the early history of the Reformation ; and to the place the Psalter still occupies in the rituals of different Churches may be referred much of that respect for the institutions of religion and the Word of God which are found among them. The experiment of excluding the Book of Psalms from the matter of the congregation's praise has been made extensively in this country by all Protestant denominations but the Episcopalians and a few minor sects of Presbyterians—Covenanters and Seceders.

The frequent changes and enlargement of the collection of hymns in different Churches must not, we think, be referred so much to the love of novelty as to the consciousness that there are defects and wants to be supplied in every collection that has been adopted.

Comparatively few hymns are treasured up in the memory by Christian people generally, and prove always to be acceptable without palling upon the taste or becoming trite. It is singular and pre-eminently characteristic of the Book of Psalms, even where the translation has been made into doggerel rhyme, as in Rous's version, that the sentiment gives value to the language, and its frequent, yea continual and even exclusive use as the material for public praise, is not only agreeable but zealously cherished and contended for as the very thing which best meets and supplies the purposes and wants of a Christian people's praise.

The young may desire and call for poetic compositions in which sentiment is less regarded than splendor of imagery and beauty of language. But where sentiment is secondary and style and ornament of chief importance, the poetry that may be consecrated for the purposes of religious worship will not long retain its freshness and power to interest the minds and hearts of the devout who seek communion with the Father, through the Son, by the Holy Spirit. It is the thought itself, the grand and sublime, the tender and touching, the thrilling and effecting truth of redemption through Christ, and the coming glories of his coming and kingdom, that give to the Book of Psalms its value and power when intelligently employed for purposes of religious praise. The person, work, character and affecting scenes and incidents in the life of Christ, the glorious Messiah, his sorrows and sufferings, his trials and conflicts and his atoning death, the wonders of his resurrection, ascension and exaltation to the right hand of the Father Almighty, the progress and history, the distresses and persecutions, the triumph and glory of the Church, the gracious retributive providences of Jesus Christ, his supremacy and Lordship over this lower creation, and the bright scenes of joy and blessedness at his coming in his kingdom which enliven the Book of Psalms, are themes that can never prove stale and uninteresting to the Christian heart. The longer the sentiments of this Book have been studied and used for purposes of praise and supplication in the worship of God, the dearer does it become to the pious heart, and the contrast between it and other hymns becomes glaring in point of strength and richness, of grandeur and power to enlighten, confirm and invigorate the Christian faith and hope, and lift the heart up to the holy joy and conscious, dignified and triumphing communion with God.

For these and other reasons not necessary to be stated, we would respectfully urge the attention of the General Assembly and their committee to the subject of enriching our psalmody by the introduction of the Psalter, or Book of Psalms, as rendered in our common prose translation, but arranged according to Hebrew parallelism, so as to admit of their being chanted. The parallelism which forms a conspicuous feature of Hebrew poetry seems to have been specially adapted, if not designed, for this sort of music. * * *

Dr. Watts was himself greatly in error as to the views he took of the spirit and design of the Book of Psalms, which led him to style many of them "cursing Psalms," and represent them to be unsuitable to the Christian spirit. The future tense indicates often mere prophetic character, and the imperative mood judged by him as inappropriate to the Christian, when employed by the Saviour whom the literal David personated, possesses a deep significancy and gives a point and power to the denunciation contained in many of the Psalms by no means inconsistent with, but corroborative of, the faith and hopes and spirit of the evangelical worshiper. An intelligent use of the Book of Psalms for purposes of religious worship could not fail to guard congregations against the influx and influence of dangerous error and keep before the mind the glorious Saviour who apprised his disciples that "all things must be fulfilled which were written in the Book of Psalms concerning him." Luke 24 : 44.

CHAPTER XII.

During the latter half of the sixteenth and in the early part of the seventeenth century, all of the church bodies in England and Scotland encouraged the singing of Psalms by the people. In an edition of Sternhold and Hopkins of 1606 we find "that the whole Book of Psalms, with English metre, with apt notes to sing them withal, were published by them, set forth and allowed to be sung in all the churches, of all the people together, before and after morning praier, as also before and after sermons; and, moreover, in private houses for their godly solace and comfort, laying apart all ungodly songs and ballads which tende only to the nourishing of vice and corrupting of youth."

The Confession of the Puritans in 1571 decreed: "We allow the people to join in one voice in a Psalm-tune, but not in tossing the Psalm from one side to the other, with the intermingling of organs."

The Westminster Assembly of Divines beside giving us the Confession gave us this direction with reference to sacred music: "It is the duty of Christians to praise God publicly by singing Psalms together in congregations and in families. That it ought to be the chief care to sing with the understanding and grace in the heart, and that the whole congregation join, and, as many cannot read, advise the minister to appoint some fit person to read the Psalm line by line."

The following extract from Pardovan's Collections will show how the old Scottish Church in the first half of the seventeenth century regarded Psalm-singing: "It was this ancient practice of the church, as it is yet of some Reformed churches abroad, for the minister or precentor to read over as much of the Psalm in metre together as was intended to be sung at once, and then the harmony and melody followed without interruption, and people either

(249)

did learn to read or got most of the Psalm by heart, but afterwards it being found that when a new paraphrase of the Psalms was appointed, it could not at first be so easy for the people to follow, then it became customary that each line was read by itself and then sung. But now, having for so long a time made use of this paraphrase, and the number of those who can read being increased, it is but reasonable that the ancient custom should be revived according to what is insinuated in the Directory on this subject. And that such who cannot read may know what Psalms to get by heart, let such be affixed on some conspicuous part of the pulpit as are to be sung in public at next meeting of the congregation. It were to be wished that masters of families would path the way for the more easy introducing of our former practice by reviving and observing the same in family worship." With such endorsements of Psalm-singing from the churches of the mother country, and the enthusiasm of song among the churches of the continent, extending over fifteen centuries, as a historic back-ground, one is surprised in turning to the Puritans of New England to find their congregations disturbed and often torn to pieces over points in sacred Psalmody that had never before been seriously considered.

There was a considerable party in the New England churches who had in some strange way convinced themselves that it was "Popish" to sing at all in public worship. The "lining out" of the Psalms, which had been a temporary resort to make up for the scarcity of Psalm-books, and the inability of some to read, assumed a sacredness almost as serious as a divine revelation.

Because St. Paul had taught that women should be "silent" in the churches, it was considered by many as sacrilege for them to be heard singing Psalms in public worship. The efforts of some advanced spirits to reduce the discordant singing to something like order and harmony, so that the churches could really make " music " to the Lord were regarded as alarming innovations. The idea of introducing a tuning fork to give the pitch for singing, created as great a horror in the minds of many of the New England Christians as

would exist to-day in some staunch Presbyterian church, if
the pastor in his pulpit were to kneel before a crucifix, or
swing a censer in his service.   It seems almost incredible that
the whole of New England should for many years be in the
throes of an intense and distracting controversy over issues
that are to us now so trivial.   To throw oil on the troubled
waters required the most earnest efforts of the distinguished
scholars and divines of that day, and their tracts and sermons
on these church controversies as preserved by Hood, and
Gould, and Ritter, are a curious feature in the early literature of our country.

The opposition to all audible singing was not peculiar
to the colonists.   It existed among the Dissenters of old
England.   Among those who labored to dispel the delusion
was Benjamin Keach.   "Mr. Keach was obliged to labor
earnestly and with great prudence and caution to obtain the
consent of his people to sing a Hymn at the conclusion of
the Lord's Supper.   After six more years, they agreed to
sing on Thanksgiving days; but it required still fourteen
years more before he could persuade them to sing every
Lord's day; and then it was only after the last prayer, that
those who chose it might withdraw without joining in it;
nor did even this satisfy these scrupulous consciences; for
after all a separation took place, and the inharmonious seceders formed a new church at Maze Pond, where it was
about twenty years longer before the praises of God could
be endured."   A writer in the Encyclopædia of Knowledge,
intimates that this was the first church among the English
Baptists where Psalm-singing was introduced.

The Psalm-book of Ainsworth from which the Puritans
sang in their passage across the sea, in 1620, had printed with
the Psalms all the music the colonists possessed at the time
of their arrival in the New World.   Hood says: This Psalm-
book "was printed with the melodies in which they were to
be sung, placed over the Psalms.   The music was printed
in the lozenge or diamond-shaped note, without bars, and
was in the German choral style."

According to Rev. Thomas Symmes, in an essay printed
in 1723, Ainsworth's Psalm-book contained forty-four tunes.

"Now, in Ainsworth's Psalm-book there are forty-four tunes, and but four of them that I ever saw anywhere, save in that Psalm-book. And there the time is pricked as in Ravenscroft's and Playford's, at the beginning of the Psalm; or you there find a reference to the time the Psalm is to be sung in, so that all the chief musician or chorister had to do was to give the pitch and lead the tune, and all were to sing according to the notes in the Psalm-book."

Of these Psalm-tunes, Ainsworth was only the compiler, as we learn from his preface: "Tunes for the Psalms I find none set of God; so that ech people is to use the most grave, decent and comfortable manner that they know, according to the general rule. The singing notes I have most taken from our Englished Psalms when they will fit the measure of the verse; and for the other long verses I have taken (for the most part) the gravest and easiest tunes of the French and Dutch Psalmes."

In the Colonial churches in and about Salem the Psalms and tunes of Ainsworth, as we have seen, were used till 1667, and in the churches at Plymouth until 1692. This attachment for the old version grew mainly out of the love the Pilgrim fathers had for Ainsworth, the pastor of their captivity in Holland. "In their exile they had used Sternhold and Hopkins' Psalm-book, but gave it up gladly to show honor to the work of their loved pastor, and perhaps with a sense of pleasure in not having to sing any verses which had been used and authorized by the Church of England."

In 1640, the Bay Psalm-book was printed at Cambridge, and gradually supplanted all others in the colonial churches. From the confusion of historians on the subject, it is difficult for the reader to conclude whether the first edition of the Bay Psalm-book had tunes printed with the Psalms or not. Hood says: "The music used for a long time before the year 1690 was mostly written in their Psalm-books, and had been so from the first using of the Bay Psalm-book. The number of tunes thus written rarely exceeded five or six." Yet afterward he writes: "About the year 1690 there was for want of a proper supply of tunes a general dullness and monotony in the music of the church.

Many congregations had scarcely more than three or four tunes that they could sing. This great scarcity created the necessity of appending music to the Psalm-book, which was done about the year 1690 ; for Mr. Symmes says, in a dialogue printed in 1723, 'as to Hackney and St. Mary's, it has been pricked in one edition of our Psalm-books for these thirty years.' The edition to which he refers is probably the first to which music was appended. The first we have been able to find was printed at Boston in 1698. The printing of the edition of 1698 is badly done, with many errors and without bars, except to divide the lines of poetry. Under each note is placed the initial of the syllable to be applied in singing by note, with other directions for singing. The tunes are Litchfield, Low Dutch, or Canterbury, York, Windsor, Cambridge, St. David's, Martyrs, Hackney or St. Mary's, and 100, 115, 119, 148th Psalm tunes. They are printed in two parts only."

The Bay Psalm-book is interesting to music lovers because of its quaint "Directions for ordering the voice in setting these following tunes to the Psalms."

The first of these directions is : "Observe how many notes compass the tune is. Next the place of your first notes, and how many notes above and below that ; so as you may begin the tune of your first note, as the rest may be sung in the compass of your and the people's voices, without squeaking above or grumbling below."

An attempt was made by those who issued the Bay Psalm-book to have the people sing their Psalm tunes to the right Psalms. Eight of the tunes were 8s and 6s, or common metre. These "may be sung to any Psalm of that measure." Three tunes, Oxford, Litchfield and Low Dutch, were to be sung to Psalms consolatory ; York and Windsor, to Psalms of prayer, and confession and at funerals. St. David's and Martyrs were recommended for Psalms of praise and thanksgiving. There were directions also with reference to the pitch. "These six short tunes in the tuning the first note, will bear a cheerful high pitch, in regard to their whole compass from the lowest note, the highest is not above five or six notes."

"These two tunes are eight notes compass above the first note, and therefore begin the first note low."

"This one tune—One hundred Psalm tune—begin your note indifferent high, in regard you are to fall four notes lower than your first pitch note."

Our impressions as to the character of the singing among the early New England colonies will depend on the historian we are controlled by.

In the opinion of Cotton Mather, who was identified with colonial history from 1663 to 1728, "their way of singing is not marked with such disorderly clamors as were condemned by the old council of Trullo, but in such grave tunes as are most used in our nation; and it may be hoped, not without some sense of that which Zonaras gives as the reason of the Trullan condemnation, the singing of Psalms is a supplicating of God himself, wherein by humble prayer we beg the pardon of our sins. Their Psalmody is neither set off with the delicacies which Austin complained of, nor is it rendered unseemly by the exorbitances we find rebuked by Chrysostom. It has been commended by strangers as generally not worse than what is in many other parts of the world, but rather as being usually, according to Origen's expression, melodiously and agreeably. However, of later times they have considerably recovered it and reformed and refined it from some indecencies that by length of time had begun to grow upon it. And more than a score of tunes are regularly sung in their assemblies."

Of the music at the same period Rev. Thos. Walter, of Roxbury, Mass., held a very different opinion. He says of the tunes sung in the churches of his day, they are "now miserably tortured and twisted and quavered into a horrid medley of confused and disorderly noises; for want of a standard to appeal to, our tunes are left to the mercy of every unskillful throat, to chop and alter and twist and change according to their infinitely divers and no less odd humors and fancies. * * * There are no two churches that sing alike. Yea, I have myself heard, for instance, Oxford tune sung in three churches with as much difference as there can possibly be between York and Oxford."

Miss Earle gives us one of the mistakes of Judge Sewall in attempting to "set the tune." "He spake to me to set the tune. I intended Windsor and fell into High Dutch, and then essaying to set another tune went into a key much too high. So I prayed to Mr. White to set it, which he did well—Litchfield tune. The Lord humble me that I should be the occasion of any interruption in the worship of God."

Modern writers have perhaps chosen extreme cases of the crude Psalm-singing of our colonial fathers and made it out worse than it really was. At the present day there are congregations, where choirs do not lead the music, in which the tunes are just as much twisted and tortured, and where many a man misses "setting the tune well" just as Judge Sewall did one hundred and fifty years ago.

It is altogether probable that many of the first Psalm-singers of the colonies understood plain music well enough to sing by note. During the sixteenth century in old England Church Psalmody made rapid progress. In 1579 John Day published his "Psalms of David in English meter with notes for four parts set unto them"; and in 1592 Thomas Este published "The Whole Booke of Psalmes with their wonted tunes, as they are song in the churches, composed in four parts, all of which are so placed that four may sing, each one a several parte in the booke." Still earlier in the century Thomas Ravenscroft, "a fine composer and skillful contrapuntist, but also a man of learning," issued "The Whole Booke of Psalmes" and printed with them ninety-eight tunes. Ritter, in his "Music in England," tells us that to perform the part-settings in this work in an appropriate style "experienced choir-singers were needed, and, according to the best information regarding English musical matters at this epoch, such singers were then to be found in every church choir."

The Sternhold and Hopkins' version, from which the Pilgrim Fathers sang before they fled to Holland, and which must have been used to some extent in the early New England colonies, was the product of the revival of music in the sixteenth century. The first issue of this Psalm-

book, printed in 1562, had forty tunes in it, and later editions had these tunes composed in four parts and made to
be "sung to all musical instruments." The singing of
these Psalm tunes and of those in the Ainsworth edition
could not have been as barbarous as that of "the Gauls and
Alemanni in the seventh century," whose "rough voices,
roaring like thunder, are not capable of soft modulation.
Indeed, their voices give out tones similar to the rumbling
of a baggage wagon rolling down from a height, and instead of touching the hearts of the hearers they only fill
them with aversion."

In Harvard University, which was born in the colonies
within six years after the landing of the Puritans, music
was entered as one of the studies. Rev. Mr. Symmes
states in one of his discourses: "It was studied, known
and approved of in our college for many years after its first
founding. This is evident from the musical theses which
were formerly printed, and from some writings containing
some tunes, with directions for singing by note, as they are
now sung; and these are yet in being, though of more than
sixty years' standing."

The same writer makes this statement: "There are
many persons of credit now living, children and grand-chil-
dren of the first settlers of New England, who can well remember that their ancestors sung by note, and they learned
so to sing of them; and they have more than their bare
words to prove that they speak the truth, for many of
them can sing tunes exactly by note which they learned of
their forefathers, and these people now sing those tunes
most agreeable to note which have been least practiced in
the congregation "

That there should come a decline in the New England Psalmody is not to be wondered at. Within thirty-five
years after the landing of the Pilgrims in New England
Cromwell came to the throne of England, and with his accession came the rage of the Puritan against everything
that had the semblance of papacy with it. Among other
things they vented their rage against the music of the Established Church. Organs were destroyed, church choirs

dissolved and musicians were chased from the organ gallery. "All the choral books were taken from the churches and destroyed, so that when things were returned to their former state it was almost impossible to procure notes, organs, organists or singers." As Ritter states, "The art of singing the Psalm tunes in the fine arrangements of Ravenscroft and other English contrapuntists was abandoned because it reminded the people of music, the frivolous art, and the tune in its melodic simplicity only was allowed to be sung by the whole congregation. Thus music with the Puritans became a kind of sacred people's song. Having been taught to look on music as a frivolous product, fashioned by the evil designs of the Tempter, the Puritan naturally shrank back with horror from an artistic occupation that might bring upon his soul punishment unto death." This furor of the Puritans in England would naturally extend its spirit to those among the colonies and produce in them a prejudice under which the art of music, singing in parts and by note, and the very knowledge of many of the better tunes would pass into decline.

Let us add to this the difficulties of the colonists in their new home in the way of cultivating any of the finer things of settled social life. Troubles came upon them "like the plague of Egypt." Their wars with the Indians, their agitation over witchcraft, and the coming of Roger Williams, and Ann Hutchinson, and the Quakers, with their "heresies," perplexed them on every side, and they had neither time nor inclination to turn thir attention to such an unnecessary thing as music.

From the earliest days the colonists suffered for want of Psalm-books. Often only a few in each congregation would possess a copy, which brought into use the "lining out," which we have seen had been discouraged among the Reformers of the Continent and Great Britain ; and this practice, if there were nothing else, would destroy all method and harmony in Psalm-singing.

The customs of the Puritans in their worship had a tendency to quench any enthusiasm in their Psalmody. The tunes used in many of the congregations were so few that they had to sing them over twice the same Sabbath in order to complete the round of the public devotions.

As worship was held in the families of the colonists twice every day, these same tunes had to be sung over many times in each week.   In their singing in the sanctuary the people stood, and as their custom was to sing a Psalm clear through, and some of the Psalms had as many as one hundred and thirty lines, it is easy to perceive that the spirit of melody could not thrive under such embarrassments.   No wonder the tired worshipers would " twist " and "quaver " in their singing, and not come out at the end of the tune at the same time.   This decline in the sacred music in the colonies lasted for fully three-quarters of a century, and became so extreme that when the revival began, the people had come to think there was something sacred in the very crudities of their Psalmody.   The struggles to dispense with " lining out " the Psalms, and to introduce singing by method, and the use of choirs and instrumental helps, remind one of the battles of the Covenanters and Camisards with the Papists.

Says Ritter, with reference to the lining out : " In churches where they had choirs the custom gradually disappeared, though not without a struggle between the choir and the clerk.   Sometimes the members of the choir would get the better of the clerk and his party, by promptly attacking the tune of the Psalm set, in singing it through in steady tune ; but at other times the clerk, conscious of his important office, would bide his time and take revenge, like that clerk in a Massachusetts town, where the choir, having started the tune without giving the Deacon time to ' line it out,' he rose, at the conclusion of the choir's singing of the Psalm, and gravely setting his spectacles upon his nose, opened the book, saying, ' Now, let the people of God sing,' and went on ' lining out ' another Psalm."

A people who so reverenced their old tunes that they would uncover the head at the sound of them, whether in the church or on the streets, and who deemed them too sacred for any but Christians to sing, were not the people to surrender at the first sound of battle.

Strange characters were these old colonists.   A more

cultured and critical generation has delighted to call them " narrow " and " bigoted." But they were men of God. They had bared their breasts against the fury of tyrants as their Plymouth rocks had bared their front to the lashing of the sea waves. Their tunes and Psalms and Bible were dearer to them than their lives. " Rough," were they? Yes, but it was the roughness of the diamond. " Narrow," were they? Yes, but it is out of just such " narrow " Psalm-singers that Christ for thirty centuries has been preparing a " peculiar people," who shall yet fill the earth with his praise.

THE END.

GENERAL INDEX.

Acrostic Psalms, 34.

Ainsworth Henry, his character and standing, 208, author of "An Arrow Against Idolatry," s; His Psalms published in 1612, s; At once become part of the faith and worship of the Refugee Brownists in Holland, 209; Taken with the Pilgrim Fathers to the New World, s; Sole source of praise in the Colonies for 20 years, 210; Copies of the old editions still extant, s; Held in great reverence, 211; Mention of in "The Courtship of Miles Standish," s; Specimen of Psalm 1, 212; Superseded by "Bay Psalm-book," s; The Psalm tunes in it, 251.

American Presbyterian churches. Psalms in, 225; Deliverances on the Psalms and Psalm-singing by Reformed, Associate. Associate Reformed, and United Presbyterian churches, 226, 227, 228; Difficulties in the way of displacing Rous' version, 231; The Presbyterian Church not formerly a Hymn-singing Church till the present century, 234; The Psalms, under the title of Psalms, disappear, 234; Importance of keeping a jealous care over Hymnology, 235; Apostolical constitutions on Psalm-singing in the fourth century, 51.

Asaph, two musicians of that name; one of the time of David; the other of the time of Babylonish captivity; both of them composers of Psalms, 23-24.

Ascetics, sing the Psalms, 69.

Augustine on the metres of the Psalms, 32; On the Psalms, 60.

Barlesnnes, his private Psalms, 52.

"Bay Psalm-book," first printed in 1640, 212; Mather's account of it, s; One of the first books printed in the Colonies, 213; where and how printed, s; Its

"Admonition to the Reader," 214; Revised by Dunster and Lyons, 214; Universally adopted in Colonial churches, 216; Passed through 70 editions, 217; Copies rare, s; Specimen of Psalm 133, s.

Bede, the English Psalmist, 149; His early life, 150.

Benedict, his reformation in the monastic rules, 70.

Beza, Theodore, his versification, 113; What he says of the singing of the Psalms in Paris, 117; Version of Marot and Beza revised, 129.

Buchanan, George, Scotch Psalmist; His Psalms written in Latin, 183; Knox's testimony to, s, that of Leissier, Mackenzie and Orme, 184; His Psalms a class book in the schools, s; Inspire Isaac Watts, 185; Selection from, s.

Calvin, his commentary on the Psalms, 109.

Camisards, their desert worship, and their Psalm-singing in battle, 126.

Carlyle on Psalm-singing in the Reformation, 95.

Canonization of saints, use of Psalms in, 79.

Catholics in France and Psalm-singing, 120.

Charlemagne, his attachment to the Psalms, 77.

Children instructed in the Psalms, 149.

Chrysostom, on Psalm-singing in his bishopric, 51, 52.

Columba, carries the Psalms with him to Great Britain, 70.

Coverdale, Bishop, his "Ghostly Psalms" published in 1539, 158. Author's address, 159; His versifications number only thirteen, 159; conforms them to the music of the "ungodlie ballates" of the day, 159.

(260)

Crawford, Rev. Jno., on use of Psalms in modern times in Eastern churches, 62.

Crusades, why they drew so largely from the monks, 73; Psalms in, 81.

David, The Psalmist of Israel, 20; Irving's eulogism of, 21; Author of seventy Psalms, 22.

Diane de Poictiers, her love of the Psalms, and her persecution for it, 118.

Divination, use of Psalms in, 78.

Dominic, St., his self-inflictions by reciting Psalms, 72.

"Dundee Psalms," 182 versified by the Wedderburn brothers, s; Prepared for the tunes of the continent, s; No common metre in them, s; Psalm LI. as sung by Wishart on the night of his arrest, 183; Sung among Scotch till substituted by version of Sternhold and Hopkins, 186.

Elizabeth, Queen, English Psalter dedicated to her in 1559, 155; Encouraged Psalm-singing, 156; Versified Psalm Fourteen, 159.

Ethan, a leader in David's choir, 24.

Eusebius, opinion of Hebrew poetic measure, 32.

Festivals, Jewish, use of Psalms in, 39.

Field meetings among the Calvinists of the Low Countries, 135; Use of Psalms in them, 135; Motley's description of, 136; Use of Marot's version, 139.

Gauge days, Psalms in, 77.

Heman, a leader in David's choir, 24.

Hopkins, Jno., the associate of Sternhold in the English Psalmbook in Liturgy of 1556, 162.

Horsley, Bishop, on the collecting of the Psalms, 27; On Hebrew poetry, 33.

Huguenots, their devotion to the Psalms and their sufferings for it, 123; Grasse on their singing, 147.

Hymns, best German ones modeled after the Psalms, 103.

Illumination of Psalms, 73.

James I. moves for revising both Bible and Psalm-book, 190; Calderwood speaks of his undertaking, s; The King himself attempts paraphrasing the Psalms, 190; Beattie on the King's Psalter, 191; Efforts of King Charles to have the Royal Psalter introduced among the Scotch, 191, 192.

Jerome on the Hebrew poetry, 32; On Psalms, 61; His Psalter translated into English, 152.

Jones, Abner's, version, 221. Its numerous versifications, 222; Specimen of Psalm, 23, s.

Jones, Sir W., applies Arabic metres to the Psalms, 33.

Josephus, his opinion of the character of Hebrew poetry, 32.

Julian, his persecution of the early Christians, 56.

Justinian, his polyglot Psalter, 88.

Kitto, on Rhyme in the Psalms, 33.

Korah, "sons of," authors of ten Psalms; and singers in the Temple choir, 24.

"Lining out" of the Psalms forbidden by a French Synod, 129.

Lobwasser his German Psalmbook, 105.

Lowth, Bishop, on the Acrostic Psalms, 34.

Luther, the German Psalmist, 100; His exposition of the Psalms, 101; His metrical Psalms largely used, 103; Their influence, 104; His "Eine Feste Burg ist unser Gott," 104; His love of music, 143; A composer, 144; Supports duty of Psalm-singing, 144.

Marot, French versifier of the Psalms, 111; His first versifications printed in Rome in 1542, 112. Their enthusiastic use, 114; Persecutions of Marot, 118.

Mather, Cotton, his "Psalterium Americanum," 218; Arranged without rhyme, s; Selection from Ps. 116, s.

Meibomius professes to have discovered the lost system of Hebrew metres, 33.

Monasteries, use of Psalms in the worship and discipline of, 64, 71.

Montagu, his versification of Psalm, 100; In Acrostic, 35.

Mosheim, on Psalm-singing in the Primitive Church, 44.

Nestorians, use of Psalms at the present day, 61.

Notker, his Psalms in the Teutonic specimen of, 86.

Paul, of Samosata, suppression of Psalms, 53.

Poetry of the Psalms. 30.

Polyglot Psalms, 86, 88.

Printing, first work from the new type a Psalter, 87; Promotes extensive use of Psalm, 92.

Psalms—Testimonials to — Henry V. of England, Joseph Addison, Salmasius, Humbolt, Darnley, Burleigh, Dickson, 13; Henry Stephanus, Herder, John Mueller, John Jacob Moser, 15; Lamartine, Schlegel, Kitto, Horne, Jonathan Edwards, 16; Gilfillan, Taylor Lewis, St. Basil, St. Ambrose, Augustine, 60; Jerome, 61; Luther, 101; Calvin, 109, Dr. Owen, 202.

Psalms — Authorship — Moses, author of Ninetieth Psalm, 18; David, author of seventy Psalms, 22; Asaph, author of twelve Psalms, 23; Heman, author of one Psalm, 24; Ethan, author of one Psalm, 24; "Sons of Korah," authors of ten Psalms, 24; Many composed during or after captivity in Babylon, 25; Westcott's objection to Maccabæan authorship, 25; Collecting of, 26; Bishop Horsley, on the collecting of the Psalms, 27; Prophetic of Christ, 28; Designed as a Book of Praise, 29; Character of their poetry, 30; Acrostic Psalms, 34; Use of in Jewish Church, 35; Use of Psalms in war, 38; Use of in Jewish festivals, 39; Use of in Primitive Church, 44; Psalms sung at the institution of the Lord's Supper, 49; Their wide distribution in the fourth century, 50; Psalm-singing a pastime, 51; Singing of Psalms condemned, 54, 118, 123, 139; Liturgical use of, 54; in burial of the dead, 56; Sung during the Arian persecution, 58; Old MS. on Papyrus from fourth century, 59; Use of in the dark ages, 64; use of Psalms in the Monasteries, 64; Among the ascetics, 69; Carried to Ireland and Scotland by Columba, 70; Use of in Monastic penalties, 71; In the illuminating and illustrating of manuscripts, 73; In perambulating, 77; In divination. 78; In canonization of the Saints, 79; In unction at sick beds, 80; In dedication of churches and cemeteries, 80; In devotions over the dead, 80; In the crusades, 81; Versions of, 82; First printed book a Psalter, 87; In the Reformation, 90; In the singing of the multitude, 93; Among the Waldenses, 96; The Hussites, 99; Luther's version, 102; Use in modern Lutheran churches, 105; Use of in countries bordering on Germany, 106; Use of among Swiss and French, 107; Among the nobles at the French court, 115; License to sing them by Henry IX., 119; Use of authorized by French Synod in 1559, 128; In a French Liturgy of the modern Huguenots, 130; In the Low Countries, 134; Decline in Psalm-singing in German in later times, 145; Among the English people, 149, 154; Psalm-singing commended by Cuthbert, 150; Extends to the service of the established church, 157; Wide use of in the homes of the people in the seventeenth century, 179; Picture of a Scotchman's family worship from, "Cotter's Saturday night," 179; Psalm-singing in English and Scotch armies, 179; A Covenanter communion, 178; Distate of the Scotch for the Royal Psalter of King James, 192. The Psalms in the Westminster Assembly, 193; Determination of its commissioners to have only a close rendering, 198; Sung at battles of Dunbar and Drumclog, 203; Psalms and Psalm-singing in New England, 207; Used at the departure of the Puritans from Holland, 209; First notes of praise on the New England shores, from the Psalter of David, 210; Psalm-singing among the American Indians, 222; Translations into dialects of, 223: Selection from Elliot's Indian Psalms, s; Use of Psalms in American Presbyterian churches, 225; An enactment restricting the Psalmody of Reformed Presbyterian church to the Psalms only, 226; Same in Associate church, 227; In Associate Reformed church, s; In United Presbyterian church, 228. Present version of United Presbyterian church, when adopted, 229, 230; Its merits, 230; The beginning of the movement in the Presbyterian church to substitute other than a close rendering of the Psalms, 231; Difficulties in the way, s; Memorial of Detroit Presbytery, 246.

Publia, beaten for her singing of Psalms, by Julian, 57.

Puritans, in Old England use no particular version of Psalms, 207; Versions of Merrick and Sandys, and Barlow and Rous, all have their friends, s; In time the Psalms and Hymns of Dr. Watts displace all others, 208; Sacred music among them, 249; Their Confession on Psalm-singing, s; Their scruples as to women singing; As to "lining out" the Psalms, 250; The character of their singing, 254; Difficulties of its cultivation, 256.

Quindreda, Psalm-book of, 82.

Rhyme, invented since the composing of the Psalms, 31.

Reformed churches of France and Switzerland, peculiarity of their Psalmody, 107.

Reformation, Psalms in, 91.

Rous, Francis, author in part of Rous' version, incipient movement for this Psalm-book, 193, 195; His character, s; Refers to his work, 196; After seven years of revising is adopted, 198; Still in use, 200; its merits, s; Specimens of their crudeness, 201; Attempts to have his version introduced into the English Episcopal church, 164; Use of in American churches, 203; Sung at battles of Dunbar and Drumclog, s; Testimonials to, 204; Revised and improved by American churches, 228; Singing Rous' Psalms and loyalty to the colonial cause synonymous, 231; Dr. Tayler Lewis on the Scotch Psalms, 239.

Sandys, George, an English Psalmist; composes his Psalms by the James river, 168; Montgomery's compliment of his Psalms, 169; His version of Psalm 29, 169.

Scotch The, Psalm-singing among, 177; the Psalmists of foreign birth, s; Lack of musical enthusiasm, s; History of Psalmody in the homes and churches of the people, 178; A Covenanter communion, s; Family worship, 179; Psalms in camp life, 180; Psalm-singing began early, 181; "Dundee Psalms," 182; The love of the Scotch for Buchanan's Psalms, 185; Adopt the Psalms of Sternhold & Hopkins, 186; Act independently of the English, 187; Scottish Psalter completed, 1564, 188; Used in Holland, 189; Movement for a new version, s; Resist the introduction of the Psalter of King James, 191; Scottish Kirk slow to adopt Rous' version, 198, 199; Rous' version among the Covenanters, 202; Pardovan on the Scotch Psalmody, 249.

Spanhiem on Psalm-Singing in the Primitive Church, 44.

Sternhold, Thos., one of the versifiers of the Psalms that came to be bound up with the English Liturgy, 161; Use of this version in New England, 165.

St. Patrick, the apostle to the Irish, his exercise in the Psalms, 151.

Tate and Brady, versifyers of the "New Version," that took the place of the "Old Version" in the English church, 169; Introduced under sanction of William III., Dec. 3, 1696; Their version first used in the churches of London, 170; Opposition to use of the "New Version" by the masses, 171; Testimonies to "New Version" by Compton, Drake, and British Encyclopedia, 171.

Temple Service, use of Psalms in, 35.

Tertullian, on use of Psalms in the African churches, 50.

Tholuck, his translation of 134th Psalm, 38.

Toulouse, council of, forbids translations, 86.

Tours, council of, its canon on Psalm-singing, 68.

Trinitarians, singing the Psalms in palm groves of Syria, 59.

Troubadours, their influence in the revival of Psalmody, 94.

Tunes sung to Psalms in Germany, 142; Luther preparing them, 145; In France, 146; In England, 156, 208; Mason, on Reformation Psalm tunes, 147, 179; Psalm tunes of Colonies, 251; Directions for singing them, 253; Character of it, 254.

Versions of Psalms, 82; In Hebrew, 82, 84; In Greek, 83; In Italic, 83; In Gallican, 83; In German, 85; In Slavonic, 85; In Norman French, 86.

Versions metrical, by Martin Luther, 103; By Ambrose Lobwasser, 105; By Marot, 111; By Beza, 113; By Peter Dothen, 139; In Dutch rhyme, by Philip de Marnix, 140; By Dirk Rafael Kamphuyzen, his paraphrase of Psalm 133, as translated by Longfellow, 141; Anglo Saxon version, by Aldhelm, 149; By Bede, 149; Translation of Jerome's Latin Psalter, into Anglo Saxon, 152; Richard Rolle's English version, 152; His rendering of Psalm 23, 153; Coverdale's metrical version, 158; Hunnis' "Seven Sobs for a Sorrowful Soul in Sin," 160; Version of Sir Thomas Wyatt, 160; Version of Thomas Sternhold and John Hopkins, 161; The "Old Version" of Sternhold and Hopkins continued in use in England till Restoration, 164; Still authorized by United Church of England and Ireland, 165; Criticisms on the version of Sternhold and Hopkins, 165; Specimens from Psalms 78, verse 46, and Psalm 74:12, 166; Version of Archbishop Parker, 167; Lord Bacon's versifications, 168; Baxter's paraphrase of 1692, 168; Versifications of Withers and Sandys, p. 168; Version of Tate & Brady, 169; Version of Dr. Isaac Watts, 171; Version of the Wesley Brothers, 175; Testimonial of Chas. Wesley in rhyme to the Psalms, 175; Version of Joseph Addison, 175; Version of James Montgomery, 176; Lord Byron's 137th Psalm, 176; "Dundee Psalms," by the Wedderburns, 182; Latin Psalms of George Buchanan, 183; Scottish Psalter, 188; Psalter of King James, 191; Rous' version, 193; Gaelic version, 204; Psalms 1, in the Gaelic, 205; Translated into the Welsh, 205; Into the Irish language, 206; Ainsworth's version, 208; "Bay Psalm-book," 212. "Psalterium Americanum," 218.

Waldenses, Psalm-singing among, 96.

Watts, Isaac, his Psalms and Hymns, 171; His Psalm-book, with Hymns published in 1719, 171; His motive in versifying the Psalms, 172; Extensive use of, 172; Criticisms of, 173; His Cenotaph, erected 1846, 174; Largely used in New England, 220; Allowed by Presbyterian church in 1787, s, Dwight's revision of, 221.

Westcott, his objection to the Maccabæan authorship of Psalms, 25.

Westminster Assembly, convened by the English Parliament, June 12, 1643, 193; Competitive versions before it, 194; Subject of new version first before the House, 196; Scotch commissioners slow in taking part, 197; Finally adopt a new version, 199.

Zwingle, his influence in the singing of Psalms in the Reformation, 103.